THE
BACHELOR

Tilly Bagshawe is the internationally bestselling author of fifteen previous novels.

A single mother at seventeen, Tilly won a place at Cambridge University and took her baby daughter with her. Now married to an American and a mother of four, Tilly and her family divide their time between the bright lights of Los Angeles and the peace and tranquillity of a sleepy Cotswold village.

Before her first book, *Adored*, became an international smash hit, Tilly had a successful career in the City. Later, as a journalist, she contributed regularly to the *Sunday Times*, *Daily Mail* and *Evening Standard* before turning her hand to novels, following in the footsteps of her sister Louise.

These days, whenever she's not writing or on a plane, Tilly's life mostly revolves around the school run, Boy Scouts and Peppa Pig.

To find out more about Tilly Bagshawe and her books, visit www.tillybagshawe.co.uk

D1052679

Also by Tilly Bagshawe

Adored
Showdown
Do Not Disturb
Flawless
Fame
Scandalous
Friends & Rivals

The Swell Valley Series
One Summer's Afternoon (Short Story)
One Christmas Morning (Short Story)
The Inheritance
The Show

Sidney Sheldon's Mistress of the Game
Sidney Sheldon's After the Darkness
Sidney Sheldon's Angel of the Dark
Sidney Sheldon's The Tides of Memory
Sidney Sheldon's Chasing Tomorrow
Sidney Sheldon's Reckless

Tilly Bagshawe

THE
BACHELOR

HARPER

HarperCollins*Publishers*
The News Building
1 London Bridge Street
London SE1 9GF

www.harpercollins.co.uk

A paperback original 2016
2

A catalogue record for this book
is available from the British Library

ISBN: 978-0-00-813281-1

Set in Meridien by Palimpsest Book Production Limited, Falkirk, Stirlingshire

Printed and bound in Great Britain by
Clays Ltd, St Ives plc

For Nonny, with love.

Acknowledgements

Thanks once again to the amazing team at Harper Collins and especially to my editors, Kimberley Young and Claire Palmer. Also to my wonderful agents, Hellie Ogden in London and Luke Janklow in New York, and to all at Janklow & Nesbit who have helped and guided me from the very beginning of my writing career and been there every step of the way. Finally thanks as always to my family, especially my children, Sefi, Zac, Theo and Summer. And to my husband Robin – thank you for our wonderful life.

The Bachelor is dedicated to my dear friend Sonya Walger, aka Nonny, who makes everything about living in LA just that little bit better. Thanks for saving my sanity so many times Nons. I hope you enjoy the book.

TB 2016

The

Tittlesc

Vicarage

Preedy's High

Furlings Estate

Old Vicarage

St. Hilda's Church

Village Green

Fox

Cricket Ground

St. Hilda's School

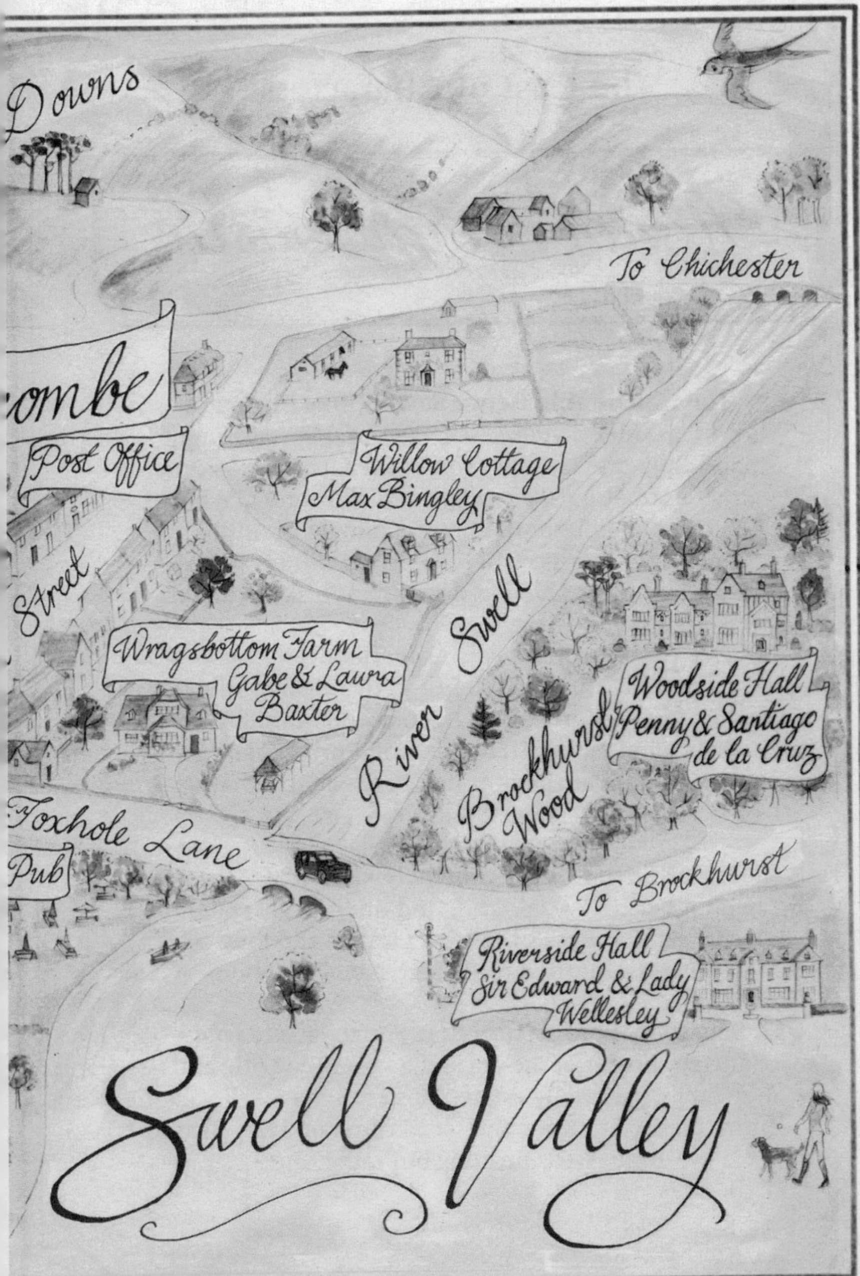
Downs
combe
Post Office
Street
Willow Cottage
Max Bingley
To Chichester
Wragsbottom Farm
Gabe & Laura
Baxter
River Swell
Brockhurst Wood
Woodside Hall
Penny & Santiago
de la Cruz
Foxhole Lane
Pub
To Brockhurst
Riverside Hall
Sir Edward & Lady
Wellesley
Swell Valley

The Cast of Characters

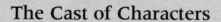

Hanborough Castle

The Honourable Henry Saxton Brae England's most eligible bachelor. Tall, dark and devastatingly handsome, the younger son of the late Lord Saxton Brae. Former tennis prodigy and all round playboy. Recently bought the breathtakingly beautiful Hanborough Castle where he lives with his fiancée **Eva**, and his beloved Irish setters Whisky & Soda.

Eva Gunnarson Swedish supermodel du jour – the latest face and body of La Perla lingerie. Blonde and willowy, effortlessly gorgeous and infinitely kind. Finally capitulated to Henry's second proposal and now lives with him at Hanborough between international modelling shoots.

Georgina Savile Unaffectionately known as 'Skeletor' behind her back – tall, thin and unendingly spiteful. Henry Saxton Brae's business partner and long-time mistress. Married to **Robert**, a crashing bore.

Sebastian, Lord Saxton Brae Squat, fat and bald – current holder of the ancient Saxton Brae title and Hatchings, the family estate. Master of the Swell Valley Hunt; married to **Kate**, the social climbing **Lady Saxton Brae**. Well-meaning but rather dull.

New York

Graydon James Internationally renowned
and sought-after interior designer –
as flamboyant and cut-throat as his interiors
are understated and breathtakingly expensive.

Flora Fitzwilliam Graydon James's right-hand
woman, having landed a job at GJD straight
out of the prestigious Rhode Island School of Design.
A petite bombshell with her Puerto Rican mother's
curves and her English father's blond colouring.
Despite having no family and no connections,
has somehow snagged one of the Upper East Side's
most eligible men, **Mason Parker**.

Mason Parker Darling son of an old East Coast money
family, with estates in Westchester County and an
impressive portfolio of real estate in the city. A blond
and preppy Wall Street banker, he looks like a Brooks
Brothers' advertisement and is about as interesting.

Fittlescombe

Barney Griffith Former corporate lawyer, current aspiring novelist. Handsome though unkempt, broad-shouldered and sandy-haired, Barney and his rascally border terrier Jeeves are as charming, scruffy and good-natured as each other.

Laura Baxter Successful screenwriter and producer, wife to **Gabe** and mum to Hugh and Luca.

Gabe Baxter Local Fittlescombe heart-throb, TV presenter and family farmer with big ambitions.

Jennifer Clempson Local vet with girl-next-door looks and a mischievous streak, recently married to **Bill Clempson**, the vicar.

Santiago de la Cruz Preposterously handsome cricket star. Played for England, Sussex and Fittlescombe. He is completely smitten with his wife, **Penny**, whom everyone adores.

Angela Cranley Ex-wife of Brett, mother to Logan and Jason. Angela lives at Furlings, the former ancestral home of Tatiana Flint-Hamilton with her long-term partner **Max Bingley**, the headmaster at St Hilda's, the village school.

PROLOGUE

Henry Saxton Brae was admiring his business partner's considerable assets.

'Harder!' she commanded. 'I'm almost there!'

Her eyes were closed and her breathing ragged. Her pretty, elfin face was twisted into an expression of intense concentration as she willed herself to orgasm.

Henry felt a moment's deep loathing, first for George and then for himself. Then he closed his own eyes and erupted inside her, his fingers digging painfully into the small of her back as they both came.

'Naughty,' Georgina chided him, turning to rub the bruises already forming above her buttocks as she dismounted, with an insufferably smug look on her face. Every time they did this, George had 'won' and Henry had 'lost'. She delighted in the power she had over him; her ability to goad him into sex, even though she knew deep down he despised her.

'Robert's bound to notice. What am I going to tell him?'

'I'm sure you'll think of something,' Henry muttered

bitterly, pulling up his jeans. 'Lying's never exactly been a problem for you.'

'Or you, darling,' George shot back.

They were lying on the floor of Gigtix.com's London offices, the internet box-office company that Henry Saxton Brae and Georgina Savile had founded together three years ago. It had made both of them fabulously wealthy, but it had also bound them together in what was becoming an increasingly toxic relationship. George's recently acquired husband Robert, a barrister of quite earth-shattering banality, was far too unimaginative ever to suspect anything might be going on behind his back. But Eva, Henry's girlfriend, was beginning to get suspicious.

Not girlfriend, Henry reminded himself guiltily. *Fiancée*.

Why had he given in to George again? Why? What compulsion kept driving him to cheat on the woman he loved, and who was a thousand times more beautiful than malicious, manipulative, spiteful George Savile, or any of his other meaningless flings?

'I'm serious,' George pouted, examining her bruises more closely. 'How would you like it if I sent you back to Ikea with scratches all over your back?'

'Don't call her that,' Henry snapped. 'Ikea' was Georgina's nickname for Eva, because she was Swedish and, in George's mind, disposable. Looking at his Patek Philippe watch, Henry felt his anxiety levels rise still further. 'I have to go. I'm going to be late.'

'For what? Your curfew?' Georgina taunted, slipping a ridiculously tight pink T-shirt over her nude push-up bra.

'For the village fete,' said Henry, grabbing his car keys from the desk. 'I'm supposed to be giving out prizes.'

George threw her slender neck back and laughed loudly.

'I'd forgotten you're playing the country gentleman now. How priceless!'

'I'm not playing,' said Henry.

Henry had bought Hanborough Castle, the Swell Valley's most idyllically romantic estate, six months ago, and now lived there full time with his bride-to-be. The whole thing was ridiculous. Taking Henry Saxton Brae out of London was like taking a killer whale out of the ocean. Henry was a predator, not a pet.

'Run along then,' George taunted. 'The lord of the manor mustn't be late for the fete.'

Henry stormed out, slamming the office door behind him.

Only once she was alone did George's triumphant smile fade and the familiar melancholy, deflated feeling take hold. Henry would come to his senses one day. George felt sure of it. But it was hard waiting sometimes.

She'd hoped her wedding to Robert would be the wake-up call Henry needed. But he'd seemed not to care at all. George was pretty sure he was faking his indifference. But it was still hard. Henry's engagement to the awful, vacuous, goody two-shoes Eva Gunnarson had been even harder. George had grown used to him screwing around. He was one of England's most eligible bachelors, after all. Rampant promiscuity went with the territory, and George knew that the one-night stands meant nothing to him. But Henry's new-found devotion to that Swedish bitch was different. That had changed everything.

Eva wouldn't win, though. Not in the long run. Henry would soon tire of country life, and of her. And when he did, Georgina Savile would be there to claim her prize.

He still needs me, George thought, caressing the bruises on her back again, but lovingly this time. *I'm his drug. We're each other's drug.*

PART ONE

CHAPTER ONE

'I can't believe how many people turned up. In this weather! It's like a bloody monsoon.'

Max Bingley huddled under an oversized umbrella with Angela Cranley, surveying the rain-soaked quagmire that was this year's Fittlescombe Fete. Swell Valley's prettiest village always held its annual fete in the lower field at Furlings. The Georgian gem of a house had once been the family seat of the Flint-Hamiltons, but was now the home of Angela and Max, Fittlescombe's happiest unmarried couple, who were delighted to carry on the tradition.

'I know,' said Angela. 'How much of the turnout do you think is down to the lovely Ms Gunnarson?'

They both turned to look at this year's cake-baking marquee, already full to bursting and with a loud and rowdy queue huddled and dripping outside.

Max grinned. 'Somewhere in the ninety per cent range I'd say. We should rope in a supermodel to judge the cakes every year.'

Eva Gunnarson, the latest face (and body) of La Perla

lingerie and a regular on the pages of *Maxim* and *Sports Illustrated*, was the supermodel in question, recently engaged to the Honourable Henry Saxton Brae. A former Under-21s England tennis champion, Henry was considered almost as much of a pin-up as his girlfriend. He was as tall, dark and handsome as Eva was blonde, willowy and generally physically perfect. The combination of his good looks, charm, immense wealth and old, aristocratic family name saw Henry regularly named in *Tatler* as one of England's most eligible bachelors, and for the last five years he'd been renowned as a playboy on the London social scene.

But all that had changed since the couple's engagement, and with both of them moving to Hanborough and taking up country life. They had thrilled the entire Swell Valley this year by announcing their intention to restore Hanborough Castle as both a family home and working estate. Eva had made an effort to get involved in the village between her hectic international modelling jobs. But Henry Saxton Brae himself had been maddeningly elusive, and today seemed to be no exception.

Inside the marquee, temperatures were rising, not just because of the heaving mass of bodies straining to catch a glimpse of Eva Gunnarson looking effortlessly gorgeous in a pair of skinny jeans and a tank top.

'The cakes are going to get damaged. You must keep people *back*, Vicar. My spun-sugar daisies are extremely delicate. Icing like that doesn't make itself, you know.' One of the ladies from the WI was haranguing the vicar.

'No, of course not.' The Reverend Bill Clempson mopped his brow uncomfortably. Picking up a loudhailer he shouted ineffectually into the throng, 'If I could ask everybody to step back from the display itself . . . '

'Would you like me to help, Vicar?'

Gabe Baxter, another local celebrity and Bill Clempson's one-time arch nemesis in the village, pushed his way to the front of the crowd around the cake stall. Relations between Bill and Gabe had improved since Bill had married his wife Jenny, who used to work as a vet up at the Baxters' farm and had always got along well with both Gabe and Laura, his wife. But the vicar still didn't completely trust Fittlescombe's most lusted-after farmer.

'I think we've got things under control.'

Ignoring him, Gabe grabbed the loudhailer, handing the vicar his sticky plastic pint of warm beer.

'Move *back*, please. Everyone move *right back* from the tables.'

Then he walked forwards with his arms outstretched. The crowds, who'd ignored Bill, immediately retreated a good five feet. It was like watching a slightly pissed Moses part the waves in the Red Sea.

'Thank you! That was marvellous.'

Gabe looked up to see Eva Gunnarson standing before him.

'I'm Eva.'

'Gabe.' With an effort he pulled himself together enough to shake her hand. Gabe was besotted with his wife, Laura, but Eva was disarmingly gorgeous, and he had had three beers. She had a lovely, natural face up close, Gabe noticed, the kind that looked more beautiful without much make-up. *Wholesome*. With her long tousled hair pushed back from her face in tumbling, golden waves, the future Mrs Saxton Brae looked younger than she did in her magazine pictures.

'So is your fella going to put in an appearance today? You do realize half the women in this village are besotted with him. I'm including my wife in that.' He didn't mention that Laura had also said of Eva, 'She's so gorgeous that you want to hate her but you can't. Which almost makes you want to hate her *more*.'

'I can't blame people for fancying Henry,' she said good-naturedly. 'He's gorgeous. And yes, I *hope* he's coming today.' She looked at her watch anxiously. 'Timekeeping's not his strongest suit. But he did promise me.'

'Don't waste your time talking to this guy.' Santiago de la Cruz – Sussex cricketing hero and a good friend of Gabe's – suddenly appeared, inserting himself between Gabe and Eva and kissing the latter on both cheeks as if they were old friends. Dark-skinned and blue-eyed, with just a hint of grey creeping in at the temples of his oil-black hair, Santiago had once been something of a player himself, in a past life, before he met and married his angelic wife Penny. 'He barely even lives here any more, you know. Spends half his time in London.'

'That is not true!' Gabe protested, although it was. Laura's TV production company had really taken off in the last two years, and they didn't spend as much time in the valley as they used to. 'I was bloody born here, unlike some Johnny-come-latelies I could mention.'

'Penny was born here,' Santiago countered.

'Penny de la Cruz? Are you her husband?' Eva smiled, delighted to have made the connection.

Santiago nodded. 'You've met?'

'Just briefly. She mentioned she's an artist and that she's got some sketches of the castle she did ages ago. She very kindly offered to frame one for us as a moving-in present.'

'That sounds like Penny.' Santiago positively glowed with pride. The de la Cruz marriage was a very happy one.

People are so nice here, thought Eva, watching Gabe and

Santiago cackle away at each other's jokes like two naughty schoolboys. Angela Cranley had been lovely to her earlier too, telling her funny anecdotes about Graydon James, the designer Henry had hired to work on Hanborough, and who had once built a house for Angela's ex-husband Brett.

'He used to shimmer about the house like Liberace, in trousers so tight they were more like ballet dancer's tights. In the end Brett couldn't take it any more. He asked him if he wouldn't mind covering up a bit, or words to that effect. Graydon just looked at him and said, deadly serious, "For your information, Mr Cranley, *the cluster* is being worn much further forward this year." It took a lot to shut my ex-husband up, I can tell you, but that did it.' Angela wiped away tears of mirth.

Eva already felt sure that the move to the Swell Valley was going to be the start of a new life, a much happier life, for her and Henry.

She pictured the two of them at this same village fete five years from now – married by then, of course – and perhaps even with a child running around. A gorgeous little boy, just like Henry . . .

Eva looked at her watch again.

'We'll have to start without him,' Max Bingley complained to Richard Smart, an old prep-school friend of Henry's and another new local face. Richard had recently accepted the position as Fittlescombe's new GP, and with his wife Lucy was renting Riverside Hall in Brockhurst from Sir Eddie and Lady Wellesley, who were spending the year abroad.

'I know. And I agree,' he told Max. 'Henry does have a lot of brilliant qualities, honestly. But I'm afraid punctuality's never been one of them.'

'Who do you suggest we rope in to give out the prizes?' Max asked.

Richard looked around, scanning the muddy field for inspiration.

'What about Seb?'

Both men looked across at Henry's elder brother Sebastian. Squat, fat and balding, with a voice so offensively upper class he sounded as if he had an entire plum tree crammed into his mouth, Seb Saxton Brae was as well meaning as he was dull.

'He is a lord. And master of the Swell Valley Hunt,' Richard reminded Max.

Seb and Henry's father, Harold, had died unexpectedly last year, making Sebastian the youngest Lord Saxton Brae in four generations. He and his wife Kate had moved into Hatchings, the family's impressive estate (though not in Hanborough Castle's league), the day after the funeral.

'Oh, go on,' said Richard. 'Ask him. He'd love to do it.'

Max sighed. Beggars really couldn't be choosers. And, at the end of the day, it was only the raffle prizes.

Picking his way through the mud, Max waved at Seb. 'Lord Saxton Brae? I wonder if I might have a word?'

CHAPTER TWO

'I don't understand. I *want* a pool. I am damn well *having* a pool. What kind of a goddamn summer house doesn't have a goddamn swimming pool?'

Lisa Kent's over-plumped, chipmunk-cheeked face positively twitched with anger. The ex-wife of billionaire hedge fund-founder Steve Kent, Lisa was used to getting her own way. Indeed, ever since her husband traded her in for a (much) younger model, getting her own way had become something of a *raison d'être* for the former Mrs Kent. If Lisa weren't so utterly obnoxious, Flora Fitzwilliam would almost have felt sorry for her. As it was, however, Flora felt sorry for herself. Being Lisa Kent's interior designer was about as much fun as having a dentist's drill slowly inserted into a rotten tooth. The fact that Lisa was building her house on Nantucket Island off Cape Cod, Massachusetts, during the coldest, wettest May that anybody could remember, didn't help matters.

How do people live here? Flora wondered. *I'd kill myself.*

Luckily her prison sentence on the Cape was almost at

an end. This time next month Flora would be in England, thank God, working on the job of her dreams. She held on to that fact like a drowning man to a raft, as Lisa ranted on.

'The thing is,' Flora explained patiently, once she could get a word in edgeways, 'you're right on the cliff here. Erosion up on Baxter Road is a huge issue, as you know. Digging foundations for a pool would seriously compromise . . . '

'I don't *care* what it would compromise! I'm paying you to fix these problems.'

Actually you're paying Graydon James, my boss, Flora thought. *You probably have dry-cleaning tickets worth more than my wages on this project.*

But she kept this thought to herself, sticking doggedly to the facts at hand.

She tried a blunter approach.

'If you try to dig a pool, Lisa, your house will fall into the ocean. I'm sorry, but that's what will happen. You knew this when you bought up here. That's why we never drew up plans for a pool when we did the garden design.'

Lisa's pretty green eyes narrowed. 'Karen Bishop has a pool.'

Flora sighed.

Her wealthy client had been a theatre actress in her youth, a great beauty by all accounts. She still maintained a lithe, yoga-toned figure, and her blonde highlighted bob brought out the fine bone structure that no amount of fillers could ruin completely. But these days Lisa Kent looked expensive rather than beautiful. Well put together. *Groomed.*

Like a dog, Flora thought, a little unkindly.

It would help a lot if she smiled from time to time.

'Karen Bishop lives on Lincoln Circle,' Flora explained.

14

'Exactly. Right on the cliff.'

'It's a different cliff, Lisa.' Really, it was like trying to reason with a tantruming toddler. 'Different geography. Different building codes.'

'I don't care! Karen always thought she was better than me, even before the divorce. I won't have her and William lording it over me at the Westmoor Club because my stupid designers couldn't build me a stupid swimming pool. I mean it, Flora. Fix this. Fix it!'

Lisa Kent jabbed a diamond-encrusted finger in Flora's general direction and stormed back into her half-built house.

Flora bit her lower lip and counted to ten.

Don't take it personally. Do not take it personally.

The reality was, Lisa Kent was an unhappy, embittered woman. She'd given the best years of her life to a man who'd discarded her like a used condom at the first signs of ageing, moving on with his new wife and new life without a backward glance. No house, no pool, no diamonds would ever make up for that humiliation.

Flora Fitzwilliam, on the other hand, was engaged to be married to a wonderful, kind, handsome, intelligent, rich man. Mason Parker was the best thing that had ever happened to her, period. The second best thing was her job. At only twenty-three, straight out of design school in Rhode Island, Flora had landed her dream job, *the* dream job in interior design, working for the great Graydon James in Manhattan.

Graydon James, designer of the new Gagosian Gallery in San Francisco and the stunning limestone and curved glass Centre des Arts in Paris. Graydon James, who had built New York's 'Nexus', a neoclassical hotel voted 'Most Beautiful New Building in America' by *InStyle* magazine and

World of Interiors' 'Top Luxury Hotel' for three years in a row. Graydon James, whose vision could vary wildly from project to project, but always within the context of clean lines and a famously pared-down aesthetic, an alchemy that no other living designer could ever quite seem to match. From private homes to libraries, from Spanish nightclubs to Middle Eastern palaces, Graydon was a design master long before his lifestyle brand propelled him into the ranks of the super-rich and made him a household name from Dubrovnik to Dubai.

All Flora's classmates at RISD had been spitting with envy when she'd landed the job with Graydon James.

Of course, most of them envied Flora anyway. Not only was she uniquely talented as a designer, with a true artist's eye, but she was also the most lusted-after girl on campus. Which wasn't to say she was necessarily the most beautiful. At only five foot two, with her Puerto Rican mother's curvaceous figure – tiny waist, big boobs, big bum – and her English father's blond colouring, Flora was more of a Fifties pin-up than a modern-day model. Plenty of girls at RISD were taller, thinner and more classically pretty. But Flora's brand of seaside-postcard sauciness was a huge hit with all the men. One ex-boyfriend observed that Flora always looked as if she should be winking, sitting on a sailor's lap and wearing his cap at a jaunty angle (with not much else on underneath).

There were always malicious rumours flying around during her college years, that Flora had flirted with her RISD professors to achieve her top scores. But at least no one could accuse her of flirting her way to the top with the famously gay Graydon James. Only last year James had been quoted in *Vanity Fair* talking about his 'vagina allergy' and the fact that ninety per cent of his workforce were very young, very handsome men.

When Graydon looked at Flora Fitzwilliam, all he saw was talent.

True, the pay was terrible, barely a living wage. And true, the hours were endless, and many of the clients were abusive and unreasonable, just like Lisa Kent. But Flora was working with Graydon James. *The* Graydon James, design genius and now heir apparent to Ralph Lauren's taste and lifestyle empire, thanks to an aesthetic as chic and classically understated as Graydon himself was flamboyant and loud. Many people found it bizarre that someone as flamingly gay, extravagant and attention-seeking as Graydon, with his penchant for Cavalli silk shirts, heavy eyeliner and preposterously young lovers, could produce houses and hotels and museums of such breathtaking simplicity and *class*. But Flora understood perfectly. Through his art, Graydon fulfilled a yearning that he could never satisfy in his own real life. There was a peace to Graydon's designs, however grand, a calm constancy that spoke of history and permanence and beauty and *depth*. The spaces Graydon designed were the antidote to his shallow, excessive, restless party life.

His art was his escape. Flora, of all people, could understand that.

Now, three years into the job, she had become Graydon's right-hand woman. Now Graydon James asked *her*, Flora Fitzwilliam, for advice on designs. He relied on her, entrusting her with major projects like Lisa Kent's thirty-million-dollar Siasconset beach house. And next month Flora would be starting work on probably the single most coveted job in international interior design: the restoration of the idyllic Hanborough Castle in England's famously beautiful Swell

Valley. Professionally, artistically, the Hanborough job was a dream come true.

At least it would be, just as soon as her Nantucket nightmare was over.

I must not complain, Flora thought, gazing out across the Siasconset bluffs at the roiling grey waters of the Atlantic.

She'd been here a week now, staying at a quaint little guesthouse in town, but Nantucket's famous charm seemed to have eluded her. In fact Flora found the island deeply depressing, with its grey, clapboard houses, cranberry bogs and miles of windswept beaches, not to mention the sour-faced locals, who always seemed to glare at you as you passed, as if you were engaged in some deeply personal dispute with them, but no one had bothered to tell you what it was. Everyone here seemed to be at war with everyone else. The über-rich residents of Baxter Road, like Lisa Kent, were daggers drawn with the local fishermen and year-round islanders, who resented them shipping in tons of sand, at vast expense, to try to shore up their crumbling properties. Flora couldn't imagine living in such a poisonous atmosphere of envy and loathing every day. It seemed to her as if the grey clouds gathering in the May skies were heavy not with rain, but with the islanders' petty resentments and grievances. A thunderstorm would do all of them good.

The situation with the 'Sconset bluffs would be funny if it weren't so tragic – the arrogance of rich New Yorkers believing they could hold back the mighty Atlantic Ocean. That a big enough cheque would stop global warming in its tracks and save them and their precious beach houses from inevitable disaster. Talk about the foolish man building his house upon the sand! You couldn't make this stuff up.

The site foreman turned to Flora. 'What do you want me

to do? We can't start digging a pool. The town hall will shut us down in a heartbeat.'

'Of course you can't,' Flora agreed. 'I'll talk some sense into her.'

The foreman raised an eyebrow. He liked Flora. She worked hard and got on with it, not like most of the poncey designers out here. Of course, it didn't hurt that she looked like Marilyn Monroe. But she'd clearly bitten off more than she could chew with this Kent bitch.

'Good luck with that,' he said to Flora. 'And until you get her to change her mind? What should I tell my guys?'

'Tell them they can take the day off. As many days as it takes, in fact. Mrs Kent will pay for their time. She can afford it.'

CHAPTER THREE

Snaking his way through rain-slicked country lanes, Henry smiled as he eased his foot down on the accelerator of his new Bugatti Veyron, delighting in the roar of the engine as the car surged forwards. The Veyron was the man-made equivalent of a leopard, he decided. Or perhaps a black panther was a better analogy. Dark, sleek, elegant and insanely powerful. Henry loved it.

He felt the last flutterings of guilt in his chest over his latest slip-up with Georgina. But they soon faded, like the dying wingbeats of a trapped butterfly. Guilt was a waste of time. Eva didn't know, and what she didn't know wouldn't hurt her.

He would do better next time.

He *did* feel bad about missing the fete, mostly because he knew Eva really cared about all that 'community spirit' bollocks. Traffic out of London had been so horrendous that not even the mighty Veyron could have got Henry to Fittlescombe on time. But Seb had already texted to say he'd filled in with the raffle prizes. So all was well that ended well.

At thirty, Henry had the world at his feet. He was successful, rich, intelligent, handsome and charming – when he wanted to be. He was engaged to be married to one of the most desirable women in the world, who also happened to be deeply kind and loyal, two qualities Henry himself had been known to lack. And then there was Hanborough, the icing on the already mouthwatering cake that was Henry Saxton Brae's life.

Despite all his success, there was still a part of Henry that felt like the younger son. Growing up, he had always known it would be Seb who would inherit the family estate in its entirety; Seb who would one day become Lord Saxton Brae. Henry was fond of his elder brother. It was hard not to be. For all his outward pomposity, Sebastian didn't have a mean bone in his body. But on some deep, subconscious level, it was important to Henry to own a house that was better than his brother's, better than Hatchings. And not just a house. An estate. Something with land and a future, that could be left to future generations.

The problem was that this dream home had to be in the Swell Valley, the most beautiful part of England, in Henry's opinion, and the part of the country where the Saxton Braes had lived for generations. That left precious few options, and although some were on a par with Hatchings, none really outshone it in terms of grandeur.

Hanborough Castle was easily the most impressive house in the county. Moated, and of Norman origin, with extensive medieval additions, it sat atop the South Downs at the end of a mile-long drive, with incredible views that stretched from the sea to the south right across the entire Swell Valley to the north. There were oak trees in Hanborough's vast swathes of parkland that were believed to date back to the

Conquest. Unfortunately, the entire estate had been gifted to the nation in 1920. As far as anybody knew, there was no mechanism for the house ever to return to private hands.

But Henry Saxton Brae rarely took 'no' for an answer. Somehow, nobody quite knew exactly how he did it, but apparently it involved an offshore trust and a large chunk of Gigtix's shares as collateral, he had pulled strings with English Heritage and the relevant government department, and emerged as Hanborough's new owner and saviour. Budget cuts had seen the property fall into serious disrepair over the last twenty years. Henry was one of the few individuals with both the money and the inclination to bring Hanborough back to life.

The rain had finally stopped and twilight was softly falling over the Sussex countryside as Hanborough shimmered into view.

God, it's beautiful, Henry thought, gazing at the shadowy turrets, like something out of a fairy tale. Graydon James, the designer, was arriving next week to begin the restoration. The plan was that next summer, after a traditional church wedding at St Hilda's, Henry and Eva would host a star-studded reception up at Hanborough, to officially launch the castle as a family home, and to begin their lives as man and wife.

It would be a new start for the estate, and for Henry.

He would be responsible. Faithful. Married.

The end of his bachelor days.

And only a year to go . . .

CHAPTER FOUR

'Forget it, Graydon. You don't take me seriously!'

Graydon James lay back against a riot of purple and peach silk cushions on his vintage B&B Italia daybed and watched Guillermo, his latest toy boy, pack. If by 'pack' one meant strutting around Graydon's apartment naked, pouting and tossing one's long, blue-black, Indian Brave mane of hair with gloriously theatrical panache while occasionally throwing a T-shirt into a Louis Vuitton Weekender.

'Don't be a drama queen, William,' Graydon drawled in his famously deep, gravelly, smoker's voice. 'You know I value your talent.'

'Yeah, right,' the young man grumbled. 'All eight inches of it.'

'Don't sell yourself short.' Graydon grinned. 'Closer to ten, I'd say. When you make an effort.'

'Piss off,' the boy hissed.

He's even more magnificent when he's angry, Graydon thought. At sixty-five, Graydon James's libido was not what it used to be, but his artist's eye could still appreciate the male form, especially when presented in such an exquisitely chiselled package as Guillermo.

Graydon knew people mocked him for his young lovers. That they saw him as a sad old queen, desperately clinging to the vestiges of his own, long-lost youth. Those people could all go fuck themselves. Graydon knew the truth: he was a huge success; rich, famous, preposterously talented. The rules of the hoi polloi did not apply to him. If he wanted a twenty-year-old lover, he would buy himself one, just the same way he bought himself a slice of chocolate cake or a couture smoking jacket or anything else that brought him pleasure.

Graydon James lived for pleasure. Yet, at the same time, he enjoyed a challenge, romantically as much as profession- ally. It wasn't Guillermo's young, perfect body that made Graydon feel alive so much as moments like this one. The drama. The tension. The *passion*. Sex was all well and good, but nothing beat the addictive thrill of romance. Hope and despair. Agony and ecstasy.

Graydon patted the seat beside him. 'What do you *want*, William? Exactly? Come and talk to me.'

'It's Guillermo,' the boy smouldered. 'And you know what I want.'

Graydon patted the seat again. Guillermo narrowed his eyes briefly, then trotted to his master's side like a chastened puppy.

'I want the London job. The castle.'

Graydon shook his head. 'It's impossible. Hanborough's a huge project. You can't possibly manage it alone.'

'I wouldn't be alone though, would I?' Guillermo put a hand suggestively on the old man's thigh. 'You could come with me.'

'Only part time.' Graydon closed his eyes as the boy's fingers crept higher. 'I can't leave New York for too long. Besides, I'd go mad. I loathe the countryside. You do realize Hanborough Castle isn't actually *in* London? It's in the middle of nowhere. You'd hate it.'

'I want that job.'

Guillermo's dark brown eyes locked with the great designer's. *A challenge*. Graydon's pupils dilated with desire.

'I'm a good designer, Graydon.' Guillermo coiled his fingers around the old man's hardening cock and squeezed gently.

No, you're not, thought Graydon. But it was hard to hold on to the thought as Guillermo's fingers began to move and the waves of pleasure built.

Flora Fitzwilliam was a good designer, perhaps a great one. Flora was Graydon's protégée, and he had already as good as promised the Hanborough job to her.

He'd first come across Flora's work by chance when an important client, a minor member of the Rockefeller clan, had dragged him along to some ghastly charity event at the Rhode Island School of Design. Flora was one of the graduating class whose portfolios were being showcased. Graydon only had to see her fabric prints and a single chaise longue to realize he'd found a pearl among swine, a rare and precious diamond in the rough. The bold simplicity of Flora's designs, her eye for light and her pure aesthetic, elegant and classic but with a wonderful youthful twist, reminded him of his own, best early work. Flora Fitzwilliam had something that Graydon James had once had, but lost. That was the brutal truth. Graydon could choose to be envious, or he could harness Flora's magic and use it to revivify his own vast but flagging brand. He could subsume her talent, polish it up a little, and present it to the world as his own. Better yet, if he managed the girl properly, she'd be grateful to him for doing it.

A few cursory enquiries into Flora Fitzwilliam's background told him all he needed to know. Born wealthy and privileged, Flora's family had lost everything when her father had been sent to jail for fraud. The penury and shame that had followed had destroyed Flora's mother. But the teenage Flora was made of stronger stuff, and had turned to art and ambition to drag her out of the morass. She was a girl after Graydon James's own heart: ambitious, artistic, and profoundly insecure. *She knows what it's like to have a good life and then lose it*, Graydon thought. *She won't want to risk that again.*

He was right. By artfully combining carrot and stick – the dangled chance of promotion and responsibility, along with the constant threat of being replaced – Graydon had managed to tie Flora's star to his own over the last three years, with a nigh on unbreakable bond.

It wasn't so much that she had earned the job restoring the magnificent Hanborough Castle (although she certainly had done that). It was more that Graydon knew Flora would hit the ball out of the park, then roll over meekly when he, Graydon, took the lion's share of the credit for her work. Well, perhaps not meekly. But she'd accept it in the end. There were other advantages too. Flora had been to boarding school in England, and understood the English upper classes and their tastes far better than Graydon. Henry Saxton Brae, Hanborough's new owner, was closer to Flora's age. Plus, if Flora was on site at Hanborough, Graydon didn't need to worry about rushing straight back to New York, a city it pained him to leave as much as it hurt to abandon a lover.

Unquestionably, Flora Fitzwilliam was the best person for the job.

On the other hand, Flora was not able to do the things to his dick that Guillermo was about to.

Decisions, decisions . . .

Running his hands through the boy's hair, Graydon murmured, 'I'll see what I can do.' Then he pulled Guillermo's head down into his lap, groaning with satisfaction as his young lover got to work.

Mason Parker looked up from his Mac when he heard the key in the lock.

'Flora? Sweetheart? Is that you?'

'No. It's an axe murderer.' Flora dropped her suitcase in the hallway with a loud thud and walked into the bedroom.

Sprawled on top of the bed in his immaculate bachelor pad on Broadway and Bleecker, wearing a pair of Ralph Lauren boxer shorts and a faded James Perse T-shirt, and with his blond hair still slick from the shower, Mason looked as preppily handsome as ever. He did, however, close his computer hurriedly when Flora walked in.

Flora grinned. 'Was that a porn slam?'

'Of course not.' Mason blushed. 'Don't be ridiculous.'

'You won't mind if I take a look then,' Flora said archly.

Before Mason could stop her she'd reached across the bed and grabbed his MacBook Air, flipping it open to reveal a screenshot of some very boring-looking graphs. 'Bloomberg? Really? Wow. I guess it's true what they say: While the cat's away, the mouse will check out bond yield curves.'

'You sound disappointed.' Mason looked hurt. 'Would you rather I were watching porn?'

'Of course not. I'm only teasing.'

Wrapping her arms around his neck, Flora kissed him on the mouth. He tasted of toothpaste and his skin smelled of soap, the same Roger & Gallet variety he always used.

The truth was, Flora sometimes wished that Mason *would* watch porn. Or lose his temper, or wear the wrong kind of shirt to an event, or forget to clean his teeth. Something, anything, to make him more normal, more fallible – more like her. Other Wall Street bankers spent their days manip-ulating the Libor rate or insider trading. Why did Mason always have to be so *good*?

But of course she was being silly. Flora loved Mason, and she knew how lucky she was to have him. He was smart, handsome and kind, not to mention loaded. Manhattan's pretty, blonde, gold-digging socialites had always been drawn to him like moths to a flame. *But he chose me*, Flora reminded herself. *The girl with no money, no family, no connections. He loves me*.

Mason's family, the Parkers, were old East Coast money, with estates in Westchester County and an impressive port-folio of real estate in the city. OK, so Mason wasn't wild and rebellious and unpredictable, like Flora's beloved father Edmund had been. But Edmund Fitzwilliam had wound up in jail at forty and dead at forty-six. Hardly an example Flora wanted her future husband to emulate.

'I wasn't expecting you back till next weekend,' Mason said, extracting himself from Flora's embrace and climbing into bed, pulling back the covers for her to slide in next to him. 'What happened to the Wicked Witch of Nantucket?'

'Oh, she's still there. Probably sending out her flying monkeys as we speak,' said Flora, stripping off her clothes and leaving them all in a pile on the floor, earning herself a disapproving look from Mason, although he quickly cheered up when she climbed naked into bed, coiling her slender legs around him like a snake and pressing her magnificent, soft breasts against his chest.

'Actually, Lisa's all right,' Flora said, while Mason pulled his T-shirt over his head, revealing a taut, athlete's body. 'She saw sense on the pool in the end, and she let me go early because there's really nothing for me to do on site right now, other than keep her company.'

'Hmmm,' Mason murmured, burying his face in Flora's ample cleavage. He'd missed having her around these last few weeks, and he really didn't care about her Nantucket client, or anything other than getting inside her.

This time next year they would be husband and wife, and Flora would be too busy with babies and running a household to worry about her so-called 'career'. Fannying about with cushions and paint swatches was all very well as a hobby, but Mason struggled to take Flora's ambitions as an interior designer seriously. If she wanted an outlet for her artistic, feminine side, she could redecorate their Hamptons beach house to her heart's content.

'The poor woman's terribly lonely,' Flora went on. 'Her husband did such a number on her. I think she's lost all her confidence since the divorce. It's sad.'

'Oh, come on,' Mason murmured, slipping an eager hand between Flora's thighs. 'She knew what she was getting into. No one marries a guy like Steve Kent for love.'

This was probably true, but it still made Flora wince to hear Mason say it.

'That's a bit cynical, isn't it?'

Mason looked up from her breasts. 'Flora?'

'Yes.'

'Please stop talking.'

Swinging his leg across Flora's tiny body, Mason positioned himself above her, propped up on his elbows. Then, with no further foreplay, he eased himself inside her, closing his eyes and thrusting his hips in the familiar rhythm. Flora closed her eyes too and tried to return his excitement. Mason wasn't a bad lover. And she *had* missed him, a lot. But for some reason she was finding it hard to get into the mood. Probably because Graydon had called earlier and left her a cryptic message. Something about 'shifting priorities'. Flora couldn't say why, exactly, but his voicemail had left her with a sinking feeling. Despite her position as Graydon James's protégée, insecurity dogged her constantly, gnawing away at her happiness like a persistent rat chewing its way through an elevator cable. One day, Flora feared, the rat would triumph, the cable would break, and she would fall from the dizzy heights of her present position and plummet back into utter oblivion. *Where you belong*, a voice in her head added spitefully.

'You OK, honey?' Mason murmured, flushed from a climax that Flora hadn't even noticed.

'Hmm? Oh, yes. Of course.' She kissed him. 'Wonderful.'

She would be tough with Graydon this time. She wasn't going to let him dick her around. After dumping her on Nantucket for the last month, he damn well owed her, and he knew it, 'shifting priorities' or not.

'No way, Graydon. No fucking way!'

Graydon watched Flora Fitzwilliam pace in front of his desk like a caged lion, her oversized breasts heaving up and down with indignation as she stalked back and forth. With her elegantly coiffed blonde hair, bright red lipstick and killer heels, Flora had made an effort to look businesslike this morning. *She's trying to project confidence*, Graydon thought, almost pityingly. *To appear in control.* It was a touching effort, but quite doomed, and deep down they both knew it. There would only ever be one captain of this ship, and it wasn't Flora.

'You promised me Hanborough Castle,' she seethed. 'You *promised.*'

'I know I did, my dear,' Graydon conceded. 'But this is a business. And in business one must be pragmatic. Lisa Kent simply *adores* your work. She's hinted at multiple future commissions, but only if you're at the helm.'

'I'll talk to Lisa,' Flora protested. 'She'll be fine.'

Graydon's face hardened. 'You'll do nothing of the sort. For heaven's sake, Flora, you should be flattered.'

'Well, I'm not,' Flora hissed. 'I'm not flattered and I'm not stupid either, Graydon. This is a total stitch-up. It has nothing to do with business.'

'What on earth do you mean by that?'

'Who's doing the Hanborough job?' Flora demanded accusingly.

'I don't see what that's—'

'Who have you given it to, behind my back?'

'I'll be working on Hanborough myself,' Graydon muttered. 'At least to start with.'

'Oh! *To start with.* And after that?'

Graydon James glanced out of the window at the New York skyline. He did at least have the decency to look sheepish when he answered Flora's question.

'After that Guillermo's going to be keeping an eye on things.'

Flora looked as if her head might be about to fly off her body.

'Guillermo? That would be Guillermo with no experience,

not to mention no bloody talent, would it? Guillermo who you just happen to be sleeping with?'

'That's enough, Flora.' Graydon's voice was like ice. 'My private life is not your concern. I'm prepared to make a lot of allowances for a talent like yours. But you needn't start thinking you're indispensable.'

Flora turned away from him. She was shaking, but now it was as much from fear as from anger. *This was unfair. This was so unfair.* Graydon's private life shouldn't be her concern. But he made it her concern when he stole jobs from under her nose and handed them on a plate to one of his toy boys.

On the other hand, this was his company, his brand. He could sack her in an instant if he wanted to. She knew she'd gone too far.

'I'm sorry.' When she turned back around there were tears in her eyes. 'You're right, I shouldn't have said that. But Hanborough Castle . . . It's the project of a lifetime.'

'A lifetime is a long time. There'll be other Hanboroughs, my dear,' Graydon said, handing her a tissue, sympathetic and avuncular again now that Flora had been suitably brought to heel. 'It might not seem that way now, but there will.'

Flora looked at him, stricken. 'No, there won't,' she said quietly. 'Other projects, maybe even other castles. But not like this.'

Graydon James said nothing.

Flora was right. Hanborough Castle was *the* most romantic, most stunning house he had ever come across in his long and illustrious career. Restoring it truly was a once-in-a-lifetime commission.

If only it were in New York, he'd have done it himself.

Flora left the room, and Graydon did his best to stop the nagging doubts from creeping in.

That intoxicating little slut Guillermo had better be worth it.

CHAPTER FIVE

Eva Gunnarson stood by the drawing-room window at Hanborough, watching Henry stride across the lawn, followed by the two Americans.

It was hard not to laugh looking at the three of them: Henry, so masculine and handsome and English in his dark green corduroys and brushed cotton shirt, leading the way, while Graydon James and his pretty-boy sidekick, Guillermo, scurried along behind him like two gaudily dressed puppies.

Working as a model, Eva spent much of her professional life around gay men. But it was a long time since she'd met anybody quite as camp as Graydon. He'd arrived last night, wearing what could only be described as a rhinestone boiler suit and shoes with a little heel, like a flamenco dancer's. He was only staying a week – after that the younger designer would be overseeing things for a month or two – but had nonetheless arrived with *eight* matching suitcases in hand-stitched leather, his initials stamped on to each one in solid gold.

'Have you ever seen such a flamer?' Henry asked Eva

in bed last night, in a distinctly horrified tone. Henry was very old-school when it came to things like that. *Time was when men were men, and pansies things that grew in the field . . .*

'What did you expect?' Eva smiled. 'This is Graydon James. Everyone knows he makes Elton John look macho.'

'Do you think he's . . . you know? With that other chap?'

Eva laughed loudly. Henry's face was hilarious. As if he'd just seen a particularly revolting spider crawl out from under the covers.

'I have no idea. But try not to think about it, darling. Just remember why you hired them. Graydon James is the best in the world.'

This was true. It was Brett Cranley who'd recommended Graydon for the Hanborough Castle job, but Henry had known Graydon by reputation long before that. The whole world knew Graydon James. Just having his name attached to your project gave a property a cachet that translated into millions of dollars of added value.

Graydon was the best, and Henry Saxton Brae only ever worked with the best.

Watching Henry now, pointing out some architectural feature or other to the great designer, Eva felt a surge of love for him. It had been a difficult week. She'd been so cross with him for bailing on the village fete that they'd ended up giving one another the cold shoulder for days.

Work was Henry's excuse for everything. As he was the one who'd moved them all the way out here, Eva felt that the least he could do was to help her in her efforts to fit in.

'You embarrassed me!' she told him.

Henry just shrugged. 'You shouldn't be so easily embarrassed. It was only a stupid raffle.'

'Stupid to you, maybe. But you made a commitment, Henry.'

'Seb was there, wasn't he? He was happy to do it. No one cares except you, Eva.'

In the end, as usual, it had been Eva who'd cracked first, even though Henry was in the wrong. He could keep up the silent treatment indefinitely, but Eva needed affection and companionship the way a plant needed sunlight and water. She'd reached over and touched his arm in bed one night, and of course then he'd pounced on her like a cat on a mouse and proceeded to have sex with her with the sort of crazed intensity only Henry was capable of. Over the two years they'd been together, Eva had learned to draw immense comfort from the desperation of Henry's love-making. He approached her body every time like a man who'd just come out of prison. There was a profound need-iness there, which was reassuring given how arrogant and aloof Henry could be in other ways.

He's a complicated person, Eva told herself. *But he loves me. And I love him.*

I understand him.

In Eva's opinion, it was Henry's childhood that was respon-sible for what some people might see as his character flaws. Growing up as the second, neglected son of a great old family had left him with a burning impetus to succeed, to make his own way. All those years training to make it as a tennis star had taught him iron discipline, but they'd also taught him to be selfish, to trample down the competition whatever it took. Eva blamed his being sent away to boarding school at seven for his emotional coldness, and his parents' divorce for his manipulative side.

'Give it a rest, Sigmund,' Henry would say, whenever she

brought these theories up. Henry wasn't a big believer in psychoanalysis, especially not when practised by his own girlfriend. He'd fallen for Eva because she was stunning, and because she loved him unconditionally. But if she needed something to fix, she should take up charity work. Or buy a model aeroplane kit. Henry used to love those at school.

A buzzing on the side table made Eva jump.

Henry's mobile.

She picked it up without thinking and touched the new WhatsApp message. Instantly she felt her chest tighten and a lump rise up in her throat. The thumbnail picture was of a busty, dark-haired girl Eva had never seen before. *Marie J.* The message read:

'Where r u handsome? Missed u this week. Again. When u back in London? M', followed by a whole string of emoji winks and hearts, the sort of thing a schoolgirl would send.

Don't jump to conclusions, Eva told herself. But it was hard. Especially after that 'again'. She started scrolling back through *Marie J*'s chat history. There were far too many 'handsomes' for her liking, but nothing a hundred per cent conclusive of an affair. Yet—

'What are you doing?'

Eva spun around guiltily. She hadn't heard Henry come inside, but suddenly there he was, standing right behind her.

'I might ask you the same question,' she shot back, unable to help herself. 'Who's Marie?'

'I'm afraid you'll have to be more specific than that, sweetheart,' Henry drawled. 'May I have my phone, please?'

'No!' Eva was shaking now, her eyes welling with tears. She was leaving for a modelling assignment tomorrow morning and the last thing she wanted to do was fight with Henry. Not until she had an explanation. 'I want to know who Marie J is. And why she's missing you and asking when you're going to be back in London. I can't go back to this, Henry. I just can't!'

'Eva,' Henry's voice softened. 'For God's sake. Marie J is a stupid little girl who works at the wine bar on Ebury Street. I'm one of her regulars.'

'Regular whats?!' Eva blurted hysterically.

'Regular customers. At the bar. You've met her.'

'No, I haven't! I've never seen her before in my life!'

'Yes, you *have*,' Henry insisted patiently. 'You've just forgotten. Because she's instantly forgettable. Eva, I am not shagging the girl behind the bar at Ebury's. Give me some credit.'

Eva hesitated. She wanted to believe him. She did believe him. Mostly. But with Henry's past it was difficult to rebuild trust.

'How does she have your number?'

'She asked me for it and I gave it to her.' A note of exasperation was creeping into Henry's voice.

'Why?'

'Why not? Christ, if I went through your address book right now, how many blokes' names do you think I'd find on there? D'you think I'd know all of them? Of course I bloody wouldn't.'

This, Eva supposed, was true.

'You want to know about paranoia, try dating a supermodel,' Henry quipped. Taking the phone gently out of Eva's hand, he slipped it into his pocket. Then he wrapped his arms around her tightly. 'I love you,' he whispered in her ear.

'I love you too.'

'Nothing's going on.'

Eva exhaled into him, relief flooding through her like the antidote to some deadly poison. Breathing in the lemon and patchouli smell of Henry's Penhaligon's aftershave, she felt a sudden rush of longing, and was just thinking of taking him back up to bed when Graydon James and Guillermo appeared in the drawing-room doorway.

'Yoo-hoo!' Graydon yodelled, gesturing at Henry like someone trying to bring a plane in to land. 'Sorry to interrupt you two lovebirds. But Guillermo and I are done for now in the great hall. We were hoping you might show us up to the attic rooms? Talk us through your vision for the old servants' quarters? If you can spare him, Princess.'

He winked at Eva, who grinned back. Graydon seemed fun. Unlike Guillermo, who stood around pouting a lot and looking bored, like a typical male model.

'Of course.' Eva wriggled out of Henry's arms. 'I was about to take the dogs for a walk anyway.'

'Jeeves! *Jeeves!* Get back here this instant, you stupid furball!'

Barney Griffith cupped his hands around his mouth like a loudspeaker as he bellowed into the wind. His Border terrier ignored him completely, and continued charging up the chalk hillside towards a field full of sheep.

Tall, broad-shouldered and sandy-haired, with a freckled complexion and merry, hazel eyes that lent him a permanently boyish look, Barney could have been very handsome if he weren't so permanently unkempt. Clutching his most prized possession, the trusty Nikon D100 camera that had cost him a month's wages back in the days when Barney had wages, he ran after the dog, giving himself a stitch almost immediately. In his defence, despite the fact it was almost June, a month of solid rain had left the Downs muddy enough to make walking without boots a fool's errand. Consequently, Barney wasn't exactly dressed for sprinting, in wellies and an old pair of canvas gardening trousers. But, even if he'd been in Lycra and Nikes, the truth was that he had become horribly unfit. There was a lot to be said for his new life as a novelist living full time in the countryside. But it did involve a lot of sitting on one's arse eating Jaffa Cakes. At least when he'd been a City lawyer he'd had a corporate gym membership. He'd never used it, of course, but just having the card in his wallet had probably burned off a few calories . . .

'For Christ's sake, Jeeves!' Panting like an asthmatic pensioner, and with sweat pouring down his face, Barney rounded the crest of the hill just in time to see a ravishingly attractive blonde emerge from the woods. She was very tall and wearing a yellow sundress with wellies that served to emphasize both her slender waist and absolutely endless legs. Two immaculately groomed Irish setters trotted obediently at her heels, their bracken-red coats gleaming and rippling in the wind, as if they were auditioning for a dog-food commercial.

'You haven't seen . . . ' Barney gasped, his soft Irish brogue coming in fits and starts. ' . . . a scruffy . . . terrier . . . have you? The little sod's . . . run off.'

'I'm afraid not,' the goddess replied. She had the faintest touch of some sort of accent, and looked vaguely familiar, in an untouchably beautiful sort of way. 'Would you like me to help you look?'

Just then, a tired but not remotely sorry-looking Jeeves dashed back to his master, hurling himself headlong into

Barney's ankles in a frenzied attempt to make himself acquainted with the Irish setters, who both kept their eyes fixed on the horizon with regal disdain. It was like watching a tramp trying to chat up a pair of movie stars. The Gabor sisters in their heyday, perhaps.

Clipping Jeeves's lead firmly back on, Barney finally caught his breath.

'Thanks for the offer.' He smiled up at the goddess. 'But he's back.'

'So I see.' The goddess smiled back. 'I'm Eva, by the way.'

Eva! Of course. The bra girl, getting married to what's-his-chops, with the castle.

'Barney. Barney Griffith. I'd shake your hand but I'm sweating like a racehorse.'

'That's all right. It's a beautiful day for some exercise.' Bending down, Eva ruffled Jeeves's matted fur affectionately. Barney noticed the absolutely enormous diamond on her engagement finger. Talk about the Rock of Gibraltar. That thing must have cost more than his cottage.

'Your dog's terribly sweet,' she said. 'What's his name?'

'Jeeves. He's yours.' Barney offered her the lead. 'I'm not even joking. He's such a little sh . . . troublemaker. Not like your dogs.' He looked admiringly at the setters, sitting calmly by their mistress's side. 'They're perfect.'

'Thanks. This is Whiskey and this is Soda. They're good girls but they're Henry's dogs really.'

'I like them less already.' Barney grinned. It was odd. She really was incredibly pretty, yet for some reason he found himself talking to her like an old friend, without the usual pit-of-the-stomach nerves that usually plagued him when he fancied a girl. When he first met Maud, he'd barely been able to string a sentence together.

Why was he thinking about bloody Maud again?

Barney's girlfriend of just over a year had recently dumped him, for good this time it seemed. By email.

'I can't support this charade any longer,' Maud had written. (As if she'd supported it up till now!) 'You're not a novelist, Barney. You're an unemployed corporate lawyer, fannying around on a computer. Throw away your future if you want to, but don't expect me to come with you.'

Barney had begun at least eight different drafts in response. He wasn't throwing away his future, he was following his heart; a concept Maud might understand better if she had a heart of her own.

'Not everything can be measured in pounds and bloody pence!' he started one note. But, of course, he hadn't finished any of them.

Maud was right. How could he call himself a novelist when he couldn't even finish a sodding email?

Turning his attention back to Eva's dogs, he asked, 'How do you keep them that shiny? I mean, are they even real?'

Eva giggled.

'I'm serious. How many times a day do you have to wash them? Or I daresay you have live-in dog-washers up at the castle, do you?'

'Not quite.'

It was nice to run into this funny, chatty Irishman. Nice to get out of Hanborough and clear her head. Eva had believed Henry earlier, about the flirty WhatsApp message. But, walking through the woods alone, doubts had already begun to creep in.

About a year ago, Henry had had a string of affairs. Well, more one-night stands really, but they'd still wounded Eva deeply. She'd just plucked up the courage to leave him when he'd broken down in tears, promised to change his ways for good, and proposed. That was the first proposal, and it had taken all Eva's willpower to refuse. At that point, Henry's remorse was just words. But in the months that followed he'd bought Hanborough, moved to the country (out of temptation's way?), and proved his devotion to Eva in myriad ways, both small and large, culminating in a second proposal, complete with a mahoosive eight-carat diamond. This time Eva had said yes.

Now she was here, planning their wedding and helping Henry's designers pick out wall colours and fabrics. She simply couldn't face it if the cheating started again.

'Well, I'm heading down towards Brockhurst,' said Barney. 'I'll see you around, I'm sure.'

'I'll walk with you,' said Eva, slightly to his surprise, falling into step beside him. It occurred to Barney that perhaps she was lonely. Maybe it was true what they said about supermodels being so intimidating that nobody ever spoke to them? Then again, she lived with her hotshot, heart-throb fiancé, so maybe not.

'I'm not really out here for the exercise,' Barney admitted, making sure he kept Jeeves on a tight lead as they picked their way down the steep slope.

'No?'

He shook his head. 'I like to say I walk for inspiration. I'm a writer, you see. But I'm actually just skiving off the book.'

'You write books?' Eva sounded impressed.

'Theoretically,' said Barney. 'I'm *supposed* to be writing *a* book.'

'A writer *and* a photographer?' Eva looked at the Nikon hanging around his neck. 'That's pretty cool.'

'Oh, no.' Barney flushed. 'Photography's just a hobby.'

'Oh my goodness!'

At that moment, seemingly out of nowhere, a pack of foxhounds erupted all around them, followed by a thunderous clattering of hooves. Pulling Whiskey and Soda close, Eva flattened herself against a tree, watching awestruck as the red-coated riders swarmed through the copse and then out again into open countryside. She recognized her brother-in-law-to-be, Sebastian, leading the charge, but he was far too focused on his quarry to notice her.

'Don't they look marvellous?' Eva turned to Barney breathlessly, as one by one they galloped off across the Downs, the hounds crying frantically in front of them, obviously close to a kill. 'We don't have anything like this in Sweden. Did you see the fox?'

'No.' Barney looked considerably less enthused. 'But I hope the poor little sod got away.'

'Oh. You don't like hunting?'

'I hate it. It's cruel, it's riddled with snobbery, and it's downright bloody dangerous. They practically trampled us to death back there.'

Eva said nothing. This was clearly an exaggeration, but there was no mistaking the strength of Barney's feelings. She wanted to change the subject, to return to the easy, chatty conversation they'd been having before. But, before she had a chance, Barney abruptly announced he had to get back to work, turned around and left her, with only the most cursory of goodbyes.

Eva watched him go feeling curiously deflated. He'd seemed so nice before.

Whistling for the dogs, she turned around herself and began the long tramp back to Hanborough. It was weird to think that this time tomorrow she'd be in Milan on a shoot, in a world about as far removed from this one as possible.

Perhaps it would do her good to get away for a while? The whole text thing had left a sour taste in her mouth. And things always improved between her and Henry after they'd spent some time apart.

Graydon James sighed with relief as the bellboy showed him into his suite at The Dorchester.

It wasn't his beloved Manhattan. But at least he was in London, free from the cloying silence of the Swell Valley, with all its ghastly green hills and sheep and fresh air. How did people live there? Young, beautiful people in the prime of their lives, like Henry Saxton Brae? It was a crime against humanity that that boy was straight, but even Graydon knew a dead horse when he saw one. He was too old for futile flogging. Too old, as well, to cope with Guillermo's relentless bitching and whining about being 'left out of the process' at Hanborough.

'He only ever talks to you,' Guillermo had pouted at Graydon last night in bed, sulking like a toddler about Henry's preference for the organ grinder over the monkey. 'He's never once asked my opinion on anything. Not the plans for the master suite, not the Venetian finishes, not the fabrics. Nothing! It's like he thinks I'm your lackey.' He gazed down sullenly at his taut, dancer's abs, his huge cock lying limp and slug-like between his legs, sulking like its owner.

'Well, you are,' Graydon shot back nastily. He'd had enough of tiptoeing around Guillermo's ego. He had the damn job, didn't he? 'Like it or not, I'm the boss. Clients like to deal with the boss. It makes them feel they're getting what they paid for. If you can't handle that, you're in the wrong job, sweetheart.'

An architect had already drawn up plans for the structural restoration of the castle, but Graydon had made it a condition that he and his team would run the entire project, from foundations to flower arrangements. As project manager, Guillermo would be working eighteen-hour days and getting his perfectly manicured hands seriously dirty. The fact that he was already complaining about the client, not to mention contributing nothing to this crucial first week of site meetings, did not bode well.

'I'm going up to town for a few days,' Graydon informed him curtly. 'Little Miss Wonder-Tits is off on a job, so you'll have Handsome Henry all to yourself. See if you can convince him you're more than just a pretty face.' Grabbing Guillermo's hand, Graydon placed it firmly on his cock. 'And see if you can convince me that I haven't made a big mistake in trusting you with this.'

In fairness to Guillermo, the sex was still good. But Graydon was tiring of the attitude.

Throwing his case down on the bed, Graydon ordered himself a double espresso with cantuccini from room service – that was something else that sucked in the countryside. Coffee. Henry Saxton Brae drank Tesco instant. If there were ever any question about his sexuality, that cleared it right up. Idly checking his messages, Graydon ignored the one from his accountant, noted three from Flora, pleading to be allowed to leave Nantucket, and one from a prospective client, a Russian oligarch with a positively palatial house in London, opposite Hyde Park. He stopped abruptly at one from *World Of Interiors*.

'*Good afternoon, Mr James. My name is Carly di Angelo. We're doing a cover piece for our September issue on the world's most beautiful city apartments. We were wondering, would Flora Fitzwilliam be prepared to talk to us about West Fifty-Sixth Street? I've tried contacting her directly but can't seem to get through. I understand she's on an island somewhere . . . '*

Graydon rang back instantly.

'Miss di Angelo? Graydon James. Yes, I'm afraid Flora's not available at present. But it just so happens I'm in London and I'd be very happy to talk to you about our work at West Fifty-Sixth. Perhaps you weren't aware, but I actually lead the design team myself?'

He hung up, purring with pleasure.

Graydon hadn't done a stitch of the work on Luca Gianotti's stunning Manhattan penthouse apartment. It had all been Flora, from start to finish, and the baseball legend had been ecstatic with the results. But the project had been commissioned under the GJD – Graydon James Designs – brand. As far as Graydon was concerned, that made West Fifty-Sixth Street his. Just as Hanborough would be his, and Lisa Kent's Siasconset folly, and anything else that his staff worked on.

If Flora, or Guillermo, or any of the ingrates didn't like it, they could spend the next thirty years building their own fucking empires. None of them would ever have amounted to anything without the great Graydon James.

Graydon glanced at his diamond-encrusted, special-edition Cartier Roadster, an accessory so dazzlingly flamboyant it might make a rap mogul think twice. He was meeting the lovely Miss di Angelo at The Wolseley in two hours. Just enough time for housekeeping to press his shirt while he popped to the spa for a mini-manicure.

God, it was good to be back in civilization.

CHAPTER SIX

Henry Saxton Brae was in a foul mood.

First, the stupid little girl from the wine bar whose WhatsApp had almost caused him serious problems with Eva had refused to go quietly and was threatening to sell details of her 'affair' with Henry to the *Daily Mirror*. (Actually a few nights of drunken, broom-cupboard shagging that had finished months ago.)

'Go ahead,' Henry told her scathingly. 'Only plebs read the *Mirror*. No one I know will have the faintest idea you even exist.'

But in the end he'd been forced to drive down to London and try to reason with her (Henry's lawyer having pointed out patiently that it wasn't, in fact, a crime to publish things that were true, and that no court in the land would grant Henry an injunction).

Having talked Marie down from the ledge, Henry had been 'summoned' to Hatchings by his brother's godawful social-climbing wife, Kate, a painfully middle-class, over-grown pony clubber with a highly developed superiority complex, for a 'vitally important' family meeting. This turned out to be some utter guff about giving money to the Countryside Alliance for a pro-hunting 'war chest' to be used in the catastrophic event of a new Labour government.

'This is life-or-death stuff, Henry,' Sebastian announced pompously, and without even a hint of irony. 'Our generation are the last line of defence. We're the bloody Normandy beaches.'

Henry rolled his eyes. 'Oh, come on, Seb.'

'You don't seem to realize. Hunting could be *wiped out* in this country,' Lady Saxton Brae added dramatically, and entirely unnecessarily. 'Gorn. For ever!'

Kate had an unfortunate habit of talking down to her husband's wealthier, much more successful brother. She resented it deeply that Henry had bought Hanborough and moved back to the Swell Valley (*'our* valley') in an attempt to usurp Sebastian's position as head of the family. She was also clever enough to realize that Henry looked down on her socially. Her ascension to the title of Lady Saxton Brae had changed nothing in her brother-in-law's eyes.

'What *you* don't seem to realize, Kate,' Henry yawned pointedly, 'is that I don't give a fuck.'

'I say now. Steady on,' Sebastian muttered uncomfortably. The new Lord Saxton Brae loathed confrontation, especially within the family. 'We all care about the hunt. About preserving our traditions.'

'Why don't you pay for it, then?' Henry asked bluntly. 'Instead of coming begging to me?'

'Nobody's *begging* anybody,' Kate hissed.

Her back was arched, like a cat's. Henry noticed that her once pretty face was becoming more lined with age. When she was angry, like now, it wrinkled up even more. Pretty soon her puckered, furious, cat's-arse mouth would disappear altogether. She did have a good figure, but today, as so often, it was swamped in a shapeless Country Casuals dress that made her look at least twenty years older. Combined with the hectoring, schoolmarm manner, she wasn't doing herself any favours.

'You know very well we aren't cash rich like you are.'

'That's one way of putting it,' said Henry, deliberately goading her now.

'Keeping Hatchings running has to be our first priority!' Kate looked as if steam might be about to come out of her ears. 'You have no conception of the pressure your brother's under. This is a huge estate.'

'I know. I was born here.'

'Sebastian supports the hunt in countless other ways.'

'But you expect me to write the cheque. Is that it?'

'It's not for us, dear boy,' said Sebastian. 'It's for future generations of Englishmen. We must all do our bit. Your country needs you, and all that.'

In the end, for Seb's sake, Henry had made a donation, but he was so furious at being hijacked, and particularly at his sister-in-law's arrogant assumptions, that he'd refused to stay the night.

'Oh, but you must stay,' Kate announced patronizingly after dinner. 'We insist, don't we, darling? Sebastian and I want you to think of Hatchings as your home, Henry.'

'I don't *think* of it as my home. It *is* my home,' Henry replied witheringly. 'But luckily not my only one. Being "cash rich" does afford one certain options in life, you see. I'll see myself out.'

By the time he got back to Hanborough it was after

midnight. A full moon cast an eerily milky shadow over the castle's ancient stones, and the still water of the moat shimmered like molten silver.

Henry used to ride over to Hanborough as a boy and play hide-and-seek among the Norman ruins. It was a paid attraction in those days, and open to the public, but all the staff went home at six o'clock and, as the house was empty, nobody thought to lock it. Sometimes, before important tennis matches, when his nerves were at their peak, Henry would close his eyes and visualize Hanborough. It had always been his happy place. Made for him. Meant for him. Waiting for him. Yet always tantalizingly out of his reach.

As an adult, even after he made his fortune, he'd never really believed he'd be able to own it. But now here he was.

He'd never made it to the top as a tennis player, a failure that still haunted him, despite everything. But owning Hanborough Castle was one dream that Henry had made come true.

Only two lights were on tonight, both in the West Wing, the most modern part of the castle, built in 1705. Henry had agreed to allow Guillermo, the weird, poof designer Graydon James had left in charge in his absence, to stay on site for the first couple of months, until works were properly under way. Henry wasn't a fan of Guillermo's. He found him sullen and uncommunicative, entirely lacking in his boss's charisma and flair. But Graydon had assured him the boy was a brilliant designer, and very capable when it came to managing contractors, architects and the like.

'If he's doing his job properly, he won't have time to go home,' Graydon told Henry, which was reassuring given the astronomical fees Henry was paying to have GJD take on the restoration.

Luckily it was a big house. Guillermo had his own bedroom, living area and small kitchen in the West Wing, while Eva and Henry had their living quarters in the old medieval hall, which made up the southern aspect of the castle, overlooking Hanborough's magnificent deer park. There was no reason for their paths and Guillermo's to cross.

Pushing open the ancient, two-foot-thick wooden door, and heading up the spiral stone steps to his bedroom, Henry wished Eva were home. He was proud of her career and her huge success as a model. But he always missed her when she was away.

Henry and Sebastian's mother Gina had died of breast cancer when Henry was eleven and Seb had just turned twenty. Even before she died, Henry had spent little time with her. Gina Saxton Brae was a famous socialite, hostess and much sought-after party guest, and though she loved her sons, no one could have described her as a 'hands-on' mother. Lord and Lady Saxton Brae employed excellent and devoted nannies for that sort of thing. Henry didn't consider his childhood to have been unhappy. But he had grown used to missing his mother, and her early death had certainly been a turning point in his emotional life. There was a certain maternal quality to Eva – nurturing, one could say – that formed a strong part of his attraction to her. For all his infidelities, Eva remained the mother ship, and Henry always felt slightly lost when she wasn't with him. The loneliness didn't last long tonight, though. Slipping under the sheets, Henry suddenly realized how dog-tired he was. All the tension with Marie J, and the frustration of his trip to Hatchings, must have drained him more than he'd realized. Within minutes he was in a deep, dreamless sleep.

The noise that woke him wasn't loud. More of a gentle rustling than anything else. But some sixth sense told Henry this wasn't the June breeze through the leaves of the elm trees outside his window, or the scurrying of mice in the castle eaves.

Something was wrong.

Someone was in the house.

He sat bolt upright and listened.

There it was again. Rustling, with a faintly clinking, metallic edge, as if someone were slowly sweeping their hand through a vat of beer-bottle tops. It was coming from across the hall. Eva's dressing room.

Without stopping to think, Henry leapt out of bed stark naked and – grabbing the nearest heavy object to hand, a solid marble bedside lamp – ran screaming into the dressing room to confront the intruder.

'Aaaaaaaagh!' Henry yelled, the lamp raised over his head, ready to slam into the burglar's skull.

'Aaaaaaaagh!' Guillermo screamed back, dropping to his knees and cowering in abject terror. He was wearing a ridiculous pair of purple silk pyjamas. Above him, on the dressing table, Eva's jewellery box was open, her rings and necklaces spread out messily across the lacquered wood. 'Don't kill me! Please! I . . . I . . . didn't know you were home.'

Henry looked from Guillermo to the jewellery then back again.

'So I see. You filthy little thief!' He lifted the lamp higher. Guillermo cringed like a dog about to be beaten by its master. His mediocre career had always been hampered by the distraction of his cocaine habit, which he couldn't fund on Graydon's measly wages alone. But even Guillermo could see that this was unequivocally the death knell. Henry's nakedness somehow made him seem even more menacing, like a savage warrior, his enormous, trunk-like dick swinging right at Guillermo's eye level.

'It's not what it looks like!' Guillermo stammered desperately.

'Oh yes it bloody well is,' roared Henry. 'Get out of my house.'

'Of course. I will.' Scrambling to his feet, Guillermo backed away from Henry, edging himself around towards the door. 'I can assure you this is all a misunderstanding, but I'll . . . I'll leave first thing in the morning.'

'*Now!*' Henry bellowed. 'Get out *now*, before I call the police to come and get you. Or worse.' He narrowed his eyes meaningfully.

Darting past him like a pyjama-clad eel, Guillermo bolted down the hall towards the West Wing, sobbing hysterically.

Henry stood there for a moment in shock.

Did that really just happen? Had Graydon James's gigolo boyfriend really just tried to pocket a handful of his fiancée's diamonds?

Talk about brass fucking balls!

Still, every cloud had a silver lining. Or, in this case, two. The useless Guillermo would be gone for good. And the price of Hanborough's restoration works were about to be cut in half.

First thing in the morning, Henry would call Graydon James and renegotiate.

Smiling, he went back to bed.

CHAPTER SEVEN

Flora Fitzwilliam stood on the lawn in Lisa Kent's idyllic Siasconset garden and looked up at the house with real pride.

It was finished, at last. Painful as this job had been on many, many levels, Flora had to admit that the finished product was beautiful. The house itself was clad in traditional grey clapboard tiles. Thanks to Nantucket's strict building codes, the materials were a given. But the fluid way that the building seemed to flow downhill at the rear, with each storey's decks tumbling into the next, like a waterfall, or perfectly tiered paddy field, each one affording breathtaking views across the Atlantic Ocean – that was all Flora. As were the formal gardens: the flowerbeds overflowing with plump hydrangeas, delicate roses and glorious sprays of lavender that filled the whole plot with their heavy, intoxicating scent. The exquisitely constructed dry-stone walls, leading down to a private beach staircase, each riser carved lovingly from local limestone, all the way down to the soft white sand.

Inside, the house was just as beautiful, simple and pared

down, despite Lisa's initial insistence that she wanted something grand and opulent.

'This *is* opulent,' Flora had insisted, presenting an initially horrified Lisa with a headboard for the master suite made of driftwood. 'What could be grander than the ocean? Than nature, right outside your window here, in all her glory. Your husband needed gold and marble to feel he lived in luxury. But his house was your prison, remember? This is *your* house, Lisa, your palace. A palace of light! Let it breathe. Let it sing.'

OK, so maybe she'd got a little carried away. But the point is, it worked. Lisa Kent had ended up with a stunning home, traditional yet unique, full of space and light. With its white wood and uncut stone, its subtle mix of textures, and of course ocean views from every room, the entire building was a testament to hope.

Lisa adored it. Draping her arm around Flora's shoulders as if she were an old friend, she stood staring at the house with her, quite overcome with emotion.

'You've changed my life,' she told Flora, her eyes welling with tears. 'Really. It's perfect.'

'I'm glad you like it,' said Flora. 'But you changed your own life, Lisa. You broke free from your marriage. That took courage.'

'I guess that's true.' Lisa brushed away a tear, conveniently forgetting that it was Steve who had left her, not the other way around, and that she'd been frogmarched back into single life like a condemned woman to the gallows, kicking and screaming.

'This was your vision. Your dream. I just helped you realize it, that's all.'

Flora could afford to be generous. The job had been a triumph in the end, despite her disappointment over

Hanborough. It would be a great addition to her portfolio. And tomorrow she was leaving Nantucket for good and heading off to the Bahamas with Mason for a much-needed romantic holiday.

As always on a project, Flora had become subsumed, to the point where she knew she'd been neglecting her fiancé. It wasn't just the endless flying back and forth to the island. Even when she was home in Manhattan she was only half there, only half connected to Mason. He was up for partnership at the bank this year, and Flora knew he needed her to be there more, turning up to functions, having lunches with the other partners' wives.

'Think of it as training for when we're married,' he'd told her, jokingly, although Flora couldn't help but feel that deep down he meant it. And, of course, she *did* want to support him in his career. She just wasn't sure she was ready to give up her own, a subject on which Mason had begun dropping heavier and heavier hints.

We can cross those bridges when we come to them, Flora thought. *He probably only resents my work because it's been so all-consuming lately.*

Yes, this vacation would do them both the world of good.

She said goodbye to Lisa and was getting into her rented Jeep when her cell phone rang. It was Graydon. For once Flora was happy to hear from him. After all, she had nothing but good news to report from Nantucket; another very satisfied client and a triumphant conclusion to what had been a difficult project.

'Hey, you!' she answered brightly. 'How's Merry Olde England?'

'I need you here,' Graydon hissed. 'Now. Immediately. How soon can you be on a plane?'

Flora had only ever heard him this agitated once before, when a powerful French fashion conglomerate had made a hostile bid for GJD. That had been a truly awful few weeks, but it had taught Flora a lot about her boss. Including when not to cross him.

'What's happened?' she asked cautiously.

'I'll tell you what's happened,' Graydon seethed. 'That duplicitous, giftless cretin Guillermo only got caught rifling through the family silver at Hanborough.'

'No!' Flora gasped.

'I swear to God I will ruin him! I will flay him alive! The client woke up to find him elbow deep in his girlfriend's jewellery. Can you credit it?'

Flora couldn't. She was also finding it hard to stifle a laugh. She knew giving a job as prestigious as the Hanborough restoration to a muppet like Guillermo had been a mistake, but not even she had imagined it would come to this. Talk about karma.

'I need you to take over.'

'You still have the job?' Flora was incredulous. 'After *that*?'

'For now,' Graydon admitted grudgingly. 'And at vastly reduced rates, I might add. But what could I do? If this were to get out and go around the industry it could devastate our reputation. Everybody knows we have the Hanborough Castle commission. To lose it now would be disastrous. Henry Saxton Brae's got me over a barrel and he knows it.'

Flora tried not to visualize the divine Henry Saxton Brae having Graydon James over a barrel.

'I've told him I can't oversee it personally, not full time. I had to draw the line somewhere,' Graydon huffed.

Flora let the full import of this statement sink in. She

allowed herself a short but intense moment of deep, personal satisfaction.

'You want me to take over the project?'

'What? Of course I want you to take it over!' Graydon barked. 'I'm not flying you to England for a fucking vacation, Flora!'

Vacation.

The Bahamas.

Mason.

For a moment a dark cloud of foreboding hovered ominously over Flora's happiness. They *did* need a vacation. And Mason really *was* her priority.

But she and Mason had their whole lives together to look forward to. There would only ever be one chance to restore Hanborough Castle.

'I'll catch a flight to London tonight,' she heard herself telling Graydon. 'I'll see you in the morning.'

'Good,' Graydon said gracelessly, and hung up.

Mason Parker gripped the steering wheel of his Tesla Model S tightly and gritted his teeth, keeping his eyes on the road ahead.

'You're mad,' said Flora.

'No, I'm not,' Mason grumbled. 'I'm disappointed.'

He was driving her to JFK, something he'd hoped to be doing tomorrow, en route to their long-planned Bahamas vacation.

'I'm disappointed too. But what was I supposed to do?' Flora asked plaintively. 'Turn down the job?'

Mason shrugged sulkily.

'Oh, come *on*,' said Flora. 'If you'd been asked to work on some deal at the last minute, or to fly to meet an important client, you wouldn't say "no".'

'That's different,' said Mason, taking the exit for the airport and immediately running into a solid wall of traffic.

'How is it different?' Flora bristled.

'Because my job actually pays the bills,' Mason snapped, in a rare loss of self-control. '*Our* bills. I'm sorry, Flora, but I'm done pretending our careers are on some sort of an equal footing.' He paused meaningfully before the word 'careers', putting it in audible quotation marks. 'I work really hard and I don't think it's too much to ask that when I plan, and pay for, an expensive vacation, my goddamn fiancée comes with me.'

Flora opened her mouth to speak then closed it again.

I work really hard?

What, and I don't?

She was angry, but at the same time she knew that she was the one who had let Mason down. She was the one who'd changed their plans at the last minute. It was only natural that he should be disappointed.

Reaching out, she put a conciliatory hand on Mason's leg. 'We'll do it another time, honey. Soon, I promise.'

'I'm doing it next week,' said Mason.

'You're still going?' Flora failed to keep the surprise out of her voice. 'On your own?'

'Sure. Why not? The villa's already paid for and I closed my deal. The Coateses are gonna be out there, so I won't be on my own. And Chuck and Henrietta.'

Flora's stomach lurched unpleasantly. Charles 'Chuck' Branston was Mason's best buddy from Andover, and would be best man at Mason and Flora's wedding next year. His sister Henrietta had always held a torch for Mason, and made no secret of her dislike for Flora, although Mason claimed not to see it.

Oh God, Flora thought miserably. *He'll be mad at me, and drunk half the time, and she'll be all over him like a rash. In a tropical paradise.*

What am I doing? What am I doing?

Mason pulled over and turned off the engine. How had they gotten here already?

'Please don't be mad,' said Flora, this time with tears in her eyes. 'I love you so much.'

'I love you too.' Mason softened, pulling her to him, inhaling the sweet, gardenia scent of her Kai perfume. 'I'm only mad because I miss you, Flora. I want you with me. Now. All the time.'

'I want that too,' Flora whispered, relief flooding through her. He wasn't going to run off with Henrietta Branston. She would get things started at Hanborough, then fly back and make it all up to him. Everything was going to be OK.

They both got out and Mason lifted Flora's case out of the trunk.

'Maybe we should bring the wedding forward?' he said, setting it on the ground.

'Bring it forward?'

'Sure, why not? We could do it at Christmas.'

'Christmas?' Flora stammered. '*This* Christmas?'

'I know it's quite soon.' Mason grinned, slipping an arm around her waist. 'But just think, by this time next year we'd already be married and settled. How great would that be? You might even be pregnant.'

Flora forced herself to smile, shutting out the *clang, clang* of prison doors closing.

'OK, well, let's think about it.' She kissed him. 'I'd better run. Don't want to miss my flight.'

'Don't talk to any boys on the plane!' Mason yelled after her.

'I won't,' Flora called back, waving and smiling till he was out of sight.

By the time the plane finally took off, engines roaring as it shook and juddered its way up into the clouds, Flora was so physically and emotionally exhausted she fell instantly asleep.

When she woke up three hours later, drenched with sweat after a horrible dream, the cabin lights were off. For a moment Flora felt the blind panic of not knowing where she was. But as the familiar sights reasserted themselves – blanket-covered passengers, smiling, red-skirted stewardesses – she exhaled, tipping her chair back and trying to relax for the first time in at least twenty-four hours.

It wasn't easy.

Going back to England was a big deal for Flora, even without the tensions with Mason. The dream hadn't helped.

It was the same dream she'd had hundreds of times before. She was back at Sherwood Hall, the English girls' boarding school where she'd been so happy until the awful day her father had been arrested for fraud, and her world had collapsed around her like a straw house in the wind. She was walking up to the auditorium stage, about to receive the prize for Art & Design, when two things happened. First, her halterneck dress somehow untied itself and fell off, leaving her standing in front of the entire school naked. And second, Georgie, Flora's most hated enemy at Sherwood, had popped up out of nowhere and started taking photographs, tossing her long blonde hair behind her and laughing spitefully as Flora frantically tried to cover herself with her hands.

God, that laugh. It was as if Georgie were right there in the Virgin Upper Class cabin with her, tormenting her, taunting her about everything from her transatlantic accent to her clothes to her weight to her (nonexistent at that time) love life.

'You know what they say about Flora: it's easy to spread.'

How many times had Flora heard that 'joke' at school? Hundreds? Thousands?

Georgie was far prettier than Flora, at least in Flora's opinion. Yet she must have perceived Flora as some sort of threat. Either that or she was just a sadist who enjoyed humiliating people. Come to think of it, that was actually perfectly possible.

Before Flora's dad went to prison, her Sherwood friends would stick up for her and protect her from the worst of Georgie's barbs. But, after that, there was nothing. Everybody dumped her, like a hot lump of coal. The life Flora had believed she had – her friends, her family, her school, her entire place in this world – had evaporated like water spilled on a stove, instantly and completely. Sherwood became every bit as much of a prison for Flora as Mount McGregor Correctional Facility had been for her poor dad. Although Flora's sentence was shorter. Unable to pay the fees, her mother had been forced to withdraw her and enrol her in public school back in New York. That would turn out to be a different form of prison.

But the point was that Flora had never been back to England since that awful time.

Until now.

Of course, now everything was different, she told herself firmly, pressing the call bell for the stewardess and ordering herself a belated dinner of steamed chicken and saffron rice.

She was an adult now. Engaged to be married, happy, successful, flying into Heathrow first class on a ticket paid for by the great Graydon James. She was coming back to work on her dream job, restoring Hanborough Castle. Hanborough would be a career game-changer for Flora Fitzwilliam, the start of a new and, hopefully, much more profitable chapter in her life as a designer.

You're not at Sherwood now, Flora reminded herself, taking a sip of the ice-cold Chablis that had arrived with her meal. *Georgie and her gang of bullies can't touch you now. None of them can.*

She'd seen all the films on offer and wasn't in the mood for TV, so after dinner she wandered down to the Upper Class bar and picked up a couple of magazines. Flipping through *Tatler* a few minutes later, she was amused to find a profile of her client, Henry Saxton Brae, in the 'Ten Hottest Aristos' feature. It seemed to Flora that the bar was embarrassingly low in this particular category, with most of the men on offer looking distinctly chinless, weedy and unappealing. Henry, however, was undoubtedly a looker, with dark hair and perfect features, slightly hooded eyes that gave him a predatory look, and a curl to his upper lip that was at once disdainful and sexy. He had a good figure too, tall and lean, no doubt a testament to his days as a teenage tennis star. His girlfriend, the model Eva Gunnarson, pictured with him at the end of the piece, was even more wildly beautiful, all flowing limbs and hair, like some exotic, landbound mermaid.

But it wasn't Eva, or Henry, that had Flora reading the piece over and over, poring lovingly over each page. It was the pictures of Hanborough in the background, with its moat and turrets, its crumbling keep and chapel tumbling against the grand Georgian style of the West Wing, more country house than castle on this one side. There was something charmingly higgledy-piggledy about the place, despite its indisputable grandeur. Flora loved the way that different generations had simply added their own touches, building on and over and around the original structure, which had clearly been intended as a fortress. Part palace, part battlement, part idyllic family home, Hanborough Castle was truly iconic, as English as toast and Marmite in some ways, and yet almost French or Italian in terms of its many romantic flourishes.

Flora felt adrenaline flood her veins at the thought of stepping inside. This time tomorrow she would literally be crossing that drawbridge and stepping into history. She, Flora Fitzwilliam, would add *her* vision to Hanborough, tying together all its different strands and styles, its quirks and its beauty and its majesty, evolved over a thousand years to meet here, now, in this moment.

She felt like a princess in a fairy tale. But it wasn't a prince who had swept her off her feet, or made her dreams come true.

This is my moment. My chance. The pinnacle of my life as an artist.

The last chapter of Flora's life in England had ended in misery and shame. It was time to write the next one. Time to create her own happy ending.

CHAPTER EIGHT

The moment Flora stepped off the plane it started to rain. Lightly at first, just a few small drops dancing off the tarmac. But by the time she'd been through Customs and made it out to the Hertz car rental, sheets of water were bucketing down from menacing, charcoal-grey sky.

Tired, and unused to driving on the left-hand side of the road, never mind with her windscreen wipers going full pelt, Flora managed to take two wrong turns getting out of Heathrow and ended up going the wrong way around the M25. By the time she got back on track heading towards the Swell Valley, she was stressed, frustrated, and more than forty minutes late for her first site meeting with Graydon and the client.

'Where are you?' Graydon's voice, low and gravelly and demanding, echoed around Flora's car like a bear growling in its cave.

'I'm on my way,' she said. 'The traffic's terrible.'

'I didn't ask for a fucking traffic report,' Graydon barked at her. Someone had woken up on the wrong side of bed this morning. 'Just make sure you get there on time. Something came up in London so you're going to have to meet Henry solo.'

Flora fought back the urge to scream. Or to ask Graydon whether what 'came up' was in fact some tart of a male stripper's ten-inch hard-on, while she'd just flown halfway across the world to try to salvage the most prestigious job GJD had *ever had*, after Graydon's last lover had just screwed it up royally.

'Is there really no way you can be there?' she asked, more in despair than expectation. 'If the client's expecting both of us—'

'The client's just secured my services for a pittance,' Graydon snapped.

You mean my services, thought Flora, although she was wise enough not to say so.

'He'll get what he's given.'

'All right, but can you at least talk me through the . . . key points?' asked Flora, grinding the car's gears noisily into fifth. She hadn't driven a stick since college and could barely see three feet in front of her in this rain. 'What are his main . . . concerns?'

'Oh, you know, the usual,' Graydon said airily. 'He wants the place to look magnificent, without compromising the history. And he wants it done yesterday. He's open to suggestion, creatively.'

'Really?' Flora perked up. Henry Saxton Brae had a reputation for arrogance, as well as for being controlling. She'd assumed he'd be one of those young clients who think they're really an architect and who weighed down projects with their endless impractical demands. 'He doesn't have a wish list?'

'Oh, well, you know, somewhat,' muttered Graydon. Flora could hear muffled voices in the background on his end of the line. And laughter. 'You'll be fine. Just don't be late. And don't nick anything.'

He hung up.

Clearly Graydon's panic over holding on to the Hanborough job had subsided since yesterday. Was it really only yesterday when he'd called her? Picturing herself in Lisa Kent's Siasconset garden, Flora felt as if it were a week ago at least.

The clock on her dashboard said 11 a.m.

She would be late. That much was a fact.

The only question was by how much.

Oh well. It couldn't be helped. Hopefully Henry Saxton Brae would understand.

Flora finally arrived at Hanborough at half past one, a full hour late for the meeting. As luck would have it, she wasn't the only one.

'Mr Saxton Brae's been held up at a meeting, I'm afraid,' a smiling, slightly plump, middle-aged secretary informed her, scurrying out to the car as soon as Flora pulled up. 'He shouldn't be long now. Can I offer you a cup of tea while you wait?'

'That would be lovely, thank you.'

The rain had finally stopped, and it seemed to Flora as if the clouds had parted just for her as she followed the secretary across the drawbridge and walked through the ancient portcullis into the castle proper. Outside, sunlight fell in thick, bright shafts onto the honey-coloured stone, and bounced back off the swollen waters of the moat. Inside, however, all was dark and cold and damp. Magnificent, in its own way, with its high ceilings and winding stairwells and tapestry-hung walls. But distinctly lacking in light.

We'll have to do something about that, thought Flora, although for the moment she wasn't sure what. A mug of tea arrived, along with a Hobnob biscuit. Not until that moment had Flora realized how hungry she was. Wolfing down the biscuit, she distracted herself from her rumbling stomach by wandering down the halls, mug in hand, trying to get her bearings while simultaneously taking a mental photograph of her first impressions of each room and feature.

First impressions were vital, in Flora's opinion. It was so easy to lose sight of the essence of a house, or any building for that matter, once it became too familiar. Part of the designer's job was to keep hold of that freshness, those first ideas and thoughts and emotions that assailed you when you walked through the door. Because that was what future generations would see, long after she and Graydon and Henry Saxton Brae were gone.

'What the hell are you doing in here?'

Flora jumped and spun around, promptly spilling half a mug of tea all over a priceless Persian rug.

'Oh my God, I'm so sorry!'

She was standing in the drawing room, examining a rather wonderful antique harpsichord that had been inexplicably shoved into a corner, when Henry Saxton Brae surprised her. In a dark suit and blue shirt open at the neck, but with an Hermès silk tie dangling from his long fingers, he'd obviously just come from a business meeting. Flora's first impressions of Henry were that he was incredibly handsome – far better looking than he was in the pictures – and incredibly angry.

He was also incredibly rude.

'Where the fuck is Graydon?'

'He got held up. In London. I'm Flora Fitzwilliam.' Flora put down the mug and offered Henry her hand. 'I just flew in from New York. I'll be overseeing the project at Hanborough and I'm incredibly excited to—'

'No.' Ignoring Flora's proffered hand, Henry looked her up and down, like a horse he'd been considering buying but now found wanting. 'I don't want you. You can go.' And with that he turned around almost casually and left the room.

It took Flora a moment to recover. But only a moment.

Running out into the hallway, she called after Henry's retreating back. 'Excuse me.' When Henry didn't answer she raised her voice. 'Hey!'

Henry turned around, still scowling.

'If you have a problem working with me, the least you can do is have the courtesy to tell me what it is,' Flora said defiantly.

Henry took a step towards her. He was still giving her the 'appraising a racehorse' look, although this time it was marginally less dismissive.

'You're too young,' he said bluntly.

'I'm twenty-six.' Flora drew herself up to her full five foot two. This seemed to amuse Henry, if the small smile playing around the corners of his lips was anything to go by.

'Exactly. I told Graydon I needed somebody experienced.'

'I am experienced,' Flora said firmly. 'I'm also the best designer at GJD. By miles,' she added, jutting her chin out defiantly.

Henry's smile grew. 'Is that so?'

'Yes, it is,' said Flora. Her dream job was slipping through her fingers. This was no time to play the shrinking violet. 'If you'd read my references—'

'I don't have time to read references,' said Henry.

He was in a bad mood because George had just lost them an important deal, the match he'd been hoping to watch at Queen's this morning had been rained off, and to top it all off that infernally arrogant queen Graydon James had sent his minion to a site meeting without him, blowing Henry off for some spurious 'emergency' up in town. The truth was that Henry had already decided to nix Graydon's girl just to teach the arrogant sod a lesson before he'd even laid eyes on Flora. Then he'd walked in, seen how young she was, and felt even more justified about pulling the trigger.

But now he was having second thoughts. He liked the girl's confidence. And Graydon had said she was the best of the best. From the beginning the great designer had always talked Guillermo down, emphasizing that he'd be overseeing everything at Hanborough personally. But he'd described Flora as 'Phenomenal. A unique talent.' And when Henry asked if she was as good as he was, Graydon had replied, 'She's the best I've ever seen.' Henry got the sense that he meant it, and that compliments probably didn't come easily for an ego like Graydon James's.

'What's your name again?' Henry asked Flora. The smile had disappeared and the look of disdain was back.

'Flora.'

He looked at his watch. 'All right, Flora. I'll walk you around the castle, but I don't have long. You've got thirty minutes to impress me.'

Arrogant dick! thought Flora. *You'd need a lot more than thirty minutes to impress me, asshole.* But she reminded herself that she was here for Hanborough, not its spoiled prick of an owner.

'And a few ground rules,' Henry went on. '*If* you get the

job, you'll be working for me, not with me. This isn't a fucking commune.'

With a heroic effort, Flora managed to keep her face neutral.

'And I don't want you living on site. Under any circumstances. Not after what happened last time.'

This was too much. Flora flushed scarlet.

'If you're suggesting I'm a thief, Mr Saxton Brae, then I'm sorry but I'm afraid I have no further interest in this position.'

'Of course I'm not suggesting that,' said Henry. He'd noticed she was shaking. He'd obviously hit a nerve, although he wasn't sure why, exactly. 'I simply meant that Eva and I value our privacy.'

'As do I,' Flora said crisply. 'That won't be a problem.'

Flora's father had been a thief. Well, a fraudster. But it amounted to the same thing. She'd spent most of her teenage years suffering for his crimes; tainted, distrusted, guilty by association. She would never let that happen again. Certainly not because of a low-life, pilfering scumbag like Guillermo. Nor would she condescend to be judged by the likes of a snob like Henry Saxton Brae.

'Good,' Henry said briskly, regaining control of the conversation. 'We're on the same page, then. Follow me, please. And if you could try not to ruin any more of my rugs . . . '

The next three days were a complete whirlwind, so much so that Flora completely forgot to call Mason.

'You're still alive, then?' he quipped, when she finally answered *his* call on Wednesday morning. Flora was standing in her 'new' home, actually a fifteenth-century cottage in the tiny hamlet of Lower Hanborough, surrounded by a sea of John Lewis boxes. 'I was starting to worry your plane had gone down in the Bermuda triangle or something.'

'Sorry. I should have called,' said Flora, distractedly trying to unpack a desperately needed coffee machine from its Fort Knox-like packaging. 'I can't tell you how insane things have been since I got here.'

She briefly filled Mason in on Henry Saxton Brae's arrogance and rudeness, Graydon's disappearing act, and the whirlwind of winning the job, meeting contractors, finding and moving in to Peony Cottage and trying to come up with an initial design plan, all within the space of thirty-six hours.

'He sounds like a total douche,' said Mason, after Flora told him about Henry's 'you work for me, not with me' line.

'He is, unfortunately,' Flora agreed. 'But you know what they say. Every douche has a silver lining. In this case it's Hanborough. I mean the castle is just . . . beyond. And the valley and the village and this cottage . . . Oh my God, Mason, you would die if you saw it. It's like a little doll's house with all these beams you have to duck under and creaky stairs with original boards and a cute little garden that looks as if it was planted by Mrs Tiggy-Winkle. You would love it.'

'No, I wouldn't.' Mason laughed. 'I'd spend the whole time whacking my head on the ceiling and pining for ESPN. But I can hear how much you love it. I'm happy for you, Flora.'

He means it, thought Flora. She could hear the smile in his voice, along with the lapping Caribbean waves in the background. *He's so kind and understanding. I really am the luckiest girl on earth.*

'Have you thought any more about what we talked about?' asked Mason.

'What's that?'

'Moving the wedding forward?'

'Oh!' Flora put down the half-opened coffee machine and frowned. 'Well, yes. Sort of. I mean, I'd like to. But it's just, you know, logistics. I'm here. You're there. Christmas is really soon.'

'We'll get a wedding planner. They can do logistics. You just show up and marry me.'

Flora laughed. 'I'm not sure it's quite that simple, honey.' She looked up at the kitchen clock, a heavy, turn-of-the-century wooden affair with a loud, ominous tick you could never quite turn into background noise. 'Shit! I'm really sorry, Mason, but I have to go. I've got a meeting up at the castle in, like, ten minutes.'

'That's OK,' said Mason, sounding distracted himself all of a sudden. Was that a woman's voice Flora could hear in the background? 'I have to go too. Henrietta's organized a boat trip.'

'That's nice of her,' said Flora through gritted teeth. *Maybe she could fall overboard?*

'I know, isn't it? We're all headed to some private island for lunch. It should be great. I'll call when I'm back in New York, OK, honey? Don't work too hard.'

'I won't,' said Flora. But Mason had already hung up.

She'd left Peony Cottage in a fluster, feeling anxious and not a little depressed about the thought of Henrietta Bitch Branston whisking her fiancé off to some fancy island for a romantic picnic. But as soon as Flora crested the hill at the top of Hanborough's long, tree-lined drive, her worries floated away like seeds on the wind.

It was as if the castle exerted some strange kind of magic

over her; some heady, hypnotic pull. Perhaps the Normans had known something Flora didn't when they positioned it here? She wasn't a big believer in mysticism, energy lines and feng shui and all that nonsense. But there was no question that simply being at Hanborough promoted a deep sense of wellbeing. It made Flora feel calm and content, the architectural equivalent of smoking a really mellow joint.

Or perhaps, more prosaically, she felt relaxed because it was a glorious June day, Henry was away until tomorrow morning, and he'd taken his secretary, the sweet Mrs French, with him. That meant Flora could have her meetings in peace – two contractors were preparing their bids this morning. After that, Flora was free to roam the castle and grounds alone, letting her creativity flow. The prospect made her feel excited, like a teenager on her first, unchaperoned date.

The contractor meetings were mercifully brief. The first guy, a leering middle-aged wide boy named Brian Hunter, was a definite no. Having first asked Flora to 'fetch her boss', he then expressed frank amazement that Flora was in charge, and proceeded to patronize her for the next twenty minutes, taking only short breaks from comments like, 'You leave that to me, love. I'm the expert' or, 'With respect, darling, you're not an architect, are you?' to drool at Flora's tits. (It was warm today, and Flora had made the mistake of wearing a lowish-cut army-green tank top and Bermuda shorts. On another woman these would have looked unremarkable, but on Flora's pneumatically pint-sized figure, they were more temptation than Brian Hunter could bear.)

The second man, Tony Graham, was better. Older and a bit of a stickler for detail (with his monotone, accountant's voice, it was fair to say Tony wasn't going to bowl anybody over with his charisma), he was also professional and thorough. Equally importantly, he was prepared to follow directions. A lot of contractors thought they knew better than the architects or designers, but Graham seemed content to stick to the spec. Flora liked him.

Even so, she was thrilled when Tony's van finally pulled out of the drive and she was alone at last. With a sketchpad and pencil in hand, she wandered inside, deciding to start at the top, in the old servants' quarters, and work her way down.

Two hours later, with a fat wodge of notes and sketches under her arm (there was so much potential here, beyond what was in the original architect's plans), she'd made it as far as the master bedroom suite above the old chapel.

There were plenty of larger, grander rooms in the castle. Clearly Henry and Eva had chosen this one for its romantic feel rather than its square footage. The medieval arched windows, complete with mullioned panes, made you feel like Rapunzel when you looked out of them, and the leaning floor and uneven, original wood-panelled walls imbued the space with a real sense of history. An antique Elizabethan four-poster bed completed the look, although glancing at it Flora felt sure it would work far better turned ninety degrees, to give its occupants a view across Hanborough's parkland. Or was it too low for that?

Slipping off her espadrilles, Flora lay back on the bed, twisting her head to the right and craning her neck to see if one could, in fact, look out whilst lying down.

'Oh my God. Oh my *God*! Who are you?'

Flora sat up to find a blonde Amazon standing in the bedroom doorway. She had an embroidered overnight bag in one hand and a small Chanel purse in the other. Even in no make-up and wearing a tatty pair of boyfriend jeans and a white T-shirt, she was instantly recognizable as Henry Saxton Brae's supermodel girlfriend, Eva Gunnarson.

'I'm Flora.' Flora blushed, hopping back down off the bed and feeling like a dwarf next to Eva. 'I'm the new designer. You must be Eva.'

Eva glared at her. 'What were you doing in our bed?'

'Oh. That.' Flora blushed as it suddenly dawned on her how it must have looked. 'I was measuring. I was, er . . . trying to see the view.'

'Henry!' Eva pushed past her, storming first into the master bathroom, then into the dressing room. 'Henry! Come out, you coward!'

Flora watched mortified as this beautiful girl opened wardrobes and slammed them shut again, tears streaming down her face. Finally she dropped to her knees and actually looked under the bed, before turning furiously back to Flora.

'Where is he?'

'He's not here.' Flora looked at her pityingly.

'Don't lie to me!' Eva screamed. 'Just how stupid do you think I am?'

Then suddenly, and without warning, she burst into explosive tears.

'Oh gosh. Oh, no, please don't. This is my fault. I didn't know you were coming back today.'

'Evidently!'

'No! No, no, no. Look, Henry really isn't here. He's at a meeting. In Birmingham. Mrs French has gone with him.'

Eva looked confused. 'Mary? How do you know Mary?'

'She let me in, when I arrived last weekend,' said Flora. 'She gave me a cup of tea and I spilled it on your rug. Look, I really *am* the designer. And I really *was* measuring your bed height. For the view. There's nothing . . . Henry and I . . . I mean I would never . . . I'm engaged!' she finished desperately, waving Mason's stunning ring in Eva's general direction.

Eva looked from Flora's ring to her face and back again. Then she sat down on the edge of the bed with her head in her hands.

'Oh God. I'm sorry. Of course you are. I'm turning into one of those women.'

'What women?' asked Flora.

'Pathetic, jealous, paranoid women. Women who don't trust their own partner.' She looked up at Flora miserably. 'You must think I'm such a fool.'

'Not at all,' said Flora truthfully. 'It's my fault entirely. I can only imagine what I'd do if I came back to my apartment and found a strange chick in my fiancé's bed.'

Eva giggled. It all seemed rather ridiculous suddenly.

'Flora, right?'

'Right.'

'Eva.' They shook hands. 'Let's never tell Henry about this.'

'Never!'

Flora smiled broadly. She had a funny feeling that she and Eva were going to become friends. She just wondered how someone so vulnerable and nice had ever made it to the top in the cut-throat world of modelling? Or why she would choose to throw herself away on a smug, arrogant jerk like Henry Saxton Brae.

'We're having a dinner party next Saturday night,' Eva announced suddenly. 'Just a few local friends, nothing fancy. You must come.'

'Oh no. I mean, thank you. But I wouldn't want to intrude,'

Flora said, remembering Henry's graceless comment about he and Eva 'valuing their privacy' and Hanborough not being a commune. Clearly he wasn't the sort of man who considered his interior designer to be a social equal. 'Besides, I have a ton of work to do. I'm still playing catch-up on the project. You have an incredible home, and I want to do it justice.'

'And I'm sure you will,' Eva said kindly. 'But you have to eat. We'll expect you next Saturday. Eight o'clock.'

'I still don't understand why you had to invite her,' Henry grumbled.

It was an hour before the party, and he was standing in front of the bathroom mirror, shaving. Stark naked after a shower, other than the white beard of shaving foam covering the lower half of his face, he looked as beautiful as ever, a Michelangelo sculpture in warm, damp flesh.

I'll never stop wanting him, Eva thought. *Never.*

'I didn't have to invite her. I wanted to. She's nice.'

'She's stroppy,' said Henry. 'More to the point, she's an employee.'

Eva frowned, adjusting the straps on her pretty, vintage sundress. 'You sound like a Victorian. She's a designer, not the man who comes to empty the bins. And, by the way, her fiancé's very rich. Mason Parker. I googled him. He comes from a very upper-class American family.'

'There's no such thing,' Henry said dismissively. 'Americans don't understand about class. And who's this other bod you've asked?' he added, before Eva could object to this last remark. 'The random dog-walker?'

'He's a writer. His name's Barney, and he's also nice.'

'How do you know?' Henry asked reasonably. 'You've only met him once.'

'Twice,' Eva corrected him. 'I ran into him again the day before yesterday. So tonight will make three times. We need to meet some new people, darling.' Walking up behind him, she ran a hand lovingly over Henry's bottom.

'I don't see why,' said Henry, rinsing off his face. Splashing on some aftershave, he started to get dressed.

He wasn't thrilled about spending an evening with Graydon James's number two and some random Paddy whose only claim to fame was that he obviously fancied Eva. But the real fly in tonight's ointment was the fact that George Savile and her deathly dull husband Robert were coming. Evidently Henry had invited them months ago, to show off Hanborough, and forgotten all about it. But after his recent relapse, the thought of having Georgina – loose-lipped and drunk – under his roof and at the same table as Eva was enough to make him want to break out in hives.

As far as Henry was concerned, this evening couldn't end soon enough.

'Good to see you, mate.' Richard Smart handed Henry an embarrassingly cheap bottle of wine as he stood in front of Hanborough's grand portcullis. 'Shame about this place, though. Bit of a shithole, isn't it? Did you realize that bit's actually falling down?'

He gestured behind him to the ruined northern tower and battlements.

Henry grinned. He loved Richard. Other than gaining a few inches in height, and a seriously fun and amazing wife, Lucy, he hadn't changed at all since Henry first met him at pre-prep school when they were both five years old. He had the same cheeky smile, the same sandy blond hair that managed to look permanently dirty and unbrushed, no matter what he did to it, the same puerile but undeniably funny sense of humour. As a country GP, with a modest inheritance from his oil-executive father, Richard was comfortably off, but he'd never come close to the sort of fame and success that Henry had enjoyed. Not that he cared. Richard Smart didn't have an envious bone in his body. In fact it was Henry who sometimes begrudged Richard his perpetually sunny nature. As Lucy put it, 'If Rich got any more optimistic, he'd have to be sectioned.'

'You're late,' said Henry.

'Naturally,' said Richard. 'That's how you know it's us and not aliens who've stolen our bodies.'

'Archie threw up,' Lucy added helpfully over his shoulder.

Archie was either one of their sons or one of their dogs. Henry couldn't keep up with the Smart menagerie. Every time you turned around some new yet-to-be-domesticated creature seemed to have joined the household.

'Well, thank God you're here,' said Henry. 'It's like the house of bloody horrors in there.'

Richard leaned forward to hug him, but Henry assumed a look of mock disgust. 'Not *you*, you big pleb. No one's pleased to see you. It's your wife I'm interested in. You don't think anyone would ask you to dinner if it weren't for Lucy, do you?'

'Probably not,' Richard admitted, watching impassively as Henry scooped Lucy up into his arms and made a big show of kissing her while she laughingly told him to get lost. In cut-off jeans and a slightly stained Madonna T-shirt, Lucy Smart had taken the evening's casual dress code to its limits, but she still managed to look lovely, exuding warmth and mischief like a naughty schoolgirl. With her short, tomboyish haircut and long, slightly off-kilter nose, Lucy was sexy rather than pretty. But she had the sort of confidence that made both men and women love her. Henry had also always got the impression that Lucy was seriously highly sexed, although Richard had never said so, and that was one question even Henry didn't have the balls to ask.

Putting Lucy down, he read the label on Richard's wine. Then he led the two of them into the castle, holding the bottle at arm's length and dropping it into the moat with a satisfying *plop* on the way, without breaking stride.

'Oi!' complained Richard. 'That was Tesco Finest!'

'Exactly,' drawled Henry. 'I love you, Rich, but I can't let you poison us. Not all of us anyway.'

Leading them into the kitchen – they still didn't have a table large enough for the formal banqueting hall, and Eva preferred kitchen suppers anyway – Henry made the introductions.

'Everyone, this is Lucy Smart and some guy she took pity on.'

Richard walked around the table, smiling and shaking hands with everyone.

Henry went on, 'This is Barney Griffith, a friend of Eva's. And Flora, who's taking over the restoration work at Hanborough.'

Christ, thought Richard, looking at Flora's impressive assets squeezed into a figure-hugging dark green shift dress. *What happened to the gay guy? Eva had better watch her back there.*

'You know my brother and his wife, Kate?' Henry went on.

'How nice to see you again,' Kate said regally, offering her hand to Lucy Smart like a duchess awaiting a kiss of submission.

'Hi!' Lucy smiled, ignoring the hand and hugging her, an

experience Kate appeared to enjoy about as much as having lemon juice squirted into her eye.

Henry looked with irritation at the two remaining empty chairs.

'We're still waiting for the Saviles.'

Richard Smart rolled his eyes. 'George is coming?'

'Sadly,' muttered Henry.

Richard knew Henry's business partner, Georgina Savile, of old, and had always disliked her. At school, girls like Georgina – the ones who were too pretty to bother making an effort – had always made a beeline for Henry, looking through Richard as if he didn't exist. George's husband Robert was all right, but a crashing bore, always banging on about his latest case, which usually involved tax or shipping and was never a nice juicy celebrity divorce, or a murder, or something you might actually want to talk about at a dinner party. Unchivalrously, Richard took the seat next to Flora's, leaving Lucy beside the Saviles' empty chairs.

'Hello.' Richard grinned at Flora. 'You are absolutely bloody gorgeous.'

Flora laughed loudly. She'd forgotten how direct English men could be.

'Er . . . thank you?'

'Richard Smart. You can trust me, I'm a doctor.'

'Flora Fitzwilliam.'

They shook hands. 'So where are you from, Flora Fitzwilliam? And what are you doing here? I detect an American accent.'

'How do you *do* it, Holmes?' Lucy teased him from across the table.

'I'm from New York,' said Flora. 'Well, I live in New York. With my fiancé,' she heard herself blurting, unnecessarily.

'Git,' said Richard. 'I hate him already.'

'Leave the poor girl alone, Rich,' said Lucy, adding to Flora, 'If he annoys you, just hit him.'

'Let's eat,' said Henry, leaning over and helping himself to a large scoop of Jansson's Temptation, a delicious Swedish dish of potato and onion with cream and anchovies that was one of Eva's specialities.

'Shouldn't we wait for Robert and George?' asked Eva.

'Definitely not,' said Henry, kissing her on the mouth. (Rather too ostentatiously in Barney Griffith's opinion, although nobody else seemed to mind.) 'If they're rude enough to show up late, we can be rude enough to start without them. Besides, I'm starving.'

Christ, he's arrogant, thought Barney. He wasn't sure why exactly, but there was a vibe about Henry Saxton Brae that he didn't like one little bit. The cut-glass accent didn't help. But it was more than that. Something to do with the possessiveness of that kiss, as if Eva were a car or a diamond necklace, a trophy to be paraded. There was just a certain assumption, an entitlement to all of Henry's gestures, looks and words that spoke of a deeply ingrained sense of superiority. He didn't seem like Eva's type at all.

Still, it was all good stuff for the novel, Barney thought, knocking back his second glass of better-than-decent claret: dinner in a castle, Henry being dastardly, Eva being good and wholesome and bewitching, an exquisite but fragile glass doll.

Barney had been astonished last week when Eva Gunnarson had tracked down his cottage, knocked on the door and invited him to dinner. (Why did that sort of thing – random dinner invitations from supermodels – never happen when other people were around? Like his ex-girlfriend

Maud, for example?) So astonished that he almost said no, on some sort of weird, self-defeating autopilot. The thing was, Barney barely knew Eva. They'd bumped into each other once or twice walking the dogs, and somehow he found she was wonderfully easy to talk to, but that was it. Astonishing as it seemed, this stunning girl was clearly lonely.

She needs a friend, Barney told himself. And it wasn't as if he had so many better things to do on a Saturday night.

In any case, he was delighted he'd got over himself and agreed to come, as it turned out he wasn't the only singleton invited. Eva, God bless her, had sat him next to the new interior designer for Hanborough, an absolute cracker of a girl and very much Barney's type: petite, blonde, curvy, and with the sort of boobs that frankly made a man happy to be alive. She was American (nobody's perfect), but so far at least she seemed to have a very English sense of humour, not to mention a wonderfully unexpected, raucous laugh that made her sound like a French truck driver.

Flora. Fabulous Flora.

He'd only met her five minutes ago, but Barney was already infatuated.

The first course was almost over by the time a clattering in the hallway announced that the last two guests had finally arrived.

Eva got up to go and greet them but Henry put a hand on her arm.

'Leave it. They know where to go.'

He seemed angry at George, which was odd as he was the one who'd invited her, and he never normally minded about lateness, being perpetually late himself. Still, Eva had long ago given up trying to figure out Henry and Georgina's relationship. They clearly worked well together in business, although outside of work they fought. A lot. Eva had always had the feeling that George didn't like her very much, but Henry was at pains to deny this.

Glancing up she smiled at Flora, who smiled back. What a great girl she had turned out to be! Having her around the place these past two weeks had been like a breath of fresh air. For the first time, Eva felt involved in the changes being made at Hanborough.

'It's going to be your home too, you know,' Flora told her. 'Your children's home. If you don't like something we're doing, or you've had an idea we haven't thought of, you need to speak up.'

Perhaps it was odd to put it in these terms, but for the first time Eva felt as if she had an ally against Henry. Not that Henry was the enemy, of course. Eva loved him more than anything, more than life. But he had such a strong personality, such a forceful way of expressing himself. Sometimes it was easy to get lost in his shadow.

On the other side of the table, poor Lucy Smart was being talked to death by Sebastian on the only subject he ever spoke about – hunting. Eva saw the look of relief and gratitude on Lucy's face when the Saviles walked in, mercifully stemming the flow.

'So sorry we're late,' George announced, not looking remotely sorry. 'Traffic was just ghastly.' She'd pulled out all the stops tonight and looked utterly ravishing in skintight black leather biker trousers, a ribbed vest that showcased her perfectly toned and slender arms, and sexily spiked Gucci heels that *tap-tapped* on the flagstone floors like metallic raindrops whenever she moved. Hovering behind her in the Fulham uniform of green jeans and checked Hackett shirt, and looking chinless and awkward, was her husband Robert. He reminded Barney of a nervous zookeeper presenting some exotic but dangerous animal to the crowds.

Just as this thought entered his head, Barney felt Flora's hand in his. Before he had time to feel ecstatic about it, she started digging her nails painfully into his palm.

'No!' she whispered. 'Oh God, please no!'

'What?' Barney asked, wincing, but loath to reclaim his hand. 'What's wrong?'

Before Flora could answer, George let out a little shriek.

'I don't believe it!' She pointed at Flora. 'It can't be! Flora Fitzwilliam? What on earth are you doing here?'

'You two know each other?'

Henry scowled at George. It was bad enough that she'd showed up late, dressed like a slut and doing everything possible to divert every ounce of attention in the room onto herself. But now she was claiming some sort of connection with Flora. He didn't know why that should annoy him so much, but it just did.

'We were at school together,' Flora said through gritted teeth.

'Old school friends?' Seb piped up. 'How marvellous. Where was it?'

'Sherwood,' said George, tossing her long blonde hair backwards luxuriantly.

'And we weren't friends,' Flora added meaningfully. 'Not at all.'

Henry looked at Flora with increased respect.

'Well, we barely had time to be, did we?' trilled George, tap-tapping her way over to the empty seat closest to Flora's.

'Poor old Flora got chucked out after her daddy was caught with his hand in the till. How long did they give him again?'

'Eight years.' Flora's face was frozen. Under the table she tightened her grip on Barney's hand.

'Oh, so he's been out for ages now then,' George said breezily, adding, 'Pass the wine would you, Henry darling? I'm parched.'

'He never got out. He died in prison.'

Flora's voice was like a funeral bell, ringing out across the table. Everyone looked at one another awkwardly. Only Henry met Flora's eyes, with an unexpected flash of sympathy.

'I was eleven when my mother died,' said Henry. 'You never get over it.'

'No,' Flora agreed, surprised and touched that Henry would understand. 'You don't.'

Meanwhile, George helped herself to the remnants of Eva's potatoes and two large slices of roast beef.

'What a sad story,' she said, in a tone that made it clear that she gave not even the slightest fraction of a shit. 'But do tell. What brings you to Hanborough, Flora? I'm quite fascinated. You are a dark horse,' she added to Henry, reaching across the table and squeezing his arm in an unduly intimate way. 'Keeping her a secret.'

Henry retracted his arm as if he'd been scalded. 'Don't be silly, Georgina. There's no secret.'

Bloody hell, thought Barney. *What's going on there?*

'Flora's our new designer,' said Eva, sensing the tension around the table but not exactly sure about the cause of it. 'She'll be overseeing the entire restoration. And she is quite brilliant.' She smiled warmly.

'I'm sorry, did you say your father went to prison?' Seb's

wife Kate piped up in horrified tones, belatedly catching on to the conversation just as the rest of the table was hoping to move on.

'Fraud,' said George, slicing gleefully into her beef.

'How shocking,' Kate thundered.

'And how awful for you,' Lucy Smart said to Flora kindly. 'Did you really have to leave your school?'

'I didn't mind that part so much,' said Flora. 'School had become pretty much unbearable anyway.' Her eyes bored into George's like lasers. 'But it was a rough time in our lives. I try not to think about it.'

'The chap we're renting our house from went to prison,' Richard Smart announced cheerfully, trying to lighten the mood. 'Eddie Wellesley. Nice bloke, actually.'

'Wasn't that fraud too?' asked Seb tactlessly.

'Tax evasion,' piped up Robert Savile, the first words he'd spoken since he and George arrived. 'I come across quite a few evasion cases in my practice, actually. The last one I worked on . . . '

And he was off, succeeding where Eva had failed and dragging the conversation away from Flora at last.

For the rest of the meal, no one returned to the subject of Flora's past, although George took every opportunity to take digs at her present.

'I thought you said Graydon James was redesigning Hanborough?' she asked Henry.

'He was. He is.'

'So how did you manage to end up with Flora? I don't understand.'

'A restoration like this is a long-term project,' Henry answered, tight-lipped. He didn't know what George was playing at exactly, but he didn't like it. Everything was a power game with her. 'Graydon was never going to be able to oversee it personally.'

'Oh, I see. So he sent one of his juniors? That's a shame. I hope he cut your bill.'

'It's not a shame at all,' said Eva. 'We're delighted to have Flora here. Aren't we, Henry?'

'Delighted.'

Henry's blue eyes flashed at Flora, and he smiled in a way that made her throat go dry. *I can't figure him out*, she thought. *One minute he's being arrogant and obnoxious. And the next he's sticking up for me.*

'You know, Graydon James worked on two of my friends' houses and he did *all* the work himself,' George went on, apparently hell-bent on irritating Henry. 'You remember Lottie Calthorpe?'

'No,' Henry scowled.

'Silly! Of course you do,' trilled George, smiling. 'Graydon did Lottie and William's place in the Hamptons, and he was on site the entire time. Then again,' George added smugly, 'Lottie has never been one to accept second best.'

'Nor am I,' said Henry, leaning over and making another great show of kissing Eva. George's smile died on her lips. Barney Griffith simply felt sick, and dirty, as if he'd been press-ganged into watching some sordid peep show.

As soon as pudding was over, Flora made her excuses and bolted out to her car like a bat from a burning belfry. Barney followed, just managing to tap on the window of Flora's rented Volkswagen Touareg before she drove off.

'Are you OK?' he asked, rubbing his sore hand. There were welts in his palm from where Flora's nails had almost drawn blood. 'That was seriously weird.'

'I'm fine,' Flora exhaled. 'I just wish I'd known she was coming.'

'George?'

Flora nodded. 'I wish I'd been prepared, that's all.'

'Did you know she was Henry's business partner?'

'No! I mean, I knew he had a partner called George Savile, but I assumed it was a guy. She was called Georgie Lynne back when I knew her. She made my life hell at school.' Flora shook her head bitterly at the memories. 'I'm not sure I'd have taken this job if I'd known it meant running into Georgie again.'

'That's ridiculous,' Barney said robustly. 'Of course you'd have taken the job. School was a lifetime ago. And, even if it weren't, you can't let bullies like her get the better of you.'

'Can't you?' sighed Flora. She felt defeated suddenly, and horribly low. This guy Barney had been really sweet all evening. But all she wanted right now was to talk to Mason; to feel his safe, comforting arms around her.

In one short evening, Georgina Savile had managed to poison what should have been one of the happiest, most triumphant moments of Flora's career. Redesigning Hanborough Castle! Coming back to England, to the glorious Swell Valley, not as an exiled fraudster's daughter but as a success in her own right. Why, *why* did that loathsome, manipulative bitch have to be Henry Saxton Brae's partner? Of all people! It wasn't fair. After tonight it was only a matter of time until the entire valley knew all about Flora's dad and her history, the dark past she'd worked so hard to transcend and forget.

She turned on the engine.

'Thanks for being so nice this evening,' she said to Barney.

'My pleasure.'

'And sorry about your hand.'

'Oh!' He gave a brave, it-was-nothing shrug. 'My pleasure again.'

'I'd better get to my bed. Early start tomorrow.'

'OK,' said Barney, reluctantly stepping back from the car. 'Well, sleep well. It was lovely to meet you, Flora.'

'And you.'

Barney stood and watched as Flora drove away.

That's the girl I'm going to marry, he thought.

CHAPTER NINE

Summer rolled into the Swell Valley late that year, slow and heavy and swollen with sticky heat like a river of molasses about to burst its banks. But when it finally came it brought record temperatures and an oppressive humidity that made it feel more like a Floridian mangrove swamp than the Sussex countryside.

While the local villagers sweated, cooling themselves off with ice lollies from the Preedys' shop or cold jugs of Pimm's from The Fox, up at Hanborough Castle the work never stopped. Flora had even started to lose some of her famous curves simply from running around the site all day, overseeing work and shouting directions till her throat was hoarse.

Tony Graham, the contractor, was efficient and on the ball, but he did have a habit of making a drama out of a crisis and niggling over the very tiniest details, right down to which brand of nails Flora wanted for the new joists. He also had the world's most annoying, nasally voice, so grating that it had begun to creep into Flora's nightmares. When

Eva was around, Flora at least had a friendly face to talk to, or share an occasional snatched lunch with up at the castle. On rare occasions, Barney Griffith might join the two of them, or drag them down to The Fox for an after-work drink. But then Barney would be sucked back into the black hole of his book, and Eva would jet off to another photo-shoot somewhere exotic, leaving Flora with only Mono-Tony, as she'd christened the contractor, for company.

Apart, of course, from Henry.

Ever since the awful night when George Savile had turned up to dinner and done her best to humiliate Flora in front of her new client and his friends, Flora had struggled to get a handle on Henry. Her first impressions of him had been wholly negative. He seemed rude, arrogant, selfish and a snob. Six weeks working for him up at Hanborough had confirmed that Henry certainly could be all of these things – and worse, if Eva's suspicions and tabloid gossip were anything to go by. Henry Saxton Brae's reputation as a womanizer was legendary, and though he'd yet to be caught cheating since getting engaged to Eva, Eva's first meeting with Flora had made it clear that not even his fiancée would have put it past him.

But there was another side to Henry, too. He'd defended Flora when George attacked her that night, and on other occasions since. (It was astonishing how frequently George seemed to 'drop in' at Hanborough, for someone who purported to live in London.) Flora had also noticed how soppy Henry could be with his dogs, Whiskey and Soda, when he thought no one was looking, hugging and tickling them and sneaking them cuts of prime fillet steak from the fridge. Yet whenever Eva was around, he ignored the dogs completely, always letting her walk them alone, almost as if he were deliberately trying to conceal his affection.

One time Flora had walked in on him in the study, rolling around on the floor with the two Irish setters, giggling like a kid. Henry had flushed beet-red and leapt to his feet, as embarrassed as if he'd just been caught romping with a porn star.

'I was just . . . I was, er . . . did you want something?' He smoothed down his hair and did his best to regain his usual sang-froid.

'Only to show you these.'

Flora unrolled her finally finished plans for the new library. When she took over the Hanborough project from Graydon and Guillermo, the idea had been to restore the old library – a vast, wood-panelled room with Victorian stained-glass windows, like a chapel, but riddled with rot and in a worse state of repair than anywhere else in the castle. Restoring this room alone would account for almost a fifth of the entire budget. When Flora had suggested a smaller, much more romantic library in one of the original towers, based on Vita Sackville-West's idyllic study at Sissinghurst, Henry had leapt at the idea.

'Sissinghurst is one of the few school trips I remember from my prep-school days,' he'd told Flora. 'They had a pond there that was so covered in bright green algae, it looked like a lawn. I went running down the path and plunged straight into it. Got the shock of my life! My mother said I smelt like a sewer rat for weeks afterwards.' His eyes lit up, as they always did on the rare occasions he mentioned his mother. 'Anyway, I loved that library, with the winding stairs and the Persian rugs and the old globe. Like living in a lighthouse.'

'I think we could do a spectacular lighthouse library here,' said Flora. 'And for a fraction of the cost of restoring the old one.'

Flora had spent untold hours perfecting the new designs, delighted that Henry seemed as enthusiastic about the idea as she was. But now, standing in his study with the plans spread out on his desk, she felt unaccountably nervous.

Would he like them? Had he changed his mind?

Her nerves intensified as he leaned over the drawings, frowning as he studied each one intently.

Oh God, thought Flora. Perhaps she'd over-egged the Sissinghurst thing. It was only an inspiration, after all. Flora's library was a lot cleaner and simpler, a lot more modern.

'You don't like it,' she blurted.

'No,' said Henry, still glued to the plans, still frowning. 'I'm afraid I don't.'

Flora bit her lower lip. *Damn it.* She'd already gone out on a limb with Graydon on this. Graydon had always felt more comfortable with the original, grander, much more expensive library, but had caved in when Flora insisted the client shared her vision. Surprisingly, Flora and Henry seemed to have a lot in common when it came to taste in architecture and interiors. Eva preferred a much more modern and, to Flora's mind, urban aesthetic. But Flora and Henry frequently saw eye to eye about Hanborough, something else that had helped Flora warm to him.

Not this time, though.

'I don't like it,' Henry repeated. Looking up at her, his frown was now almost a scowl. 'I bloody love it.'

'I'm sorry?' said Flora.

Henry grinned, pulling her into a hug and twirling her around, to Flora's combined delight and astonishment. 'You're a genius, Flora Fitzwilliam! It's perfect.'

'Oh, I'm so glad!' Flora exhaled.

'It's warm. It's intimate,' said Henry. He'd set her back

down on the carpet, but his hands were still resting loosely on her hips. All of a sudden Flora felt intensely aware of his physical presence: the scent of his aftershave; the way the fabric of his shirt strained slightly against his muscular arms. And his eyes, which had gone from embarrassed when she first walked in, to angry, now had a playful, teasing look to them that Flora found she had no idea how to handle.

Looking down at her, he smiled and said gruffly, 'I can climb up there when I'm under attack. Lock myself away.'

'Are you often under attack?' Flora heard herself ask, in a voice that was not quite her own.

'Sometimes.'

Was it Flora's imagination, or did his hands just tighten around her hips?

'Well. It will be somewhere to retreat to, then. Every home should have a retreat,' she replied briskly, doing her best to sound professional.

'I never retreat.'

Henry's upper lip curled arrogantly, the same way it had the day Flora first met him. She'd loathed his arrogance then. Now she felt something else, something thoroughly disconcerting. 'But it'll be the perfect space to plan my counter-attack.'

Smiling, he released her, and walked around to the other side of the desk.

What just happened? thought Flora. Had they been talking about her new library? Or something else entirely?

Gathering up her plans, she left, the disconcerting feeling still hovering unpleasantly in the pit of her stomach.

About two weeks after Flora's encounter with Henry in the study, Graydon James decided to pay an impromptu site visit to Hanborough. Eva, back from her latest *Sports Illustrated* shoot in Australia, insisted that Graydon stay at the castle as their guest.

'That way you can spend a few days and really get a sense of what Flora's been achieving here. Henry and I both just *love* her,' she'd added loyally, winking at Flora, who wished the ground would open up and swallow her.

They were all in the formal drawing room at Hanborough. 'All' being the operative word. Henry, still in tennis whites after an early morning game with Richard Smart, was nursing a large gin and tonic by the window, looking less than thrilled by Graydon James's unannounced and typically flamboyant arrival. Graydon, now on his third Bellini, had shown up in an open-topped pink Porsche 911, wearing a preposterous 1930s golfing outfit consisting of plus fours and a peach sweater, teamed with a dreadful Sherlock Holmes cap. Eva was there, boho chic in a bright orange cotton kaftan that would have looked like a curtain on anyone else, while Flora was looking pale and tired in boyfriend jeans and an old shirt of Mason's tied at the waist that she basically lived in these days. George Savile, minus her dreary husband this time, had just 'dropped in', again, for lunch, looking typically chic in a Stella McCartney jumpsuit and sky-high heels. She greeted Graydon with a screech of delight and the sort of ecstatic hug usually reserved for a husband returning from war.

'Graydon! Thank *goodness* you're here to liven things up a bit,' George trilled, linking arms possessively with the great designer in a clear message to Flora that the two of them were *great* friends, and that she'd better watch her back.

Flora had arrived for lunch tired, and now felt utterly exhausted. Graydon's guest appearance was absolutely the last thing she needed. Clearly Eva thought she was doing Flora a favour by inviting Graydon to stay at the castle, and telling him how much they loved Flora's work. She wasn't to know how pathologically jealous Graydon was of other designers, even his own staff, and how paranoid of having his thunder stolen. Especially by Flora.

'Well,' Graydon beamed, first at George and then at Eva. 'I must say it's nice to be made so welcome. If you're really sure it's no imposition, I'd love to stay a couple of nights. I loathe the drive back to London, and The Dorchester's become so corporate these days, don't you think?'

'Oh, dreadful,' George agreed with a shudder. 'I wouldn't put my gardener up there. The place is alive with Russians.'

'There's a perfectly good pub in Fittlescombe. They've got rooms,' Henry muttered, too quietly for Graydon to hear but loudly enough to earn himself a reproachful look from Eva.

'It's no imposition at all. We'd be delighted to have you.'

'In that case, I think I might stay too,' said George. 'Make a house party of it. If that's all right?' She fluttered her eyelashes innocently at Eva.

'Not really,' thundered Henry.

'Of course it's all right,' said Eva, simultaneously. She'd never warmed to George. She'd tried, many times, but Henry's business partner always had a knowing, sour look on her face when talking to Eva, as if she were laughing at some private joke that Eva strongly suspected was at her expense. Despite this, Eva continued to be hospitable and to hold out repeated olive branches to Georgina. One day, she felt sure, her kindness would pay off, and George would realize that Eva was a decent person and that she made Henry happy.

'We'd love to have you. There are plenty of rooms, after all.'

'Even if it is still a building site!' George laughed, adding teasingly, 'But I suppose genius can't be rushed, eh, Flora?'

Die. Thought Flora. *Die, die, die, you poisonous, manipulative cow.*

Flora couldn't understand why George kept showing up like a bad smell when it was clear that Henry didn't want her here. Or why either Henry or Eva put up with it.

The only thing she knew for sure was that it was going to be a very, very long few days.

Flora's first official walk-through of the site with Graydon began at eight o'clock the next morning. It did not go well.

No doubt irked by Eva's lavish praise of Flora's designs the day before, Graydon systematically ripped into every last inch of her work. Nothing was good enough. The fixtures in the guest bathroom suites were too modern. The window dressings in the state rooms too traditional. The reclaimed stone Flora had used for the floor in the great hall was too expensive. The oak boards in the master bedroom too cheap.

'And as for this *folly*,' Graydon jabbed a gold-ringed finger at the new library plans in derision. 'This will have to go.'

'It can't,' said Flora, aghast. They were standing just inside the castle doors, in a room known as the hall. A long refectory bench lined one wall. Flora sat down on it wearily. 'Henry loves it. It's his favourite room in the entire castle. Plus it represents a huge saving over the original plan.'

'I don't care what it represents,' Graydon snapped, sitting beside her. 'I'm not having my name associated with that piece of kitsch.'

Flora's eyes widened. Coming from a man wearing an aqua-blue sweater with two felt puppies appliquéd on the front, this was a bit rich.

'Besides,' Graydon added, his tone softening slightly, 'Henry Saxton Brae is not the only person we're trying to please here.'

Flora looked puzzled. 'What do you mean?'

'The International Designer of the Year award is being held in London next year,' said Graydon. 'It's been moved forward to June, which means all submissions must be put before the judges by April.'

Flora looked at him blankly. The Hanborough restoration would not be close to finished by April. The plan had been to get everything but the South Wing completed by next August, in time for Henry and Eva's wedding. At the current rate of progress, even that was going to be a stretch.

'You're not thinking of entering Hanborough?'

'I'm not thinking about it, no,' Graydon said caustically. 'I'm doing it. Or, rather, we're doing it. Together.'

Flora opened her mouth to protest but Graydon wasn't finished.

'I happen to have two close friends on the panel. It's going to be a much more avant-garde group of judges than in previous years. We're going to have to rethink a lot of the plans here if we want to have a shot at winning. Introduce some much more innovative, modern elements. Think sustainability. Eco-friendly. Old meets new.'

Flora imagined Henry wincing at every one of these expressions.

'Take a look at these.' Flipping open his MacBook Air, Graydon showed Flora a slide show of images. One was of a steel-framed barn with a retractable glass roof. Another of a Plexiglas tunnel connecting the East and West wings of the castle at the rear.

Flora shook her head. 'There's just no way. For one thing, Henry's a traditionalist. He'll never agree to anything like that.'

'Then you must make him agree,' said Graydon, unyielding.

'Even if I could, this stuff is all way over budget,' protested Flora. 'And you want it done by next *April*? At the rate we've been going we'll struggle to get the current plans finished by next August.'

Graydon fell silent for a moment, his lips pursed.

'Perhaps I made a mistake in entrusting you with a project of this significance,' he said at last. 'Our mutual friend Mrs Savile confided in me that you've been struggling.'

'I have *not* been struggling!' Flora said hotly. 'And Georgina Savile is no friend of mine.'

'Hmmm,' Graydon mused. 'Well, you do look terribly tired, Flora. I have a new fellow working for me in New York, Riccardo. Perhaps it makes sense for him to take over from here? I know he's chomping at the bit for a challenge.'

Flora could instantly visualize Riccardo, no doubt Graydon's latest squeeze.

'Sure,' she quipped. 'That's a great idea, Graydon. Because Guillermo worked out so well.'

Graydon's eyes narrowed. 'I don't owe you this job, Flora.'

'No, you don't. But you gave it to me, and I've done all you asked – and more. *And*, Henry and Eva love me,' Flora said defiantly. 'They would have to agree to any change in designer and, I'm telling you now, they won't. Not in a million years. So if you want the slightest chance of getting these changes made, or entering Hanborough for the

International Designer of the Year award, the fact is, Graydon, you *do* need me. You do.'

She was quivering with rage, glaring at Graydon, daring him to deny it. For a moment Graydon glared back, equally furious. Then, to Flora's surprise, he smiled.

'Thank goodness,' he said. 'I'd started to think the old, ambitious Flora Fitzwilliam was gone for ever. So, we're on the same page? Winning International Designer of the Year will mean more for your career than it will for mine, darling.'

'You'd share the award with me?' Flora's eyes widened. 'I mean, we'd enter Hanborough together?'

'Of course,' Graydon said breezily. 'As a team. My brand. My vision. Your hard graft. What do you say?'

Flora's mind raced. She made a mental list of pros and cons. The cons list was considerably longer.

Graydon's plans were frankly hideous, a betrayal not only of Henry and of Hanborough, but of Flora's own artistic integrity.

Changing tack so radically and aiming for an April completion would mean working even harder than she was now, which scarcely seemed possible.

It would also leave her even less time for Mason – fewer trips home, and no time at all to focus on planning their wedding.

On the pros side, if by some miracle they pulled it off, she, Flora Fitzwilliam, would be International Designer of the Year. Her name and Graydon's, side by side, as equals.

'OK.' She smiled back at Graydon. 'I'm in.'

'Wonderful,' the old man purred. 'So, how do you plan to convince our friend Henry to change his plans and double his budget?'

'I don't,' said Flora.

Graydon frowned. 'What do you mean?'

'I have a better idea.' Flora smiled cryptically. 'Trust me.'

'What do you think?'

Flora and Eva were sprawled out in old-fashioned deck-chairs in the back garden of Peony Cottage. It was a glorious, baking hot summer afternoon and Flora had asked Eva over specially for tea and cake. 'I have something I want to show you privately,' she'd told her up at the castle, the day Graydon flew back to New York. 'Shall we meet at my cottage? Around four?'

Eva was entranced by Flora's cottage, with its simple, cool whitewashed walls and artfully placed earthenware, and its overblown but exquisite back garden, bursting with sweet-smelling clematis and honeysuckle, its beds crowded with pretty pink roses and towering hollyhocks in white and pink and deep purple, the colour of overripe plums.

'It's like a Kate Greenaway postcard,' she sighed. 'Like something from a hundred years ago.'

'It's beautiful, isn't it?' agreed Flora. 'I love it here. It's my sanctuary.'

'Lucky you,' said Eva. 'I mean, obviously I'm incredibly blessed to live at Hanborough. Who wouldn't want to wake up in a fairy-tale castle every day, right?'

'But?' Flora prodded.

'Well. It's Henry's home, really,' said Eva.

'What do you mean?'

'Just that here, at Peony Cottage, you can do what you like. You've made it your home because you designed all the interiors yourself. Don't get me wrong, I love what you're doing up at Hanborough,' Eva explained hastily. 'It's just that you're doing it. You and Henry. Not me.'

Flora beamed. This couldn't be going more perfectly.

'That's exactly why I invited you over,' she said. 'You've hit the nail on the head. Graydon and I both felt that you've been excluded from the design process up till now, and that maybe what we've been doing up at the castle is a bit . . . ' She searched around for the right word. 'A bit simplistic – a bit one-dimensional, shall we say – as a result. Take a look at these.'

Slowly, one by one, Flora walked Eva through Graydon's revised plans. Naturally far more of a modernist than Henry, Eva was instantly drawn to the stark, minimalist, even industrial style of the party barn, with its steel and glass and light. 'It looks very Swedish,' she observed approvingly. Within half an hour, Flora had as good as convinced Eva that the designs were her own – or at least that she and Graydon had merely 'anticipated' her vision.

'I know Henry wants Hanborough to feel like your home too,' said Flora. 'That's why he moved here, after all. So the two of you could make a life together.'

'That's true,' Eva mused, flipping longingly through the new plans.

'But you need to speak up for yourself,' Flora told her. 'I can't do it. If I showed Henry these plans, he'd shut me down immediately. But *you* can. And I really think you should.'

Eva nodded, taking another sip of Earl Grey tea from Flora's shabby-chic china cup. Flora noticed she had left her fruit cake completely untouched. Being a world-famous lingerie model did have some disadvantages, apparently.

'You're right,' said Eva boldly, tucking the plans under her arm. 'I can't complain about being left out of the process if I never tell Henry what I want. Thanks, Flora.'

Standing up to her full five feet eleven, towering over Flora, she hugged her goodbye. 'And thanks for asking me over today. I really appreciate your friendship. I hope you know that.'

'Likewise,' said Flora, suppressing a mighty wave of guilt.

She felt bad, using Eva so blatantly to get these design changes past Henry. But it was the only way. Henry and Flora had such similar tastes; if Flora presented them he would smell a rat immediately. Plexiglas tunnels and party barns were definitely not Flora's style. And the International Designer of the Year award was not going to win itself.

'I'm sorry,' Henry told Flora two days later, re-presenting her own plans to her over coffee in the castle kitchen, 'I know these are big changes. And I know they're godawful. But it means so much to Eva. I want to at least meet her halfway.'

'I understand.' Flora nodded sympathetically. 'You realize it's a lot more money?'

Henry shrugged. 'Money's not a problem. Don't tell your bloody boss I said that,' he added quickly.

'Of course not,' said Flora, trying her best to look loyal and supportive. Once again she successfully suppressed a pang of guilt. She was surprising herself by how good she was becoming at this manipulation lark. Perhaps she'd learned more from Graydon James than she realized?

'I'm not having the tunnel,' Henry said firmly. 'It looks like a fucking small intestine.'

Flora laughed loudly. She wouldn't tell Graydon that either, although she wanted to.

'But I told her yes to the barn.'

'OK,' said Flora. 'I'll put the change orders in to Tony and we'll get started.'

Draining her coffee, she was getting up to leave when Henry put a hand on her arm.

'I appreciate your work here, Flora. I really do,' he said earnestly. 'And what a good friend you've been to Eva. She needed a friend here.'

'Thanks,' Flora said weakly. 'She's a lovely woman.'

'Yes,' agreed Henry. 'She is. Far too lovely for me.'

Not even Flora could hold back the guilt that time as she slunk away.

CHAPTER TEN

For the next ten days, Flora barely slept. After speaking to an ecstatic Graydon, she dealt with an irritated Tony Graham ('More money's all very well, Miss Fitzwilliam, but my men aren't miracle workers. We can't erect a complex structure like this from scratch in that timeframe. Not with all the other work we have to finish on the place.' To which Flora's response had been a pithy: 'Try.'). She started spending sixteen-hour days up at the castle, followed by at least two hours of admin and emails at home before collapsing into bed, exhausted but often too wired to fall asleep. She was invariably already awake when her alarm went off at six each morning, with ideas and potential problems on site racing through her head like unwanted rallycross drivers.

'You need a day off,' said Eva one Friday afternoon, catching an increasingly skinny and haggard-looking Flora slumped against the portcullis, jerking in and out of an involuntary sleep. 'I mean it. If I see you up here tomorrow I'll have Henry set the dogs on you. No one can function like this. Go home and sleep.'

'I can't sleep,' Flora replied, honestly.

'Then do something else. Something fun. Disconnect. Seriously.'

Somewhat reluctantly, Flora agreed, booking herself into Petals, the new hairdresser's-cum-beauty salon on Fittlescombe High Street, for highlights, a haircut and a desperately needed mani-pedi on Saturday morning.

Converted from the old village bakery, and run by a sixty-five-year-old matron called Doris and her sweet but dim daughter Denise, it wasn't exactly Vidal Sassoon. But needs must. Flora had caught sight of her toenails in the bath a few nights ago and almost had a heart attack.

'I look like a Hobbit,' she'd told Mason on their daily Skype call. 'Bilbo Fitzwilliam.'

'No, you don't. You look beautiful,' Mason said loyally. 'I just wish I could see you in the flesh. Man cannot live by Skype alone, you know.'

It was a familiar refrain, and a fair one. Flora had been promising to fly home for a few days for months now. It wasn't that she didn't want to. Just that every time she thought she might have a window, more work miraculously materialized.

'I know,' said Flora. 'I'll book something. I promise.'

'When?'

'Soon. Very soon.' She meant it. She missed Mason horribly. Seeing him on the computer, lying in bed in their apartment, felt surreal. Flora worried that their life together in Manhattan was starting to feel like a distant dream. A part of her past, rather than her future.

'Is the water all right for you?' Denise was asking, plunging Flora's battered feet into a plastic washing-up bowl that she'd filled from the sink, while her mother, Doris, folded foils into Flora's hair.

'Hmm? Oh, yes. It's fine.'

'I'll bring you a couple of wedding magazines, shall I?' Denise said cheerfully.

'Oh, that's OK. I don't really—'

Ignoring Flora's protests, Denise deposited *Modern Bride* and *Wedding Fever* into her lap. 'A little bird told me Eva Gunnarson's not the only bride-to-be up at the castle.' Denise winked, her heavy false eyelashes coming down onto her over-Botoxed cheeks like shutters. 'You must be well excited.'

'The wedding's not till next summer,' said Flora, flipping politely through the magazine pages and trying to look interested. 'I haven't had time to think about it much, to be honest with you.'

Flora suspected that Eva herself was the 'little bird'. Desperate for some sisterly solidarity, and feverishly excited about her own wedding to Henry, she was forever shoving bridal magazines under Flora's nose, or emailing her images of flower arrangements or veils. Right this moment, in fact, Eva was supposed to be meeting with the vicar to discuss something or other about her and Henry's nuptials – also not scheduled until next summer, but in Eva's mind this was 'practically tomorrow'. She simply couldn't understand why Flora hadn't started trying on dresses already. 'Any good seamstress will need at least six months' lead time, you know,' she told Flora seriously, in the manner of someone delivering a hurricane warning to someone refusing to leave their home.

While Denise did her best to return Flora's feet to human status, Flora sipped her PG Tips and pretended to read her magazines, whilst secretly tuning in to what was going on around her. A very old woman sitting under an old-fashioned dryer in the corner, having her remaining wisps of hair 'set' into tight, white curls, turned out to be old Mrs Griggs, mother of Mrs Preedy from Fittlescombe's eponymous village shop. Her loud, derogatory comments about her son-in-law's business acumen, fashion sense, and failures as a father – 'he wouldn't say boo to a goose, that Preedy. Lets them kids walk all over him' – left no one in the salon in any doubt as to her firmly held opinion that her daughter could have done better. 'Beautiful she was as a youngster, my Val. She looked like Marilyn Monroe.'

Flora was still struggling to imagine the hefty, boot-faced Mrs Preedy as a young siren, when another conversation claimed her attention.

Two younger women, who Flora vaguely recognized as mothers from the local primary school – she'd seen them pushing buggies towards the village green at pick-up time – were having their hair washed side by side by Doris's two juniors, gossiping loudly to drown out the sound of the water.

'He really is gorgeous, isn't he? Much better looking than Gabe Baxter,' said one.

'D'you think so?' observed her friend. 'I dunno. He's a bit smarmy. I think it's the posh voice.'

'You wouldn't need him to talk though, would you?' the first girl cackled. 'It's like David Beckham. "Stop squeaking, David, and get on with it!"'

Both women laughed.

'They're both dirty dogs though, aren't they? Beckham's slept with everything in a skirt and Saxton Brae's no better. I wouldn't trust him as far as I could spit.'

For the first time Flora realized they were talking about Henry.

'I heard he's got a new bit on the side,' said the first woman. 'Someone local apparently.'

'Really?' The friend turned her head, earning herself a squirt of warm water in the eyes. The junior passed her a towel. 'Someone besides that snooty Savile woman, you mean?'

'What, Skeletor?' Both women laughed again.

'She's awful, isn't she? God knows what Henry sees in her. I mean, why would you sleep with a flat-chested cow like Georgina Savile when you've got Eva Gunnarson at home?'

Flora froze.

It wasn't that she couldn't imagine Henry cheating on Eva. With his arrogance, and raging sense of entitlement, he probably viewed having a mistress as no more than his due, par for the course for an eligible bachelor like him. But an affair with George Savile? That she couldn't imagine.

He can't be, she told herself. *They're business partners. Besides, Henry hates George. Every time she comes to Hanborough, he looks as if he can't wait for her to leave.*

Although, come to think of it, an affair would explain George's frequent visits to the castle. Flora tuned back into the women's conversation.

'So who's his new bit of crumpet?' asked the friend.

'Dunno,' the first woman said. 'Nobody does. They're being very discreet, apparently. But I hear she's married.'

The friend sighed dramatically. 'Poor old Eva Gunnarson. Just goes to show, even if you're a supermodel, you can still get your heart broken. Men like Henry Saxton Brae will still shit on you.'

'Only if you let them,' said the first woman. 'If you ask me, Eva should give him his marching orders.'

'Yeah, but d'you think she knows?'

'Course she does! Everyone knows. D'you think Posh Spice didn't know? She just wanted the lifestyle, didn't she?'

Their conversation moved on to the Beckhams and footballers' wives in general. But Flora sat in utter shock. Was this true? How could she have spent so many weeks at Hanborough and not heard so much as a whisper of these rumours before now? Then she remembered that today was the first time she'd been anywhere *except* Hanborough, or passed out on the couch alone in Peony Cottage, for almost a month. You couldn't hear rumours if you never talked to anyone.

She was still thinking about Henry and George and Henry's other mystery lover, if such a person actually existed, when Doris led her over to the basins to have her highlights rinsed out.

Unable to face another bridal magazine, Flora distracted herself by picking up the latest copy of *Vanity Fair*. It wasn't until she was back in her chair and halfway through her blow-dry that she saw it.

'Oh my God!' she said out loud. 'Oh my *God*. How *could* he?'

'Everything all right, my love?' Doris asked her, still working her magic with the round brush.

'No,' said Flora. 'Not really. In fact, not at all.'

The scheming, lying bastard!

The Reverend Bill Clempson shook Eva Gunnarson's hand warmly and watched as she sauntered happily back down the vicarage's garden path to her car. She really was a quite inordinately beautiful girl, and even lovelier in her anticipatory, prenuptial glow. Henry Saxton Brae was a lucky man.

'Take a bloody picture, why don't you? It'll last longer.'

Jennifer Clempson, Bill's wife, loomed in the doorway with a face like thunder. To say that Bill adored Jen would be an understatement. She was truly the miracle of his life. They'd first met when Jen was working as the vet on *Valley Farm*, Gabe and Laura Baxter's reality show that had caused a huge schism in the Swell Valley when Bill first arrived in the parish. Bill had been leading his flock in protest against the show and its intrusive TV crews, when Jen had deposited a truckload of manure over his Mini Cooper, covering it completely. Never in Bill's wildest dreams had it occurred to him that, from this inauspicious start, this gorgeous, kind, accomplished, confident young woman might one day become his wife.

And yet she had. Not just that, but she was now four months pregnant with his child! Their child. Truly the Lord had blessed him.

However, it would be fair to say that perhaps pregnancy didn't bring out the absolute best in Jennifer Clempson.

'It's not very vicarly behaviour to stand there checking out your parishioner's perfect, supermodel arse, you know,' Jen grumbled.

'My darling, I wasn't "checking out" anything,' said Bill. 'I was actually just thinking how happy Eva seems. Like we were before our wedding.'

'Hmmm,' said Jen, grouchily.

Bill placed a hand lovingly on her emerging bump. 'You're so beautiful.'

'It's not very vicarly to lie, either,' said Jen. 'I look like a dyspeptic frog with a beer belly and you know it.'

'Nonsense,' said Bill. 'You look lovely. Like a . . . like a . . . ' For an awful moment his mind went completely blank. What were pregnant women supposed to look like? All he could think of was the word 'glow'.

Glow-worm.

Electric eel.

In desperation he blurted out, ' . . . like a beautiful dolphin.'

'Like a dolphin?' Jen's eyes widened. 'I look like a bloody dolphin?'

Then, thankfully, the clouds broke and she grinned, then laughed, kissing her relieved husband and rolling her eyes. 'That is the crappiest compliment ever, Bill.'

'Sorry.' He blushed.

'No, I'm sorry. I'm just in a bad mood. I can't move five yards without wanting to throw up. So why was she here?'

'It was supposed to be their first spiritual preparation session. I try to do five hour-long meetings with all couples-to-be, just to make sure they understand the sacrament. But Henry couldn't make it, unfortunately.'

'Why not?' asked Jen.

'Oh, I don't know. Some last-minute business meeting or other. It's amazing the excuses people will make to avoid looking honestly at their spiritual lives.'

'Or to avoid telling their fiancées they're off shagging someone else,' said Jen, raising an eyebrow knowingly.

Bill frowned. 'You shouldn't repeat that sort of gossip, darling. Remember, you *are* the vicar's wife now. We have a position to uphold.'

'I wonder what position Henry Saxton Brae's upholding *right now*?' Jen grinned. 'D'you think it's the wheelbarrow?'

'Jennifer!'

'Oh, don't be so po-faced!' said Jen. 'You know as well as I do that man's like a dog in heat. While Eva's hanging around our living room talking to you about lace and hymns, he's off somewhere having his wicked way with his mystery mistress. Who do you think it is?'

'You sound like a bad daytime soap opera.' Bill kissed her indulgently.

'Oh, come on. You must have an idea.'

'I need to go and work on my sermon.'

'How about "Thou shalt not covet thy neighbour's wife"?' Jen called after him. 'That's a good theme. Or perhaps it should be "cover" in Henry's case, seeing as he's already at it.'

Bill shook his head. He too had heard the rumours about Henry's philandering. But he chose not to believe them. In the Reverend Clempson's book, even infamous playboys were innocent until proven guilty.

Perhaps 'trust' should be this Sunday's theme?

Lucy Smart fought her way off a packed Tube train at High Street Kensington, emerging onto the equally crowded street.

Had London always been this much of a zoo? Or did it seem worse to her now that she and Richard had traded their big house in Battersea for a new life in the country?

From the start Lucy had had mixed feelings about their move to the Swell Valley. Like Richard, she'd always loved the beauty of the place, and adored spending weekends and half-term holidays at her parents' farm near Fittlescombe. She also bought into the idea of the boys growing up closer to nature, with more space to play outdoors and ride and fish and build camps and do all the things that she used to love as a child, and that her boys rarely got to do when they'd lived in London.

But . . . (There always had to be a but.) As a GP, Richard had instantly plugged into village life, and the children had had their new school to keep them occupied; at their age, school was a whole world in itself. It was only Lucy who ever felt the oppressive weight of time on her hands. Only Lucy who ever gazed out of the window at Riverside Hall, the Wellesleys' idyllic house, which she and Richard had rented to get out from under her parents' feet, admiring the glorious view over the Downs while simultaneously longing to be able to pop out to Starbucks and go and meet a girl-friend, or go to Zara on a spur-of-the-moment shopping spree, or do any of the hundreds of little things that one could do in London, but couldn't in the country.

It didn't help that Richard was wildly unsympathetic.

'Of course you can go for coffee in the country. You just do it at people's houses, that's all, and not in some dreary American dump on the Wandsworth Bridge Road.'

'People's houses? Like whose?' Lucy shot back.

'I don't know. Henry and Eva's?' said Richard.

'Henry and Eva' was Richard's answer to everything. Lucy had tried to explain that, nice as she was, Eva really wasn't exactly a kindred spirit. 'Come on, darling. What do I have in common with a twenty-five-year-old Swedish lingerie model?'

'Great tits?' Richard offered helpfully.

'I'm serious.'

'So am I!'

'Just because Henry's your friend doesn't make Eva mine.'

'Well, make friends with some of the mums at school then.'

'I'm trying!' Lucy said, exasperated. 'It's not that easy.'

'I don't see why not.'

'That's because you don't have to do it. Dickhead,' said Lucy. 'Most of them have known each other for years. I don't fit in.'

Lucy adored her husband, but he could be terribly blinkered at times. It was as if he had decided they were going to be happy living in the country; ergo, they *were* happy. Any feelings Lucy might have to the contrary were teething problems, the inevitable bumpiness of a transition from one life to another. He had made an effort to invite London friends down for the weekends, mostly for Lucy's sake. But, ironically, that only made it worse. Even listening to friends moan about traffic on the Cromwell Road school run had the power to make Lucy feel homesick. Which was, of course, ridiculous.

I am home, she told herself. *Wherever Rich and the kids are is home*.

But, try as she might, she couldn't stop the tendrils of some dark mood, some nameless depression creeping in. Lucy was thirty-five, five years older than Richard, and in a myriad small ways she was beginning to notice her body ageing. Nothing catastrophic. Just the usual fine lines around the eyes, the inevitable slight sagging in her breasts, the faint latticework of stretchmarks across her once taut and perfect stomach. Rich, God bless him, never saw her as anything other than beautiful. But Lucy couldn't quite shake the feeling that this was her last chance; these were her last years as a vibrant, attractive, sexual woman in her prime. And that she was wasting them, locked away in a country house like Miss Marple, crocheting. (Metaphorically, obviously. Lucy wouldn't know what to do with a crochet needle if world peace depended on it.)

Trying to explain any of this to Richard was like shouting

flat-pack assembly instructions in Urdu to a deaf mute. Lucy was perfect. Their life was perfect. Any minor problems that arose, Richard would solve by loving Lucy even more. And so, guiltily, Lucy had let it drop.

Hailing a cab, Lucy headed for her sister Pippa's flat in Notting Hill. Normally, any trip to London was cause for celebration, but today Lucy felt jumpy and anxious, a mood that stayed with her all the way to Pippa's place.

Answering the door with her packed weekend bag over her shoulder and her passport clutched in one hand, Pippa Fullerton took one look at her sister and put the holdall down. 'Are you all right? You look so pale! What's wrong?'

'Nothing,' Lucy assured her. 'Long journey, that's all. What *are* you wearing, Pip?'

Pippa was eight years younger than Lucy and still lived a life that revolved around Ibiza and parties and DJ boyfriends who all had names that sounded to Lucy like dogs, or cheap makes of car. The last one was called Fontina, sometimes referred to by Pippa as 'Mr F'. Richard would always enquire after him by turning to his sister-in-law and asking loudly, 'So how is what's-his-name? Ford Cortina?'

Today Pippa was off to some obscure festival in the south of France, and was dressed, as far as Lucy could tell, like an extra from a 1970s episode of *Dr Who*, in a tiny orange skirt, paisley shirt tied at the waist and floppy straw hat.

'It's boho,' she said breezily. 'Are you sure you're all right? You look awful. Oh God, you're not up the duff again are you?'

'No! Definitely not! Why would you say that?'

Lucy pushed past her, taking a look at herself in the hall mirror. Had she put on weight? Perhaps she shouldn't have eaten that giant Pret baguette at Charing Cross Station earlier? But Pret was yet another thing she missed about London, and the siren call of the Chicken Caesar baguette had been more temptation than Lucy could resist.

'No reason.' Pippa shrugged. 'You just look as if you might vom, that's all. Anyway, if you're sure you're all right I'd better run. Don't want to miss my flight. EasyJet are such Nazis these days. You know where everything is, right?'

Without waiting for an answer she was gone, swirling out of the flat like a whirlwind and leaving Lucy, mercifully, alone.

She's right, Lucy thought, re-examining her complexion more closely in the mirror. *I do look green.*

Dashing into Pippa's minuscule bathroom, she rubbed some bronzer into her sallow cheeks and powdered the worst of the sickly shine off her nose and chin. She realized then that her hands were sweating.

What am I doing? I'm not cut out for this. Maybe I should forget the whole thing and get the first train back to the country before I make a total fool of myself.

The doorbell rang. Pippa had obviously forgotten something. She'd always been scatterbrained. All the weed she smoked didn't help.

'I thought you said you were late?' Lucy shouted, running back to the front door and yanking it open, still brandishing the make-up brush in her hand like a magic wand.

'Actually, I'm early.' Henry Saxton Brae stood on the doorstep looking as relaxed and confident as Lucy did terrified. 'Can I come in?'

Barney Griffith was sitting at his usual table in the snug bar at The Fox, Fittlescombe's finest (and only) village pub, enjoying a drink with Eva. The two of them had become good friends over the course of the summer, and Barney often hung out with Eva during Henry's many absences. For a guy who worked for himself, it struck Barney that Henry Saxton Brae made a hell of a lot of business trips. But he kept this opinion to himself.

Eva was looking ethereally lovely, drinking Perrier water and lime and turning over a single crisp in her fingertips without ever actually eating it. Barney, meanwhile, was looking as cheerfully dishevelled as ever, indulging himself in a delicious pint of stout (his second) and a packet of pork scratchings (his third). There had to be *some* advantages to being an unemployed writer over a world-famous model and sex symbol. Whatever La Perla actually was, Barney was confident it didn't involve a lot of pork scratchings.

Barney was halfway through asking Eva's advice on a problem with his plotting when the front door swung open and a wildly flustered-looking Flora Fitzwilliam burst in.

'Vodka and tonic, please. Double,' she announced, marching straight up to the bar. She hadn't seen Barney or Eva, but Barney had seen her. In a tight New York Yankees T-shirt and frayed denim miniskirt, with her hair freshly streaked blonde and her skin tanned to a light caramel from all the long days on site up at the castle, Flora looked even sexier than usual.

Barney brightened visibly. 'Did you ask her down here?' he asked Eva. 'I haven't seen her in weeks.'

Eva shook her head. 'I would have, if I'd have thought she'd come. I did tell her to take the day off though, try to decompress. She's been working like a maniac on these new designs.'

'She looks amazing,' Barney sighed. Eva looked at him pityingly. It was sweet the way he blushed and went all self-conscious whenever Flora was around. Sweet, but dangerous. Eva had become extremely fond of Barney. He needed to fall in love with someone single, not waste his time mooning over a girl who was already engaged to a rich and handsome New York banker.

Eva beckoned Flora over.

'We didn't expect to see you here.' She smiled beatifically. 'Your hair looks lovely, by the way.'

'Lovely,' Barney agreed.

'Never mind my damned hair,' Flora seethed. 'Take a look at this!'

Disgusted, she hurled the copy of *Vanity Fair* that she'd 'borrowed' from the salon down on the table.

'"Young Hollywood Comes of Age",' Barney read the cover headline. 'Is that so terrible?'

'Page twenty-two,' said Flora. 'And twenty-three, -four and -five. Graydon, my *asshole* of a boss and so called fucking *mentor* just sold me down the river. Again!'

'I don't understand,' said Eva. 'What's he done?'

'Only gone and given some puff piece of an interview taking all the credit for Baxter Road. I sweated blood over that job!'

Barney and Eva turned to the offending article. It took them a few moments to piece together what had happened, flitting between the text and Flora's expletive-laden rant about her boss. Apparently Graydon James had taken all the credit for a house Flora had designed and built for one of GJD's clients, a rich Manhattan socialite by the name of Lisa Kent, giving an interview to *Vanity Fair* about the project without so much as informing Flora.

'Five months of my life,' Flora fumed. 'Five months away from Mason; five months dealing with Lisa's neuroses and

122

meltdowns on that godforsaken island. And he doesn't even *mention my name*. Neither of them do! I mean, listen to Lisa, right here,' she grabbed the magazine back. '"*I'm so grateful for Graydon's vision. He truly is the best in the world and this house is a testament to that.*" I'm sorry, what? *Graydon's* vision? I designed that house! I picked out every bloody throw pillow, and every last nail.'

'Isn't that what happens, though, when it's someone else's business?' Barney said bravely.

'What do you mean?' Flora's eyes narrowed.

'Only that, at the end of the day, it is Graydon's name on the door, not yours. It's his brand that got you the commission in the first place, and that's going to add value to this lady's property. The house wouldn't be featured in *Vanity Fair* if it weren't for Graydon James. Would it?'

Flora looked at him, incredulous. 'So that makes it OK to lie? To take credit for something you didn't do?'

'No, of course not,' said Barney, thinking how utterly magnificent Flora looked when she was angry, and trying hard not to picture her naked while he was trying to string a sentence together. 'I'm just saying—'

'What? What are you saying?' Flora demanded.

'That if you want control, you need to work for yourself.'

Flora leaned back and exhaled. She didn't want to hear it. But Barney was right.

'You say Graydon's done this before?' Barney went on.

Flora nodded.

'What happened then? Did you call him on it?'

'Yes, of course,' said Flora. 'I was furious. We had a screaming row.'

'And what happened after that?'

'Well, nothing,' admitted Flora. 'He pretty much used the

same argument you just did. That it was his name on the door and he could do what he liked.'

'And you accepted that?' asked Barney.

'I had no choice!' Flora's voice was rising again in frustration. 'He holds all the cards and he knows it.'

'Not true,' said Barney. 'You hold some cards. You're just too scared to play them. No one's going to give you control of your own life, Flora. You have to take it. That's why I left my law firm,' he added, taking another long, slow sip of his stout. 'One of the reasons, anyway. Pork scratching?'

'Sure,' said Flora, emptying the entire remnants of the packet into her mouth and swallowing the lot. 'Wow, those are good.'

'Aren't they?' Barney beamed. A girl after his own heart.

'This is different though,' said Flora, washing down the salty pork with a hefty slug of vodka. 'I can't just set up on my own.'

'Why not?'

'Yes, why not?' Eva seconded Barney. 'Henry and I would hire you in a heartbeat, with or without Graydon.'

'That's sweet.' Flora smiled gratefully. 'But if you did that, Graydon would sue me. Fire me, and then sue me.'

'How?' Barney asked. 'The man doesn't own you.'

'Professionally, he sorta does,' said Flora. 'He may not hold all the cards, but he holds enough. My contract is very clear on non-competes. I cannot work for a rival firm, or set up on my own, within three years of leaving GJD. And I can never solicit former GJD clients, or work for anyone introduced to me by a GJD client, past or present.'

'That's ridiculous,' said Barney. 'That wouldn't be legal here.'

Flora shrugged. 'It's legal in the US.'

Eva's phone buzzed loudly.

'It's a text from Henry.' She beamed, showing the screen to Flora.

All he had written was a cursory: 'Love you. Miss you. Back tmrrow.' But it was enough to light Eva up like a firework. She wandered outside to text him back, leaving Flora alone with Barney.

'Why don't you start a business here?' said Barney, returning to their earlier conversation. 'If it really is impossible in America?'

'Because.' Flora drained the last of her vodka. 'My whole life's in New York. Remember?'

She waved her engagement ring at Barney.

'That's not your whole life, I hope,' he said, frowning. 'There's more to you than who you marry, surely?'

'Oh, well, of course,' said Flora, sounding more irritated than she'd meant to. 'That's not what I meant. I just mean I have commitments. Back home.'

But Barney wasn't listening. Instead he was waving at Penny de la Cruz, who was sitting a few tables away with a girlfriend. 'Pen!' he shouted across the bar. 'Come and meet a friend of mine.'

Penny floated over, a vision in a long, tie-dye skirt with bells on the bottom and a series of layered vests and shirts, the effect of which was to make her look like a wafting, human-sized feather.

'Penny's a local artist. Local legend, really,' Barney explained to Flora. 'She's about to open a new gallery in London.'

Penny made a face. 'Well, it might be a bit too soon to say that! We haven't even exchanged on the space yet,' she told Flora.

'Yes, but you will,' said Barney. 'And when you do you're going to need a kick-arse designer to get the place looking as amazing as your paintings. Right?'

'In an ideal world, yes,' admitted Penny.

'Well, Flora here just happens to be a kick-arse designer.'

'Who works for someone else,' Flora reminded him.

'Who's thinking about setting up on her own,' Barney told Penny firmly. 'She designed this house.' He shoved the *Vanity Fair* article under Penny's nose.

'Oh my goodness!' said Penny, marvelling at the light-filled opulence of Lisa Kent's beach house, captured in page after page of glossy, beautifully shot pictures. 'Did you really?'

'Well, I—'

'Yes, she did,' said Barney. 'Her boss has her on some ridiculous American contract saying she can never ever do her own projects, but no English court would uphold it. You can trust me on that,' he looked authoratively at Flora. 'I'm a lawyer.'

'Ex-lawyer,' piped up Eva, who'd just walked back in.

'And didn't you tell me you used to specialize in tax cases?' Penny added.

Barney waved a hand breezily at both these objections. 'The point is, the two of you should get to know each other.'

'I'd like that,' said Penny. 'Any friend of Barney's is a friend of mine. And, really, this house is divine. You must be so proud.' She handed the magazine back to Flora.

'Thanks.' Flora smiled back. She liked Penny. It was impossible not to. 'I worked hard on it actually.'

'Well, it shows. Anyway, lovely to meet you.'

'And you.'

'I'd better get back. I'm afraid I'm being rather rude to my friend.'

'See?' said Barney, as Penny drifted back to her table.

'See what?' said Flora.

'How easy it is! I just got you your first client.'

Later that night, in bed at Peony Cottage, Flora stared at the ceiling, her mind racing as usual.

Of course, Barney Griffith's idea had been ridiculous. So ridiculous that she hadn't bothered to mention it to Mason when they Skyped an hour ago. What was she going to do, move to England and start a design house? First stop, Penny de la Cruz's not-even-bought-yet gallery, next stop global domination? I mean, please. The whole thing was obviously just bar talk. Bravado, designed to cheer her up.

And it *had* cheered her up. Barney was good at that. Eva, too, and Penny. They were all such nice people.

Unlike the treacherous Graydon James.

Just thinking about Graydon sent the tension flooding back into Flora's body like an intravenous shot of resentment. Only two weeks ago she'd lied to Henry, shamelessly used Eva, and sold out her own artistic integrity to rush through the new plans for Hanborough that Graydon hoped would win them the International Designer of the Year award.

But what if it wasn't 'them'? What if it was 'him'?

What was to stop Graydon taking all the credit for Hanborough Castle, the way he had with Lisa Kent's project on Baxter Road? Flora wouldn't put it past him. She wouldn't put anything past him.

Barney's words floated back to her. *'No one's going to give you control of your own life, Flora. You have to take it.'*

Yes, but how?

Manipulating clients was one thing. Lisa Kent, Henry and Eva, none of them held the same life-or-death power over

Flora that Graydon had. Graydon James had made her, professionally. And he could also destroy her.

But it wasn't just fear that made it so hard for Flora to stand up to Graydon. It went deeper than that, deep into parts of her psyche Flora would rather not look at. Flora's feelings towards her boss were deeply tangled, she now realized, and probably said as much about her as they did about Graydon. He was part father figure, part tyrant, part idol and part oppressor – a Jekyll and Hyde character, darkness and light all rolled into one.

Graydon could be so stubborn and selfish and unreasonable, it took your breath away. And yet, Flora reminded herself, he could also be generous. *A bit like Henry* – the thought flashed through her mind, quickly dismissed. Graydon had been the most influential force in her adult life – he had plucked her from utter obscurity, after all, and spoon-fed her commissions that most of her RISD contemporaries could only dream of. At the end of the day, if it weren't for Graydon James and the faith he'd shown in her talent and potential, Flora wouldn't be here. It was thanks to Graydon that she was lying in this antique walnut bed in this beautiful cottage, in this idyllic valley, working on Hanborough Castle, her dream job. The fact that Flora knew all this but was still cursing his name just went with the territory. Graydon protected her, but at the same time he kept her where he wanted her: trapped.

Barney's voice again:

'It is Graydon's name on the door.'

'If you want control, you need to work for yourself.'

Flora tried to focus but she soon lost her mental thread. She was very tired. Ideas, words and images were beginning to blur into one.

Flora thought again about the two gossiping women at the hairdresser's, and what they'd said about Henry having multiple mistresses, possibly including George. It was a testament to how deeply Graydon's *Vanity Fair* betrayal had affected her that this toxic piece of news had entirely slipped Flora's mind earlier when she ran into Eva and Barney in the pub. She still wasn't sure what to believe. She pictured Eva's face when she'd got Henry's text tonight, transformed with love by just a few typed words. Mason's texts never had anything near that effect on Flora. Was that weird? She was pleased to get them, of course. But was she supposed to look all luminous and transfixed at his every word? Was that what 'true love' really was?

What had Barney said, when she'd shown him her ring?

'That's not your whole life, I hope. There's more to you than who you marry.'

More to me than who I marry, thought Flora.

More to me . . .

Sleep overwhelmed her at last.

Lucy Smart lay in her sister's bed, naked and exhausted in Henry Saxton Brae's arms.

'You are so. Incredibly. Beautiful,' Henry told her, planting kisses slowly from her shoulder along her collarbone to the tops of her breasts.

Lucy stroked his thick black hair and stared at the ceiling.

'You only want me because you can't have me.'

'*Au contraire*,' said Henry, his lips moving agonizingly slowly towards her left nipple. 'I just had you. And I still want you.'

His hand was wandering lower now, the backs of his fingers grazing her taut stomach before burrowing back beneath the silky mound of her pubic hair. Henry loved that Lucy still had hair down there. Eva only had the tiniest of landing strips, which he'd always thought he preferred. But somehow, on Lucy, the more natural look felt wildly erotic.

Closing her eyes, Lucy let the pleasure crash over her, washing away the guilt, at least for this moment. She knew it was wrong to be with Henry. Desperately wrong. But his desire and persistence had overwhelmed her. This beautiful, sexual, incredibly desirable man might be the last person ever to want her like this. That was too much temptation for Lucy to resist.

'I'll never leave Richard,' she murmured, her excitement building despite herself.

'I'll never ask you to,' said Henry, grabbing her hand and placing it on his rock-hard cock.

'This is just sex.'

Henry grinned. 'The four most beautiful words in the English language.'

'I mean it,' Lucy blurted, suddenly panicked. 'I love him.'

Henry stopped smiling and looked her deep in the eye. 'So do I,' he said truthfully. 'You have my word. Richard will never, ever know.'

As he eased inside her, it suddenly dawned on Lucy that he hadn't mentioned Eva.

Not once.

CHAPTER ELEVEN

Flora quickened her pace as the music on her headphones reached a crescendo, turning her jog into a full-on sprint as she approached the top of the ridge.

It was a stunning day, warm and clear and blue-skied. The Downs spread out beneath her like an emerald quilt, shot through with the bright blue thread of the River Swell snaking its way along the base of the valley. Bending over, Flora stopped to catch her breath, allowing the clean country air to fill her overworked lungs.

She'd started running again a few days earlier, at Mason's suggestion. 'It always used to de-stress you in New York. You used to put in close to half-marathons after a bad day with Graydon, doing laps of Central Park, remember?'

Flora had forgotten. But he was right. Back in New York she made it a point of honour never to miss her Tuesday and Thursday SoulCycle classes. She usually found time to squeeze in at least one Tracy Anderson at the weekend too. But since she'd come to England, the combination of her long working hours, the lack of any form of gym for miles around, and now the colder weather meant she'd barely exercised in months. Thanks to her fondness for Tesco Finest sticky-toffee pudding, Flora had been more horrified than surprised when she'd stepped on the scales at Peony Cottage to discover that the ten pounds she'd lost over the hot, exhausting summer, running around the site at Hanborough like a blue arsed-fly, had all been gained back, with a few to spare.

'It's all in your boobs,' Eva had said encouragingly when Flora moaned about the return of her curves. 'You look great.'

This was a typically kind response from the Swell Valley's answer to Gisele. But Flora couldn't help but notice that Eva was very slowly eating some sort of organic mung bean salad at the time. No doubt she'd be following that up with a big glass of distilled air and a delicious bowl of ice chips.

There was no getting around it. It was time to start running again.

Incredibly sweetly, Mason had had a new set of state-of-the-art Bose headphones delivered to Peony Cottage the very next day, along with an iPod loaded up with everything from Wagner's 'Ride of the Valkyries' to 'Eye of the Tiger'. With no more excuses, Flora had set off into the woods and hills. Despite being horrified at her lack of fitness, especially on the first day, it was astonishing how quickly she felt her spirits lifting and the pain of Graydon's most recent betrayal begin to heal, or at least to fade.

Slipping off her headphones, she took a moment to take in the beauty of her surroundings and listen to the twitter of birdsong in the trees and the wild rushing of the river.

Seconds later the tranquillity was broken by a loud shout from the valley floor. Then another. It was a man's voice, very loud and – though Flora couldn't make out what he was saying – distinctly panicked.

Running down the hill, she took the footpath into the copse that led straight to the river. 'Hello?' she called out to whoever might be there. 'Is everything OK?'

But rounding the next corner, she saw at once that it wasn't. Henry, waist deep in water, was on one side of the river, a look of utter desperation on his face. Behind him on the bank, one of his Irish setters was tethered to a birch tree. The other dog, Flora saw to her horror, was trapped in some sort of sluice or drainage pipe on the opposite bank, its sleek head intermittently appearing as it strained frantically for escape before disappearing again beneath the gushing water.

'Soda!' Henry yelled futilely over the din. 'Stay!' Looking up at Flora with tears in his eyes, he shouted, 'Every time she struggles she gets jammed deeper in. She's going to drown!'

'What happened?' asked Flora, already taking off her sneakers. 'How did she get in there in the first place?'

'She went after a stick.' Henry sounded utterly distraught. 'It's my fault. I wasn't paying attention and she went in before I could stop her. The current's too strong. I've been trying to reach her but I can't.'

Without thinking, Flora stripped down to her knickers and sports bra and plunged into the icy water. Henry watched wide-eyed as she started to swim, her small but curvaceous frame astonishingly powerful in the water. Within ten seconds she was closer to Soda than he'd managed to get in the last horrendous two minutes. But at the mouth of the pipe the pull of the water was overpowering. Flora ended up clinging to the root of a willow on the far bank so that she wouldn't be swept downstream.

'Cross at the bridge!' she shouted to Henry.

He hesitated. The rickety footbridge was about fifty yards upstream. By the time he got there, crossed, and got back to where Soda was trapped, it might be too late. Flora's own position didn't look too safe either. But he couldn't see any better options.

'Just go!' Flora yelled.

Scrambling up the muddy bank, Henry ran along the river and over the bridge as fast as his waterlogged jeans would let him, tearing the skin on his forearms to shreds as he plunged through brambles and undergrowth to get to the sluice pipe. Flora manoeuvred herself directly underneath the entrance to the pipe opening. Soda was nowhere to be seen.

'She's gone!' Henry wailed. 'You need to get out of there.'

Lying on his stomach along the top of the pipe, he reached a hand down to Flora.

'No,' panted Flora. 'I can see her.'

'Are you sure?'

'I think so. If I grab her forelegs and pull, can you reach down and grab her from above?'

'I don't know!'

'Try,' said Flora. Before Henry could say anything else, or even process what was happening, she had slipped completely beneath the water.

'Flora!' he screamed.

The next thing he knew, Flora reappeared, her head thrown back and her arms extended, straining wildly, her feet wedged against the river bed, pulling Soda's front half out of the sluice pipe like a reluctant dance partner. It was their only chance. Reaching down, Henry wrapped both arms around the dog's underbelly and heaved with a strength he didn't even know he possessed.

The dog gave a wild, terrible yelp of pain before shooting out of the pipe with an almighty 'pop', like a champagne cork. With Soda in his arms, Henry flew backwards, collapsing onto the ground and slamming his head painfully on the base of a tree trunk. By the time he sat up, Flora was already about twenty feet downstream, pulling herself up to safety before collapsing, exhausted, onto the bank.

Soda stood up, sneezed, shook herself off and looked around, slightly baffled by all the commotion now that the danger was past.

'You stupid sod,' said Henry, unable to stop the tears of relief coursing down his cheeks as he pressed them into the setter's sodden fur. 'Don't ever do that again.'

Holding on to Soda firmly by the collar, he squelched over to where Flora was still lying, panting, on the ground.

'Are you OK?' he asked. 'I can't believe you just did that. Thank you so much.'

'You're welcome.' Rolling onto her side, Flora smiled at him. Her face was streaked with mud, there were leaves in her hair, and her wet underwear clung to her bottom like particularly raunchy gift-wrap. Despite the seriousness of the situation and the magnitude of what Flora had just done, Henry felt himself in danger of getting aroused just by looking at her. She had the exact opposite body type to Eva, but there could be no denying that she was an extremely sexy girl.

'You could have drowned,' he said.

'Nah,' said Flora, propping herself up on one elbow. 'I'm a pretty good swimmer.'

'You're bloody amazing,' said Henry, stroking Soda's head lovingly. 'I really can't thank you enough. She'd be dead if it weren't for you.' Watching from the opposite bank,

Whiskey whimpered loudly, then barked as if to say, 'Hey, what about me?'

Henry grinned. 'We're coming, lass. Give us a minute.'

'You really love them, don't you?' said Flora, looking at Henry quizzically.

'Of course,' Henry replied.

'Why do you act like you don't give a shit when Eva's around? Or when anyone's around for that matter?'

'I don't know what you mean,' Henry lied.

'Yeah, you do,' said Flora. 'It wouldn't kill you to let your guard down once in a while. You are allowed to have feelings, you know.'

Henry frowned, his eyes still locked with disconcerting intensity on Flora's. Soaked in river water, with his black hair plastered to his head, he looked sleek and predatory, like a wet mink. Their faces were so close, it would have been the easiest thing in the world to lean forward and kiss him. Appalled, Flora felt a rush of blood to her groin.

'You've just been completely heroic,' Henry drawled. Could he sense the heat between them? 'Don't ruin it by going all schmaltzy and American on me. I couldn't bear it.'

Flora shivered, and not only from cold. 'I need my clothes,' she said, blushing.

'I couldn't disagree more,' said Henry, his eyes roaming lazily over her almost naked body.

'Clothes!' said Flora, laughing to try and break the tension. 'I just saved your damn dog and you're going to let me die of hypothermia?'

Henry sat up and snapped out of whatever it was that had just happened. 'No. Of course not. I'll go and get them.'

He smiled, but it was a controlled smile. Polite. Distant.

The moment of closeness, of intimacy or attraction or . . . something, had passed. The spell was broken.

Standing up, he walked back towards the bridge, never loosening his grip on Soda's collar for an instant.

He loves those dogs, thought Flora. *He is capable of love. I wonder why he's so deathly afraid to show it?*

CHAPTER TWELVE

Flora yawned loudly. God, she was tired. That flight back from New York was a killer. And it wasn't as if she'd had much sleep the night before.

Opening the car window as she approached Peony Cottage, she let in a cool blast of evening air and tried to wake up. It was September, and autumn had arrived in the Swell Valley with a bang. Overnight, it seemed, temperatures had fallen by a good twenty degrees. A distinct chill now hung in the air, intensified by strong flurries of wind that blew leaves from the trees and whipped branches to and fro like the waving arms of teenage fans at a rock concert. Flora had only been gone five days – it was only ten days since her encounter with Henry and the dogs in the river, which almost felt like a dream now – but in that short time the last dregs of summer seemed to have drained completely from the landscape. She'd returned to a valley already changing from lush green to faded brown, its blue skies replaced by heavy, brooding clouds that matched Flora's mood.

New York had been amazing. Going home, seeing Mason, making love again for the first time in almost three months. She'd been working so hard since she got to Hanborough, Flora hadn't fully realized how much she'd missed that. Missed Mason, and their apartment and their friends and their life together. Her fleeting attraction to Henry Saxton Brae that day at the river had clearly been a symptom of loneliness, possibly combined with the adrenaline of the moment, nothing more. From now on, she vowed, she would go home at least once every six weeks. Either that or Mason would fly to her. Long-distance love sucked.

Not everything about the trip had been easy. She'd had a major showdown with Graydon about the *Vanity Fair* article, although as usual he'd somehow ended up turning the thing around to make it out that Flora was in the wrong.

'Lisa Kent *was* my client. And I *did* come up with the original design for Baxter Road.'

'Which was changed completely by the time the house was actually built!' Flora protested. 'Every room in those pictures was my work, Graydon. You never even mentioned me.'

'Of course I mentioned you,' he'd told her testily. 'So did Lisa, for that matter. It was the magazine that chose to focus on me. Because, like it or not, my dear, it's my name that sells copies, not yours.'

He'd then proceeded to rip into Flora about what he called the 'slow progress' at Hanborough.

'I didn't step in when you changed the plans for the great hall. Even though we both knew you'd need new Listed Buildings Consent. I let you run with the idea because you swore to me you could complete on time.'

'And I will,' said Flora. 'Henry gave me a deadline of the first of July.'

'I don't give a fuck about Henry!' Graydon roared. '*Our* deadline, *the* deadline, is April, for the International Designer of the Year award. I thought I made that crystal clear months ago.'

'You mean back when you also said I'd be named as the co-designer on Hanborough?' Flora challenged him defiantly. 'That you wouldn't take all the glory, the way you just did with Baxter Road?'

Graydon had actually thrown her out of his office for that. It wasn't until the next day that they made peace. But, even then, it was very much on Graydon's terms.

'Your job, your only job, is to get Hanborough finished on time. Are we clear?'

Flora nodded.

'Once you can show me that the works are on schedule, and once *I'm* happy with the quality of your designs – assuming that I am – then we'll talk about credit.'

That night, over dinner at Minetta Tavern, Mason had tried to be sympathetic, although his advice was the same as it always was.

'Just tell the miserable old queen to stick it. You don't need him, Flora. You don't need to work at all. It's my job to take care of you, angel. I just wish you'd let me do it.'

For the first time, Flora had started to wonder if maybe Mason was right. Why *did* she work so hard, when she didn't have to? She'd always told herself it was because she was an artist. And artists need to express themselves, to work, to create. But deep down she knew there was another, darker reason. When her dad had gone to jail, and then died, and later when her mom had shrunk back into her shell like some pathetic, dried-up snail, Flora had learned the hard way how to rely on herself. She'd survived on her own, worked hard on her own, got into RISD and landed the job with Graydon James, all on her own. Self-reliance sounded like a good thing, like a character strength. But really it was just another name for fear. For the terror of losing everything, again.

Things are different now, Flora told herself.

I have Mason. I can trust Mason.

Mason is not like dad.

She'd flown back to England feeling deeply conflicted. Perhaps the restoration of Hanborough Castle really would be her last job as a designer, not just for Graydon, but altogether? Her last hurrah before married life as Mason Parker's wife – cared for, cherished and loved. She couldn't decide whether the idea of letting it all go made her depressed or relieved. In a strange sort of way, it seemed to do both. But, either way, it felt more important than ever now that Hanborough should be a success. More than a success. A triumph. And that Flora should be credited for her efforts.

Arriving at Peony Cottage at last, she dragged her case up the garden path and unlocked the front door. Fighting her way through a mountain of junk mail and small parcels, most of them fabric swatches or paint samples she'd ordered before she left, she scooped up an armful of what looked like actual post, dumped her case at the foot of the stairs and wandered into the kitchen to make herself a cup of tea.

Sitting down at the tiny wooden table, Flora began opening letters. There was a small gas bill for the cottage, a request for money from Prisoners First, a charity helping prison inmates and their families that Flora had long supported, and an invitation to dinner next week from Barney Griffith.

'Welcome back!' he'd written inside. 'Come over on Friday. Small group, v casual. Vodka and pork scratchings both provided.' The card was a quite stunning photograph of Hanborough in the dawn light, taken from the valley below. Barney had taken the picture himself and was obviously a much more talented photographer than he'd let on.

Finally there was a large brown envelope containing a detailed bid for the new masonry works to the great hall. Page after page of numbers and spreadsheets and addenda swam before Flora's eyes.

She looked at the clock on the wall.

Six fifteen p.m.

There was still time to pop up to the castle now, take some measurements for the stonework and check on progress, before exhaustion truly kicked in.

Taking a quick slug of tea, shoving the paperwork back in its envelope and grabbing a KitKat out of the larder cupboard for energy, Flora tucked the envelope under her arm and hurried back out to her car.

Flora arrived to find Hanborough unusually quiet. No cars were parked in front of the portcullis. Even when Henry and Eva were away, the gardeners and Mrs French – Henry's secretary – were usually milling around somewhere. But today the staff must have gone home early.

Letting herself in with her own keys, Flora shouted into the great hall, her voice echoing off the stone walls like a ping-pong ball. 'Hello? Anybody home?'

'In here.'

Henry's voice came from the kitchen. It sounded rough, as if he'd just woken up. Flora put her head around the door to find him sprawled in the tatty old armchair next to the Aga. Still in his hunting gear – the Swell Valley must have been out today – but with his shirt untucked, riding boots kicked off and his red jacket draped over the back of a kitchen chair, he looked unusually dishevelled. His face and chest glistened with sweat and his black hair was pushed messily back from his forehead. He had a half-drunk tumbler of whisky in his hand and a brooding, dark look in his eyes. Flora was horrified to find herself thinking how sexy he looked.

'When'd you get back?' he asked, looking up at Flora with an intense, if somewhat glassy stare. From his expression and the slight slur in his voice, Flora surmised that the glass in his hand was not the first he'd had tonight.

'Just now.' She kept her own voice deliberately brisk and businesslike. 'Sorry to disturb you. I just popped in to check on a few things and take some measurements.'

'You're not disturbing me.' Henry smiled broadly. 'Have a drink.'

'Oh, no thanks. I'm fine,' said Flora. She felt flustered suddenly, and regretted coming up here. Why on earth hadn't she left it till morning? 'I'll just run into the great hall to get what I need and leave you in peace.'

'Don't be silly. Sit down,' said Henry. 'I'm fed up with peace. Eva's in Paris working and I'm bored shitless.'

'Even so, I—'

'Sit!'

He was still smiling. Deciding it would look churlish to refuse him, Flora perched awkwardly on a wooden chair. Hauling himself to his feet, Henry grabbed a glass down from the cupboard and poured her a whisky, ignoring her gestures of protest.

'How was New York?'

'It was good.' Flora sipped the whisky tentatively.

'You saw your fella?' Henry sat back down, stretching his

long legs out in front of him. Flora noticed the way his thigh muscles bulged beneath the tight fabric of his breeches. 'Mr Perfect?'

'Why do you call him that?' Flora felt annoyed.

'Just something Eva said. About him being one of the good guys. Kind and understanding and . . . all that.' He waved a hand vaguely, as if concepts like kindness and understanding were bizarre, otherworldly concepts that he'd never quite understood.

'Yes, well. Mason *is* very kind,' Flora said primly. 'It was wonderful to see him. And long overdue.'

'He must miss you.' Henry gazed down at the amber liquid swirling in his glass.

'I hope so,' laughed Flora.

'Do you miss him?'

'Of course I do.' She frowned. 'All the time.'

'All the time?' said Henry. 'Wow. You don't show it. When you're working, I mean.'

'Well, you know, not *all* the time, like every minute of the day. I mean, we have our own lives. Obviously. Mason's very supportive of my career.'

An awkward silence fell.

Why the hell am I being so defensive? thought Flora.

She changed the subject quickly. 'So, have I missed anything while I've been away? What's been happening here?'

'If you mean at Hanborough, I don't really know.' Henry drained the last of his drink and poured himself another. 'I've been away a lot. In town. I get lonely staying here when Eva's away.'

Do you? thought Flora. *And just how do you deal with that loneliness, I wonder?*

'I've been working,' said Henry, as if reading her mind. 'There's a lot going on at Gigtix.'

'How's your business partner?' Flora was amazed to hear herself asking. Georgina Savile was the very last person she wanted to talk about. But she seemed to be suffering from some bizarre form of Tourette's this evening. Maybe it was the jet lag.

'George?' Henry looked equally surprised by the question. 'George is George. She's a nightmare, as we both know. But she's great at what she does.'

'Which is?'

'Raising money,' said Henry. 'When we started the company, everybody believed the bubble had burst for online auction-based sites. But Georgina just radiated this self-belief from the start. Investors loved her. They still do. She's . . . ' he cast around for the right word. 'Single-minded.'

'Hmmm,' said Flora bitterly. 'That's one way of putting it.'

She would never forget the single-minded way Georgie Lynne, as she had been then, had ruined her life at school, picking on her mercilessly at the worst time in her life.

'I know she's been rude to you when she's been here,' said Henry. 'I'm sorry about that.'

'It's not your fault,' said Flora.

'No, but still. She should never have said those things at dinner. About your father, I mean.'

Flora stiffened. How on earth had they got into this?

'No, she shouldn't.'

She looked away. When she turned back to Henry, she found he was staring at her intently, searching her face as if it held the answer to some nameless riddle. It was quite disconcerting.

145

'Why *does* George come to Hanborough so often?' she asked.

'What do you mean?'

Flora shrugged. 'Just that she's here a lot. And yet you don't seem to like her any more than I do.'

Henry's jaw tightened. 'It's complicated.'

'Is it?' Flora found herself hoping more than ever that the rumours about an affair weren't true.

'We run a company together,' said Henry. 'That throws you into each other's path socially, more than you might like. It's a bit like having a child with an ex.'

Flora raised an eyebrow. 'Is Georgina an ex?'

'No.'

Henry looked her right in the eye in a way that made Flora's stomach flip over unpleasantly.

'Well,' she stood up, pushing her drink aside. 'On that note, I guess I'd better take those measurements. It's been a long day and I need my bed.'

Henry nodded glassily. It wasn't until Flora reached the door that he called after her.

'Flora?'

She spun around. 'Yes?'

'About your fiancé.'

'Mason?' Flora's eyes narrowed. 'What about him?'

'Do you ever feel as if he's too good for you? Too good a person, I mean?'

Flora contemplated taking offence, then thought better of it. She and Eva had had a few conversations about their respective relationships over the course of the summer. Flora probably had said words to this effect in one of them, about Mason sometimes being so saintly it was hard to measure up. Eva must have mentioned it to Henry. In the grand scheme of things, that wasn't a big deal.

'Sometimes,' she said. 'Yes. But he also makes me want to be a better person. And that's a good thing, right?'

Now it was Henry's turn to look away. 'It is if you can be. But what if you can't? What if you're just *not* a good person? Can a bad person and a good person ever be happily married, do you think?'

'I don't believe in bad people,' Flora told him, suddenly serious. 'We can all change.'

She wasn't sure if they were still talking about Mason, or Eva, or what exactly Henry was getting at. But she had the strong feeling they had strayed into dangerous waters.

'Can we?' Closing his eyes, Henry ran his hands through his hair. 'I'm not so sure.' For an awful moment, Flora thought he might be about to cry. But then he sat forward and exhaled loudly, laughing again. 'Eeeugh. Ignore me,' he said. 'I'm drunk and talking out of my arse. Goodnight, Flora. I'm glad you're back.'

'Goodnight, Henry,' said Flora.

What a strange mixture of a man he was. Rude, yet thoughtful; arrogant, but bizarrely vulnerable too.

Poor Eva had her work cut out for her there.

Barney Griffith hovered over the Nespresso machine in his tiny cottage kitchen, surreptitiously sneaking glances into the next room.

He was, if he did say so himself, quite the matchmaker. Flora Fitzwilliam and Penny de la Cruz were getting on like a house on fire.

It had been five days since Flora had returned from New York and, to Barney's delight, accepted his invitation to dinner. Ever since that night at The Fox, Barney had been determined to get Penny and Flora together again, and to further the idea of Flora starting her own business.

Barney's plan was simple, if not entirely altruistic. Flora couldn't work for herself in the States. She would therefore start a business here, become wildly successful, break up with her American boyfriend, see the light (at some point), fall in love with Barney, marry him, and keep him and Jeeves in the style to which they both fervently hoped to become accustomed.

'You have no chance with Flora, Barn,' Eva told him bluntly, being cruel to be kind before she left for her latest Paris trip. 'I talk to the girl almost every day and I'm telling you, she's in love.'

Barney put his fingers in his ears and started to hum. 'No she's not. No, no, no, no, no. Nope.'

'I mean it.' Eva tried to look serious. 'I don't want to see you get hurt.'

Barney shrugged. 'Can't help it. Love is blind.'

'And deaf apparently,' said Eva. 'You'll find someone else, someone who's meant for you. I thought I was in love tons of times before I met Henry. And now look at me!' She beamed, holding her whopping engagement ring up to the light.

Barney loved Eva, but it was tough to take love-life advice from someone so self-evidently delusional. So he waited for her to leave and then set his plan in motion, inviting both Flora and Penny de la Cruz for dinner, along with his old lawyer friend Kenneth Bay, whose job was to make up the numbers, eat, then slope off back to London early so that Penny and Flora could talk business.

'Can't I stay for coffee at least?' Ken had asked plaintively half an hour ago, looking longingly over his shoulder at Flora as Barney physically thrust him out of the back door.

In fitted Hudson jeans and a bottle-green turtleneck sweater teamed with shiny black spiked-heel boots, Flora looked ridiculously sexy tonight, like Scarlett Johansson on a really, really good day.

'No.'

'You do realize you are never going to pull that girl?' Ken said bitterly, regretting his earlier promise to eat and run.

'Yes, I am,' said Barney.

'No, you're not. She's way out of your league.'

'Doesn't matter. I'm a writer. Hot women love writers,' said Barney. 'It's like models and rock stars.'

'No, it isn't!'

'Yes, it is. Look at that writer guy Cate Blanchett married. He's no oil painting.'

'Andrew Upton? He's a world-famous playwright,' said Ken. 'Not a sad git living with his dog in Sussex with half a novel stuffed in his bedside drawer.'

'That's it,' said Barney. 'I just removed you from my thank-you speech at the Booker Prize. Now sod *off*,' he added, slamming the door in his old friend's face before Ken could distract him any further from his mission, and turning his attention to the coffee.

'What do you think he's *doing* in there?' Penny asked Flora, listening to the endless clinking of china and rattling of spoons coming from the kitchen. 'He's taking for ever.'

'I'm not sure.' Flora sipped the remnants of her Sangiovese and nibbled on one of Barney's rather delicious home-made truffles. For such a big lug of an Irishman, he was quite the Marcus Wareing in the kitchen. 'I can't quite shake the feeling I'm being set up.'

'You are,' Penny said cheerfully, chucking another log on Barney's fire and settling down next to Flora on the sofa.

'In the nicest possible way, though. Barney wants me to hire you to design my new gallery. We exchanged last week, while you were in New York. Can you believe it's ours now?'

Grabbing her MacBook Air off the coffee table, Penny clicked open more photographs of her new space, a vast if slightly desolate-looking loft on the wrong side of Battersea.

'Santiago says it looks like a multi-storey car park,' said Penny, gazing at each image adoringly, like a new mother cooing over pictures of her child. 'But obviously he has no idea what he's talking about.'

'Obviously,' agreed Flora.

'Spaces aren't beautiful to my husband, unless they're green and have a pavilion at one end,' said Penny. 'But what do *you* think?'

'I think it has huge potential,' said Flora.

'But?' Penny frowned.

'But nothing!' Flora laughed. 'It has huge potential. I'd need to see your work, though, to get a better sense of why you chose it. What does it say about your art? What do you want it to say?'

Penny refilled both their glasses. 'I want it to say: "Please buy this painting for an astronomical sum of money."'

Flora laughed.

'But at the moment I think it's saying something more along the lines of: "Help! I need an amazing designer who will work for next to no wages as my owner is broke, but who will help me achieve my" – what did you say again? – my "huge potential".'

Flora popped another chocolate into her mouth and sucked on it contemplatively.

'I'd love to do it,' she began.

'Really?' Penny said hopefully.

'Really. But I can't,' said Flora. 'Even if I didn't have contract issues, not to mention a wedding to go home for, I literally have no time. Hanborough's like a black hole of work.'

Penny's face fell. 'I understand. I mean, I can imagine. The castle *is* enormous.' She looked at Flora wistfully. 'But don't you think, sometimes, it would be nice to get out of the Swell Valley? To have a reason to come up to London? Do some new things, meet some new people? Perhaps it's different with painting, but I find I get terribly stuck in a rut creatively when I only have one thing to focus on.'

This was sort of true. Flora's routine of work, eat, sleep, work was not exactly conducive to creative brilliance. On the other hand, she barely had the energy for the work she was being paid to do, never mind dangerous freebies that could never ultimately lead anywhere . . .

'Coffee, ladies.'

Barney walked in bearing a chipped, plastic tray with three mismatched china mugs on it. There was something about Barney's relentless scruffiness that Flora found endearing. Mason would rather die than present his guests with a tray like that. On the other hand, she knew she could never live the life of the impoverished artist that Barney seemed so bizarrely attached to. Art was important to Flora, but not at any cost. She wondered idly whether Barney still had any savings from his former life as a lawyer – and if so, how fast they were running out.

'Flora can't do it,' Penny summarized, with a sigh of resignation. 'She's too overstretched at Hanborough.'

'Too overstretched to manage the whole project,' said Barney. 'But you could knock up a few sketches, surely? Just to give Penny some ideas.'

Flora scowled at him. She didn't appreciate the use of the phrase 'knock up', as if sketching out the interior design for a London gallery were as easy as whipping up an omelette.

'And maybe you could do something for Flora in return?' Barney suggested to Penny, ignoring Flora's evil eye. 'A portrait, perhaps?'

'Oh, yes!' Penny clapped her hands together. 'I'd adore to paint you. We could do it in the nude if you like. As a wedding present for your husband.'

This wasn't at all what Barney had had in mind. The whole idea was to get Flora to forget her American fiancé, not to spend every Friday night at Penny's, stripping off for the guy.

Luckily, Flora seemed to feel equally awkward.

'Oh, I don't know about that,' she muttered, blushing scarlet. Mason's idea of a suitable wedding present would be something along the lines of a pair of Tiffany candelabra or a first edition John Steinbeck. Flora was as sure as she could be that the last thing on earth he would want to receive was a nude painting of her. In fact, she could practically hear his disapproval from here.

'For God's sake, Flora! We can't possibly hang it. What if my mother came to stay?'

'You'd look incredible, I promise you,' said Penny. 'I wouldn't do a Lucian Freud on you.'

'It's very kind, but I really couldn't impose.'

'It's no imposition.' Penny warmed to her theme. 'It'd be an honour to paint you.'

'I wouldn't have time for the sittings.' Flora's voice grew increasingly desperate. 'But I'll happily do some sketches for you,' she blurted out. Anything to get Penny to drop it. 'That's no problem.'

'Really? Would you?' Penny's kind face lit up. 'Oh, that's amazing! Thank you so much.' She hugged Flora, letting out a little squeal of excitement. 'And thank you, Barn, for introducing us.'

Flora shot Barney a look that clearly said, *Yeah. Thanks for nothing, buddy.*

'I'll arrange a time for you to come up to London and see it,' Penny beamed. 'We'll have lunch at The Latchmere. Oh, it'll be such *fun!*'

Flora forced a smile. How had she been bamboozled into this? She considered backing out quietly in a few days' time, but one look at Penny's face and she knew she couldn't let her down. It would be like kicking a puppy.

Bloody Barney.

On the other hand, it *would* be fun to come up with some ideas for a London gallery. Flora had never designed a gallery before. And Hanborough had become terribly all-consuming.

Perhaps a change would be as good as a rest?

Eva couldn't believe her eyes when she landed at Heathrow and saw Henry waiting for her in Arrivals.

'You came to meet me! You never come to meet me.' Her eyes lit up. Then, almost instantly, a cloud of worry fell over her face. 'Is everything all right?'

'Of course everything's all right. Why wouldn't it be?' said Henry, pulling her into his arms and kissing her passionately in front of the gawping crowds. Of course people recognized England's most glamorous engaged couple, and more than a few were snapping pictures on their phones.

In a thin black cashmere sweater and jeans, clean-shaven for once and smelling of toothpaste and Acqua di Parma cologne, Henry looked and felt heavenly. Closing her eyes,

Eva inhaled him, reassuring herself that he was hers, that nothing was wrong.

That was the problem with infidelity. No matter how long ago it was, or how fully you forgave the other person, total trust was never quite possible ever again. There would always be that tiny hairline fracture, invisible to the naked eye, but at risk of cracking open at any minute.

Henry comes to pick me up and I assume something's happened. That he must be feeling guilty. Or that he's leaving me. I panic.

Eva didn't want to be that person – the insecure, needy fiancée. But holding back her doubts was a constant battle.

Taking her hand in his, Henry walked her out to the car, the clicking of cameras and flashing of phones following them with every step. Even in her off-duty uniform of black jeans, sneakers and a white T-shirt paired with a Rick Owens leather jacket, Eva still managed to radiate glamour.

I'm so lucky to be with her, Henry thought, for the thousandth time. *What the hell is wrong with me?*

He'd been with Lucy Smart again last night, briefly, in one of the derelict outbuildings on the Hanborough Estate. Their affair was becoming dangerously addictive, like slipping into an alternative reality in which both of them were free, the rest of the world didn't exist, and nothing mattered except each other, their bodies, the moment. Henry had tried endlessly to untangle what it was that drew him to Lucy. Perhaps the fact that, unlike Eva, she didn't love him, didn't need him. Too often, Eva's devotion felt like a millstone around Henry's neck, compounding his guilt and his growing feelings of panic about the commitment he was about to make. With Lucy there was no commitment, no weight dragging him under. But the relationship had other problems. Lucy was already talking about ending their fling.

'No one's been hurt yet. No one knows,' she told Henry last night, after their brief but passionate encounter. 'I think we should quit while we're ahead.'

She was right, of course. But for some reason the thought of her walking away, back to Richard and their happy, stable domestic life, filled Henry with utter misery.

'Not yet,' he pleaded, burying his head between her thighs to drive the point home. 'Please.'

It pained him to realize that he was envious of Richard. Envious of the love that he and Lucy shared, notwithstanding Henry and Lucy's current dalliance. Henry loved Eva, but they'd never had that stability, that calm, contented companionship that Richard seemed to have achieved so effortlessly with his wife. And it was Henry's fault entirely that they didn't. Eva was nothing if not stable. Endlessly kind, devoted, faithful, forgiving. If Henry couldn't make it with Eva, he couldn't make it with anyone. But perhaps that was exactly it. He *couldn't* make it with anyone. Richard, Lucy and Eva were all fundamentally good people. Loyal people, even if Henry had managed to tempt Lucy temporarily into his bed. Henry wasn't. He was fundamentally flawed. Broken. Incapable of lasting happiness. So he leapt instead at fleeting joy, of the kind that Lucy offered him, all the sweeter because it wouldn't and couldn't last.

One day, and probably soon, Henry knew that Lucy Smart would file him away under 'regret' and return to her real life, never to think about him again. At least, not in that way. Henry found this idea simultaneously painful and intoxicating.

'I've got something to show you.'

They'd left the airport now and were pulling on to the M25. Reaching into the back seat of Henry's vintage, woodgreen Bentley S2, Eva unzipped her case and pulled out a carefully wrapped package.

'For me?' Henry raised an eyebrow.

'Sort of.' Eva smiled, opening the box and carefully removing layer after layer of lovingly folded tissue paper. 'For us.'

At last she pulled out a very fine, exquisitely worked piece of lace. Holding it up to the light, you could see some faint yellowing at the edges, presumably from age. But it seemed to go on for ever, yards and yards of beautifully embroidered needlepoint.

'It was my grandmother's wedding veil.' Eva stroked the fabric lovingly. 'My father sent it to me from Stockholm as a surprise. They found it when they were packing up the summer house in Skåne.'

'That was kind of him,' said Henry, keeping his eyes on the road.

'It'll bring us good luck,' said Eva, smiling and placing her hand on Henry's thigh. 'Farmor and Farfar were married for almost sixty years when Farfar died.'

A muscle on Henry's neck twitched involuntarily.

'We won't need luck,' he said, covering Eva's hand with his. 'I love you.'

Eva felt suffused with happiness.

It really was going to be all right.

'I love you too, Henry.'

Flora ran through the woods, sweat pouring down between her shoulder blades. Reaching the bottom of the steep slope that ran from the end of Peony Cottage's garden all the way to the banks of the River Swell, Flora turned sharp left and began climbing again, through the woods that marked the boundary of the Hanborough Estate. Although not officially public footpaths, generations of local villagers had walked and ridden through the Hanborough woods. The track Flora followed was well worn, if a little slippery after the recent rain. At this time of the evening – by the time Flora had finished work, Skyped Mason, changed and got out of the house, it was already past seven – she had the place to herself, but the dwindling light combined with the natural shade from the overhanging trees made it hard to see where one was going.

Two more miles, thought Flora, *and I'll turn around*. She still had a mountain of emails to get through this evening, and the burning sensation in her thighs was getting beyond a joke. *OK, maybe one more.*

Reaching the top of the rise, she was about to make another right, deeper into the trees, when a strange sound stopped her in her tracks. It was loud and high-pitched and sudden. She heard it a second time, and then a third. The hairs on Flora's forearms stood on end.

There could be no doubt about it. The sound was human. Human and female. Someone, a woman, was being attacked.

Pulling out her phone, Flora checked for a signal but there was none. Her mind raced. Should she surprise the attacker, or run directly for help? On the one hand an unarmed, exhausted girl of five foot two was unlikely to be of much physical help to this poor woman, whoever she was. She needed real help. The police. On the other hand, the perpetrator might run off if surprised. And by the time Flora got back to her cottage and a phone, it might be too late.

The screech came again.

Shit.

Using her phone as a light and holding it low to the

ground, Flora made her way gingerly through the under-growth towards the sound. Maybe if she could just see what was going on she could hit the guy over the head with something. A branch? In any case, she couldn't just stand there while some poor woman was being raped or murdered.

After about twenty yards, the thick ground cover of ferns and brambles began to thin out. Flora saw what looked like a derelict barn or store of some sort, nestled in a clearing. It was hard to imagine a more secluded or desolate spot. You would never know a building was here, unless . . .

There it was again. The noise. But this time it was accom-panied by some scuffling and heavy breathing. And then a lower, more masculine sound, almost like a . . . a grunt?

Oh God! Flora felt sick. Someone *was* being raped. Looking around desperately, scanning the forest floor for a possible weapon, she saw a biggish stone, about the size of a large grapefruit. Racing forwards before her fear got the better of her, holding her phone in one hand and the stone in the other, Flora ran around to the far side of the building, where the noises were coming from.

What she saw next would never leave her.

Lucy Smart, spread-eagled against the wall, her skirt pushed up around her hips and her underwear around her ankles. And behind her, totally naked and thrusting himself violently into her like an Exocet missile, was Henry Saxton Brae. Lucy had her eyes closed, utterly lost in the moment and Flora now recognized her screams as cries of pleasure. Henry, however, clearly sensed himself being watched. Without stopping or even slowing the frenzied rhythm of his thrusts, he turned his head around, his eyes wide open, and looked right at Flora.

It was the most mortifying, and *longest*, moment of Flora's adult life. It felt as if the two of them stood there staring at one another for hours. At last, incredibly, it was Henry who broke the spell, turning away from Flora and continuing to fuck his best friend's wife as if nothing had happened. As if Flora wasn't there. As if she hadn't seen them.

Her heart pounding, and not knowing what else to do, Flora turned and ran.

'I'm coming!'

Barney wiped his wet, soapy hands on his jeans – Jeeves had got to the box of expensive Belgian chocolates that his godmother had sent Barney for his birthday last week, and proceeded to crap spectacularly all over the cottage – and raced to the door.

Flora, his second visitor in less than an hour, stood panting and dishevelled on the doorstep. In running gear, splattered all over with mud, and with twigs and bits of bramble literally stuck to her hair, she looked as if she'd been to war.

'What on earth's happened?' Glancing down, Barney saw the scratches on her arms and feared the worst. 'Did someone attack you?'

'Henry . . . ' Flora gasped, doubling over as she fought to catch her breath.

Barney's brows knitted into a deep scowl. 'Henry? Henry Saxton Brae tried to hurt you?'

Flora shook her head, too weary to explain. She'd run all the way from the Hanborough woods to Barney's cottage, because it was closer than her own and because she needed to talk to someone about what she'd seen. Should she tell Eva? As a friend, all Flora's instincts screamed that she should. If the shoe were on the other foot and Mason were the one having an affair, Flora would definitely want to know.

On the other hand, the idea of being responsible for

shattering not only Eva's happiness but Richard Smart's too was not a pleasant one. Flora didn't know Richard or Lucy well, but they'd both seemed like such lovely people. Plus they had children. Not to mention the fact that speaking up would mean the end of Flora's Hanborough job. The whole thing was a giant cluster-fuck.

How dare Henry put her in this position?

Turning around like that, as if the fact he'd been caught didn't even matter; as if he already knew what Flora was going to do – or not going to do. The revolting arrogance of the man! And to think, she'd actually started thinking there was more to Henry Saxton Brae than met the eye. That, deep down, there might actually have been a good man lurking in there somewhere.

So much for that theory.

'No one attacked me,' she told Barney, finding her voice at last as the oxygen rushed back into her lungs. 'I saw Henry—'

'What about Henry?'

To Flora's horror, Eva drifted into the hallway. In a flowing gypsy skirt and flat boots, with a gossamer-thin cashmere sweater loosely belted at the hips, she looked like an angel, or the heroine of some Pre-Raphaelite epic poem. The smile she gave Flora radiated happiness and peace. Flora's stomach lurched.

What the hell was she doing here?

'He hasn't been giving you a hard time, has he?' Eva asked. 'If he has, just tell me and I'll sort him out. No one knows more than I do how hard you've been working up at . . . My goodness, are you OK?' Belatedly Eva noticed the state Flora was in. 'You look terrible.'

'I'm fine.' Flora plastered a stupid grin onto her face. 'I've just been for a run. Thought I'd pop in and see Barney. I won't disturb you though.' She turned to leave.

'No, stay!' Barney urged her. Even with his house smelling strongly of a mixture of dog poo and Dettol, he was keen for Flora to come inside. Whatever it was she'd wanted to tell him about Henry, surely the fact that she'd come to *him* was some sort of a good sign?

If only Eva hadn't been here, Flora would have come in and confided in him. They would have shared a secret, an intimacy of sorts. Barney felt himself getting more and more cross. Really, it was too much, the way these supermodels just dropped in for tea whenever they felt like it, tearing a man away from his novel-writing and dashing his romantic chances to smithereens, without so much as a by your leave.

'Yes, do come in,' Eva was cajoling Flora. 'You look like you could use a bit of a sit-down.'

'Exactly,' said Barney.

'And you're not disturbing anything.'

'Nothing at all,' he reiterated.

'We were just having a cup of tea, weren't we, Barney?'

'We were.'

They're like an old married couple, thought Flora.

'Besides,' Eva smiled knowingly, 'I want to know exactly what Henry's been up to.'

No, you don't, thought Flora, the sick feeling in her stomach returning. *You really don't.*

'Another time,' she said hurriedly. And before Barney had a chance to stop her, she ran off, taking the back road up the hill to Hanborough and the safety of her own cottage.

Henry pulled in to the side of the lane, turned off his engine and sat alone in the darkness, waiting.

Why did it have to be Flora who saw them? Flora, whose good opinion meant so much to him, for some reason he'd never fully been able to fathom. That look of horror on her face, seeing him with Lucy. It was a combination of revulsion and, almost worse, deep, deep disappointment, and it would haunt Henry for ever. He knew he ought to be grateful that it had been Flora and not Eva who'd caught them. But he wasn't. Not at all.

When he'd turned away from Flora in the woods, tried to block out that look of hers by pretending she wasn't there, he'd done so not out of arrogance, but out of shame and utter, abject panic. He'd been weak. Horribly, pathetically weak. It was that, more than anything else, that he needed to put right now.

In some strange way, he and Flora had always been equals. He'd tried to take the upper hand in the relationship when they'd first met, but he'd failed, and that was OK. Equal was good. Equal was refreshing.

Subordination, however, was not to be borne. Henry had dealt Flora the upper hand this evening and he must, at all costs, get it back.

If Flora was going to hate him, so be it. Hatred he could deal with. But not disdain. Not from her.

He looked at the dashboard clock impatiently.

Where the bloody hell was she?

Too tired to run any further, and nursing both a sore ankle and a pronounced stitch in her left side, Flora slowed her pace to a jog, then a walk. By the time she finally reached her garden gate it was nearly nine o'clock at night, cold and completely dark.

Fumbling in her pocket for her keys, she jammed it into

the lock, but her fingers were numb with cold and she couldn't seem to work the door open.

'Let me.'

Flora screamed, jumping out of her skin. Emerging from the shadows like a night stalker, Henry had crept up behind her, grabbing her keys with one hand and blocking her escape with the other.

'Shhh,' he whispered in her ear, unlocking the door and bundling the two of them inside before Flora could scream again, or hit him, or react in any way. Only once they were inside and Henry had closed the door behind them and switched the hall light on did she turn on him.

'Get out!' she hissed. 'How dare you come into my house? Ambush me like a fucking burglar.'

'I'm sorry about that. I needed to talk to you.'

'Yeah? Well, I don't need to talk to you. I mean it, Henry. Get out. You make me sick!'

Henry leaned back against the door and looked at her calmly. 'Do I? Why?'

'*Why?*' Flora repeated, incredulous. His nonchalance was truly infuriating – the ultimate insult. Everything about his body language, the relaxed way he extended his leg and rolled his ankle to and fro, spoke to Flora of his deep-seated selfishness, his utter lack of remorse. 'You're engaged to be married, Henry. To a lovely, incredible girl who you don't deserve.'

'That's true,' said Henry. 'We're not married yet, though.'

'Lucy is,' Flora shot back. 'To your *best friend*! My God, Henry. Don't you have any boundaries?'

'I hate it when you start speaking American,' Henry quipped, with a confidence he was far from feeling. 'And as a point of fact, I have very clear boundaries. You crossed them tonight when you decided to trespass in my woods.'

'You're not funny.' Flora looked at him witheringly. 'No one's laughing.'

'No. I know.' Henry looked at the floor. For the first time he showed the slightest hint of being chastened.

'You don't care about anyone except yourself, do you?' Flora said furiously. 'I can see why you and Georgina Savile found each other.'

Henry looked up sharply. 'I'm nothing like George.'

Flora laughed out loud. 'Of course you are! You're two selfish peas in a pod. That's why you're screwing her as well, isn't it?'

The words were out of her mouth before she even knew she planned to say them.

Henry's eyes narrowed. 'No,' he drawled. 'If you must know, I fuck George from time to time because I loathe her.'

Flora flushed with a mixture of embarrassment and anger.

'With Lucy it's different.'

'Oh. I see. So you sleep with your best friend's wife from time to time because you love her? Is that it?'

Flora's voice dripped with sarcasm. But when Henry answered he was deadpan.

'I do love her. I love Eva too. It's complicated.'

'No, it isn't,' said Flora. 'It's very, very simple. You're a selfish asshole who thinks with his dick and to hell with the consequences. I really, really want you to leave my house now.'

Moving past her into the tiny cottage kitchen, Henry pulled out a chair and sat down at the table. Picking up a saltcellar in the shape of a pheasant, turning it over slowly in his hand, he said, 'I can't do that, I'm afraid. Not until I know what you're going to do.'

Gritting her teeth, Flora sat down opposite him.

'Are you going to tell Eva?'

The question was neither angry, nor pleading. Like Henry's expression it was impassive, unreadable. *Does he want me to tell Eva?* Flora wondered. *Is he like one of those serial killers who's secretly hoping to be caught?*

'I probably should,' she said.

Henry exhaled slowly, his shoulders dropping with relief. That 'probably' spoke volumes. Equally important, he and Flora were negotiating again now like equals. He'd achieved his goal.

'But you won't.'

'Not for your sake,' Flora hastened to add.

'No. For yours, I imagine,' said Henry. 'You want to keep the job at Hanborough.'

Flora considered denying this but then thought better of it. One of them might as well be honest.

'I do, yes. This restoration's very important for my career.'

'You're ambitious, aren't you?' Henry smiled. 'I like that in a woman.'

'I don't give a toss what you like,' Flora snapped, appalled at herself for the momentary flash of desire she'd felt when he smiled at her. No wonder Lucy Smart had been seduced by him. The man should have a government health warning tattooed across his forehead. 'And Hanborough's only part of the reason,' she pressed on. 'Eva's my friend. That's the bottom line, I guess. I don't want to see her hurt.'

Henry stood up, apparently satisfied. 'OK. Well, thank you.'

'Don't thank me. Like I said, I'm not doing it for you.'

He nodded, heading for the door.

'I'll see you up at the castle tomorrow, then?'

'Yes.'

Flora closed her eyes. She felt bone-tired all of a sudden, a combination of all the physical exertion and stress.

'Henry?' she called after him as he unlatched the door.

He turned around silently.

'You will end things with Lucy now, won't you?'

Henry looked at Flora. Then he looked around the room, his gaze fixing for a moment on a still-life painting of some vegetables that Flora had hung over the fireplace. One of the few splashes of colour in the otherwise whitewashed room, the picture naturally drew the eye.

'I like what you've done with this place,' said Henry, flashing her the smile again. 'You're a great designer.'

'It can't end well, you know,' Flora told him.

'Goodnight, Flora.'

Henry left, closing the door behind him.

CHAPTER THIRTEEN

Flora burst into GJD's London offices on Tite Street, a tiny, harassed figure almost completely obscured by the mountain of large shopping bags she was carrying.

'Has the call started yet?' Dumping the bags unceremoniously on the lobby floor, like a camel shedding its packs, Flora looked at Katie, the receptionist, nervously.

'No. You're lucky. He's late.' Katie smiled. 'They're all upstairs in the conference room, waiting.'

'Thank God for that,' Flora exhaled, eschewing the ancient lift and taking the office stairs two at a time. 'Be an angel and shove all that stuff in a cupboard somewhere for me, would you?' she called over her shoulder, gesturing vaguely at the bag mountain.

It had been a frenzied morning, racing around Chelsea Wharf with Eva looking at tiles and curtain fabric and reclaimed brass bath taps and God knows what else for the castle's new master bedroom suite. Living in their little bubble in the Swell Valley, it was easy to forget quite how famous Eva Gunnarson was in the real world. Spending a morning in London with Eva was quite an eye-opener. Flora was amazed by the numbers of people who approached them as they made their way through the Design Centre, wanting to take selfies with Eva or get her autograph or simply to say hello. All types of people too: rich Chelsea businessmen, teenage girls with their own dreams of making it as models, housewives, builders; even an adorable couple in their eighties who recognized Eva 'off that advert on the telly' and just wanted to give her a hug and remind her to eat properly. Eva was her usual patient, gracious self with all of them, but Flora found the constant interruptions incredibly irritating. Couldn't people see they were busy?

By noon it was clear she was going to be late for the conference call with Graydon. Then, at the last minute, Flora had decided to swing by the Battersea site of Penny de la Cruz's new gallery and drop off a couple more sketches, making herself even later.

Despite having subzero free time, coming up with sketches for Penny had become Flora's new hobby, a much-needed stress reliever after the long days spent up at Hanborough, avoiding Henry's eye. To say things had been tense since Flora's discovery of Henry and Lucy in the woods would be an understatement. Twice, Richard Smart had 'popped by' unexpectedly, and Flora had bolted out of the house like a rabbit down a hole, poleaxed with guilt.

'You don't need to run away from him you know,' Henry had chastised her afterwards. 'He'll think something weird's going on.'

'Something weird *is* going on,' Flora reminded him caustically. 'Or should I put that in the past tense?'

'You should mind your own business,' said Henry. 'And I'll do the same. Ask me no secrets, Flora.'

It was even worse when Georgina Savile came to Hanborough, ostensibly to talk business with Henry, although recently George had made a big show of ingratiating herself with Eva.

'Oh, I *love* what you've done with the chef's kitchen,' George exclaimed, when Eva showed her around. 'I'd never have thought pink would work in here, but it's spectacular. You are *clever*.'

'Actually, it was Flora's idea . . . ' Eva began, smiling at Flora who was sitting at the table, engrossed in her work.

'Uh uh uh. No!' George wagged a finger playfully in Eva's direction. 'Now you really must stop doing that. Putting yourself down. Henry's told me how hands-on you've been with all of the design here.'

'Well, I have made a few suggestions,' Eva admitted.

'More than a few!' George's fake smile threatened to take over her entire elfin face. 'Much more. This is your design, Eva. Flora's just here to act as a channel for *your* creative vision. Isn't that right, Flora?'

'If you say so.' Flora smiled tightly at George.

'You wouldn't be a poppet and make us some tea, would you?' George asked, as she led Eva back to the drawing room. 'I'm absolutely dying for a cuppa, but I'm longing to see the rest of the changes Eva's made.'

'Oh, no, no, no, it isn't Flora's job to make us tea!' Eva said, embarrassed.

'It's all right,' said Flora. 'I'm making one myself.'

'You see?' George trilled, taking the unsuspecting Eva by the hand with a forced girliness that made Flora want to throw up. *When was the last time those fingers were wrapped around Henry's cock?* 'Flora doesn't mind.'

'Well, I do,' said Henry, pulling Eva into an embrace and

kissing her, pointedly, in front of George. 'Flora's a professional and she's trying to work. Make your own bloody tea.'

George had laughed it off, with an eye-roll and an 'Oh, Henry!' But not before she'd looked daggers at Flora – as if any of this awful charade were her fault!

It was a relief to come to London, but as usual there was never enough time to fit everything in, especially not illicit trips to Penny de la Cruz in Battersea.

'I feel like a spy, delivering secrets to the enemy,' Flora told Penny as she handed over the sketches. Penny was sitting cross-legged on the floor in a pair of paint-splattered overalls, eating a picnic lunch of Fortnum & Mason game pie, a delicious-looking plum cake, and drinking champagne, with a disconcertingly attractive blond man.

'I do hope I'm not the enemy.' She smiled at Flora. 'This is my good friend Gabe Baxter.' She introduced the blond. Flora bent down to shake his hand.

'Gabe, this is Flora Fitzwilliam, my secret squirrel designer. She escaped from the dungeons at Hanborough Castle to bring me these.'

'They're bloody good,' said Gabe, flipping through Flora's sketches admiringly. 'Do you ever do common-or-garden houses? Or only castles? I ask because Laura and I just bought a new place on Clapham Common. Great house but everything's dark brown. We think the last people employed a mole to decorate it. Possibly a mole from 1976 with an abiding passion for shag pile.'

Flora laughed. 'Unfortunately I don't get to choose my own commissions. Not yet, anyway. I work for Graydon James. Thinking of which, I'd better get back to the office now before he sacks me.'

'Really? Right now?' Penny looked disappointed. 'Can't

you join us? Gabe brought this delicious hamper over as a gallery-warming present. I know it's not really lunchtime, but we were both too greedy to wait.'

'Stay for a glass of champagne at least,' said Gabe.

'I'd love to,' Flora sighed. Gabe and Penny both seemed to be having such fun. But Graydon would hit the roof if she missed the big video conference call. He'd summoned the entire company together, all over the globe, to discuss the International Designer of the Year awards next year, and their strategy for winning the nomination. As Hanborough Castle was supposed to be the jewel in the GJD crown, Flora's presence was not so much requested as required.

'Cutting it a bit fine, aren't you?'

Conrad, a pouty twenty-two-year-old Graydon groupie with perfect cheekbones and a pronounced bitchy streak, looked daggers at Flora as she took her seat at the head of the table. Graydon kept a skeleton staff of two designers and an assistant in the London office. Conrad, preposterously, had been promoted from assistant to designer last year, prompting James Peace, the senior designer, to leave GJD in disgust. Conrad now worked alongside Frances Kingham, a timid vole of a woman who sat to Flora's left, wearing her usual expression of abject terror at the prospect of a conference call with her boss. Making up the foursome was Karin, the new assistant, who sat on Flora's right. Karin was a sweet, dumpy Swedish girl, who didn't know the first thing about design, but could type at the speed of light, was wildly efficient, and let Conrad's histrionics roll off her back like harmless drops of rain.

'If there's one thing you can rely on with Graydon, it's his lateness.' Flora smiled at Conrad sweetly.

Right on cue, the screen on the wall flickered into life

and Graydon's waxy, overfilled face loomed into view, surrounded by smaller screenshots of the other GJD offices.

'Is everybody here? Los Angeles? London? Dubai?' Graydon barked.

Various nervous echoes of assent rang around the room.

Taking the lead with a confident smile – as the chief designer on the Hanborough project, she was the most senior person on the call – Flora asked, 'So, Graydon, where would you like to start?'

'I'd like to start with you wiping that smile off your face,' Graydon said viciously. 'We are six weeks behind schedule on Hanborough and I want to know what, precisely, you intend to do about it!'

To say that the call went downhill from there would be an understatement. While Conrad preened and smirked smugly beside her, Flora took punch after punch after punch. Nothing she'd done at Hanborough so far was good enough. Her newly completed library was 'revoltingly bourgeois. If you want to do any more naff studies in taupe, I suggest you go and work for Kelly Hoppen.'

The fact that the clients were satisfied; that the library was both luxurious and textured while remaining in keeping with Hanborough's unique architectural heritage; that Flora had valiantly succeeded in keeping the works within budget: all meant nothing. All that Graydon cared about was the International Designer of the Year award. To win that, Flora would have to be far more innovative, far more avant-garde and far more attention-grabbing. Not to mention far faster.

In other words, she was to abandon completely the pared-down, clean aesthetic for which Graydon had hired her in the first place, and sell out, not just on Henry and Eva, but on her own artistic integrity.

'I want to see *trompe l'oeil*,' Graydon ranted. 'I want to see retractable roofs, I want to see connecting Plexiglas passages marrying old and new, I want to see eco-efficient materials. Mosaics. Gold!'

'Henry won't agree to any of that,' Flora replied bravely. She refrained to point out that 'gold' was probably as far from an eco-efficient material as one could possibly get, not to mention light years outside their budget. 'He hates modernist design, and he hates bling. And he certainly won't pay for it.'

'Then you must make him agree,' Graydon insisted. 'I had dinner last night with the head of the awarding committee and she told me it's going to be a very left-wing, avant-garde panel next year. Stop *asking* Saxton Brae what he wants, and start *telling* him what he needs. If you can't do that, I need to put somebody else into Hanborough who can. And soon.'

Flora could sense the pricking up of ears from her ambitious colleagues at the various satellite offices. All the older male designers resented her. Even the women thought she was wildly over-promoted. She could swear she heard the sound of knives being sharpened.

She held her own, however, fighting her corner to the end and insisting that her designs for Hanborough, while neither opulent nor crassly futuristic, were nonetheless fresh and cutting edge in their own, minimalist way. Eventually Graydon moved on to other projects, heaping praise on the Dubai team for the new five-star hotel they were building to rival the Burj Al Arab. But the call left Flora's ego bruised and her confidence in tatters.

Graydon wasn't going to replace her at Hanborough. As he'd said himself, repeatedly, he simply didn't have time.

Besides which, Flora was pretty sure Henry wouldn't stand for it. The two of them might not like each other personally, but Henry had come to respect Flora's work. They were increasingly seeing eye to eye on the direction of the works, and Flora had been nothing short of brilliant at getting Eva involved in decision-making without putting any of Henry's pet plans at risk.

Even so, Flora walked out of the conference room in a daze, like someone who has just woken up to find their house has been burned down around them.

'Are you OK?' Frances Kingham asked kindly. As senior London designer, Frances would have been the obvious person to step into Flora's shoes, should Graydon carry out his threats. But Frances could no more sharpen a knife or fight her way to a promotion than she could fly to the moon. 'I thought that library you did looked lovely.'

'Thanks,' said Flora. 'I'm fine. I'm used to it.'

'There's someone here to see you, downstairs,' Karin interrupted them.

'Me?' Flora frowned. She didn't have any more meetings planned, and wanted nothing more than to drive back to Peony Cottage, crawl under her bedcovers and die. 'Are you sure?'

Karin shrugged. 'That's what he said.'

Shit. Flora remembered. She'd told the wallpaper supplier from the Design Centre, a garrulous Cockney, that he could come by 'any time' if he came to his senses on pricing for the William Morris prints and wanted to make her a serious offer. Surely it wasn't him already? Flora really didn't know if she had it in her to enter into yet another haggling session today.

Wearily, she trudged back down to the lobby.

'In there,' said Katie, nodding towards the ground-floor meeting room and adding with a wink, 'Lucky you.'

'Oh yeah.' Flora rolled her eyes. 'It's definitely my lucky day.'

What was the little man's name again? Ian? Or was it Steve?
She pushed open the door.

Mason spun around and grinned at her sheepishly. 'Surprise!'

Flora's mouth opened then closed, then opened, then closed again.

'Aren't you pleased to see me?' asked Mason.

Flora burst into tears.

The next few hours were like a beautiful dream.

Mason took Flora back to his suite at the Mandarin Oriental. ('Our suite,' he told Flora firmly. 'I've already called Henry Saxton Brae and let him know you're taking three days' vacation.') Instantaneously she'd been trans- formed from harried underling, traipsing around after Eva Gunnarson and being publicly berated by Graydon James, to fairy-tale princess. Or, at the very least, to being a rich man's wife. Which was, of course, what she was soon to become. If this afternoon's showing was anything to go by, it was an alternative lifestyle Flora could quickly get used to.

After spending an hour stroking Mason's face, bursting into tears, and smelling him a lot, mostly to make sure he was real, Flora sank into a deep, lavender-scented bath and dozed off while Mason did some emails on the bed. Their bed. *Our bed.*

Drifting back into the bedroom in a profoundly contented haze, Flora saw three Jimmy Choo bags placed neatly at the foot of the bed and a gorgeous grey Donna Karan jersey dress laid out on the bedspread.

'The dress is from Manhattan,' said Mason, slipping a hand under Flora's towel and cupping each of her gloriously heavy, full breasts in turn. 'It's this season's and there was a hell of a wait list, but Henrietta had a friend at Barneys who helped me out. I just knew it would look perfect on you.'

'It's gorgeous,' said Flora, making a determined effort not to focus on the Henrietta Branston part – God, that girl was like a bad smell – as well as not to start bawling again. Really, she was so emotional; if it weren't a physical impossibility, she might have suspected she was pregnant.

'The shoes I picked up here. I just liked the colours.'

Feeling like a kid on Christmas morning, Flora opened the Jimmy Choo boxes, pulling out three pairs of strappy heels in hot pink, metallic blue and neon yellow. They were all divine, although none of them were at all Mason's usual style. *Has he changed his tastes that much?* thought Flora. *How long have I been away?*

'Go put them on,' said Mason, stroking Flora's hair, then sliding a hand around the back of her neck and caressing it slowly. He'd been tempted to take her to bed the minute they got back to the hotel, but she'd been so keyed up he decided to wait until after dinner. 'We have a table at Lucio at eight.'

A small, intimate restaurant on a quiet part of the Fulham Road in South Kensington, Lucio was famous for serving the best tiramisu in London, if not the world. After a delicious meal of Burrata Caprese and lobster '*fra diavolo*', washed down with a wonderful bottle of Brunello, Mason and Flora shared the rich, creamy pudding in a state of sated bliss.

Flora had spent the first two courses yabbering away endlessly to Mason about Swell Valley gossip: Henry's infidelities, her guilt about not telling Eva, Georgina Savile's bitchiness, the weirdness of seeing Richard Smart dropping by the castle and yukking it up with Henry, while knowing what she knew about Henry sleeping with Richard's wife.

'The irony is, she seems terribly nice,' Flora told Mason. 'Lucy, I mean. She must be out of her mind to risk it all for Henry. I mean, the man has no scruples. None whatsoever . . .'

Mason listened patiently, nodding and reassuring, making comments when the conversation seemed to demand it. He waited while Flora told him all about Barney Griffith, the would-be writer she'd befriended, and the artist wife of the handsome cricketer who was opening some gallery or other. He did a heroic job of hiding his utter lack of interest in any of these people – people he would almost certainly never meet and whose lives were a million miles removed from his own. But the effort was worth it. By the time the ambrosial tiramisu arrived, Flora was all talked out, nicely buzzed from the food and wine, and as relaxed as she would ever be.

Mason decided to strike while the iron was hot.

'I spoke to your mother last week,' he said, as casually as he could. 'About the wedding.'

Flora dropped her spoon with a clatter. 'You spoke to *my* mother?'

Flora's mom, Camila, lived as a semi-recluse in a small apartment in Brooklyn, subsisting on a diet of Walmart ready meals and disappointment. Her life consisted of daily visits to church, online bridge (she was a very talented card player), and a lot of daytime television. Flora's repeated efforts to persuade her to get out more, contact old friends or take any sort of interest in Flora's own life had been met with total rejection. 'I'm happy as I am' was her mom's mantra, a statement so self-evidently untrue it broke Flora's heart. As for Flora's engagement, having gloomily pronounced that matrimony always 'ended in tears', especially marriage into a 'snobby, rich family' like the Parkers, Camila had specifically asked not to meet her daughter's intended, and expressed her wish not to be involved in any of Flora and Mason's wedding plans. At this point, Flora was by no means sure her mother would even attend the wedding.

'I want her to be a part of it, Flora,' said Mason. 'She's the only family you have.'

'I agree,' said Flora, touched that Mason would go to so much effort for a woman who had been less than welcoming to him or his family. 'But you know what she's like. Even talking about the wedding brings her out in hives.'

'I know. But I think part of that is because things have been so uncertain and up in the air. We hadn't decided on a venue or a date or anything when we told her. Then you disappeared, first to Nantucket and then to England. Your mother's been through so much turmoil in her life, Flora. I think more than anything she wants to know where she stands.'

Flora raised an eyebrow. First the jazzy shoes. Now the amateur psychology. What had happened to her straight-as-a-die, conservative boyfriend?

'So,' Mason went on, 'I told her we'd set a date. That we're getting married on the fifteenth of April, at St James's Presbyterian in Westchester. The reception will be at my parents' estate, and all she has to do is turn up and look beautiful. She was actually really happy.'

Flora sat there, stunned.

'One of us had to make a decision.' Mason shrugged, only slightly sheepishly. 'I figured, as you were overwhelmed with Hanborough, I'd better do it.'

A million thoughts, feelings and emotions assailed Flora all at once.

The fifteenth of April was too soon. Much too soon.

It was also the month submissions had to be in for the International Designer of the Year award.

Graydon was going to go ballistic.

On the other hand, it did feel kind of nice to have things settled at last. To have someone else – Mason – take control; make all the decisions that she, Flora, couldn't make. And the work at Hanborough Castle would have to be finished by then.

Perhaps Flora had more in common with her mother than she realized?

And really, at the end of the day, what could Graydon do about it? People had a right to get married. They had a right to a life of their own.

Right?

'Flora?' Mason reached for her hand anxiously across the table. 'Are you OK? Are you mad at me?'

'Mad at you?' Flora shook her head. 'No. I'm not mad. A little surprised, maybe. I figured we'd discuss all this when I came home for Christmas.'

'Christmas is going to be way too busy,' Mason said firmly, his confidence returning as he saw that the alpha-male approach seemed to have worked. You could never quite tell with Flora. 'We have a whole string of parties to attend at the bank. My senior partners are starting to think I made you up.' He laughed. 'Plus my mother wants to throw two formal engagement celebrations for us, one in the country and one in town, at the club.' 'The club' was the Metropolitan Club, probably Manhattan's oldest and most self-consciously elitist private members' club. 'And of course we'll need to invite *your* mother too,' Mason added.

'Right. OK,' said Flora, trying to imagine Camila in the hallowed surroundings of the Metropolitan Club, surrounded by the Parkers' *Mayflower*-descendant friends.

She knew she was being steamrollered. Yet, in an odd way, it was a relief.

At least if Mason took charge of the wedding and their New York life, she'd be free to focus solely on Hanborough and the International Designer of the Year gong that she hoped to share with Graydon. All the work and stress and exhaustion would be worth it if, this time next year, she had that award.

And, of course, if she'd become Mrs Mason Parker. Although that part hopefully wasn't an 'if'.

Mason squeezed her hand.

'I love you so much, Flora.'

'I love you too.'

'Let's go to bed.'

Back in their suite at the Mandarin, Flora tried to relax as Mason undressed her. Unbuttoning his shirt, she ran her hands over his smooth, firm chest. It felt wonderful. *He* felt wonderful. And yet there was a certain awkwardness there, an unfamiliarity that made it hard to get into the mood, at least in the beginning.

It had been the same when Flora went back to New York. The first couple of times they'd made love they'd both had to work to rediscover each other's rhythms. *That's normal,*

Flora told herself. *That's what happens when you spend time apart. There's always that initial feeling of bumpy re-entry.* Sex had been fine in the end on that trip and it would be fine now. She just had to stop overthinking things.

She was naked now, and Mason was down to his striped J.Crew boxer shorts. Scooping her into his arms, he carried her over to the bed like a groom carrying his bride over the threshold, and began kissing her breasts, his tongue flickering over her nipples the way she'd always liked it. Flora ran her fingers through his preppily short blond hair, sighing with pleasure as he began to slide downwards, kissing her ribs and belly and taking delicious, nibbling little bites at the tops of her thighs.

'I've missed you,' he breathed, slipping both hands under her bottom to lift her slightly before burying his face between her legs.

Flora closed her eyes and squirmed with pleasure.

This was new too. Mason was a good lover, but he'd never been big on foreplay, and especially not on oral sex. Flora could count on the fingers of one hand the times he'd been down on her.

Oh God. A horrible thought occurred to her. *Has he been unfaithful? Has he been with someone else? Is that why he wants to bring the wedding forward? And why he showed up here, out of the blue? Out of guilt?*

Feeling Flora's muscles tense, Mason looked up. 'What's wrong?'

'Nothing,' Flora said quickly. 'Nothing's wrong.'

I'm being ridiculous. Mason wouldn't cheat. He's straighter than straight, the most trustworthy person I know.

She'd been spending too much time with Henry Saxton Brae, that was the problem. Henry, with his good looks and

181

his charm and his absolute lack of morals of any kind.

Reaching down so her hands were on Mason's back, she coaxed him upwards, guiding him inside her. The foreplay was nice, but she wanted him to make love to her the way he usually did. To close her eyes and sink back into the familiar rhythm that was theirs and theirs alone. Mason smiled as if to say, 'Are you sure?' But he didn't need to be asked twice. Hard as a rock already, he flipped Flora over onto her stomach and thrust deeply into her, groaning with pleasure as she gyrated her hips back against him.

After a few minutes, Flora felt her own climax starting to build.

Then, to her utter horror, she found herself thinking about Henry. First an image of him screwing Lucy Smart up against the wall of the barn jumped, unbidden, into her mind. Then she remembered his eyes boring into her own; the liquefying, awful feeling of desire mixed with loathing in the pit of her stomach; and his voice, so revoltingly arrogant.

'*You're ambitious. I like that in a woman.*'

Mason didn't like Flora's ambition.

He was fucking her harder now, and faster, his movements getting more and more urgent as he was about to come. At last he climaxed, his fingers gratefully clutching the soft, pillowy flesh of her incredible breasts.

'Flora!' he moaned.

Flora screwed up her eyes and tried to block it out, but the image of Henry Saxton Brae's triumphant, obnoxious face wouldn't budge. It was still there, squatting in her mind's eye like an unwanted cuckoo chick, shattering the safety of her nest, when she came too, gasping for breath as Mason collapsed on top of her.

'Well, that was pretty amazing,' Mason panted, laughing.

Turning over, Flora buried her head in his neck. 'I love you. I really do love you, Mason.'

'I hope so,' he replied, still laughing. 'Because in a few short months, you're gonna be stuck with me for life.'

CHAPTER FOURTEEN

The Reverend 'Call-me-Bill' Clempson clapped his gloved hands together and stamped his feet against the cold.

Being vicar of a place like Fittlescombe had its advantages, naturally, but also its trials. It was November now, hunting season, and Bill's Swell Valley parish had distinctly divided views when it came to the morality or otherwise of chasing foxes around the countryside in the hope of having them ripped to shreds by a pack of slavering hounds.

The arguments on either side of this debate were as old as the valley itself. The pro-hunt lobby argued that foxes were pests, a bane to farmers, chicken fanciers and anyone who owned a dustbin. They also played the 'tradition' card, equating fox hunting with an English rural way of life already under attack from ignorant city dwellers, who seemed to view the countryside as some sort of theme park designed for their benefit.

The antis, in turn, saw the bloodthirsty pursuit of a single, innocent animal by scores of riders and hounds, intent on killing for no better reason than their own pleasure, as nothing short of barbarism. Hunting had no place in a modern, civilized, animal-loving society, and tradition be damned.

Considering himself both a liberal and a voice for the underdog – in this case, the fox – Bill sided firmly with the latter group. Unfortunately this alienated him not only from at least fifty per cent of his parishioners, but also from his wife, Jen.

'I've never heard such anthropomorphic twaddle,' she'd told Bill earlier that morning. 'Foxes are a menace.'

He'd been outlining his views on the sanctity of life in the kitchen at the vicarage, while preparing a Thermos of Bovril and a large round of ham and cheese sandwiches to take with him to today's meet at The Fox. Along with Barney Griffith, Angela Cranley, and a small but vocal group of anti-hunt protestors, Bill was going to gather on the village green and generally make a nuisance of himself, annoying the huntsmen.

Bill sighed disappointedly. 'I know we don't agree on this, Jenny. But I hope I can rely on your support.'

'Sorry.' Waddling over from the sink, Jen kissed him on the cheek. Enormously pregnant, she'd started to look not unlike a human puffball mushroom. Everything that *could* swell *had* swelled, and her hormones were teetering on tsunami levels. 'I'm with the red coats all the way on this one. Besides, Gabe has already invited me to the meet.'

'Gabe Baxter?' Bill spluttered. 'I hope you said no!'

Bill had had numerous run-ins over the years with Jenny's old boss. Although the two had officially buried the hatchet, it was fair to say that relations between them would never be warm.

'Why would I say no? If I weren't such a heifer I'd ride

185

out with them. As it is, I've loyally agreed to support the cause by eating some free meat pies and knocking back some port.'

'You can't drink *port*. Not in your condition. And not at ten o'clock in the morning, for heaven's sake,' Bill said sanctimoniously.

Jen's eyes narrowed. 'Watch me.'

So now Bill stood – cold and, so far, completely alone – on the village green opposite the pub car park, a desultory stack of 'Say No to Cruelty!' placards at his feet, watching the first huntsmen and their followers arrive.

'Sorry I'm late.' Barney Griffith, out of breath and looking even scruffier than usual in a filthy Barbour jacket, dark blue fishermen's sweater with holes in it and a pair of what looked like canvas trousers tied at the waist with string. 'I had a bit of a . . . erm . . . wardrobe malfunction this morning.'

'So I see,' said Bill.

'Get down, you little focker!' Barney shouted at Jeeves, his even scruffier Border terrier, who was half-heartedly cocking his leg on his master's shin. 'Sorry, Vicar. Didn't mean to swear.'

'You didn't have a belt?' Bill asked, glancing disapprovingly at the string holding up Barney's trousers. He was more concerned with the boy's appearance than his language. With so many in the village already viewing the anti-hunting activists as ruffians and troublemakers, it didn't help to have prominent members such as Barney show up looking like tramps.

'Jeeves chewed it up months ago,' Barney explained cheerfully. 'I only really need it with these trousers, which I hardly ever wear. But I put my other trews on to wash last night, and the sodding machine broke. Started making weird gurgling noises and now the door won't open.' He glanced around the green. 'Where are the others?'

'I have no idea,' griped Bill. 'Coming, I hope, and soon. We're going to be ridiculously outnumbered as it is.'

'They'll be here,' said Barney confidently, clapping a hand across Bill Clempson's back. 'You know your trouble, Vicar? You don't have enough *faith*.'

Lord Saxton Brae, aka Henry's older brother Sebastian, mounted Elijah, his stocky but surprisingly fast grey stallion, at the back of The Fox's car park and surveyed the scene around him approvingly.

If inheriting his father's title and the struggling family estate at Hatchings were the greatest responsibilities of Seb's life, his position as master of the Swell Valley Hunt was easily his greatest pleasure. Nothing could ever quite beat the excitement of turning out on a crisp, clear November morning like this one. The smell of horseflesh, the excited barking of the hounds, the warm, jolly feeling of camaraderie amongst huntsmen and riders and followers as the meet began to gather and swell. Seb was often accused of being a snob, and fox hunting the ultimate snob's sport, toffee-nosed and out of touch. But as Seb looked around at today's turnout, he saw people from all walks of life crowded happily in The Fox's car park and beer garden, sipping the landlord's excellent (and free) hot toddies and fortifying themselves with steaming game and venison pies. Even better, a quick glance across the green revealed that barely a handful of antis had turned up – miserable, joyless spoilsports in Seb's opinion. Perhaps the tide of public opinion was finally swinging back in favour of field sports? *About bloody time.*

Kate, Seb's wife, was about twenty feet away, also

mounted and chatting to Eva, who was on foot. Seb felt a surge of pride watching her. In her new tight white breeches and fitted black hunting jacket, with her hair tied back and netted in a chic chignon beneath her hat, she looked a knockout. Her bay mare, Starlight, was also easily the prettiest horse there. As she should be, the price Seb had paid for her. He was pleased to see Kate and Eva getting along. Henry could be quite prickly with his sister-in-law. Seb hoped that marriage to Eva would take off some of his little brother's rough edges and improve Saxton Brae family relations.

'Hello, Master. Good turnout.'

Gabe Baxter rode up cheerfully on the dirtiest horse Seb had seen in some time. Not that its master looked much better, in a tatty tweed jacket with holes in and a thoroughly threadbare pair of jodhpurs. Trotting along behind him was a small blond boy on a fat little pony, grinning from ear to ear.

'I don't think you've met my son Hugh. It's his first time.'

Seb beamed. 'How marvellous!' He wasn't a natural with children, but it was always good to see a new generation taking an interest in the hunt. 'How do you do, Hugh?'

'How do you do?' The small boy shook his hand solemnly, a look of excitement and determination on his freckled face.

'Hello, monster!' Riding up behind him, Santiago de la Cruz lifted Hugh right up out of the saddle, tickling him under the arms, before plonking him back down again.

'Hi, Uncle Santi!' Hugh grinned.

Turning to Gabe, Santiago asked, 'Laura let him come, then? How'd you swing that?'

'With difficulty.' Gabe rolled his eyes. 'She's still convinced he's going to break his neck. She's over there.' He nodded towards the pub, where Laura stood chatting with some of her old Fittlescombe girlfriends, intermittently stealing anxious glances at her eldest son. 'If I bring him back with so much as a scratch, she'll divorce me.'

'Yeah, well. At least she's not an animal-rights nutter. Penny's the bloody Che Guevara of foxes.'

Gabe laughed. 'Over on the green, is she? Looks like poor old "Call-me-Bill" needs all the help he can get. Even his wife's abandoned him,' he added, waving at the hugely pregnant Jen who was chatting to Henry Saxton Brae while simultaneously shovelling pies into her mouth like a human conveyor belt. Catching Gabe's eye, she waved back.

'Pen's not a placard waver, thankfully,' said Santiago. 'She prefers to waft around among the enemy, radiating disapproval.'

'Speaking of radiating,' said Gabe, sotto voce, 'the future Mrs Saxton Brae's not looking too shabby this morning.'

Still politely listening to Lady Saxton Brae (Kate was explaining at great length to her why Henry should do more to support the West Swell Valley), Eva did look particularly fetching this morning in a pale grey cashmere sweater that clung to her in all the right places, and tight black corduroy trousers tucked into a pair of gleaming black riding boots, of the kind that never actually went riding. Her long blonde hair was loose and blowing in the breeze. She was easily the most attractive woman at the meet, and quite possibly on planet earth.

'No,' Santiago agreed. 'I wouldn't let Laura catch you looking if I were you, mate. Sounds like you're on thin ice as it is.'

'True,' Gabe agreed, reluctantly averting his eyes from the vision that was Eva Gunnarson.

'Five minutes, chaps,' Seb announced brusquely, in his

best military manner, riding off to check on the hounds who'd just been let out of the hunt van and were swarming around the car park excitedly, tails wagging like metronomes. 'Good luck, Hugh.'

'Thanks.' Hugh grinned back.

'You're supposed to call him "Master",' Gabe whispered in his son's ear. 'Or Lord Saxton Brae.'

'Why?'

'Because he's a pompous arse, and he likes it,' Santiago explained.

Hugh giggled. 'You said arse.'

'Don't tell your mother,' Santiago and Gabe said in unison.

Finally escaping from Kate's clutches (Eva knew Seb's wife meant well, she just wished Kate would stop labouring under the illusion that she, Eva, controlled any aspect of Henry's behaviour), Eva looked around for Henry in the throng. By now the crowd had grown too big for The Fox's modest car park and beer garden and was spilling out onto the lane.

The small gaggle of anti-hunt protestors had also grown, although not to the same extent. About twenty people were now rallying behind the vicar, whose reedy voice was magnified by his handheld loudhailer as he preached about St Francis and the importance of protecting all God's creatures. Seeing that Barney was with them, struggling to control Jeeves who was straining wildly at his leash and looked in imminent danger of garrotting himself, Eva crossed the battle lines and went over to say hello.

'It's turning into a nice morning,' she said, kissing him on the cheek.

'Not for the fox it isn't,' Barney said, ungraciously.

'Honestly, I don't know how you can fraternize with that lot.' His eyes narrowed in the general direction of the meet. 'Bloody Hooray Henrys.'

'"That lot" includes my fiancé and a number of my friends. And yours, I might add,' Eva reminded him crossly. 'I was going to invite you to the drinks we're having up at the castle this evening, but if you're going to be grumpy and boring, I'll leave you to it.' She turned to go.

'Sorry,' said Barney, putting a hand on her arm. 'I can't come to a hunt drinks. But it's sweet of you to ask me, and you're right, there's no excuse for grumpiness. I'm afraid I didn't get much sleep last night.'

'Oh? Why not?' asked Eva.

Barney ran a despairing hand through his hair. 'Lots of reasons. The book's a bloody disaster, for one.'

'I'm sure it isn't,' Eva said kindly.

'It is. It's haunting me.'

'Well, if you're worried, why don't you show it to somebody? Get some feedback?'

Barney's eyes widened with horror. 'Feedback? Are you serious? The state it's in now, I'd rather stick a hot poker up my arse.'

Eva frowned. Barney did have a way with words, whether his novel was any good or not.

He'd failed to mention the other main reason that he'd slept so poorly, namely the fact that he'd been wracked by erotic dreams about Flora Fitzwilliam. Flora's American boyfriend, who'd seemed so far off and unreal when Barney first met her, now seemed to be popping up everywhere like some malevolent jack-in-the-box.

'Flora not with you?' he couldn't help himself asking.

'No. She's working, as usual. Ever since she came up with

the new plans for our party barn, it's been more full on than ever. I think she knows Henry has mixed feelings about the barn. It's terribly modern and it's costing a fortune. I think Flora's feeling the pressure a bit.'

'If Henry doesn't like it, why did he agree to it?' asked Barney.

'For me, I think.' Eva smiled. 'I love the new barn. I think it's rather Swedish with all the steel posts and the retractable roof that opens to the night sky. It's not totally finished yet, but we're having a drinks party there tonight, to try it out.'

She glanced across at Henry, who was looking even sexier than usual in his hunting gear, his muscular thighs gripping the sides of his horse with languid, effortless grace. Worryingly, though, he appeared to be arguing heatedly with Kate.

Judging from Henry's hostile body language, Kate must have made the mistake of trying to harangue him the way she'd harangued Eva earlier. She'd picked the wrong day to bend his ear, that was for sure. Henry had been in a foul mood all morning. For some reason Eva couldn't understand, he'd seemed irritated to learn that Richard and Lucy Smart were both coming out with today's hunt, even though this was hardly news; the Smarts were West Swell Valley regulars, and Richard was supposed to be Henry's best friend. But when Eva asked if the two of them had fallen out, Henry bit her head off, snapping angrily, 'Of course we bloody haven't. Why on earth would you ask something inane like that?'

Eva hoped the day's hunting would put him in a better mood, before tonight's big drinks up at Hanborough. She felt guilty even thinking it around Barney, but she found herself rather hoping today's quarry didn't make it. Nothing cheered Henry up quite so much as winning, even if it was against a fox.

Just then, Jeeves triumphantly broke free from Barney's grip, somehow contriving to slip his wiry head out of his collar like a canine Houdini.

'Shit,' muttered Barney. 'JEEVES!'

Racing across the road like a hairy bullet, the terrier narrowly avoided being trampled to death by one of the huntsmen before launching himself in a frenzy at one of the pack bitches, who promptly turned around and bit him. Within moments it was pandemonium. As various hounds and hunt followers' dogs piled into the fight, a number of the jumpier horses took fright, including Hugh Baxter's pony, who reared dangerously, narrowly missing Jen Clempson's head with its front hooves.

'Fuck!' yelled Barney, racing across the road and trying to fight his way through the snarling tangle of hounds and dogs.

'Jenny!' The vicar went white and dropped his loudhailer, racing after him.

Laura Baxter, also ashen-faced after the rearing incident, rushed over to Hugh and bravely grabbed hold of his pony's bridle, doing her best to calm the frightened animal as the noise and mayhem escalated. 'Are you all right, darling?'

'I'm fine, Mum,' said Hugh. In fact his heart was pounding nineteen to the dozen. Sparky had never reared before. But he knew his mother was looking for any excuse to stop him going out today, and he couldn't bear to give her one with only minutes to go until the off.

Meanwhile, Barney had finally reached the dog fight. Unfortunately Henry Saxton Brae was a few seconds ahead of him and had already dismounted and plunged into the fray, extracting a wriggling and pugnacious Jeeves roughly by the scruff of the neck.

'Is this your damned dog?' Henry glared at Barney accusingly.

'I'm afraid so. I'm terribly sorry. Thank you for pulling him out of there,' said Barney, reaching for Jeeves.

'Don't thank me,' Henry snarled, holding the Border terrier further away from his master, dangling him above the barking pack like a tasty morsel of meat. 'I've got a good mind to let them finish him off. Or to throw him into the river. Preferably with a rock tied around his leg. If you can't control your dog, you shouldn't bloody be out here in the first place.'

Barney tensed. He'd been quite prepared to apologize, but Henry's arrogant tone knocked the humility right out of him.

'You don't get to say who should and shouldn't be out here, you arrogant prick. Just because you bought a castle, it doesn't make you the fucking king.'

'Really?' Henry drawled. 'By that logic, just because you're Irish, it doesn't make you a fucking peasant. And yet, apparently, it does.'

'Give me back my dog,' Barney said slowly.

'Or what?' Henry sneered, an ugly smile forming on his handsome face as he swung a now terrified Jeeves in the air like a Frisbee. 'You'll set the vicar on me? I'm quaking in my boots.'

'Henry,' Richard Smart said sternly. 'Stop being a penis. Give the man his dog back.' Richard and Lucy, both hunt regulars, had ridden over to see what all the trouble was about. Lucy was also looking at Henry with a horrified expression. She'd never seen this ugly, vindictive side of him before. It wasn't at all pleasant.

'Here.' Laughing, Henry threw poor Jeeves at Barney with a lot more force than was good for him. Only by a miracle did Barney manage to catch the dog without injury. 'Take him and good riddance.'

Barney stood and glared at Henry. Complete silence had fallen suddenly. You could have cut the tension with a knife. Then a hunting horn rang out and the spell was broken, Seb Saxton Brae wisely taking the opportunity to sound for the off.

'I hope Eva comes to her senses and leaves you,' Barney hissed at Henry through gritted teeth, slipping the collar and lead back onto his traumatized terrier.

'For a penniless pacifist Paddy like you, you mean?' Henry's upper lip curled. 'I wouldn't hold your breath.'

And with that he rode off, but not before stopping in the lane and making a point of bending down low to kiss Eva passionately on the lips. Unable to break through the crowd, she'd missed his big fight with Barney, and couldn't understand why Barney glowered at her, stomping right past her as Henry rode away, marching back to his cottage with Jeeves without saying a word.

Flora drew her heavy knitted scarf more tightly around her and shivered. She was standing in the party barn at Hanborough, a building that, if only he knew it, Flora had come to hate even more than Henry did, watching the caterers set up for tonight's 'casual' post-hunt drinks. Observing the silver service, white linen tablecloths and immaculately cut crystal glassware all being unpacked, Flora wondered what a formal drinks party might look like in Henry and Eva's world. Not since last Christmas at Mason's mother's house in Connecticut had she witnessed preparations quite so out of proportion to the event planned. But Eva was so excited at the idea of entertaining as Hanborough's chatelaine, it was hard to begrudge her the extravagance. Especially as burning money was apparently Henry's latest craze.

The barn Flora was standing in, and that Henry in no sense wanted or needed, had cost him a cool million pounds to build so far, and it wasn't even finished yet. Despite the fact that she had designed every inch of it, and had persuaded Eva to adopt the plans, Flora was not at all keen on the structure. She'd conceived the plans for it purely to satisfy Graydon James, who had no thought in his head beyond satisfying the International Designer of the Year award committee. To Flora the new plans were overly modernist, full of gimmicks, ludicrously expensive, and not in keeping with the history, majesty and simplicity of Hanborough Castle. But Eva had loved the changes. For some inexplicable reason, the new designs reminded her of home, although Flora could think of no example of Swedish architecture that looked remotely like this.

Eva floated in just as Flora was directing a man with a vanload of trestle tables to the back of the barn.

'How was the big meet?' Flora asked, trying to muster some enthusiasm. She felt so tired and depleted – ever since Mason had gone home she'd barely slept and found it hard to focus on anything except work.

'It was fine. Very busy,' said Eva, idly picking up a hydrangea stem from one of the flower arrangements and stripping away a dead leaf. 'You need to eat more, you know.'

Eva had noticed that Flora's weight seemed to fluctuate markedly depending on her mood. Thinner tended to mean more unhappy. Today Flora's skinnier than usual frame was drowning in an oversized Guernsey sweater that Barney Griffith had given her after the first frost.

Barney was becoming a good friend, and one of the few people Flora could really relax around. He walked Jeeves past Peony Cottage most days, often stopping for a chat when Flora was just getting home from Hanborough. Thankfully he'd given up badgering her about starting her own business, or asking how things were going with Penny de la Cruz's London gallery. They weren't going, and if the current rate of progress at Hanborough was anything to go by, they never would be.

'You're not exactly Rosie O'Donnell yourself,' Flora replied good-naturedly. 'So who was there?'

'Oh, pretty much everybody,' said Eva. 'Seb and Kate, obviously. Penny and her husband. I must say he's very good-looking in an older man sort of way.'

'Santiago?' said Flora. 'I suppose so. I think his friend Gabriel Baxter is a lot handsomer.'

'He was there too, out with one of his little boys. They looked adorable together,' said Eva. 'Who else? The Smarts. Henry's been in a very odd mood with them lately, have you noticed? He's been avoiding Richard like the plague.'

'Has he?' Flora flushed guiltily, feigning innocence. She hated being complicit in Henry's dirty secrets, but what could she do?

On the plus side, Henry's affair with Lucy did seem to have cooled. Flora hadn't seen them together in weeks, although she got the sense it was Lucy who was keeping her distance, rather than Henry. She hoped he hadn't fallen seriously for his best friend's wife. Sometimes working at Hanborough and being around Henry and Eva was like watching a train crash in slow motion. Little by little, inch by inch, they were sliding off the rails, and poor Eva seemed to have no idea.

'The vicar and his wife were funny,' she babbled on, oblivious to Flora's worries. 'She was on our side, at the meet, while poor Bill was over on the village green with Barney and a few other stragglers, chanting "save the fox". I did feel sorry for him. Anyway, I've invited them both tonight. I do hope they come, although I daresay the vicar might feel it's against his principles. Do you think he will? Barney's already said no.'

'Oh,' said Flora, disappointed. Barney's presence was the only thing that would have made coming out tonight bearable. She was just wondering how offended Eva would be if she pleaded tiredness and ducked out too, when Eva shocked her by announcing baldly, 'You do realize he's in love with you?'

'Barney?' Flora laughed nervously. 'Don't be ridiculous!'

'He asked about you today,' said Eva. 'He always asks about you.'

'That doesn't mean anything,' said Flora. 'We're friends.'

'So are we,' said Eva, raising an eyebrow, 'but he doesn't buy me sweaters.'

'Only because he knows you already have a closet full of Chanel ones. I have lower standards.' Flora stroked her navy blue Guernsey appreciatively.

'You know I'm right,' said Eva, refusing to let it go. 'Just be careful, that's all. He's a nice guy.'

Flora stood there dumbfounded.

I know he's a nice guy, she wanted to say. *I'm a nice girl. But there is nothing – nothing – going on between me and Barney Griffith!*

But by the time the words had made it from her brain to her lips, Eva was already gone, off to catch up with the hunt and see if she could get a glimpse of Henry in action.

'Candles?' Another delivery man tapped Flora on the shoulder.

'Hmm?' Flora turned around, distracted.

'Candles. Where should I put 'em?'

'Wherever you like,' Flora said wearily. 'Mrs French, the PA, should be around here somewhere. Small, efficient, almost certainly wearing tweed. Ask her. I'm going home.'

Eva reached for her Ray-Ban aviators as a dazzling ray of winter sun burst through the windscreen of her Range Rover, blinding her. Despite Henry's grumpy mood this morning, she felt profoundly happy. The scenery might have had something to do with it. The Swell Valley looked magnificent in winter, its frosty fields glittering beneath cloudless blue skies and its ancient woodlands starkly beautiful, stripped of their leaves. The River Swell, ice cold and crystal clear, was running high after the heavy autumn rains, and even the cold, shrill wind felt welcome, blasting away all that was old and rotten and overblown and heralding a new, uncluttered day.

It felt like a new day for Eva, too. As if, at long last, the disparate pieces of her life were starting to come together. Having just shot her first L'Oréal campaign, the holy grail of beauty endorsements and a game-changer financially, her career was at an all-time high. She was going back to her native Sweden for Christmas, something she could hardly contain her excitement about. Yet, at the same time, she was finally starting to feel settled here in the English countryside, with friends like Barney and Flora and Penny and even Jen Clempson making her feel less like an appendage of Henry's and more like a person in her own right. Thanks to Flora, she now had a real say in the works at Hanborough too, which made the castle feel like her home for the first time, and not just Henry's.

Last but not least, there was Henry himself.

Something had changed between them. Something good, notwithstanding his occasional moodiness. The tide was turning in their romance; in little ways, like him driving to the airport to meet her, or the way he'd kissed her at the meet today; and in big ways, such as deferring to Eva on the new barn. That was huge. A year ago there would have been no way Henry would have done that: let Eva have something truly her own, at Hanborough, even though it wasn't to his taste.

He'd changed. Matured. Grown less selfish.

He was starting to think of them, not just of him.

He's trying to learn how to be married, Eva thought happily.

Not before time, of course. But better late than never.

Once they were married, Eva felt sure he would open up to her more. This thing with Richard Smart, for example. Whatever was bothering Henry about Rich, he would share it with her eventually. Loving a man like Henry took an immense amount of patience. But Eva did love him, deeply. She understood that wounds received in childhood could take a very, very long time to heal. And when someone like Henry *did* confide in you, when they *did* make an effort to love, and trust and give, it felt more wonderful and precious than anything else on earth.

When Eva had tried to explain this to Barney Griffith the other day, he'd told her she sounded like a battered wife.

'It's so good when he stops punching me in the face! It

almost feels like a massage!' Barney had teased her, in his appalling attempt at a Swedish accent. Eva had laughed it off at the time, but afterwards Barney's words had stung. Who the hell was he to offer advice about romance anyway, never mind to preach to others from on high? Eva hadn't noticed any rings on his fingers. Just a mooning, love-struck fascination with Flora, a woman as utterly unavailable to Barney as she was.

Today, though, she pushed all thoughts of Barney and his caustic comments out of her mind. Life was wonderful, and Eva intended to cherish every second of it. Turning sharp right into Brickyard Lane, she drove up to the top of the rise and was rewarded with a magnificent view of the hunt erupting out of the woods into open country, the pack leading the way, tearing down the valley in full cry in pursuit of their quarry.

Seb Saxton Brae was one of the first to emerge on Elijah, his magnificent silver grey stallion, a horse as sleekly muscled and elegant as Seb himself was fat, round and inelegant, at least in the saddle. With his short legs flapping at Elijah's sides and his ruddy farmer's face a parody of determined concentration, he reminded Eva of an old Thelwell cartoon. Not even his beautifully cut, red master's livery could save him from looking like an overweight bank manager who'd been kidnapped by some sadistic friend and plonked down in the middle of a fox hunt for a dare. It really was quite incredible to think that Sebastian and Henry had come from the same gene pool.

After Seb, the riders poured out of the woods thick and fast. Eva was no horsewoman, but you could tell at a glance the good riders from the bad. Santiago de la Cruz made it look like ballet, his still-athletic body at one with the powerful animal beneath him as they thundered across the field. Gabe Baxter, on the other hand, seemed to be having all sorts of difficulty controlling his mud-encrusted bay mare, while his son Hugh galloped on ahead at an eye-watering pace on his squat little pony, grinning broadly and half standing in his stirrups as they careered across the countryside. Eva felt a pang of anxiety watching him, leaning so far forward along his pony's neck that he looked in imminent danger of flying headfirst into the nearest ditch. No wonder poor Gabe looked so panicked.

A stream of huntsmen and riders followed, most of whom Eva didn't recognize. She couldn't see Henry among them, or Kate, Seb's wife. And at least two of the whippers-in seemed to be missing. There must be another group of them somewhere, separated from the main pack. Perhaps she should turn back and look for them?

Restarting the engine and swinging her Range Rover around, she caught sight of Richard and Lucy Smart, side by side at the very back of the hunt, leaning into one another and giggling like a couple of teenagers.

They look so happy, Eva thought wistfully. *So at ease in each other's company. I hope Henry and I look like that after nearly ten years of marriage.*

Heading back towards Hanborough, Eva peered over the tops of the hedgerows and flint walls, looking for any sign of Henry and the others, but there was none. Following the hunt by road was always tricky. There were so many different directions the riders could have gone in, especially when the hounds had a scent and were following a fox that might zigzag wildly, doubling back on itself multiple times before going to ground. Experienced riders, or those with a daredevil streak like Henry, often took different routes across country from the core of the hunt, deliberately seeking out higher jumps or more challenging terrain. Eva felt a flicker of anxiety. She did hope Henry hadn't overreached himself and had a bad fall, or got himself into some other trouble. Hunt accidents were rare, but when they happened they could be devastating.

Eva tried not to think about Christopher Reeve as she arrived back at the foot of Brickyard Lane. The castle was about a mile up the hill to her right, past Hanborough 'village', if you could dignify the smattering of estate cottages with the name. On a whim, Eva turned left, towards Fittlescombe, where the hunt had started out a few hours earlier. If she didn't see any other riders after five minutes, she'd head back to the castle and check on preparations for tonight's drinks. She really ought to be doing that anyway, but the urge to catch a glimpse of Henry riding to hounds, like a prince from a fairy tale, had been too strong for the hopeless romantic in her to resist.

Coming around a blind corner, Eva slammed on the brakes, her tyres squealing painfully as the 4x4 skidded to a halt.

'Shit!' Only by inches had she missed the skittish bay mare, clattering riderless along the lane, her reins and stirrups dangling.

Eva pulled over and got out, her heart pounding. In panic, the horse had tried to turn back the way she came, but lost her footing and careered into the five-bar gate on the right-hand side of the lane, whinnying in pain as the metal bars slammed into her flank.

'It's all right,' Eva said calmly, slowly approaching the distressed animal. She recognized the mare as Starlight, Kate's horse. 'It's all right, girl.' Miraculously, Starlight allowed Eva to come closer, and eventually to take her reins. Tethering her firmly to the gatepost, Eva patted her neck, her own anxiety rising as the mare's subsided.

Something must have happened.

Kate must have been thrown.

Was she lying somewhere, injured or unconscious? Or worse?

'Kate!' Eva shouted, vaulting over the gate and starting to run across the field. 'Kate?'

There was no answer. *I'd better call for help.* Reaching into her jacket pocket for her mobile, Eva cursed under her breath. No signal. Not even a hint of a bar.

She was just weighing up whether to go back to her car and drive into Fittlescombe village to get help, or to spend at least a few minutes more searching by herself, when something caught her eye. A movement in the trees to her left. A flash of white breeches, followed by a glint of black riding boots. Someone was in there. Running.

'Kate?' Eva hurried towards the trees, arriving at the edge of the copse just in time to see her future sister-in-law, naked from the waist up and with leaves still stuck to her hair, making an undignified dash down the hill in a doomed attempt to escape detection.

Eva had barely had time to process the shock of this vision when Henry, fully dressed but equally dishevelled, emerged from behind a large oak tree.

'Eva.'

He looked at her guiltily, but said nothing. Perhaps because there was nothing to say. The scene spoke for itself. Just behind him, in a clearing between three vast oaks, Kate's shirt, hat and bra still lay strewn across the ground.

Eva stood there, stunned, staring at the discarded clothes,

then at Henry, then back at the scene of the crime. She could see it, but she couldn't believe it. Not with *Kate*. Henry hated Kate.

Henry took a step towards her, then another. 'I'm sorry,' he began. 'It was nothing. It means nothing—'

His words were the wake-up call Eva needed, a glass of iced water in the face.

'No!' She held up her hand to stop him. 'Don't come near me! Get back.'

'Eva, please.'

'*No!*'

Eva turned and ran back to her car, the engine roaring as she sped away. The last thing she saw in her rear-view mirror was poor Starlight, terrified once again, straining wildly at her tethered reins as she tried to break free. Henry laid a hand on the mare's sweat-drenched flank, doing his best to comfort and calm her, but to no avail.

She's trapped, thought Eva. *Like me*.

Only then did the tears begin to flow.

CHAPTER FIFTEEN

'All right, enough of this shit. What the hell is going on?'

Richard Smart accosted Henry in a quiet corner of the party barn, where he sat miserably nursing a large tumbler of whisky. Henry and Eva's post-hunt drinks party was in full swing. Just about the entire West Swell Valley had shown up and were enjoying themselves immensely, quaffing their host's excellent wine and gorging themselves on the cordon bleu catering while congratulating themselves on today's kill and admiring Flora's 'James Bond' touches to the new building, including the retractable roof, floor-to-ceiling glass walls and rotating rainbow LED lights.

The only people not enjoying themselves were the hosts. Eva hadn't even bothered to show up to her own party, and was conspicuous by her absence. Henry was there, but looked as if he'd rather be having root-canal surgery, and wore an expression that angrily dared his guests to engage him in conversation at their peril.

'Have you and Eva had a row?' asked Richard. 'Is that it?'

Henry stared straight ahead of him and said nothing.

'Where is she?'

Still nothing.

Richard frowned. 'Can I sit down?'

'No.'

Ignoring him, Richard pulled up a chair. 'For God's sake, Henry, what is it? You've been avoiding me and Lucy for weeks now.'

Henry looked up at him, surprised. 'That's not true,' he muttered.

'Of course it bloody is,' Richard said robustly. 'You acted like a complete tool with that dog at the meet this morning. What have you got against that chap, anyway?'

'He's a raging anti for a start,' muttered Henry. 'And he's always sniffing around Eva,' he added petulantly. First Eva, then Flora, now Richard. It irritated Henry that so many people in his life seemed to think that the sun shone out of Barney Griffith's arse.

'Oh, grow up,' said Richard. 'They're friends. Anyway, it wasn't just that. After that you went AWOL. For the entire bloody day,' he added meaningfully. 'You even missed the kill. And now you're sitting at your own party getting drunk in the corner like Suicide Sid.'

Henry gazed morosely into his whisky glass before downing its entire contents and signalling to the waiting staff for another.

'I'm not leaving till you tell me what's happened,' said Richard. 'Are you feeling all right?'

Henry sighed. There were times when he wished to God Richard weren't such a good friend and all-round decent person.

If only he could turn back the clock! If only he'd never slept with Lucy.

In Henry's mind, that was the beginning of all his current troubles. Every time he and Lucy were together, he hated himself for betraying Richard and found himself longing for a way out. And yet, when Lucy had called time on their fling a few weeks ago, he'd been devastated. Stupidly, preposterously, Henry had done what he'd sworn never to do: he'd fallen in love with Lucy. Or, rather, there was a part of what Lucy gave him that he loved, and needed. He hadn't stopped loving Eva. If anything, in a bizarre way, his affair with his best friend's wife had made him appreciate his fiancée even more. But he'd been so *angry* when Lucy dropped him, so angry at himself for needing her, and needing Eva, and fucking everything up . . . and now he'd gone and done the most stupid thing in the world, and had it off with Kate, of all people, for no better reason than that she belonged to his brother. That and the fact that she'd pissed him off royally this morning at the meet and he wanted to own her and conquer her and teach her a goddamned lesson . . . but Henry had been the one who'd learned a lesson.

There was something wrong with him. Something very, very wrong.

All the compulsive risk-taking. All the sex with women like Kate or George Savile, women Henry didn't even like. He felt like a serial killer, leaving more and more elaborate clues, desperate for someone to stop him and catch him, to save him from himself.

Well, today, Eva had.

But Henry didn't feel relief. He felt nothing but utter desolation.

He looked at Richard.

'I slept with Kate.'

'Ha ha ha!' Richard laughed loudly. 'At least you're making jokes. I suppose I should take that as progress.'

'This afternoon,' Henry said seriously. 'That's why I went AWOL. I took Kate to Gamlin's Wood and had it off with her. Eva caught us. I think she's left me.'

The smile died on Richard's lips. 'You're serious?'

Henry nodded grimly.

'Kate, as in Kate.'

'Yup.'

'As in Kate, your brother's wife? Kate, who's standing over there right now, acting completely normal?' Richard looked across the room to where Kate and Seb Saxton Brae were chatting amiably to Max Bingley and Angela Cranley, apparently without a worry in the world. 'Kate, who last time I checked, you couldn't stand?'

'I still can't stand her,' said Henry.

'So why . . . ?'

'I don't know! I don't know, I don't know, I don't *fucking* know! Because I'm an idiot. Because I turn everything good in my life into poison. But it's not enough for me to poison my own life, apparently. I have to poison everyone else's too.' Henry screwed up his eyes tight, as if trying to block out something frightening, something too awful to contemplate. Bizarrely, he found himself thinking about his mother. Then, to Richard's utter astonishment, he started to cry.

'All right, mate. Calm down.' Feeling completely inadequate, Richard put an arm around Henry's heaving shoulders. 'Don't go to pieces. Let's be practical about this. Was Eva the only one who saw you?'

Henry nodded. Wiping his eyes, he told Richard briefly what had happened. How after Eva had driven away, he'd ridden back to Hanborough, got his car and scoured the countryside looking for her, but to no avail. At six o'clock he'd decided to change and come to the drinks party, mostly because it would look damned odd if he didn't. Kate had also clearly opted to brazen things out, at least for now, changing into a demure knee-length skirt and polo neck and sticking to Seb all evening like a conjugal limpet.

'So no one else knows?' asked Richard when he'd finished.

'That depends. Eva might have told someone.'

'Who would she have told?'

Henry's head was starting to throb. 'I don't know. Does it matter?'

'It might,' said Richard. 'Think.'

'She's friends with that twat Barney Griffith,' said Henry.

Richard looked momentarily blank.

'The anti. Irish. Wannabe writer. You met him at dinner here once. Dresses like a tramp.'

The penny dropped. 'You mean the guy whose dog you tried to kill this morning?'

'That dog's a bloody menace,' grumbled Henry. 'Anyway, I doubt Eva would have said anything to Griffith. Not about this.'

'Why not?'

'She'd find it too humiliating. If she confides in anyone, it'll be another woman.'

'Who are her girlfriends, then?' Richard asked.

Henry shrugged, defeated. 'She doesn't really have any. I mean, back in Sweden maybe. But I don't know their names.'

'There must be someone local. Someone she might turn to in a crisis.' Richard was getting frustrated. 'You have to *find* her, Henry. Talk to her. Unless you *want* her to leave you and tell the whole world you've been banging your brother's wife, you need to bloody *do* something!'

Henry put his glass down and stood up suddenly.

'I know where she is,' he said, hugging Richard tightly and heading for the barn doors. 'Thank you.'

'Thank me for what?' said Richard, getting up after him. 'Where are you going? I hope you're not thinking of driving. Henry? Henry!'

'What was all that about?' Lucy appeared behind him, putting a restraining hand on his arm. She tried to keep her voice light, but she'd been watching the exchange between Henry and her husband from across the room with increasing alarm. Henry was clearly drunk and had been in a belligerent mood all day. Lucy hoped he wouldn't go so far as to spill the beans to Richard about their affair out of spite. But recently she didn't know what to expect from him. He'd been so angry when she'd cooled things off between them. So unreasonably and illogically hurt, as if he didn't already *know* that they couldn't carry on the way they had been; that the affair was eating away at both of them like a cancer. But instead of being reasonable, or kind or sane about it, he'd decided to take his frustrations out on Lucy as if she alone were to blame. As if it weren't hard for her too, to walk away.

Richard gave her such a sad, bleak look that for a moment Lucy's heart plunged to the pit of her stomach. *Oh God! Henry's told him.*

'I think Henry's having a breakdown.'

Lucy gripped Richard's arm, dizzy with relief.

'Eva might be leaving him.'

'Why?'

'She caught him cheating on her.'

The relief evaporated. Lucy went white.

211

'When?' she croaked.

'Today.' Richard dropped his voice to a conspiratorial whisper. 'And you'll never guess with who. Only Sebastian's bloody wife!'

'What?' spluttered Lucy. 'Henry's sleeping with *Kate*?'

The pain was like a dagger blow to the intestines; visceral, ugly and deep. So much for Henry's 'heartache'. His 'love' for her. All this time he'd been trying to make her feel guilty, for going back to her husband and trying to do the right thing, and meanwhile he'd been out there shagging his own sister-in-law!

'Shhh!' hissed Richard. 'Keep your voice down.'

'Sorry. I just . . . I think I'm in shock.'

Lucy looked so desolate, Richard pulled her into a hug. Lucy was trapped within his crushing arms, like two lead bars of solid guilt.

'I know. I couldn't believe it either,' he whispered in her ear. 'He's gone to try and find Eva now. See if they can work things out.'

'How?' Lucy asked, incredulous. 'How do you "work out" a betrayal like that?'

Richard shrugged. 'I dunno. But it's got to be worth a try, hasn't it? Besides, it's amazing what people can forgive when they really love someone.'

Lucy buried her face in his chest so he couldn't see the pain in her eyes.

Did he suspect about her and Henry? Had he guessed?

Oh God, what had she done?

'Yes,' she murmured. 'I suppose it is.'

Flora had just sunk into a hot, Floris-scented bath, closing her eyes and relaxing for the first time all day, when a frenzied pounding on Peony Cottage's front door signalled Eva's arrival.

Flora had been irritated with Eva earlier – her comment about Barney had seemed designed to annoy her. Quite possibly men *did* fall in love with you willy-nilly if you happened to be a world-famous lingerie model, but there was no need for Eva to make Flora feel guilty about her own friendship with Barney. The casual implication that Flora was somehow leading him on, and/or behaving in an un-fiancée-like manner towards Mason was uncalled for, in Flora's opinion. But as soon as she saw Eva's tear-stained, heartbroken face, all thoughts of their earlier conversation flew out of Flora's head.

Hugging Eva and installing her on the sofa in front of the fire, Flora sat and listened, still wrapped in a towel, while Eva told her the whole sorry, sordid story.

'I mean, Kate. *Kate!*' she repeated, over and over, between sobs. 'I don't suppose it would have mattered who it was, but Kate? Henry can't stand her. They can't stand each other. Why would he . . . ? I don't understand it.'

Flora listened and nodded and poured Eva the first of many large brandies, as well as one for herself. They sat and talked for a long time, hours, with the conversation mostly going round in circles. Flora didn't understand Henry's latest choice of lover either. Lady Saxton Brae had a face like a horse and considerably less brainpower, not to mention the fact that she was stupefyingly boring. Flora remembered hearing Henry refer to his sister-in-law as an 'antisocial climber, like poison ivy' and repeatedly expressing pity for 'poor Seb' for being married to her. What on earth had possessed him to risk it all with Eva for an afternoon of chilly outdoor copulation with Kate, of all people?

She wanted to say something comforting to Eva as a friend, but try as she might she couldn't come up with a single mitigating circumstance to explain Henry's behaviour. Clearly the man was some sort of sex addict. Or lunatic. Or both.

'It isn't the first time. Or even the second, or third,' Eva sniffed miserably. 'I've heard the rumours, about him and George. And I know there have been others. I'm not stupid.'

'So why do you stay?' asked Flora, not unkindly.

'I don't know. I love him I suppose,' Eva sighed.

'There must be more to it than that,' Flora pressed her.

'Well, there's his childhood,' said Eva. 'Losing his mother so young. That's a classic reason for men to fear intimacy.'

'And that makes it OK?'

'No, of course not. Nothing makes it OK.' Eva ran a hand through her long golden hair in exasperation. 'I don't know, perhaps I *am* stupid. Because, honestly, I thought he'd changed. Since we moved to Hanborough things have been better. Different. Henry seemed so much happier here. At least he did until a few weeks ago.'

Flora wondered how much of Henry's happiness had been down to his affair with Lucy Smart. Now that it was over, or at least on the wane, had he turned to his sister-in-law in anger, as the nearest available conquest? The whole thing was all seriously fucked up. Not for the first time, Flora wished she wasn't privy to so much inside information on Henry's extracurricular activities.

'What are you going to do?' she asked Eva.

Picking up a red damask throw cushion, Eva played idly with the silk threads on one of the tassels. 'Cancel the wedding, I suppose,' she sighed. 'I do love him. And I've tried to understand him. I really have tried so hard. But we can't go on like this.'

It was the first sign of strength Flora had ever seen from Eva. She was amazed by it, and encouraged. 'I agree,' she said, refilling Eva's glass and noticing that the bottle was almost empty. 'For what it's worth, I don't think this has anything to do with you. Some people are just not capable of being married. I used to be like that.'

'You?' Eva looked at her disbelievingly. 'I can't imagine you ever sleeping with your sister's husband!'

'No, well, I don't have a sister.' Flora smiled, trying to lighten the mood. 'I don't mean I slept around. Just that I was scared of commitment, for a long time. Like Henry. If I hadn't met Mason, I honestly don't know if I would ever have gotten married.'

'Of course you would,' said Eva. 'You're totally the marrying kind.'

Flora shook her head. 'I'm not. You only think that because you are, so you imagine everybody else is.'

'Even Henry, you mean?'

Flora gave her a 'you said it' look. 'You can't fix him, Eva. My mother spent half her life trying to fix my father, and the other half blaming herself for failing. You can do so much better.'

'Mason fixed you, though, didn't he?' said Eva.

Flora was just thinking about this and how to respond – she didn't like the idea that Mason had 'fixed' her, although perhaps in some ways this was true – when the front door burst open. Unlike Eva, Henry didn't bother to knock. Swaying in the cottage doorway, looking like a vast, drunken giant in Flora's tiny but immaculate front room, he marched over to Eva and grabbed her hand.

'I need to talk to you.'

Eva snatched her arm back. 'Go away, Henry.'

'No. I won't. I can't. Please, Eva.'

He was shaking. Looking as handsome as ever in a simple black jacket and open-necked shirt over dark jeans, with his black curls pushed back from his forehead, he gazed at Eva with a desolate, half-crazed look in his eyes. Even Flora felt sorry for him for a moment. But only for a moment.

'She doesn't want to talk to you,' Flora said, standing up and physically inserting herself between them.

'You don't know what she wants,' Henry turned on her angrily.

'I know what *I* want,' said Flora, 'which is for you to get out of my house right now. You can't just come barging in here and demand—'

Putting one hand on each of Flora's upper arms, Henry simply lifted her up and moved her out of his way, setting her down again a few feet to the left, as if she were an inconveniently placed piece of furniture. Flora would have liked to hit him, but she was in imminent danger of losing her towel, and infuriatingly needed both hands to hold it up and protect her modesty.

'Please,' Henry addressed himself to Eva again. 'Five minutes. That's all I'm asking for. Please, just hear me out.'

It took Flora a few seconds to regain the power of speech after being so unceremoniously manhandled in her own living room. By the time she'd resecured her bath towel and opened her mouth, it was too late. One look at Eva's face told her she'd already caved in.

'Five minutes. Outside,' she said, drawing Flora's throw blanket around her shoulders as if she'd just been rescued from a shipwreck. Which, emotionally, she sort of had.

Flora watched, speechless, as Henry led Eva into the garden. They left the door ajar, and Flora could hear snatches of the conversation from her position on the sofa. Raised voices. Tears. A pleading tone from Henry that she'd never heard before. At one point she thought she heard Eva fighting back, and telling him where to go. But eventually the shouting subsided. Their voices grew lower and calmer. Flora distinctly heard the words 'Christmas' and 'Sweden' and Henry, conciliatory now, saying, 'Of course. Of course we'll go home. As long as you want.'

Moments later, Flora heard a car door open and shut.

I can't believe it! she thought, waiting for the engine to start. *She can't have let him off that easy. She's going to go back to Hanborough with him, just like that?*

A rap on the door made her jump. She jumped again when she saw that it wasn't Eva, regaining control of her senses and asking to stay the night, but Henry, looking less tragic than before but still surprisingly hangdog.

'You must hate me,' he said to Flora.

'I don't hate you,' she heard herself reply.

'But you think Eva should leave me?'

Flora looked at him, wide-eyed. 'Of course I do. Don't you?'

A half-smile formed on his lips, then disappeared. 'Probably. I wouldn't marry me.'

'Exactly,' said Flora.

Henry had started walking towards her, and stood now only inches away, towering over her like a poplar tree, smelling of whisky and aftershave and night air and sweat.

'Thank you.' He touched Flora's arm.

Her heart seemed to have leapt into her throat, making speech almost impossible, and was beating so violently Flora felt sick. He was too close. Far too close.

'For what?' she managed to squeak.

217

'Taking care of her,' said Henry. 'And for not saying anything. About Lucy, I mean.'

'I know what you mean,' said Flora, who was starting to feel even sicker.

Henry turned to go.

'If you really loved her, you'd let her go. Let her find someone else,' Flora called after him. She hadn't meant to. The words just sort of rushed out.

'If I were a better person, you mean?' Henry gave Flora a look she would never forget, his eyes boring into hers with an intensity that made her knees buckle. 'Like Eva? Or your fiancé?'

Don't bring Mason into this, Flora wanted to say. *You don't even know him.* But her earlier eloquence seemed to have withered on the vine.

Henry filled the silence for her.

'I'm not a better person though, am I? I'm just me. I can't change, Flora. Neither can you. Our better halves will just have to take us as they find us.'

And with that, he left, closing the door quietly behind him.

CHAPTER SIXTEEN

Georgina Savile leaned back in her Herman Miller office chair and flipped, bored, through the pages of December *Vogue*. George already had all the winter collection pieces she wanted on order – Alison Loehnis at Net-a-Porter had sorted her out for years on the wardrobe front, which was marvellous, of course, but it did mean that one was reduced to actually reading the articles in *Vogue*, which this month were a dreary litany of 'holiday-themed' stories about as stimulating as watching paint dry. Or as listening to George's husband bang on about Gimlet, the racehorse he'd just bought for an astronomical sum of money and dropped into every conversation with the sort of enthusiasm another man might reserve for the name of a new and exotic lover.

Even in his bachelor days, George thought sadly, Robert's idea of a wild night out would have involved one too many glasses of claret at White's or the novelty of a rickshaw-ride home after an evening of *La Bohème* at Covent Garden.

Then again, George hadn't married her husband for the thrill factor. She'd married Robert because he was rich, successful, well connected and pliant. Since the day they'd met, George had chosen everything, from their wedding date and venue to which home they bought, how they decorated it, whom they invited over and whether or not they would have children. (They wouldn't.) Finally, and perhaps most importantly, she'd married Robert to send a message to Henry. That she wouldn't wait for ever. That if he didn't commit to her, someone else would. That she didn't need him.

The problem was that she did. George was used to men falling at her feet, lining up for the privilege of being the next to grace her bed. Not since her schooldays at Sherwood Hall had she experienced romantic rejection of the kind she got from Henry.

Back then George had been madly in love with Alexander Neville, a shy sixth-former with big doe eyes and a mop of unruly auburn hair, destined for great things at Oxford. When Alexander turned her down, thanks to his unrequited obsession with that tacky American sex-doll Flora Fitzwilliam, George had oscillated between fury and deep, penetrating shame. It wasn't simply that Alexander didn't want her. It was that he wanted Flora more. Even after she had been forced to leave the school in disgrace, the idiotic boy continued to write to her, mooning from afar like a lovesick puppy.

Of course, George got over it. She left school, became even more beautiful, and delighted in seducing a string of high-profile men, many of them married, all of them powerful, successful or just plain gorgeous. Henry Saxton Brae fell into all three categories. When they met, the chemistry had been instant, both carnally and intellectually. Founding Gigtix together had felt to George like the first step in their lives as a long-term couple. They were already lovers. Soon they became not just business partners but a business phenomenon, feted and interviewed all over the world as the next big thing in e-commerce, the glamorous twin ambassadors of Young British Entrepreneurship.

Although they'd never been exclusive, or announced themselves as boyfriend and girlfriend, George assumed that this would simply be a matter of time. Henry would grow up a little, realize that no one could ever match what they had in bed, marry her, and the two of them would live happily ever after. But it never happened. In fact, as the months passed, and then the years, he became increasingly bored and restless, ultimately coming to view George with something bordering on disdain. They still slept together regularly. But when he met Ikea, even that started to change. His encounters with George became less and less frequent and more and more laden with guilt on Henry's part. Panicked, George had married Robert to make Henry jealous. It hadn't worked. Two weeks later, Henry had proposed to Eva, bought Hanborough Castle, and decamped to the country.

As if all that weren't bad enough, in a cruelly ironic twist, Henry had hired Graydon James to renovate Hanborough and wound up with none other than Flora Fitzwilliam, George's old nemesis from school, as his practically live-in designer! Not only did Henry clearly like and respect Flora, but – far worse – Flora and Ikea had apparently become best friends. And, to top it all, while George was stuck sleeping next to a snoring Robert night after night, Flora was all set to marry some über-eligible New York bachelor, almost as rich and handsome as Henry but, by all accounts, considerably nicer.

George's direct line buzzed.

'Henry's here,' Charlotte, George's secretary, said nervously. Charlotte said everything nervously. Working for George she'd found it necessary to adopt the emotional 'brace position' at all times. 'Do you have time for a quick meeting?'

George slipped *Vogue* back into her desk drawer. She had nothing but time. Gigtix pretty much ran itself these days, and she only came into the office in the hope of catching Henry alone.

In the old days he would simply have knocked on her office door, or more likely just walked in. Now that they were a hundred-million-pound company, with twenty permanent staff based in the London office, things were a lot more formal.

'I have ten minutes if he wants to come up now. But that's my only window,' George lied.

'OK, I'll let him know.'

Two minutes later, Henry walked in. Dressed casually in jeans and a chocolate brown cashmere sweater, he looked tired and distracted.

'What's the latest with R-Ventures?' he asked brusquely, getting straight down to business.

George yawned, leaned back and recrossed her legs, affording him a brief but crystal-clear view of her new red La Perla knickers. 'I signed yesterday,' she said nonchalantly.

Henry turned puce. 'What? What do you mean you signed?'

George cocked her pretty head to one side in mock innocence. 'Isn't that self-explanatory?'

'How can you have signed?' Henry exploded. 'We haven't agreed terms yet.'

'Yes, we have. I agreed them.'

'Without my consent?'

George shrugged. 'I tried to reach you. Repeatedly. You don't return my calls, or emails. You're never in the office—'

'You had no right to do that deal without me!'

'On the contrary,' George shouted back. 'I have every right. One of us has to live up to our responsibilities. Ever since you bought that damned castle, you've been totally distracted. All you think about is weddings and interior design. It's like you have no balls left at all.'

'But your balls are big enough for both of us. Right?' Henry shot back.

'You said it,' said George.

Henry smiled. For the briefest of moments, the old spark flickered in the air between them. But then it was gone.

'What are your plans for Christmas?' Henry asked, changing gear and trying to return the conversation to a more civil footing. He was livid that George had done a big private equity deal without him, but part of him also knew that her criticisms were fair. He had been absent from the business recently, both physically and mentally.

'The usual.' George shrugged. 'Mustique. Robert's shooting in Scotland over New Year, though, so I might get *some* time to myself.'

She looked at Henry knowingly, but he didn't take the bait.

'I suppose you'll be at Hanborough?'

'Actually, no.' He frowned. 'We're going to Stockholm. Staying with Eva's parents.'

George laughed loudly. 'What *fun*,' she teased him. 'Meatballs and roll-mop herrings in the Gunnarsons' charming bungalow. I'll bet you can't wait.'

'It means a lot to Eva,' Henry muttered, grudgingly.

'Well, that's all right then,' George said archly. 'Are your trips to buy cheap, flat-packed furniture already planned? Or will you play that by ear, add an *extra* layer of excitement?'

'Stop,' said Henry wearily. He didn't want another argument. George was still his business partner. Somehow he had to improve things between them, to find a way other than sex to neutralize George's anger. 'We couldn't have stayed at Hanborough anyway. They found dry rot in the great hall and the entire roof of the West Wing. We're back to camping in the master suite and kitchen, which is a pain in the arse.'

George raised an eyebrow. 'I hate to say "I told you so".'

'Do you?' quipped Henry.

'But Flora Fitzwilliam's clearly not up to the job. Six months in, and they're only finding major structural problems now?'

'That was the surveyor's fault. Before Flora's time,' said Henry, already regretting bringing this up, or meeting with George at all. Somehow she never failed to make his day just that little bit worse.

'I knew her at school, you remember, and it was the same story then,' George went on. 'She never had much talent, but she was always given good grades because the male teachers fawned on her. Not that she was ever particularly pretty. She just had that same slutty, available look she has now.'

'Stop,' Henry said quietly.

'Oh, come *on*, you know what I'm talking about,' said George. 'Those great big uddery tits, like a porn star's.' She shuddered with distaste. 'It's obvious what Flora brings to Graydon James's table.'

'Is it?' Henry's voice was like ice.

'Of course it is,' trilled George. 'He gets all the gay male clients and flings Flora at the straight ones like you with her boobs hanging out. And six months later, here you are with no roof, six months behind on works and seven figures over budget! As a friend, darling, I'm telling you. Stop thinking with your cock for once – fire Flora, and bring in somebody competent. I'd be happy to introduce you to our chap, Jeremy Baines.'

'As a friend?' Henry said witheringly.

'Absolutely.' George smiled. 'Jeremy did a wonderful job on our Holland Park house. I've got his number here somewhere.'

She started scrolling through her address book.

Henry stood up.

'As a friend,' he smiled thinly, 'your Holland Park house looks like a dentist's office. Painting everything white is not my idea of design genius. I'm restoring a castle, not building a morgue.'

George gaped at him, open-mouthed.

'As for Flora, she has more talent in her little finger than you or I have in our entire bodies. The fact that you can't see that says everything about you and nothing whatsoever about her. She also works like a bloody slave. I have no intention of firing her.'

George's eyes narrowed. 'Touched a nerve, have I? So you *do* fancy her. How tragically predictable.'

'Merry Christmas, George,' said Henry, stalking out.

'You too!' George called after him furiously. 'Enjoy sunny Sweden!'

After Henry had left, George sat and stared at the door for a long time.

225

So bloody, hateful Flora had worked her magic on Henry too, had she? Cast her insidious, goody two-shoes spell? Not content with sucking up to Eva, she'd managed to enrol Henry, George's Henry, into her ever-growing fan club.

Not on my watch, George thought bitterly. *It's time somebody taught Miss Flora Fitzwilliam a lesson.*

She picked up the phone. 'Charlotte? I need a number. Get me Graydon James's private office in New York.'

'I shouldn't be eating this.'

Flora dug her spoon into a third, ambrosial mouthful of The Latchmere's sticky toffee pudding, closing her eyes as the delicious hot butterscotch sauce exploded onto her tongue like a sugar-fuelled orgasm.

'Yes, you should,' Penny de la Cruz said firmly. 'I hate to sound like a Jewish mother, but you've been wasting away recently. I'm sure Mason doesn't want a twig coming back to him for Christmas.'

Actually, Flora thought, *Mason wouldn't mind at all if I lost a few pounds.* Not that he didn't appreciate her curves, especially her boobs. But there was something borderline obscene about Flora's figure at its fullest, something almost cartoonishly sexual, that she sensed Mason was sometimes embarrassed by. As he once put it, 'It's like even when you're dressed, you're naked.' Admittedly he'd been sporting a splendid erection at the time which, combined with his admiring tone of voice, had led Flora to take this observation as a compliment. But she'd also seen him wistfully eyeing the slender, willowy girlfriends of his fellow J.P. Morgan bankers. Or perhaps she was the one doing the wistful eyeing – at least when it came to the gorgeous, sample-sized dresses they all seemed able to fit into. Being short and voluptuous made it mightily difficult to dress well at black-tie events. And this Christmas in New York would be one black-tie event after another, with Flora being paraded around by Mason's mother like some sort of prize turkey.

Luckily, notwithstanding the pudding, Flora was probably the skinniest she'd been since high school. She'd agreed to meet Penny for a long overdue lunch ('the least I can do to thank you for your sketches, especially as I'm going to use all of them at the gallery'), partly as a way of forcing herself to come up to London and do some Christmas shopping. The discovery of dry rot had turned her into a virtual prisoner at Hanborough, but her flight to New York was fast approaching, and she'd yet to buy a single Christmas present, never mind find two evening dresses to fit her, replace her greying, hole-ridden panties and ancient bras with something less shame-inducing, and get a wax, facial, pedicure and other Manhattan basic essentials, none of which were remotely available anywhere in the Swell Valley.

'Are you excited?' Penny asked, attacking her own chocolate fondant with considerable gusto. 'About going home for Christmas, I mean. I imagine New York must be terribly romantic at this time of year.'

'It is,' said Flora. 'Haven't you been?'

'Me? Oh, no.' Penny shook her head and laughed, as if the very idea were ridiculous. 'My first husband was a big believer in traditional Christmases when the children were little. That meant lots of church and carol singing and whatnot, and the Queen's speech, and me doing all the cooking and washing up. We never went anywhere.'

'I didn't know you were married before,' said Flora. 'What happened to him?'

'Paul? He ran off with another man.'

Flora gasped and went bright red. 'How awful! I'm so sorry.'

'Oh, please don't be.' Penny waved a hand airily. 'Being gay was actually one of the least awful things about Paul. I thank God every day he ran off. I'd never have found Santiago otherwise.'

Flora smiled. 'The two of you do seem terribly happy together.'

'We are,' Penny beamed. 'But he won't go anywhere for Christmas either. All he wants to do is stay in bed and eat chocolate truffles and, you know. Celebrate.' She blushed. 'He even gets annoyed if the children come home. He likes it to be just us.'

'That sounds great,' sighed Flora. She'd be looking forward to going home a lot more if Mason wasn't insisting on dragging them both out to a different cocktail party every single night. If only it were just the two of them, in a cabin somewhere. Canada, maybe. Or Wyoming. Or even here, in England, somewhere tranquil and lovely.

Barney was going to the Lake District for Christmas to stay with his sister in some crumbling stone farmhouse under a mountain. He'd shown Flora pictures, incredible images of grey skies and still silver water against a magnificent backdrop of towering crags and fells. Barney really was an amazing photographer. The place looked like heaven.

'I heard Henry's going to Sweden this year, missing all the parties,' said Penny, shattering Flora's reverie.

'Yes.'

'I assume that means things are going well with him and Eva?'

'I don't know if I'd assume that,' said Flora.

'Oh?' Penny's eyebrow went up.

'Henry has a sweet side.' She was mainly thinking of him with Whiskey and Soda. 'He can be kind and he does love her. But I'm not sure he's cut out for marriage,' Flora said diplomatically.

The conversation turned back to Penny's gallery, and Flora's work. Flora explained about next year's big design award and the pressure she was under from Graydon both to modernize the designs at Hanborough and to finish on time, which now looked like a taller order than ever with the roof problems and dry rot.

'He can't expect you to do the impossible,' said Penny, waving to a waiter for the bill.

'You haven't met Graydon,' said Flora. 'Expecting the impossible is the James family motto. But you know, this award is important to me too. Hanborough may be my last big job, and I'd like to go out with a bang.'

Penny frowned. 'Why would it be your last big job?'

'I'm not saying it will,' Flora backtracked, 'I just don't know. After I'm married, things might be different. Mason wants to have kids right away, so there's that. And his career will have to come first.'

'Will it?' said Penny. 'It sounds to me as if your career's just taking off.'

'Yes, but mine doesn't make any money,' Flora said ruefully.

'Not yet, maybe,' said Penny. 'In any case, aren't there other measures of success? I mean, look at Barney. He gave up an excellent job as a lawyer to do something he loves.'

'Exactly. Look at Barney,' said Flora. 'His cottage is freezing and all his clothes are falling apart at the seams; he's wasted a year of his life not finishing a book, and he's alone.'

'Maybe he hasn't found the right girl yet. Or the right girl hasn't found him,' Penny observed cryptically.

'Maybe.' Flora scraped the last remnants of her pudding from the bowl. 'All I know is, that sort of life would never work for me. I don't want to be poor and live in a garret.'

'What *is* a garret, anyway?' asked Penny.

Flora laughed. 'No idea. But let's never find out. Mason works hard and he can give us both a good life. I do love my job. But one has to be practical.'

Penny said nothing. But she wondered who she'd just eaten lunch with, Flora Fitzwilliam or Mason Parker?

Heading back to Battersea, she found herself hoping that Flora's fiancé really was the prince that Flora thought him to be. Penny knew better than anyone that there was no unhappiness in life quite so hard to bear as a miserable marriage.

'*One has to be practical*?' That didn't sound like a recipe for happily ever after.

Barney and Eva walked together down the hill towards Flora's cottage. It was only teatime, but twilight had already crept over the valley, spreading a blue-black blanket of stars over the bare woods and frosted grey fields.

Jeeves, who wasn't a fan of the cold, trotted along at his master's heels in an unusually subdued manner, while Whiskey and Soda raced ahead, their lean muscles rippling and their glossy coats glinting with health, even in the half-light.

'Does Henry *ever* walk his own dogs?' Barney asked, breaking his own, new rule never to bring up Eva's dickhead fiancé. His opinion and Eva's were so far removed on the subject of Henry, that the safest course was to avoid the topic altogether. 'What did he do before you two got together?'

'I don't actually know,' said Eva, whistling to the two setters to return, which they did with instant obedience. 'I think the grooms took them out. I don't mind, though. I love walking them. Anyway, it gives us a chance to talk.'

They'd reached the bottom of the hill now and stood at a gate, directly across the lane from Flora's front door. The lights were all off, other than the single lantern hanging above the front door. Clearly no one was home. Barney pulled out his camera and started clicking away. The cottage looked so tranquil, its whitewashed walls bathed softly in the last of the evening's light, and with long shadows dancing along the brick path.

'Isn't it too dark for that?' Eva asked.

'No. It's perfect. Ethereal,' said Barney, still taking shots. 'If they come out nicely I'll blow one up for Flora as a Christmas present. Remind her why she wants to stay here and not move back to New York.'

Eva rolled her eyes. 'You don't give up, do you? Try and be open to meeting someone else.'

'I will if you will.'

'You're single,' Eva reminded him. 'I'm engaged.'

'To a tosser,' Barney reminded her.

Eva scowled.

'Sorry.' Barney held his arms out wide, like a footballer admitting a foul. 'She's dreading going back for Christmas, you know,' changing the subject back to Flora as they turned left along the lane.

'Did she say that?' Eva sounded surprised. Flora had told her more than once how much she was missing Mason, and how badly she needed the break.

'Not in so many words. But when I showed her the Lake District pictures I could just tell she wanted to be there.'

'Bar*neee*!' Eva chided.

'She did! Flora loves peace and beauty. She's an artist, like me. You know I'm much more suited to her than Perry Mason, or Peter Parker, or whatever his stupid American name is. She doesn't want to waste her life being some sodding banker's wife.'

'She wants security,' Eva said bluntly. Sometimes one had to be cruel to be kind. 'I'm not saying she's a gold-digger, but not everyone can live on air and dreams the way that you can.'

'Air, dreams and Guinness,' Barney corrected her. 'There's a difference.'

He joked about it because he didn't know what else to do. Deep down, however, he had a horrible feeling that Eva might be right. Flora wanted a rich man to take care of her. Barring a miracle, rich was something that Barney Griffith was never going to be.

It was funny how Eva could be so perceptive about everybody else's love life and insecurities, and yet so blind about her own.

Then again, thought Barney as they approached Fittlescombe village, *perhaps we're all a bit like that. Perhaps that's part of the human condition?*

He was just wondering how he could work this idea into his book when the pure, beautiful sound of children's voices drifted towards them from the direction of the village green.

'What is that?' asked Eva, stopping to listen.

'I think it's carols.' Barney grinned. 'They must be practising down at the school.'

'How lovely!' said Eva. 'Let's go and listen.'

Clipping the dogs onto their leads, they hurried across the bridge onto the green. St Hilda's School stood next to the parish church. Sure enough, about twenty children clutching candles were huddled around the school gate, their high, breathless voices reciting the verses of 'O Little Town of Bethlehem'. A small but growing group of villagers, mostly drinkers from The Fox, had spilled out onto the green to listen to them. You could see people's frozen breath hovering in little puffs in front of them as they linked arms and pressed together for warmth.

'Oh, look, there's Henry!' exclaimed Eva, dashing away to join him as he emerged from the pub with Richard Smart.

Barney watched as Henry threw his arms wide, drawing Eva protectively into him, kissing the top of her head as they both stood swaying, entranced by the music, their two dogs sitting obediently at their side. It was a small gesture, nothing out of the ordinary. But it was the first time Barney had seen Henry behave in a genuine, unaffected, loving way towards his girlfriend. This wasn't another 'look at me, I bagged a supermodel' public display of affection. This was real. Heartfelt.

Barney was surprised by how jealous he felt, as if a small but very sharp knife were being twisted in his heart.

Don't be such a sad, lonely git, he told himself firmly. *Just because Flora doesn't want you, you can't go around resenting everyone who* has *found love.*

Glancing around, it suddenly seemed as if happy couples were everywhere. Santiago and Penny de la Cruz were there, arms coiled around one another like a pair of contented snakes. Laura Baxter was in stitches at something Gabe had just whispered in her ear, earning herself a stern look from a number of parents, gathered to gaze adoringly at their singing children. Outside the church, the vicar and his wife stood arm in arm: he skinny and small, she enormously round and fat, clearly about to give birth any minute. The entire scene reminded Barney of Dr Seuss's Whoville, with the whole village coming together in song, glowing with Christmas spirit.

And what does that make me? Barney thought miserably. *The Grinch?*

Closing his eyes, he let the children's voices soothe him.

'The hopes and fears of all the years, are met in thee tonight.'

Jeeves started to howl.

Gathering up his own hopes and fears, Barney turned and headed home.

CHAPTER SEVENTEEN

'There you are! I've been looking for you everywhere. Mother wants you to meet Kashi Soames and her new husband. I think she's on number five now.'

Mason Parker opened the French doors that led from the library of his parents' Westchester estate onto one of at least ten balconies and smiled at Flora. In a full-length gold evening gown with a cropped mink jacket, she was standing with her hands on the stone balustrade, looking out across the Parkers' stunningly lit grounds. A gently sloping, manicured lawn, bordered on either side by giant clipped yew hedges, led down to a boating lake. In the middle of the water, an artificial island had been built. It usually sported a fountain, but at Christmas time the water was switched off and a vast Norwegian spruce was erected in its place, professionally trimmed and sparkling with thousands of tasteful white bulbs, their reflections dancing on the still water like fireflies.

The grounds, like the house, spoke of wealth but also of class. Everything here was classical, beautiful, and just as it should be.

Everything except me, Flora couldn't help thinking.

Coming up behind her, pressing his strong body against Flora's soft one, Mason reached down and extracted a lit cigarette from between Flora's fingers.

'I thought you gave up?' he said, disapprovingly, crushing out the offending object on the stone and flicking it off the balustrade into the abyss.

'I did. But tonight's a special circumstance.'

'How so?'

Flora turned around and looked up at him, lovingly but with a hint of despair.

'Are you kidding me? I already feel like a prize pig being shown for sale at a farmers' market. Your mother must have introduced me to fifty of her friends, and every one of them looked at me like this.' Flora did an exaggerated, up-down, appraising look, narrowing her eyes and shaking her head disappointedly.

'Oh, hush,' said Mason, kissing her. 'Everyone loved you. And besides, you're not for sale. You're my pig, and you're off the market. Right?'

He made a snorting, pig noise that even Flora had to laugh at. Perhaps she *should* lighten up. But it was Christmas Eve, and all she wanted to do was get back to their apartment in the city, crawl into bed and stay there, like Penny and Santiago de la Cruz were probably doing right now. Instead they would be sleeping in one of Ruth Parker's many 'guest suites' tonight, which was like being in a luxury hotel except without the privacy. And tomorrow there would be more parties, more people to meet and smile at till her jaw ached, and yet more conversations about the wedding and how ridiculously excited she was about it, *all the time*.

'Who's Kashi Soames again?' Flora asked as Mason led

her back inside. Bing Crosby's 'White Christmas' was playing, mingling with the laughter and chatter of well over a hundred excited guests. Pine and balsam candles had been lit everywhere, filling even the grandest, high-ceilinged room with a glorious festive scent, and another huge Nordic spruce dazzled in the entryway.

'My godmother,' Mason whispered in Flora's ear. 'Very rich, very eccentric.' Looking at his watch, he added, 'And by now probably very drunk.'

'Maaaason! Daaarling!' Right on cue, a bejewelled crone wearing what looked like green silk ceremonial robes and a matching turban, made her way over to Mason and Flora. 'You've been hiding from me!'

'Not at all, Kashi. I—'

'So is this her?' The crone pointed a bony, ruby-encrusted finger at Flora, talking about her as if she weren't there. 'She's very pretty. Shorter than I expected, though. I always thought you admired tall girls.'

'Oh, Mason admired a lot of things until he met Flora,' a familiar voice trilled.

Flora's heart sank. Just when she thought the evening couldn't get any worse, Henrietta Branston appeared behind the dreadful Kashi. Henrietta had pulled out all the stops tonight in a stunning red backless gown that accentuated her tall, athletic figure, and a ruby drop necklace that drew attention instantly to her impressive cleavage. Her blonde hair was piled and pinned extravagantly on top of her head, making her look even taller. Standing next to her, Flora felt like a hobbit. Bilbo Baggins in the presence of the Ice Queen.

'But true love changes everything, doesn't it, darling?'

She kissed Mason on both cheeks, before pointedly stooping to do the same to Flora. 'My goodness, you are a long way down, aren't you?' She laughed. 'I haven't seen you for ages. Chuck and I were starting to think you'd abandoned poor Mason for good.'

Think or hope? thought Flora, forcing a smile.

'How's Merry Olde England?'

'Fine. Busy.'

'I'll bet.' Henrietta poured the remnants of her flute of vintage champagne down her swan-like neck. 'I heard you've had all sorts of problems at Hanborough. Aren't the renovations, like, a year behind schedule?'

'Renovations?' Mason's godmother piped up disapprovingly. Glaring at Flora, she asked, 'Are you some sort of builder?'

'Flora's a designer, Kashi,' said Mason. 'She works with one of the top guys in the city.'

'Who told you the castle was a year behind?' Flora asked Henrietta, all pretence at an *entente cordiale* abandoned. 'That's complete bullshit, by the way.'

She couldn't understand how Henrietta Branston knew anything about Hanborough, other than what Mason might have told her, and he would never have said they were a year off schedule.

'Well.' Henrietta smiled, ignoring Flora's hostile tone and addressing herself to Kashi and Mason as much as to Flora. '*Such* a small world. But it turns out one of my best girlfriends is the business partner of the guy who owns the castle! Can you believe that?'

'Georgina Savile?' Flora went white. She felt as if she were in the midst of some awful lucid dream. All she needed now was to look down and find she was standing there naked. 'You know each other?'

'Oh, we go way back.' Henrietta beamed. 'We met in the

Hamptons years ago, at a summer party up at Brett Cranley's place. I just adore George, don't you? She told me you guys were at school together.'

'That's amazing,' said Mason, smiling at Flora. 'What a crazy coincidence. So this is Henry's partner?'

Flora nodded awkwardly. She hadn't mentioned anything about George to Mason. Those terrible days at Sherwood Hall were a part of her life she wanted to forget, to leave behind for ever. Only now they seemed to be stalking her, in the loathsome form of Henrietta-butter-wouldn't-melt Branston.

'I know. Crazy, right?' Henrietta gushed. 'It takes six degrees of separation to a whole new level. Anyway George has been at the castle a lot, right, Flora? So she's been filling me in on all these setbacks you've been having.'

'How thoughtful of her,' said Flora through gritted teeth.

'I feel so *bad* for you.' Henrietta's attempt at a sympathetic expression was not a roaring success. 'George says Henry Saxton Brae's been spitting teeth about all the delays and the extra costs.'

'Really?' Mason looked at Flora. 'You never told me that.'

Because it isn't true, thought Flora, but she didn't want to get into any of this in front of Henrietta.

'Isn't there some, like, super-modern barn you built that Henry can't stand?' Henrietta went on. Putting a comforting arm on Flora's shoulder, she said, 'You know, you shouldn't feel too bad. George also tells me Henry can be real difficult to please.'

'On the contrary,' said Flora, downing her own champagne in one gulp, so fast that bubbles threatened to pour out of her nose. 'He's actually very easy to please. All you have to do is open your legs. Your *good friend* George Savile should know all about that. Merry Christmas, Henrietta.'

Turning on her heel, Flora stalked off.

'Did she just say . . . what I think she said?' Kashi Soames asked Mason, open-mouthed. 'How utterly appalling. And you're sure this is the girl you want to marry?'

'I hope I didn't speak out of turn,' said Henrietta, biting her lower lip in a bravura performance of hurt innocence. 'Should I go after her?'

'No,' Mason said grimly. 'It's all right. I'll go.'

Later that night in bed, Flora lay in Mason's arms, relieved that the evening was over. They'd had a stand-up row out on the lawn after the Henrietta incident. Mason could see that Henrietta was being provoking and manipulative, but he still felt deeply embarrassed by Flora's outburst. Flora, on the other hand, felt completely unsupported.

'What was I supposed to do? Sit there and take it while she told a bunch of lies about my work, and made me out to be an asshole in front of your godmother? Who, by the way, is just *horrible*.'

'I agree Kashi can be a challenge,' Mason said pompously. 'And I'm sorry Henrietta upset you.'

'Are you?' Flora demanded angrily. 'Because it doesn't look that way to me.'

'Yes,' said Mason, 'I am. But in answer to your original question, what you're *supposed* to do is be a lady, Flora. Rise above it. Show some dignity, for God's sake. I'm introducing you to these people as my future *wife*.'

Flora had been reduced to tears of frustration, unable to get Mason to see things her way. In the end they'd both given up the fight, retired to bed and had two much-needed rounds of make-up sex, which turned out to be by far the best they'd had since Flora arrived. Mason had fallen asleep

immediately afterwards, satisfied and no doubt also physically exhausted by all the tension.

Flora was very tired too, but sleep eluded her. She'd texted
her mother earlier, to wish her a happy Christmas. Checking
her phone now, she saw there'd been no response. Camila
was supposed to be coming to dinner out here tomorrow
night – Mason had insisted they invite her – but neither he
nor Flora had heard from her in days, which was worrying.
Flora prayed she hadn't fallen off the wagon again.

She did have one new picture message.

Clicking it open, she saw it was from Barney, a beautiful
shot of the lake where he was staying, with the fells behind
it covered in what looked like knee-deep snow. It was an
image from another world, almost another planet. It made
Flora smile.

First white Christmas in 12 years, he wrote. *Sister's kids all
very excited. I miss you. B xoxo*

Flora thought about how much more fun tonight would
have been if Barney had been there. *He would have backed
me to the hilt against that bitch Henrietta.*

She was about to turn her phone off when another MMS
came through. She assumed it would be another of Barney's
beautiful landscape photographs. Instead, to her surprise, it
was from Henry. Underneath a picture of himself sitting
under a plastic Christmas tree and holding up a tin of roll-
mop herrings, he had written: *Beam me up, Scotty!*

Flora laughed so loudly that Mason stirred and woke for
a moment, sitting upright before sinking back into a deep
sleep.

Poor Henry! Three weeks with Eva's sweet but deathly
dull parents in their Swedish bungalow made Flora's
Christmas look like heaven on earth.

I miss him, she was worried to find herself thinking. *I miss them all.*

Tomorrow was going to be another long day. Turning off her phone, she forced herself to go to sleep.

CHAPTER EIGHTEEN

Christmas Day dawned cold and wet across the Swell Valley. As excited children reached for their stockings and tore open the first of the day's presents, the storm that had begun as blustery winds and a few scattered showers morphed into a full-blown downpour. By the time Fittlescombe parishioners began arriving for the Christmas morning service at St Hilda's Church, half the roads in the village were flooded and the village green was a quagmire.

'The Swell's burst its banks upstream, about a mile north of Brockhurst,' Seb Saxton Brae announced gravely, holding an official hunt umbrella over his wife's perfectly hairsprayed head as they made their way into the church. 'We might all be sandbagging the village later.'

'Sod that,' Gabe Baxter said cheerfully, shaking the rain out of his hair like a dog and liberally spraying anyone within a twelve-foot radius. 'Bloody Brockhurst could do with a bit of biblical retribution after last year's cricket match.'

Feelings among Fittlescombe's cricket fans still ran high after last summer's Swell Valley face-off, when a very controversial run-out had been given against Fittlescombe's star batsman, a young man who revelled in the name of Dave Grunt, leading to Brockhurst being awarded the match.

'They should be swept away like . . . who got swept away in the Bible, Vicar?' Gabe asked Bill, who looked more stressed out than usual, decked in his Christmas finery.

'I'm sorry?' Bill asked distractedly. Jen had been having contractions half the night but was still refusing to go to the hospital until lunchtime at the earliest.

'Who got swept away in a flood?' Gabe asked again.

'Noah, you arse,' Gabe's wife Laura answered for him, dragging Gabe into a pew and away from the poor, harassed vicar, adding to Seb and Kate, 'And if Brockhurst floods, of course we'll come and help. I don't think it will, though.'

'Not Noah,' protested Gabe. 'He was rescued, wasn't he? I want to know who actually drowned. Vicar? Vicar!'

Santiago de la Cruz leaned forwards from the pew behind. 'I think it was some dickhead who wouldn't stop talking. Merry Christmas.' He kissed Laura on the cheek. 'How long are you down for?'

'A week,' Laura mouthed, as the first strains of 'Good King Wenceslas' rang out from the new and very loud church pipe organ.

At the back of the church, Lucy Smart shook out her umbrella while Richard ushered the children into one of the few remaining open pews. It always took Richard an age to get anywhere, as he kept stopping to smile and wave and 'Merry Christmas' everybody he laid eyes on, from actual friends, to the village baker, to the man he once bumped into coming out of the loos in The Fox. Watching him meet-and-greet his way along the pew, the human embodiment of bonhomie, Lucy felt a combined surge of love and guilt.

He's the loveliest man in the world. The best husband. The best father.

She hated herself for missing Henry as much as she did. Of course it wasn't really Henry she missed. It was the agony and the exhilaration. Lucy wasn't sure whether that made it better or worse.

Sex with Richard was lovely and loving and easy and fun. Sex with Henry was painful and complicated and addictive and incredible, like having an adrenaline needle plunged directly into your heart. The terrible thing was that Lucy was beginning to need both.

Unlike Henry, however, she knew right from wrong. She'd stuck to her guns since ending their affair and had done everything she could to keep away from Henry. Learning about his quickie with Kate Saxton Brae had definitely helped to harden her resolve, and before Christmas she'd almost reached a point where she felt she was over him completely, where she'd finally moved on. But, weirdly, Henry's disappearing to Sweden with Eva for the holidays had been incredibly hard for Lucy. Harder, perhaps, because she hadn't expected it. Driving past Hanborough Castle every day, knowing that Henry wasn't there, she'd felt an awful emptiness inside. Before he left, Lucy had begged him to stop texting her, especially when he was drunk, which he'd taken to doing a lot. But now that the texts finally *had* stopped completely, she was appalled by how much she missed them.

The second carol had already started. Richard was singing along loudly and tunelessly. *'The angel Gab-ri-el from heaven caaaaaame!'*

Harry, the older of their two boys, grinned up at Lucy as the chorus came around, delightedly changing the words from 'Most highly favoured lady' to 'Most highly flavoured gravy'.

Lucy grinned back at him.

I have to get a grip, she thought. But as the organ fell silent and the congregation sat down, she couldn't stop herself from wondering what Henry was doing right now.

'Aha, yes. Bra. Very good. And where would the children's rooms be in this plan?'

Eva's mother, Kaisa, was sitting in the Gunnarsons' pine-clad 'family room', poring over Flora's latest designs for Hanborough. Henry had already sat for almost an hour, bored rigid, while Eva scrolled through images of the party barn, which both her parents seemed to love as much as she did.

'I like the clean lines,' her father Erik had intoned, obviously pleased with his command of relevant architectural English expressions. 'This is actually rather Swedish,' he told Henry, smiling broadly.

Eva's parents did a lot of smiling. They were such good people, so eager to please and be pleased. Henry felt like a heel for finding them so crushingly, despair-inducingly boring. But after a week of Gunnarson family small talk, he was seriously considering slipping out while Eva took a nap and swimming back to England.

And now Kaisa was talking about children's rooms and where Eva wanted the nursery. Every well-intentioned word sounded like the clanging of another prison door.

'We haven't really thought about that yet, have we, darling?' Eva squeezed Henry's hand.

'No, not yet.'

He squeezed back. Eva was so happy here, and so happy to have him here, it was touching. She hadn't brought up the Kate incident once, which Henry knew had been hard for her. After hurting her so badly, spending Christmas here was the very least he could do for her and he knew it. He tried to return the favour by smiling till his jaw ached, helping out around the house and doing his best to show some enthusiasm for Eva's homeland.

But, by God, it was hard. The Gunnarsons didn't even live in Stockholm proper, which at least had the advantage of being a beautiful city, but in a dreary suburb that seemed to be stuck in some nightmarish 1960s socialist time warp.

Waking up on Christmas morning in a fiendishly uncomfortable futon bed in the Gunnarsons' hideously ugly guest room was not Henry's idea of fun. Nor was being dragged to a revolting breakfast of kaviar (actually some sort of god-awful fish paste) and crispbread at some ungodly hour, followed by another boring session looking at Hanborough plans around the fire. Next on the yuletide hit list would be a *spännande* trip out to the Swedish church in six-degrees-below weather. And after that, Kaisa was threatening to make 'Lutefisk' for Christmas lunch, a slimy, gelatinous fish dish which was considered a great holiday delicacy in Scandinavia, but which looked and tasted, to Henry, like a quivering plate of frozen snot.

'What did you expect, mate?' Richard Smart had replied unsympathetically to Henry's moaning emails. 'It's Sweden. These are people whose national sport is paying income tax, for God's sake. You were never gonna fit in there.'

'Didn't they invent porn?' Henry asked plaintively.

'Ah, no. That's a myth,' Richard shot back confidently. 'They actually invented meatballs.'

Henry had resisted the urge to ask after Lucy. He hadn't texted her, but that didn't stop him missing her, and the wild, abandoned way she'd given herself to him. All the sweeter, of course, because they both knew it had to end. But he'd come here to recommit to Eva, to prove to her and to himself that he was capable of being faithful, of being the loyal, loving husband she deserved. And that was what he was going to do, even if it killed him.

Giving up other women is like giving up smoking, he told himself firmly. *It's a question of willpower.*

There was no magic bullet. The only way to stop was just to stop.

He had texted Flora, mostly because he suspected she might be having a difficult Christmas too, and because she would have understood the things he found absurd about Sweden, and laughed about them with him. Eva truly was the perfect woman. But sometimes it was nice to have a less than perfect woman around: someone who could catch your eye and giggle when your mother-in-law handed you a plate of ectoplasm for lunch.

He'd checked his phone first thing this morning, hoping Flora might have replied, but there'd been radio silence from New York as well.

'You do want children, though?' Erik Gunnarson looked at Henry expectantly as he offered him a bowl of sugared almonds.

'Of course.' Henry tried to relax his jaw.

'Eva will make a wonderful mother. Don't you think?' Kaisa chimed in. 'Always she was very maternal. Even as a little girl. With her dolls.'

'*Mor!*' Eva looked embarrassed.

'I can imagine,' Henry said kindly.

'Tell us about your mother?' Kaisa ploughed on. 'What

was she like? Eva was telling us she died when you were very young?'

'That's right.' Henry stood up. He was still smiling but his jaw was in danger of going into spasm. 'I'm actually feeling a little warm. If you don't mind, I think I'll go out and get some air.'

'I'll come with you.' Eva stood up too. She could have strangled her mother, asking Henry about his mum like that, as if she were enquiring about the weather.

'It's OK.' Henry kissed her on the cheek, sensing her embarrassment. 'I just need a few minutes on my own.'

'Don't forget church!' Erik called after him cheerfully. 'We leave at ten.'

'*Absolut*,' said Henry, to approving glances all round. He'd learned that the occasional word of Swedish went a long way.

Outside, the snow had stopped falling and the wind dropped to almost nothing. The still, cold air echoed the silence of the suburban street. All the Gunnarsons' neighbours were safe and snug indoors, and a week's steady snowfall had left a thick, heavy blanket on the ground, muffling every sound except for the quiet crunch of Henry's feet as he walked.

He thought about his mother, something he generally tried not to do. Even after all these years, it was still too painful. What would she have made of Sweden, of Eva and her parents? Would she be proud of Henry's life and achievements? Or would she disapprove of his choices?

She'd have loved Hanborough, that much Henry knew. And everybody loved Eva. Although perhaps Gina Saxton Brae would have pictured a different kind of wife for her younger son? Someone English, maybe? Or someone who shared his sense of humour, like Flora?

Henry's phone buzzed in his pocket.

Pulling it out with frozen fingers, his heart skipped when he saw it was a text from Lucy.

Merry Christmas. I miss u. L.

It wasn't exactly a Shakespearean love sonnet. But it was enough.

Lucy wasn't ready to walk away either.

Despite himself, Henry felt a warm glow of happiness rush through him.

She still wants me.

Turning off his phone, he headed back inside.

'Why was Santa's Little Helper feeling depressed?' Barney's sister Claire challenged him from across the table. They were halfway through a big, boozy family Christmas lunch, and Claire's husband Michael had declared it cracker joke time.

'I don't know,' Barney said dutifully.

He was feeling a bit depressed himself. After Flora had failed to reply to any of his texts, he'd drunkenly looked at her Facebook page earlier, and been bombarded by picture after picture of her at glamorous New York parties with her ghastly stiff of a fiancé.

Terrible word that. *Fiancé.* It sounded like the sort of cheap drink you'd make with Martini Bianco or Malibu and fizzy wine from Tesco. *Make mine a Fiancé, please. With one of them little umbrellas in it.*

'Because he had low Elf-Esteem!' Claire laughed loudly. 'Geddit? Low "elf" esteem? Oh, for fuck's sake, Barn, cheer up.'

'You said "fuck"!' Barney's nephew Peter announced, with a triumphant look at his mother.

'Your mother's a fucking grown-up,' said Michael, refilling Barney's wineglass, which was the last thing he needed. 'She can say what she likes. Now eat your Christmas pudding or you won't get any presents.'

Lunch dragged on. Then it was presents round the tree, with Barney's nephews tearing at their gifts like overexcited puppies in a display of naked greed that would normally have amused Barney immensely, but this year went right over his head. Slumped on the sofa by the fire, he stared into space, there but not there, getting progressively drunker as the afternoon wore on.

At five o'clock, he slipped outside into the freezing Cumbrian weather and drunk-dialled Flora's American number.

She didn't sound ecstatic to hear from him.

'Barney? Is that you?'

He could hear loud voices all around her. *Another party.*

'This isn't really a great time.'

'I jush called . . . I . . . Merry Chrishmash,' Barney slurred.

'Merry Christmas,' Flora replied dutifully. 'Are you having fun at your sister's?'

'No. You can't marry him,' Barney blurted.

The voices in the background were getting louder. 'What?' said Flora. 'It's really hard to hear you . . . '

'I said: You can't marry . . . you know. The guy. Peter-fucking-Parker,' Barney shouted. 'You can't marry him!'

There was a pause. 'Are you drunk?' Flora asked.

'Only on love,' Barney sighed dramatically.

'You are drunk.'

'I love you, Flora. I mean it. I want to marry you!'

'I have to go,' Flora said tersely. 'Merry Christmas, Barney.'

She hung up. Barney stood in the cold, staring at the phone in his hand for a long, long time.

Shit, he groaned. *Shit, shit, shit.*

'Everything OK?' Mason asked Flora, reappearing at Flora's side just as she cut Barney Griffith off.

'Yes!' She smiled, again – the same manic Jack Nicholson smile she'd been wearing as a mask for the past three days. 'Everything's fine! How are you?'

'I'm good,' said Mason, giving her a confused look. 'Are you sure you're OK, Flora? You sound . . . weird. And you look like you've seen a ghost.'

'I'm OK,' she said. 'Just tired I guess. And worried.'

She looked over Mason's shoulder to where her mother, Camila, was deep in conversation with Mason's father, also called Mason but known to everyone as MJ. From her mother's body language – the animated Puerto Rican hand gestures, the face thrust forwards and just a little too close to MJ's, the defiant jut of the jaw – Flora could tell Camila had been drinking, probably since early this morning. In her bright print dress and cheap high heels, she looked painfully out of place amid this Waspy, conservative, republican crowd.

'I wish you hadn't asked her here,' Flora whispered in Mason's ear.

'She's your mother, Flora,' Mason said reprovingly. 'It's Christmas.'

Flora rounded on him angrily, the pressure of the last week suddenly overwhelming her, shattering her fixed-smile façade like water crashing through a dam.

'Do you think I don't know that?' she shouted.

A number of the Parkers pre-lunch guests turned to stare at them.

'There's no need to raise your voice,' said Mason, mortified. 'Let's go outside.'

It was a command, not a request. Grabbing Flora firmly
by the elbow, he dragged her into the kitchen, past the
surprised-looking staff, and out into the rear courtyard.

'What was all that about?' he asked.

He looked hurt, and Flora felt bad, but she needed to get
this out.

'You never listen to me!' she shouted, tears stinging her
eyes. 'She's *my* mother, Mason. Mine! I told you I didn't want
her here. I told you it would be embarrassing. But you insisted.'

'The only thing that's embarrassing right now is you
yelling,' said Mason.

'You see? There you go again. Not listening! Has it ever
occurred to you that maybe that's *why* I yell? So you can
hear me for once. I didn't want this.'

'Didn't want what?' Mason looked confused.

'*This!*' Flora threw her arms wide. 'All these parties. All
this fuss. Wedding this, wedding that, change for lunch,
change for dinner, "you must be *so* excited!" My *God*. It's
deafening, Mason. It's stifling. I can't breathe.'

Mason's face hardened, his lips drawing into a tight, hurt
line.

'I guess people made the mistake of thinking that maybe
you *were* excited about our wedding.'

Flora ran a hand through her hair in frustration. She tried
to explain.

'I'm excited about our *marriage*. I'm excited about you.'

'Well, you have a funny way of showing it.'

'Don't you ever wish we were spending Christmas on our
own? Somewhere beautiful and peaceful, with mountains
and lakes? Or just . . . lying in bed?'

An image of Barney at his sister's farmhouse floated into Flora's mind, followed by one of Penny and Santiago de la Cruz, wrapped blissfully in one another's arms.

'No,' Mason said coldly, 'I don't. You've been gone for seven months, Flora. Seven months! No one's seen you. No one's had a chance to celebrate. None of our friends or family. I want to mark our engagement, to share our joy. Only *you* could turn that around to sound like a bad thing.'

Flora turned away, stung.

Was he *trying* to misunderstand her?

'You've changed since you went to England,' Mason went on. 'It's like your whole head is somewhere else, all the time. The sooner you finish this damn Hanborough project the better. Maybe then we can all get on with our lives.'

He walked back inside, slamming the kitchen door behind him.

Flora stood alone, staring up at the sky, a sinking feeling in the pit of her stomach. Snow began to fall, the heavy flakes landing on her upturned cheeks like iced tears. For some inexplicable reason, she found herself thinking about Henry, and his funny text from last night.

Beam me up, Scotty.

Despite everything, she smiled.

PART TWO

CHAPTER NINETEEN

The annual West Swell Valley Hunt Ball was the highlight of the valley's midwinter social calendar. Held in January, usually about a week after New Year, to give people a chance fully to recover from their hangovers, it always used to be hosted at Furlings, back when old Rory Flint-Hamilton was still alive. But these days the idyllic Fittlescombe estate was owned by Angela Cranley and her defacto husband, Max, neither of whom were hunt supporters. As a result, in recent years the ball had moved to a variety of different venues, from private homes to grand hotels and even one year (shamefully) to Hinton Golf Club.

It was this last disastrous fall from grace that had prompted Sebastian Saxton Brae to take over as master. This year, for the first time, Seb was able to host the ball himself at Hatchings, having inherited both the house and the title from his and Henry's father.

Across the Swell Valley, and at a number of smart London addresses, the arrival of the stiff, formal invitation, embossed with the words 'Lord and Lady Saxton Brae request the pleasure of your company . . . ' had been a source of much excitement during the boring lull between Christmas and New Year. And now, at long last, the evening of the forty-third annual WSV Hunt Ball had arrived.

Lady Saxton Brae, unsurprisingly, had pulled out all the stops to ensure that Hatchings looked its best for the big event. This was not as easy as it sounded. The estate was grand – a huge, sprawling early Victorian pile, approached by a long, oak-lined drive and through impressive ten-foot-high stone gates – but it could not truthfully be described as beautiful. Despite the huge proportions of every room, the high ceilings and oversized windows and doors, there was something inexorably solid and dour and dark about the house. With its mahogany staircase and thick panelled walls, it felt institutional, like a boarding school or a particularly impressively maintained old people's home. Unlike Furlings, a house that positively begged to be used for parties with its pretty, flower-filled terraces and delicately framed rooms flooded with light, Hatchings had to be cranked into life laboriously by hand, like an old-fashioned motor car.

Despite this, Kate had done her best, hanging bright white fairy lights over the front door and lining the entire terrace and front lawn with outdoor candles in pretty glass and silver hurricane lanterns. Inside, positively enormous displays of flowers filled every room, in light, feminine shades of pink and violet and pale green. Tables had been covered with simple white linen cloths and dressed with the Saxton Brae silver, a dazzling collection dating from the early eighteenth century. Two priceless medieval tapestries by Bruges masters, depicting hunting scenes, had been moved from their usual position on the stairway and rehung in the ballroom, the hub of the night's festivities. The sound of 1930s jazz music echoed through the downstairs rooms, courtesy of a local live band, and fully liveried maids and footmen relieved arriving guests of their overcoats and furs.

'Blimey,' Lucy Smart whispered to Richard, slipping out of her grandmother's old fox fur that had seen better days and helping herself to a passing flute of champagne. 'How much do you think all this cost? Isn't Seb always saying he's "cash poor"?'

'I suppose it's all relative,' said Richard, grabbing a glass for himself along with some sort of fancy-looking beef and truffle hors d'oeuvre. 'Damn good spread though.'

'Lucy! Richard! How lovely to see you both.'

Kate glided forward, very much in ladyship mode, and kissed both of them on the cheek. In a full-length blue taffeta gown that looked like something Maggie Smith's dowager countess might have worn, and with an absolutely vast sapphire sparkling at her neck, she could have passed for a woman twice her age. She wore her hair swept up, accentuating her long nose and the horsiness of her features. Overall the impression was regal, which was clearly exactly what she was aiming at.

'She sounds like the bloody Queen!' Lucy giggled, once Kate glided away. '*High lovely to seeiyew,*' she mimicked, dropping into a deep curtsey.

'Never mind sounds. She looks like the Queen.' Richard shuddered. 'Can you imagine what possessed Henry?' he added, dropping his voice to a whisper.

'No,' said Lucy. She didn't want to talk about Henry and Kate. Especially not with Richard. Although at least comments like this one meant that Richard hadn't guessed about her own affair with Henry, which was a huge relief.

Henry was coming tonight, with Eva. They'd flown in from Stockholm yesterday, apparently, although nobody had seen them yet. It would be the first time Lucy had seen him in almost six weeks, and the combination of nerves, guilt and excitement at the prospect had released a whole swarm of butterflies in her stomach. As soon as she'd sent him her Christmas Day text she'd regretted it, cursing herself for her weakness. Yet at the same time, just seeing a response from Henry in her message folder later that day had calmed her growing panic far more effectively than any tranquillizer. In a bizarre way, that small contact had enabled her to put him out of her mind, to refocus her energies on the children and Richard.

And meanwhile, of course, Richard had been perfectly lovely and Lucy loved him more than ever. Which just made the butterflies in her stomach flap all the harder. Increasingly she felt as if she lived simultaneously in two parallel universes. It was an effort to remind herself that her children lived only in one of them.

'Hello. Happy New Year!'

A human beachball in a bright pink dress that would have made a very serviceable big-top tent for a small circus rolled up and accosted Lucy. It took Lucy a moment to recognize it as Jen Clempson, the vicar's wife. Her eyes widened.

'You're not *still* pregnant?'

'Two weeks overdue.' Jen patted her swollen belly ruefully with her fat, sausage-like fingers. 'I'm hoping to dance it out tonight.'

'Is Bill here?'

'Are you joking?' Jen spluttered, through a mouthful of mini-hot dog. 'Bill doesn't fraternize with the enemy. He's furious I came. Then again, he's furious if I so much as pop to the village shop these days. If he had his way, I'd have been chained to a hospital bed since before Christmas.'

'I'm sure he's just nervous,' said Lucy. 'First baby and all that.'

'So am I,' said Jen, not looking *that* nervous as she shovelled in two more hot dogs and washed them down with a large glass of champagne. 'If it doesn't come out soon I'm going to pop open like an overcooked baked potato. It'll be like Lord Grantham's ulcer bursting open on *Downton Abbey*.'

In the ballroom proper, the party was already in full swing. The invitations said 7.30 p.m., but guests had been arriving as early as six and many were already clearly three sheets to the wind as they ricocheted around the room, swapping Christmas holiday horror stories and bemoaning the awful weather they'd had for this year's New Year's Day meet.

'You know it's bad when the sodding antis don't even bother to turn up,' old Graham Hewson grumbled loudly to Laura Baxter.

Laura was exhausted, having just wrapped her latest reality show for Endemol, and was only here tonight on sufferance because Gabe had his eye on a future mastership.

'Old Seb Saxton Brae can't go on for ever,' Gabe had informed Laura confidently after the New Year's Day meet. 'Wouldn't you like to be married to the master of the West Swell Valley?'

Laura had pointed out that 'old' Seb was only in his forties, so actually younger than Gabriel, that he could perfectly well go on for ever, and that being married to a master of hounds was low on her list of fantasies, as it was for most women.

As so often, Gabe had ignored her and dragged them both up to Hatchings for tonight's hunt ball, insisting Laura looked 'gorgeous' in her tatty old red evening dress from Monsoon, and claiming not to be able to see her undyed grey roots or the almighty bags under both her eyes.

'I suppose the vicar had other things on his mind,' Laura said to Graham Hewson, 'what with Jenny about to pop.'

But the old man had stopped listening. Like everyone else, he'd turned to gawp at Henry Saxton Brae and Eva Gunnarson, who'd just walked in with their arms around each other, looking like a couple of movie stars.

Henry was his usual, dapper self, in an immaculately cut dinner jacket and evening trousers. His black hair positively gleamed in the candlelight, and his blue eyes danced whenever he looked at his stunning girlfriend, which was frequently. Eva, who would have looked heavenly in a sack, had positively outdone herself tonight in a cream and gold, floor-length Grecian gown, which seemed to shimmer when she moved, as if it were woven from pure light. Other than a demure scoop at the back, the fabric of the dress covered her entire body. But despite this, or perhaps because of it, the overall effect was phenomenally sexy, accentuating Eva's every curve, her long legs and high, round breasts to perfection.

'By God, that's a beautiful woman,' sighed Graham Hewson, with as much longing as a retired gardener in his eighties could muster.

'Yes,' agreed Laura, feeling older and frumpier than ever. 'She's divine, isn't she?'

'And marrying a devil,' Santiago de la Cruz whispered in Laura's ear, sneaking up behind her, hand in hand with Penny.

'Is he, really?' Laura asked, watching Henry kiss Eva lovingly on the neck. 'They look awfully happy together.'

'It's a new year,' said Penny, shrugging. 'Maybe Henry's turned over a new leaf?'

Santiago laughed loudly. 'Maybe pigs will fly.' Kissing his

wife adoringly, he added, 'You're far too nice, darling. Unfortunately, not everybody else is.'

Over at the cocktail bar, Seb grabbed his wife's hand.

'Come on, darling,' he said cheerfully. 'Henry and Eva are here. We must go and say hello.'

Seb was too busy playing host to notice the tense look on Kate's face, or the way the colour had drained from her cheeks the moment Henry walked in.

'You go. I'll talk to them later,' she said as casually as she could. 'They're being mobbed as it is.'

'Don't be silly,' said Seb, holding up a short, red-coated arm and beckoning his little brother over. 'Henry! Eva! How was Sweden?' he shouted, as they made their way over.

'Great,' said Henry, hugging his older brother with unusual warmth.

'It was lovely,' said Eva.

Trapped, Kate did her best to maintain her regal composure. It wasn't easy. The last time she'd seen Eva she'd been running away through the woods, half dressed, after her ill-judged tryst with Henry. The entire debacle felt like a bad dream now, looking back. To this day, Kate really had no idea why she'd done it. She'd been so utterly shocked when Henry made an advance that day at the hunt – shocked and, if she were honest, flattered. She'd never got along with her brother-in-law, and she was well aware that Henry looked down on her socially; that he felt Seb had married beneath him. That had always stung, probably because Kate (a raging snob herself) knew it was true. As much as she loathed Henry, she'd always longed to be accepted by him. And, of course, there could be no denying he *was* wildly attractive. Not to mention charismatic. One minute they'd been arguing heatedly, calling one another names. And the next, just like that, Henry had been tearing at her blouse like a wild animal and pinning her to the ground and . . . well, she'd simply been swept away in a moment of madness.

But then Eva had caught them. And what should have been a transitory moment had been captured for ever, preserved in the amber of all of their memories like an unwanted fossil.

Kate was no longer worried about Eva spilling the beans to Sebastian. If she were going to do that, she'd have done it at the time. But, even so, seeing her face to face for the first time was always going to be awkward.

'How was your Christmas?' Henry asked Seb, still smiling. Kate couldn't understand how he could be so relaxed. 'Did we miss any excitement in the valley?'

'Excitement?' Seb looked at Kate, perplexed. 'I don't know about that. What do you think, darling? Did they miss anything?'

Having avoided Eva's eyes for as long as she could, Kate was forced to look up now. 'Not really,' she said stiffly.

'Lady SB and I lead a quiet life, you see.' Seb winked jovially at Eva, oblivious to the tension between her and Kate. 'Not like you two jet-setters.'

'Perhaps it's not as quiet as you think,' said Eva, looking pointedly at Kate, who felt her stomach give way and lurch unpleasantly down to her feet.

'What do you mean?' asked Seb.

'Only that Kate must have been working like mad to pull off such a beautiful party,' Henry interjected smoothly. 'Right, darling?'

Slipping his arm around Eva's waist, he gently pressed into the small of her back, guiding her away. 'Shall we catch up later?' he said casually to Seb. 'I must go and say a quick hello to Richard.'

'Of course,' beamed Sebastian. 'Jolly good. They seem on good form,' he said to Kate as Henry and Eva wandered off. 'Nice of them to notice how much effort you went to. I must say, Kate, the house looks marvellous. It really does.'

'Thank you, Sebastian,' said Kate, kissing her husband on the top of his balding head, like a mistress rewarding a well-behaved dog. 'I love you,' she added, truthfully.

'Good heavens! What a thing to say.' Sebastian laughed. 'You've been watching too much American television, my dear,' he added fondly. 'We'll have to do something about that.'

Dinner was disappointing. Some sort of limpish salad with goat's cheese, followed by overboiled beef with new potatoes.

'Old potatoes, more like,' Santiago de la Cruz complained loudly. 'Who the hell did the catering? Little Chef?'

Pudding, an unimaginative but edible chocolate mousse with raspberries, was the highlight. Luckily, as Gabe Baxter pointed out, the wine never stopped flowing and, as soon as the meal was over, couples in various shades of drunkenness began hitting the dance floor.

Richard Smart literally yanked Eva out of Henry's arms and onto the dance floor.

'She's had enough of your groping, mate,' Richard informed Henry jokingly. 'She needs at least *one* dance with a real man.'

'I agree,' Henry shouted back as they disappeared into the throng. 'But I think Gabe Baxter's busy.'

'Ha ha,' said Richard.

Henry noticed Lucy sitting alone a couple of tables away,

lost in thought. In a simple black evening dress and minimal make-up, hers wasn't a striking, punch-you-between-the-eyes beauty like Eva's. But, as ever, there was something about her, a quiet confidence that was both sensual and compelling. Sensing Henry staring at her, Lucy glanced up. Their eyes locked. For a few seconds neither of them moved. Then, slowly, Henry walked over and held out his hand.

'Shall we dance?'

His voice was dry and scratchy with desire. Or nerves. Or both.

'OK. One dance.' Tentatively she let her fingers brush his.

They moved to the edge of the floor, as the band struck up Chet Baker's 'There Will Never Be Another You'. Lucy had to remind herself to breathe as Henry's warm body pressed against hers.

'So,' she asked him, 'how was Sweden? The two of you look very happy.'

'We are.' Henry was so close, his breath tickled her neck as they spun around the dance floor. 'It was a good trip. And you and Richard? How was your Christmas?'

'Good, very good,' Lucy blurted. 'Things are great.'

They danced on in silence for a moment.

'I was pleased to get your text,' Henry said at last.

'That was a mistake,' Lucy said quickly. 'I shouldn't have sent it.'

Henry looked at her, wounded. 'So why did you?'

'I don't know,' Lucy shot back, wounded herself. 'Why did you sleep with your sister-in-law?'

Henry's feet kept moving but every other muscle in his body froze.

'Richard told you,' he muttered, shaking his head.

'Richard tells me everything,' said Lucy.

'Really? Well that makes one of you,' Henry said angrily. He knew he had no right to be taking his frustrations out on Lucy. Screwing his brother's bitch of a wife had been his fault, his mistake. But the more people knew, the more likely it was that Seb would find out. Henry didn't know why, exactly, but the thought of hurting his brother crushed him like an insect under a stone.

'You are such a hypocrite, you know that?' Lucy hissed back at him with tears in her eyes. 'All the risks we took, all the betrayal. I was just another notch in the Saxton Brae bedpost.'

'That is not true.' Henry tightened his grip on her arm. 'You meant a lot to me. You still do.'

'Liar!' said Lucy, more loudly than she'd intended.

The couple dancing next to them shot her and Henry a questioning look.

When Henry spoke again, he lowered his voice to a whisper.

'You were the one who said it was over, remember?'

'So we could do the right thing! Make it up to Richard and Eva!' Lucy sobbed. Henry winced at the pain etched on her face. 'But instead you run out and celebrate by fucking your own brother's wife!'

Pulling free from his grip, Lucy walked off the dance floor and disappeared into the throng of guests.

'It wasn't like that!' Henry called after her. But she was already gone.

'Everything all right?' Eva materialized beside him, flushed and panting after an energetic dance with Richard. 'Where did Lucy run off to?'

'The Ladies, I think,' said Henry.

'Oh. Well, let's dance then,' Eva beamed, coiling herself

around him like a golden snake and pulling him deeper onto the floor.

Henry felt sick to his stomach.

Outside, Lucy ran down the drive, allowing deep, desperate breaths of cold night air to fill her lungs.

How had she been so stupid? So utterly, pathetically stupid! She'd betrayed a man she'd loved her whole adult life – a good man – and for what? For a few snatched hours of sex with a selfish child.

Oh God.

Feeling utterly wretched, she ran until her legs gave out, then walked, across the lawns and down to the stable yard, as far away from the house and lights and music as possible. Eventually, finding a less-than-totally sodden hay bale in one of the empty stalls, she sank down onto it and put her head in her hands, exhausted.

Breathe in. Breathe out, she told herself. *You aren't dying. The children aren't dying. You must get a grip.*

Just then she heard a noise. It began as a sort of low wail, of the kind an injured animal might make, then rose up into a high-pitched screech.

Lucy stopped, straining her ears to listen, but silence seemed to have fallen again. Then suddenly there was a nervous stomping of hooves and the sound was repeated, louder this time, the screech short but desperate, like a chimpanzee's alarm call.

'Hello?' Staggering out into the darkness, Lucy made her way past the various stables in turn. 'Is anyone there?'

'Here!' The voice was faint and exhausted, but clearly audible just a few stalls down. 'I'm in here!' Running towards it, Lucy pulled open the stable door and was almost flattened by an enormous, terrified mare, clattering past her and taking off at a canter towards the open fields.

In the vacated stable, crouched on all fours in the far corner, was Jen Clempson, the vicar's wife, clearly in the advanced stages of labour. Her pink tent-dress was hiked up around her hips and her face was wet with sweat and contorted with pain, although a clear expression of relief swept over her face when she saw Lucy.

'Fucking hell!' said Lucy. 'I'll go and get help.'

'No!' Jen waved at her frantically. 'There's no time. Stay.'

The groan started again as her contraction hit. It sounded like a plane taking off. Feeling useless and more than a little panicked, Lucy knelt down beside Jen and stroked her forehead, gently pulling back her hair. It felt warm and sticky. Pulling back her hand, Lucy was horrified to find it was covered with blood. Jen had a deep gash all along her hairline and a swelling the size of an egg at the front of her skull.

'What happened?' Lucy gasped.

Once the contraction finished, Jen answered, her breath coming in short rasps. She'd slipped out to say hello to the horses. Maya, the mare who'd almost killed Lucy on her way out, used to be one of Jen's patients and the vet in her had been curious to see how she was doing. When she got here, a sharp contraction had made her cry out and the horse had taken fright and lashed out, landing a hoof on Jenny's skull and knocking her out for a few minutes at least. When she came to she had been too dizzy to stand and in full-on labour. She'd been here for over an hour by the time Lucy found her.

'You really need an ambulance,' said Lucy.

'No phone,' panted Jen.

She must have left her mobile up at the party. Stupidly, Lucy had done the same. 'I can run back to the house in two minutes,' she told Jen. 'I'll be back before—'

Jen shook her head, wincing with pain. 'Baby could be here in two minutes. Please, when you see the head just . . . put your arms out.'

'Put my arms out?'

'Try and catch it like a rugby ball. And make sure the cord's not around the neck. Oooooaaaaaaagh!'

Everything happened so quickly after that, Lucy had no more time to think. She couldn't see the head. It was too dark to see anything much. Reaching down to the business end, she'd barely had time to do as she was told and hold out both her arms when a hot, wet, slippery object shot out of Jen's body like a bullet from a gun and landed in her hands.

'The neck,' said Jen, exhausted. 'Check the neck! The cord . . . '

'It's fine,' said Lucy. 'There's nothing around the neck.'

As if to prove it, the baby suddenly gave a jerk and cried loudly.

'What is it?' asked Jen, still too weak to turn over or to move at all.

'I'm sorry?' said Lucy, who was staring down at the writhing, yelling life in her arms in profound shock.

'Boy or girl?'

'Oh God. I don't . . . er . . . ' Lucy reached down. 'It's a girl.'

Jen didn't react.

'Did you hear me?' Lucy asked. 'I said it's a girl.'

Jenny groaned incoherently.

Moving gingerly down from her haunches into a more

stable sitting position, Lucy cradled the baby in her arms, grabbing a handful of straw to cover her and holding her close to her chest for warmth. The umbilical cord was still attached, but Jen seemed unable to move and Lucy wasn't sure how one was supposed to cut it.

'Luce? Is that you? I've been looking everywhere.'

Richard appeared behind her with a torch, standing in the stable doorway like the Angel Gabriel. Lucy didn't think she had ever been so pleased to see a person in her life. Out of nowhere, she burst into tears.

'Rich!'

'Jesus Christ!' he said, surveying the scene and simultaneously taking off his jacket and rolling up his sleeves, instantly in doctor mode. He knelt over Jenny. 'Is she conscious?'

'I don't know. She's been in and out. I heard her screaming,' said Lucy. 'I wanted to get help but there was no time. She has a head injury.'

'You did the right thing,' Richard assured her. Taking the baby from her, he wrapped her tightly in his dinner jacket and laid her in the straw. Then, passing Lucy his phone, he said, 'Call an ambulance. Then go up to the house and get help. Water, towels, anything. And someone should call the vicarage.'

'Right,' said Lucy, already dialling 999.

CHAPTER TWENTY

The dramatic arrival of the vicar's daughter was the talk of the valley for months to come, earning the hunt ball at Hatchings its place in the Swell Valley history books, much to Lord and Lady Saxton Brae's delight. After a nasty scare with a brain bleed, Jen had made a full recovery, and both mother and baby had been at church last Sunday for the first time, with Call-me-Bill hovering proudly, like an over-attentive mother hen.

'Did you know they've called her Diana?' Seb informed Henry delightedly over dinner at Hanborough. 'After the goddess of hunting.'

'Bollocks,' said Henry, popping his brother's balloon. 'They named her after the vicar's granny.'

'Did they?' muttered Seb, shovelling in another forkful of venison stew. 'Damn good name anyway.'

Eva was away in the Maldives on a three-week shoot for Lisa Marie Fernandez's new swimwear collection, leaving Henry home alone. Flora was back from New York now, but she seemed to be making a point of avoiding Henry whenever she was up at the castle. Lucy was also away, on a mini-break with Richard. Despite the legions of builders swarming all over the property, Hanborough was starting to feel big and lonely, so much so that Henry had taken the unprecedented step of inviting his elder brother over solo for a boys' dinner.

He was already regretting it.

'Lucky your friend Richard showed up when he did. I gather he only went out to the stables to look for his wife, who'd wandered orf,' said Seb. 'If she'd gone in a different direction, that gal might have died.'

'Yes,' said Henry. 'That was lucky.'

He hadn't seen Lucy since the night of the ball, and although the temptation to contact her was stronger than ever, so far he'd resisted. Somehow Flora's presence in the castle made him feel permanently guilty, like being haunted by the ghost of your own conscience.

'What was Smart's wife doing down there, do you think? Mike Brunner told me she'd been upset earlier, after she'd danced with you. Did she say anything?'

'No,' said Henry. 'She was fine. And Mike Brunner's a wanker. I expect she just wanted some air.'

The conversation moved on to other topics, mostly related to Hanborough and the restoration.

'You're still keen on this girl, are you? Flora?' Seb asked, helping himself to a second generous tumbler of malt from Henry's decanter.

'What do you mean, "keen"?' Henry asked, sounding more defensive than he'd meant to.

'You still like her work,' Seb explained. 'Rate her as a designer?'

'Absolutely,' said Henry.

Seb sniffed disapprovingly. 'I'm surprised.'

'Why?'

'Well, you've got to admit things have changed rather, from what you originally said you wanted. The new great hall, for instance. And all those white bedrooms in the South Wing. Not to mention that monstrosity outside.'

'Ah. The barn,' Henry sighed.

'Don't you find it rather modern? Rather *urban*.'

Seb turned the word over in his mouth like a stale piece of food.

'For a castle dating back to the Conquest, it's hardly in keeping,' he added, dabbing venison juices from his mouth with a napkin.

'I agree,' said Henry.

'You do? Then why on earth . . . ?'

'Because Eva likes it,' Henry explained. 'She wanted some more contemporary elements in the designs for Hanborough, a way to put her own stamp on the place. Flora may have helped with the sketching and what not, but she's not really responsible for the changes.'

'I see,' said Seb, in the tone of someone who quite clearly didn't.

'Anyway, you and I might not like the new designs, but apparently a lot of people do. According to Graydon James, Hanborough's got a chance of being nominated for some prestigious design award.'

Seb raised an eyebrow. 'Does that matter?'

Since when did Henry care about design awards? The castle was his home, not some GCSE art project.

'It matters to Flora,' said Henry. 'Anyway, we're still using some of her original ideas, like the Sissinghurst library in the tower and the oak-panelled master suite. And the wine cellar, with all the reclaimed flagstones.'

'Hmm. Well, that's something, I suppose,' muttered Seb.

'The finished castle will be a marriage of old and new,' said Henry. 'A compromise between Eva's tastes and mine.'

Seb smiled. 'A compromise, eh? My dear Henry! You're starting to sound like quite the married man.'

'I'll take that as a compliment,' said Henry, downing the last of his wine.

The conversation soon turned to hunting, as it always did with Seb, and before long Henry tuned out. He found himself thinking about Flora, and how much jollier tonight's supper would have been if he had been dining with her instead of his brother. Henry wasn't sure why she'd been avoiding him like the proverbial plague since she'd got back from New York. When he challenged her she'd pleaded pressure of work, but Henry could tell it went deeper than that. Something had changed between them. He missed Flora's witty, bitchy asides and the sparring matches he used to enjoy with her back in the autumn. She'd always disapproved of him, of course. But for Henry, that was part of Flora's charm. The fact that she couldn't be charmed. That she saw through him, and stood up for Eva, and called him on his shit, both great and small.

Ever since the day of the hunt, when Eva had caught Henry in flagrante with Kate and gone running to Flora as a shoulder to cry on, something had shifted between Henry and Flora. Disapproval had become dislike. At least, that was what it felt like from Henry's perspective. He was surprised by how much the thought depressed him. Flora was the first female friend Henry had ever had. Now it seemed he'd managed to lose her already.

His mobile phone started buzzing in his pocket.

'Sorry,' he said to Seb, pulling out the offending object.

He had a new picture message. Clicking it open, he saw it was a naked selfie of George, her legs spread to reveal a perfectly groomed, pale pink pussy. She was looking right at the camera, right at Henry, her pupils dilated with desire. *Can't wait to see you*, read the message.

Henry closed the image, but not before his cock had stiffened to concrete under the table. George was coming to the valley next week as a guest at some grand shooting party over at Hinton. In a weak moment, Henry had allowed himself to be bamboozled into giving her lunch at Hanborough. It was pretty clear what George expected the main course to be.

Henry hadn't slept with her in months. It felt good, like giving up smoking. But now, with Eva and Lucy both away and Flora consistently looking at him as if he were something unpleasant she'd found stuck to the bottom of her shoe, the idea of taking out his frustrations on George's lithe, available body was more appealing than ever.

'Anything important?' asked Seb.

'No,' said Henry, deleting the image. 'Nothing.'

Flora drew her parka more tightly around her, burying her face in the soft, downy fur around the hood in an attempt to keep out the worst of the freezing drizzle.

Stupidly, she'd decided to walk into Fittlescombe to buy an emergency bar of Cadbury's Fruit & Nut, her new addiction, at the Preedys' shop. Within twenty minutes of setting out from Peony Cottage, the weather had closed in. Now she was exactly halfway between Hanborough and Fittlescombe, and faced with an impossible choice that at this particular moment felt worthy of Solomon's judgement – should she abort her mission and return to Peony Cottage chocolate-less but pneumonia-free? Or press on and risk being lost like Scott of the Antarctic on her return journey?

'Flora!'

Oh Christ. That was all she needed.

Barney Griffith, dressed like a North Sea fisherman in head-to-toe yellow oilskins with a matching rain hat, darted out of his cottage garden and up the hill towards her, a bedraggled-looking Jeeves trotting reluctantly at his heels.

'I thought it was you,' he panted, rain coursing down his ruddy cheeks as he drew closer. 'Bloody awful weather. I had to take the dog out for a pee. What's your excuse?'

'Oh, well, I . . . er . . . chocolate,' blurted Flora. She hadn't seen Barney since before she left for Christmas, and had been slightly dreading running into him, particularly after his drunken declaration of love on the telephone.

'You haven't returned any of my calls,' he said, cutting to the chase.

'I've been busy,' Flora said awkwardly. 'With work.'

'Bollocks,' Barney replied robustly. 'You're avoiding me. It's because I rang you up at Christmas and made a tit of myself, isn't it?'

'No,' insisted Flora. 'Of course not.'

In reality, Barney's drunk-dial insistence that he loved her, and that Flora couldn't, under any circumstances, marry 'Peter Parker', was a part of why she'd failed to return a single phone call or email from him since she got back to England. But only a part of it.

It was Mason who'd really changed things. Changed the way Flora was with Barney, and Henry; changed the way she saw England and the valley and Hanborough and this entire chapter in her life. She could still hear his reproachful words ringing in her ears.

'*You've changed since you went to England. It's like your whole head is somewhere else, all the time.*'

It hurt because he was right. Somehow, since taking on the Hanborough project, and especially since Graydon had dangled the possibility of winning International Designer of the Year in front of her, Flora *had* changed. She'd lost sight of what really mattered in life – her and Mason. More than that, she'd begun to lose touch with the person she was before she came to the Swell Valley. Henry, Eva, Barney Griffith, Penny de la Cruz – these people had become her reality, her world, her tribe. Peony Cottage already felt like home, to a frightening degree. Even the bad things in England, like her enmity with Georgina Savile or having to keep Henry's secrets or Graydon breathing down her neck, demanding the impossible, now seemed more real to Flora than the bad things in her New York life, like her mother's problems or the flirty society girls flocking around Mason, wanting nothing more than to usurp Flora's position.

In short, she'd become disconnected. But it had taken Mason calling her on it to make Flora wake up and smell the coffee. To make her sense the danger, remember what it was that she stood to lose. Security. Happiness. Her entire future. The morning after her fight with Mason, she'd extended her visit home by two and a half weeks, braving a bone-rattling meltdown from Graydon.

'Absolutely not!' he seethed. 'You cannot possibly step away from the project at such a crucial stage. I won't allow it!'

'Then you'd better fire me and find someone else,' Flora said defiantly, knowing that he couldn't. At least, not if he wanted to stand a chance of getting nominated for the work on the castle. 'I'm not asking you, I'm telling you, Graydon. I need this time with Mason.'

Those extra two and a half weeks had been hugely healing, and gone a long way to bridging the rift that Flora had unwittingly allowed to form between the two of them. Now that she was finally back in England, she was determined not to make the same mistake twice and be sucked back into the vortex of Swell Valley life.

I work here. I don't live here.

I'm here to do a job. That's all.

Barney Griffith was just one of a series of connections that Flora was trying to break, or at least weaken to a point where it was no longer a threat to her engagement. Not that she fancied Barney. Although, of course, thanks to his drunken Christmas phone call, she had now had it confirmed that he fancied her.

'Good,' Barney said, as the rain began to fall harder, ice-cold drops bouncing off the tarmac of the lane like tiny, frozen silver balls. 'In that case you'll come in and have a cup of tea with me.'

'Oh, thanks, but I honestly can't,' protested Flora. 'I'm on an emergency Fruit and Nut run and then I really have to get home.'

'I've got Fruit and Nut,' said Barney. 'And I'll drive you home. Stay out in this and you'll catch the sort of chest cold that girls in Jane Austen novels get and drop down dead. Come on.'

He turned and marched back towards his cottage, dragging Jeeves behind him. Too wet and cold to resist, Flora found herself following. A few minutes later she was sitting by a crackling log fire, sipping a delicious mug of Lapsang Souchong tea and warming her bare feet while her wet socks dried on the rail of Barney's Aga.

'Thanks,' she said, smiling as he handed her a plate of

Mr Kipling's Country Slices. All around her, spread out across the coffee table and then spilling onto the floor, where they covered most of the living-room carpet, were Barney's photographs. They were landscapes mostly: brooding, darkly conceived shots of the valley. In one of them a dead oak tree, long since struck by lightning, clawed at the sky, its arm-like branches wreathed in thin strands of cloud, like a skeleton dressing itself for the first time in its ghostly white raiments. There were two versions of the picture side by side: one in colour and the other in black and white. In the latter version the cloud looked like a shadowy swarm of bees from which the poor tree was trying to escape.

'Those are terrific,' said Flora, forgetting for a moment to feel embarrassed about being there.

'Do you think so?' Barney brightened. Having peeled off his oilskins he was wearing a pair of dark Levi's with a thick black roll-neck sweater. The look rather suited him. He reminded Flora of a young Ted Hughes.

'That tree's at the top of the field behind my garden here,' Barney told her. 'I liked the way the cloud was sort of smothering it.'

'It's an incredible photograph. Why do you have all these pictures laid out?' Flora asked, looking around at the blanket of images.

Barney turned away, looking awkwardly into the fire.

'You'll think it's silly.'

Flora frowned. 'I'm sure I won't.'

'Penny's asked to showcase some of my work at her gallery. They're officially opening soon. She's asked me to pull together eight to twelve images of the valley as part of their first exhibition.'

'That's incredible!' Flora beamed. 'Barney, that's huge. You must be so excited.'

Forgetting her new detachment resolution, she jumped up and hugged him. Barney closed his eyes, feeling Flora's small, soft body pressed against his. She'd regained a little weight over Christmas, which was no bad thing in Barney's book, and cut her hair a bit shorter. It felt silky under Barney's chin and smelled of something floral – lavender water, perhaps, mixed with rose. Releasing him, she sat back down. Barney just stood there swaying, his senses still reeling.

'You see?' said Flora, apparently oblivious to the effect she was having on him. 'I told you you were super-talented as a photographer.'

'I'm just an amateur.' Barney shrugged.

'Only until someone at Penny's gallery buys one of your pieces,' said Flora. 'Then you're a professional.'

'I highly doubt that's going to happen,' said Barney, pouring a cup of tea for himself from the pot on the table. 'I'd be a lot more excited if someone had agreed to publish my bloody book.'

'Is it finished then?' Flora asked, innocently.

A look of dejection swept over Barney like a storm front. 'No.'

Silence descended. Flora took a bite of Country Slice and chewed it contemplatively. She was starting to feel a bit guilty about how nice it was to be here, in front of Barney's fire, eating cake and talking about art as if she'd never been away.

'How are things coming along up at the castle?' asked Barney. He didn't dare ask Flora about her New York trip, in case she waxed lyrical about how wonderful it was to be back with Perry Mason, or whatever the arsehole's name was.

'Slowly,' she said. 'Too slowly.'

Barney smiled despite himself. 'That's a shame. You'll have to stay longer, then?'

'I can't.' Flora shook her head. 'My wedding's this spring and I still have so much to do. I'm hoping Graydon will let me go back once the International Designer of the Year award is over. Whatever isn't done by then can be managed by someone else.'

Barney asked her, 'When are the awards?'

'June. Nominations are in April,' said Flora, matter-of-factly. 'I pretty much have to work twenty-four/seven until then. So don't take it personally if we don't see that much of each other.'

Barney sat down. He could feel all the happiness he'd felt when Flora hugged him seeping out of his body like air from a slow-punctured tyre.

'Graydon's flying into London at the end of this week to start lobbying for a nomination. Schmoozing the sponsors and the judging panel, lunching with design mag editors, trying to whip up interest in Hanborough. He'll be here for a site meeting next Saturday.'

'Is that bad?' asked Barney.

Flora made a face. 'It could be. Mason wants me to fly home every three weeks now for a visit, with the wedding so close and all. I'll have to ask Graydon for the time off.'

'And you think he'll say no?' asked Barney, who was starting to think he might have misjudged Graydon James. Anyone who wanted to keep Flora in England was good news in Barney's book.

'He went gonzo when I told him I was staying on in New York past New Year,' said Flora. 'I seriously thought his head was going to fly off his body.'

'Maybe now's not the best time to be abandoning s
then?' suggested Barney, as casually as he was able to. 'With
the award looming, and all that? I'm sure your fiancé will
understand. He supports your career, doesn't he?'

'Sure,' answered Flora, a little too quickly. 'Totally.'

'Well, then,' said Barney. 'I'd play it by ear, if I were you,
when Graydon gets here. No point taunting the tiger if you
don't really need to.'

Flora got up to go, padding into the kitchen for her almost
dry socks. Suddenly she felt annoyed with herself. She hadn't
wanted to talk about Mason, or Graydon, with Barney, but
had ended up doing both.

'I'll drive you back,' said Barney, getting up too.

'It's OK,' said Flora, looking past him out of the window
as she pulled on her boots and parka. 'The rain's stopped.
I'd prefer to walk.'

Barney opened the door, and watched as Flora began to
slosh her way down his garden path. 'Will you come?' He
blurted out the question. 'To the opening of Penny's gallery?
To see my stuff?' When Flora didn't answer instantly, he
added, 'The whole place has been done to your designs, you
know. You really should see it.'

'Of course,' said Flora. 'I'd love to come. See someone
pay fifty thousand dollars for your ghost tree.'

'Ha!' Barney laughed. 'I wish.'

George Savile arched her back and pulled Henry deeper
inside her.

'Harder!' she commanded. 'I want it harder.'

I don't give a shit what you want, thought Henry. But he
obliged anyway, flipping George over onto her stomach and
driving into her from behind with all the force of a runaway

ge shot forward, the top of her head
st the padded headboard.

ed. Three powerful thrusts later and they
rge's orgasm spasming through her like an
elec ent, her muscles gripping Henry's dick like a
hungry mollusc devouring its prey.

Dripping with sweat, his heart pounding, Henry pulled
out of her and flopped back onto the bed. Staring up at the
ceiling, complete with a glittering French antique chandelier,
he let his mind go blank.

They were at The Dorchester, in a quiet but luxurious
bedroom suite at the rear of the hotel. In the past, they'd
tended to make love at Henry's flat in Belgravia or in the
office. Once they'd done it in George's marital bed, but Henry
found the framed wedding pictures of George and Robert
off-putting, not to mention the godawful taupe interiors and
gold 'accents'. It was like shagging in a Kardashian's bedroom.
The way Henry saw it, if one were going to play away, one
might as well do it in style. He liked The Dorchester because
it was luxurious and the staff were discreet. He also preferred
the impersonal atmosphere of a hotel. In his mind, it kept
his 'relationship' with George, whatever that was, at a safe
distance from his real life, in a 'what happens in Vegas stays
in Vegas' sort of a way.

'I must say, I was touched you went to so much trouble,'
said George, lighting a post-coital cigarette and doing her
best, nonchalant, Lauren Bacall impression. 'A suite at The
Dorchester? For me? If I didn't know you better, I'd be
tempted to say you were turning romantic in your old
age.'

'You do know me better,' Henry said coldly. As always
after sex with George, especially like the great session they'd

just had, he felt dirty and ashamed of himself the moment it was over.

'All right then, Mr Grumpy,' said George, rolling onto her side and resting a hand on Henry's chest, smiling as if he hadn't just insulted her. 'Let's forget romance and talk business. I've got an idea for a new project for us. A fabulous idea, if I do say so myself.'

Henry frowned. They'd talked about diversifying before, and he'd reluctantly agreed to consider things that had obvious synergies with Gigtix.com. Competition had become increasingly fierce in the e-ticket space, and if they were going to keep thriving as a business, they needed to adapt. The problem was that, up till now, George's suggestions had all revolved around making large cash bids for existing companies. Buying and restoring Hanborough had seriously depleted Henry's cash reserves, and though George had offered to put in more money and cover any shortfall from Henry's side, Henry didn't like the idea of owing her, or of being viewed as the junior partner.

'I think we should launch a lifestyle brand!' George announced triumphantly.

Henry's frown deepened. 'What? You mean something like Goop? Rich, spoiled women giving tips on overpriced cashmere scarves to poor, ordinary women?'

'It's a huge business,' said George, 'and it's one of the fastest-growing sectors in e-commerce. Plus, there are no barriers to entry and its super-low cost to get started. We can use our existing customer base at Gigtix. I thought we could operate out of Hanborough – what could be more aspirational than living in a castle, after all? You and Ikea can promote it, swanning around the battlements looking glamorous.'

'Absolutely not,' said Henry.

'And if the castle wins this design award,' George rattled on, ignoring him, 'just think of the merchandising opportunities. We could sell homeware, silverware, gifts, jewellery. People would want Hanborough-style rugs and lamps – you name it. Of course, we'd need to work out the logistics. Distribution's the obvious problem, but—'

'George!' Henry cut her off. 'I said no.'

George's eyes narrowed. Her lips pursed into a tight, angry bow.

'You always say no,' she shot back. 'But guess what, Henry? This isn't just up to you. I'm not prepared to sit back and watch Gigtix.com go under because you're too scared to take the next step.'

Rolling out of bed, she began pulling on her clothes angrily.

'I've invited Graydon James to lunch up at the castle to discuss it further,' she told Henry defiantly.

'You've *what*? For fuck's sake, Georgina, it's my house.'

'Not if Gigtix goes under it isn't,' George reminded him bitterly. 'As partners, we both agreed to unlimited liability, remember? That means all our assets are at risk, Henry, your precious castle included.'

Pulling on her high-heeled Jimmy Choo boots, she yanked up the zips loudly.

'Graydon James is one of the top design brands in the world. If he'd be prepared to come in with us, to lend his name, that would be *huge*. Especially if he gets this big award for Hanborough. People would come to associate Gigtix with Hanborough with Graydon James. That's three brands for the price of one.'

Henry hesitated. He loathed the idea of using Hanborough

as a prop to flog cheap carpets and silverware online. On the other hand, he had to admit George had a point. Most firms would pay a fortune to triple their brand recognition. What George was suggesting might do that for their business for free.

'Flora Fitzwilliam did most of the design work for Hanborough,' he said eventually. 'If we do this, I want Flora involved.'

'Don't be ridiculous, darling,' said George, not bothering to look up as she hunted on the floor for a missing earring. 'No one's heard of Flora. We want the organ grinder, not the monkey.'

'I mean it,' said Henry.

'Ah, there it is!' said George, spying the earring and screwing it into her left lobe.

'She's a damn good designer and she has an incredible eye for this stuff,' Henry went on. 'If we do this, I want Flora in.'

George looked at him now. Lying in bed, his head propped up on two huge hotel pillows, he radiated entitlement like a king. She hated herself for wanting him so much. For letting him use her, screw her and discard her, like some cheap prostitute, to go running back to his boring Swedish girlfriend. But to have to sit here and listen to him demand that *Flora Fitzwilliam,* of all people, be involved in their business? George's business? That was beyond the pale.

'My God,' she muttered scathingly. 'You've got the hots for her, haven't you?'

'Don't be ridiculous,' said Henry.

'What's ridiculous is you trying to jimmy some unknown underling into a perfectly good business plan, just because she gives you a hard-on.'

'That's enough!' Henry shouted.

'Have you slept with her already?' George demanded. When Henry didn't answer she added nastily, 'You know what her nickname was at school, don't you? *Easy to Spread.* Get it? Flora? I daresay she hasn't changed much.'

Henry looked at her with utter loathing, but for once George was too angry to care.

'I'll see you for lunch on Saturday,' she said, picking up her Chanel purse and swinging it over her shoulder. 'With Graydon. Wear something nice. And try not to be *too* bloody miserable, would you? It gets dreadfully boring after a while.'

Before Henry could think of a comeback she left, slamming the door behind her.

Flora scuttled nervously along Marylebone High Street, looking over her shoulder every few minutes as if worried she might be being followed.

I'd make a terrible spy, she thought, ducking left into a winding, cobbled mews street before taking a sharp right into a wider, tree-lined avenue. *I wouldn't be great as an unfaithful wife, either. I don't know how people can stand the tension.*

The street she was on now was full of large, grand Victorian homes. Classic London, white stucco affairs, with pillared porticos and balconies outside the upper-floor windows that no one ever used. Flora quickly identified number forty-four, with its neatly trimmed hedge and new paintwork, its gleaming windows and window boxes overflowing with gypsophila and tiny blue pansies.

Smoothing down her hair and tightening the belt on her new mackintosh coat, she steadied her nerves and rang the bell.

An older man opened the front door. Handsome in a very English way, he wore a perfectly pressed chocolate brown cashmere sweater over a checked, Thomas Pink shirt, and corduroy trousers in a lighter shade of brown. He smelled of light, lemony aftershave and soap and he had a wonderful, utterly genuine smile that dissolved Flora's nerves like an Alka-Seltzer in water.

'You must be Flora. Come in, my dear. Come in.'

The older man introduced himself as George Wilkes, Jason Cranley's husband. It was Jason Cranley, only son of Brett Cranley, and erstwhile Fittlescombe resident, who had rung Flora yesterday out of the blue and convinced her to make the trip down to town today.

'Penny tells me you're a miracle worker,' Jason had told Flora. 'A design genius, she said.'

Flora had laughed. 'I'm afraid she may have stretched the truth a little there.'

'I wouldn't ask if we weren't desperate,' Jason had gone on. 'George just fired our third designer in a row. The new adoption people are coming in two weeks and we need the place to look like a family home before then. Please? Just take a look.'

The house was glorious, already finished to a very high standard, at least in Flora's opinion. Admittedly it didn't scream 'family home'. Although they already had one delightful, very placid little girl, the stark white walls and abstract sculptures, erotic sketches and chinoiserie-themed master suite in various shades of dark lacquer and murder-red were definitely more gay-art-dealer chic than Play-Doh friendly. Flora wasn't sure what the problem with the adoption agency was, though, if they already had one child?

'That's the thing,' Jason explained, arriving home late

from a rehearsal – Brett Cranley's only son was a gifted jazz pianist. 'New agency, new regulations . . . basically, it needs to look more relaxed. Less perfect.'

'You mean a bit less gay?' George chipped in, apparently amused by the whole thing.

'Honestly, he's got no idea what these adoption harridans are like. *Yes*, it needs to be less gay. And less white, and less male and less rich. We need to look like—'

'Mixed-race heterosexuals from the wrong end of Fulham who can't pay their mortgage and love nothing more than having all their furniture scrawled on by sticky-handed rug-rats?' George winked at Jason, obligingly finishing for him.

'Exactly,' said Jason. Turning back to Flora he asked, 'Can you do that?'

'Easy-peasy.' Flora grinned. She already loved Jason and George, just as Penny had told her she would. 'The problem is, I'm not officially allowed to work on my own projects. I'm under contract to Graydon James.'

'Graydon? He did my dad's beach house in the Hamptons,' said Jason.

'I know. I think your father was the one who recommended him to Henry Saxton Brae. That's how I ended up doing the Hanborough restoration and meeting Penny . . . '

' . . . who introduced you to us. How perfect.' Jason smiled.

'Well, yes and no,' said Flora. 'Like I say, officially—'

'We'll employ you unofficially,' said Jason, waving a hand in easy dismissal of Flora's contractual problems. 'Two weeks' work, on the side, cash in hand, no questions asked.'

'You sound like Del Boy.' George laughed.

'Please?' said Jason.

'Well, I—'

'A hundred thousand,' said Jason.

Flora's jaw dropped. *A hundred grand? In pounds? For two weeks' moonlighting? Just how rich are these guys?*

'OK, a hundred and fifty,' said Jason, misinterpreting her silence as some sort of negotiating technique. 'Graydon will never know, I promise. Mum's the word.'

'Shouldn't the word be Dad?' quipped George, who still wasn't taking this seriously.

'OK,' Flora blurted. *What the hell. I'll be able to buy the world's most beautiful wedding dress, and even have some savings left over for once in my life.*

Of course, it did mean that whatever small chance she'd had of flying back to see Mason had now evaporated completely. She would literally have to work through the night on Jason and George's project to get it done in time without compromising her work up at the castle. *When he sees my dress, he'll understand*, Flora told herself.

'OK, you'll do it?' Jason grabbed both of her hands and looked up at her hopefully.

'I'll do it,' said Flora, grinning. 'You've got yourself a designer.'

Graydon James walked morosely around the moat at Hanborough Castle. He'd jetted into Heathrow with high hopes, but so far his trip had been one disappointment after another. First, Cedric Brun, Graydon's old friend and most influential ally on the committee for the International Designer of the Year award, had announced he was stepping down from this year's judging panel due to 'health pressures'. As Graydon knew for a fact that this was code for Cedric slipping off to Argentina for yet another face-lift (no doubt to fix the last one, which had made him look like a baboon's arse shot with extremely unflattering light), he was less than sympathetic during their lunch at Scalini.

'Nominations are two months away,' Graydon pleaded. 'Surely you can hang on until then?'

'I can, darling,' Cedric simpered. 'But my stomach's another matter. I've been a martyr to it for years now, as you know, but it's reached a point where I simply can't focus on my work. It wouldn't be *fair* for me to stay on. Not when all the entrants have put their hearts and souls into their projects. It's time for a younger man to take my seat.'

Graydon didn't give a fuck about the other entrants. He needed a major feather in his cap now, a significant PR victory, if he didn't want a younger man – or woman, for that matter – to take *his* seat as global tastemaker extraordinaire. He'd been around long enough to know that one was only ever as good as one's last big project, one's last prestigious award or multi-page glossy magazine spread. If he played his cards right, Hanborough Castle would be Graydon's ticket to another decade at the top of the pile. It didn't help that his ace in the pack, Cedric, was busy throwing himself on the fire.

His schmoozing meetings at Condé Nast hadn't gone much better either. *Vogue Interiors* had just hired a new editor, a preposterously young lesbian named Jane Tee. Ms Tee looked at Graydon as if he were some sort of curiosity from the prehistoric era, and could barely restrain her laughter at his suggestion that she might like to devote a few pages on next month's issue to his career highlights.

'We don't do those sort of puff pieces any more, I'm afraid, Mr James,' Jane Tee said bluntly. Lesbians, in Graydon's opinion, said everything bluntly, and were a tiresome addition to their already tiresome sex. 'I'd be happy to look at any genuinely *new* work you're doing. Or perhaps showcase some of your younger designers? I hear you have quite the reputation for fostering new talent.'

'You're too kind,' said Graydon, through teeth so gritted he was in danger of losing a veneer.

Then, finally, he'd driven all the way out to Hanborough Castle for a lunch meeting with Georgina Savile, to discuss terms for some sort of collaboration on an online lifestyle business, only to be forced to sit through an embarrassing meal, during which it became apparent that Henry Saxton Brae, George's partner, was by no means on board with the idea.

'What is it you feel you can offer us at Gigtix?' Henry had had the nerve to ask him. As if he, Graydon James, had approached them cap in hand, and not the other way around!

'Don't be silly, Henry,' George answered for him, in the face of Graydon's own horrified silence. 'Graydon James is a globally recognized brand with decades of experience. As you well know.'

'And as *you* well know, GJD made a loss in the last three consecutive quarters,' Henry hit the ball back to her.

Graydon had sat and watched miserably, like a dog at a tennis match, while the two young partners fired increasingly aggressive shots at one another. At last, mercifully, the plates were cleared, Henry made his excuses, and George suggested that the two of them take a stroll around the grounds.

There was little outside to lift Graydon's spirits. A grey, freezing, early February mist hung over the castle like a shadow on an old man's lung. Flora had achieved a huge amount in the months since Graydon had last been here.

But a quarter of the building was still covered in scaffolding and in the thin, shadowy half-light of winter, the new party barn looked stark, ugly and out of place.

'I thought you said you'd discussed our collaboration with Henry.' Graydon looked accusingly at George.

'We did discuss it.'

'Well, he's obviously not interested,' Graydon snapped.

'Oh, that's just Henry being Henry,' George said soothingly. 'He knows we need to break new ground as a business. It's just that, when it comes to Hanborough, he takes everything so personally.'

Graydon made a noncommittal grunting noise, designed to express his lack of interest in Henry's emotional attachment to his new home.

'And then, you know . . . there's Flora,' George added, making a scrunched-up face.

Graydon stopped walking. 'What about Flora?'

George hesitated, biting her lower lip. 'Oh, nothing. I don't really like to say.'

'Has something happened?' Graydon pressed her.

'No, no. Nothing. Well, nothing concrete,' George corrected herself.

Graydon gave her an *out with it* look.

'The thing is, I'm rather afraid that Henry has the hots for her.'

'Is that a problem?' Graydon looked perplexed.

'It might be,' said George. 'When I floated the idea of launching a lifestyle brand, the first thing Henry did was start insisting that Flora be involved. According to Henry, Flora's done all the design work at the castle single-handedly. He made it sound as if you'd had nothing to do with it at all.' She fluttered her eyelashes at Graydon disingenuously.

'That's nonsense,' said Graydon. 'Is that what Flora's been saying?'

George shrugged. 'I don't know. But I do know she's worked very hard to get both Henry and Eva wrapped around her little finger. According to Henry, Flora's the creative genius at Graydon James.'

'That's ridiculous!' Graydon exploded.

'I know. That's what I told him,' said George. 'But Henry's under the impression that you're – now, how did he put it again?' She furrowed her brow, as if trying to remember. '"The numbers guy." That's it. That's what he called you.'

Graydon felt the bile rise up into his throat. So that's what Flora had been doing these past few months. Undermining him with the clients. After everything he'd done for that girl!

'He even said that if Hanborough did win this award you've been talking about, it really ought to go to Flora.' George twisted the knife. 'I don't know what Flora's been saying exactly. But I don't think Henry would have come up with an idea like that on his own. Do you?'

No, thought Graydon, walking on in a moody silence. *I don't.*

'I'm probably speaking out of turn,' said George, delighted by the effect her comments were having on Graydon but doing her best to hide it. 'But I've also heard that she's been taking on private commissions in London.'

'She can't!' Graydon was suitably appalled. 'She works for me. She's under contract.'

'Well, quite,' said George. 'But when the cat's away, and all that. Now, obviously, these are just rumours,' she demurred. 'I don't know any of this for a fact. But if you want me to get Henry on board with our collaboration, I think you might need to rein Flora in a bit.'

Rein her in? thought Graydon furiously. *I'll fucking strangle her.*

'And in the meantime,' George slipped her arm through Graydon's, 'I have another idea I wanted to run past you. This is nothing to do with Henry or Gigtix. It's something I thought perhaps the two of us might work on together. *Under the radar*, as it were.' She simpered.

'Shoot,' said Graydon.

George made her pitch. It was interesting, actually, but Graydon was only half listening.

Flora Fitzwilliam was stabbing him in the back, was she? Trying to cut him out of his own damn business? Wrecking what Graydon had spend a lifetime creating, like an ungrateful, greedy cuckoo in his nest?

Well, two could play at that game.

CHAPTER TWENTY-ONE

It was a Sunday night at the beginning of March and Flora was in her pyjamas on the sofa in Peony Cottage when her cell phone rang.

'Flora Fitzwilliam?' It was a woman's voice. American.

'Yes?'

'My name is Janet Kingston. I'm calling from the *New York Post*.'

'OK,' said Flora warily, putting aside her laptop. She couldn't imagine why the *New York Post* might want to talk to her.

'We're running a story on tomorrow's "Page Six" about Mason Parker's affair with Henrietta Branston. I wondered if you have any comment you'd like to make on that before we go to press?'

Flora felt a strange sensation in her limbs, as if she were suddenly weightless.

'Miss Fitzwilliam?'

She could still hear the reporter's voice, but it was muffled now, as if Flora had cotton wool in her ears or was holding her phone under water.

Mason Parker's affair . . . Henrietta Branston.

No. It didn't make sense. She'd spoken to Mason only a few hours ago and everything was fine.

'Flora, are you still there?'

'Yes. I'm here,' Flora croaked. 'I think you've made a mistake. Mason and Henrietta are old friends.'

'So, is that your comment?' Janet Kingston asked cheerfully, as if the two of them were discussing the weather.

'What? No!' said Flora. 'I don't have a comment.'

'Because I think you ought to know we're publishing pictures tomorrow that show the two of them are a lot more than friends.'

The room had started to spin. Flora clutched the arm of the sofa like a drowning woman clinging to a life raft.

'Can I take it you didn't know?'

'I have to go,' Flora mumbled, hanging up and dropping her phone onto the cushions as if it were a red-hot coal. No sooner had she let it go than it rang again, the shrill notes piercing her skull like arrows.

Mason's name flashed up on her screen.

Flora picked up. 'Hey.' She was surprised to hear the tremor in her voice.

Mason sighed heavily. 'They called you already, didn't they?'

'Just now. But it's a mistake, right?' Flora blurted. 'I mean, it isn't true.'

The silence that followed seemed to last for hours.

'I'm so sorry, Flora,' Mason said at last. 'I can't tell you how awful I feel.'

Flora stared at the phone in her hand as though she were

watching somebody else. Possibly somebody in a really cheesy Lifetime movie. The entire last ten minutes felt like an out-of-body experience. When she spoke, her voice was not her own.

'How long . . . I mean, when did it start?'

'Does it matter?' asked Mason.

'Kind of. Yeah, it does.'

Another heavy sigh. 'It started on Valentine's Day.'

Flora winced.

'Look, I'm not making excuses. I know it was totally wrong,' said Mason. 'But when you didn't fly home like you said you would, I was so mad at you. And I got drunk, and Hen was there—'

'Hen's always there,' Flora said numbly, although with less bitterness than she expected. The weird thing was, this wasn't hitting her as hard as it should be. Mason cheating on her, and not just with a random other woman, but with Henrietta Branston – it was Flora's worst nightmare come true. And yet she couldn't shake the feeling of detachment, like it was happening to someone else. *Maybe it's the shock?*

'I just . . . I didn't know if you loved me any more.' Mason's voice was breaking. 'You never come home. You shut me down every time I bring up the wedding.'

'That's not true.'

'It is true, Flora.'

For someone who's sorry, he's sure focusing a lot on my *problems*, thought Flora.

'I still love you,' said Mason, filling the dead air between them.

'OK. So is it over with Henrietta?' Flora heard herself asking, feeling more like somebody else than ever.

Mason's hesitation was brief, but it spoke volumes.

'It will be.'

'It *will* be?'

'It's complicated.'

'How? How is it complicated?' For the first time, Flora began to sound angry. 'We're engaged and you slept with another woman behind my back.'

'I know!' Mason sounded close to tears. 'And I'm sorry. But there is a context here, Flora, and you know it. We—'

'I have to go,' Flora cut him off.

'Flora, please! Don't hang up. Hear me out. You weren't here. I'm not in love with Hen, but I can't just drop her like a stone.'

Flora pressed the red button on her phone. Then she pressed it again, keeping her thumb in place long enough to turn it off completely.

Could you end a relationship as easily as you could end a phone call? With the touch of a button? Erase your life as a couple, your past, your hopes and dreams for the future?

Perhaps you could.

Feeling more unreal than ever, and not knowing what else to do, Flora locked the cottage doors, turned off the downstairs lights and went up to bed. The pills she took for jet lag were in her bathroom cabinet. Popping two into her mouth, she swallowed them with water from her tooth mug. Crawling under her covers, she waited for the pain to hit her and her tortured thoughts to start racing.

Instead she fell into a deep, dreamless sleep.

When she woke the next morning, dazzling sunlight streamed through her bedroom window, of the kind Flora hadn't seen in months. Glancing blearily at her clock, she was horrified to discover it was already after ten. She had slept for twelve hours, something she couldn't remember doing since college.

Jumping out of bed and into the shower, she allowed the warm jets of water to soothe her as the events of last night reasserted themselves.

Mason was having an affair.

With Henrietta Branston.

Page Six were running the story. It would be out by now, all over the internet. That was the worst part, Flora decided. Knowing that as soon as she switched on her phone or logged into Facebook, as soon as she emerged from the cocoon of Peony Cottage, she would be bombarded by other people's opinions and emotions. Some would be kind. Some spiteful. Many, no doubt, would be pitying, which was almost worse. But all would expect some sort of response from Flora. Anger or heartbreak or . . . something.

I don't know what to tell them, she thought, lathering zingy lime shower gel over her arms and stomach. *I don't know how I feel.*

Mason and I are not getting married. She turned the thought over in her head, examining it from every angle, waiting for the grief and pain that ought to follow. But nothing much happened. She felt sad. And tired. And something else; another, unexpected emotion that Flora was trying hard not to recognize, but that kept reasserting itself: relief.

Pulling on skinny jeans and a rust-red turtleneck sweater, she grabbed her laptop, phone, car keys and jacket and headed to work.

'I can't bear it.'

Sitting at the kitchen table at Hanborough with Henry, Eva was rereading the *Post's* piece on Mason Parker for the umpteenth time that morning on her phone. Georgina Savile had helpfully emailed it to Henry yesterday, in a message entitled, *Oh dear! Trouble in paradise* . . . Lottie Calthorpe, George's friend in the Hamptons, had wasted no time letting her know. Evidently there was much rejoicing among Manhattan's It-Girl community that Mason Parker had finally seen sense and dumped 'that chubby little Puerto Rican', as Lottie had described Flora.

'Poor Flora!' Eva shook her head sadly.

Recently returned from a modelling assignment, and looking more bronzed and lithe than ever, she was dressed this morning in a multicoloured silk shirt teamed with skin-tight bright yellow jeans. It gave Henry a hangover just to look at her. She put him in mind of a bird of paradise that had somehow lost its flock and ended up in the rainy Sussex countryside instead of the Brazilian rainforest.

'Do you think she'll come in to work today?'

'I have no idea,' said Henry, spreading marmalade on a third slice of toast. He also felt bad for Flora. She'd called in sick yesterday, the morning the news broke, and was clearly lying low. No one liked being cheated on, still less having their humiliation made public for all to see. On the other hand, a less worthy part of Henry was pleased that this fiancé of hers, this guy who Flora had always held up as being such a saint, turned out to have the same feet of clay as he did.

'Should I go over to the cottage? If she doesn't come in today?' Eva asked. She was obviously genuinely worried for her friend. 'I mean, Flora was there for me. After you and Kate . . . ' She left the sentence hanging.

Henry grimaced, as much from embarrassment as from guilt. Looking back now he had no idea what had possessed him to sleep with his brother's wife that day at the hunt. He'd had countless affairs, but that one slip with Kate had caused more grief than all of the others put together. Eva had forgiven, but not forgotten. And Henry's friendship with Flora had never recovered.

'Have you called her this morning?' Henry asked, steering the conversation back to Flora and the present drama.

'I've tried. Her phone's switched off.'

'So maybe she needs some more time.'

Right on cue, Flora appeared in the kitchen doorway. Dressed for work in a fitted riding jacket and skinny jeans tucked into boots, and with her laptop slung over her shoulder, she looked as calm and collected as ever. If she'd been crying it didn't show. There was no puffiness around her eyes, no blotchy skin or ruddy nose. Indeed, if anything, she looked better rested than usual. It was all rather odd.

'I've come to run through the latest list of change orders,' she said briskly. 'It's quite long, I'm afraid, but I need approval from one of you.'

'Are you OK?' Eva asked nervously. 'Did you get my messages?'

'I did.' Flora smiled. 'Thank you. But I'm fine.'

Getting up from the table, Eva enveloped her tightly in a sisterly hug.

'I'm so sorry, Flora,' she said sincerely. 'Have you spoken to him?'

'Briefly,' said Flora, extricating herself from Eva's well-meaning but stifling embrace.

She caught Henry's eye for a moment, but was unable fully to read his expression.

'You don't have to act brave around us, you know,' said

Eva. 'Does she, Henry? You're allowed to be upset. I mean, you were about to get married to the guy.'

'I think Flora knows that, darling,' Henry said, tactfully.

'Of course she does. Sorry,' said Eva, blushing. 'That was a stupid thing to say.'

'It's OK,' said Flora. 'Really. I appreciate the concern but to be honest I don't want to talk about it. I'd rather focus on work.'

'Miss Gunnarson?' Henry's PA, Mrs French, waddled in behind Flora. 'Madame Faubourg is here.'

'Who?' Eva looked perplexed.

'The dressmaker? From Paris. For your wedding dress fitting?'

'Oh my goodness, I totally forgot.' Eva gave Flora an embarrassed look. 'I'm really sorry.'

'For what?' asked Flora.

'It's not exactly the greatest timing,' said Eva. 'I can ask her to come back . . . '

'Don't be silly. Go. Have your fitting. It's fine.'

'Are you sure?'

'Of course I'm sure. Henry can sign off on these.'

Sitting down at the table, Flora began unzipping her laptop bag in a businesslike manner. Her relief was palpable when Eva left.

'OK,' she said, handing a sheaf of printed spreadsheets to Henry while bringing up the relevant page on her Mac. 'Let's start with the big-ticket items and move down.'

For the next fifteen minutes they were all business. Henry agreed most of the changes, although he did question the contractor's budget here and there.

'Sixty thousand on marble? What's that for?'

'Bathrooms mostly,' said Flora. 'The floors in the guest suites, also the tile bases for the outdoor showers.'

'What outdoor showers? This is the Swell Valley, not Ibiza.'

'I know.' Flora suppressed a smile. 'I think Graydon might have slipped those in.'

'Well, he can bloody well slip them out again,' said Henry. 'Have you heard from him since he went back to the States?'

'Surprisingly, no,' said Flora. 'He was acting very strangely while he was over here too. We were supposed to have a whole string of site meetings, but I barely saw him in the end. How was your lunch?'

'Boring,' said Henry. He contemplated telling her about George's plans for world domination with Graydon, but decided to leave it for now. Flora had enough on her plate. 'Listen, Flora. I know you said you didn't want to talk about it—'

'Because I don't.' Flora looked up sharply.

'I just want to say that I understand.' Reaching across the table, he took her hand. 'If you ever do want to talk about it.'

'*You* understand?' Flora looked at him angrily, withdrawing her hand. 'What do you understand, Henry? What it feels like to be totally betrayed?'

'Would that be so hard to believe?' Now it was Henry's turn to be angry. 'Do you really think you're the only person who's ever been hurt? I'm your friend, Flora. At least, I'm trying to be.'

The hurt in his eyes was obviously genuine. For a moment Flora felt remorseful. But only for a moment.

'I'm sorry,' she said caustically. 'I guess I see you as more as the betrayer than the betrayee. I wonder why that is?'

'Right,' Henry snapped. 'So I'm still the bad guy, am I? Your perfect fiancé screws one of your friends and gets himself all over the gossip columns, but it's not him you're mad at, it's me. Why *is* that, Flora? Why is it that Eva can forgive me but you can't?'

Suddenly the tears that had refused to come ever since the Page Six reporter had broken the news burst out of Flora like water from a popped balloon.

'Oh Christ,' said Henry, rushing round to Flora's side of the table and offering her a napkin. 'I'm sorry. Please don't cry. I shouldn't have said that.'

Flora shook her head vehemently. 'No. It's OK. You should. I mean, I *am* mad at you. I genuinely don't understand why you can't seem to keep it in your pants. Or why *I* have to know about it every time you cheat.'

'That wasn't exactly by design,' said Henry, stroking her hair as she blew her nose loudly into the napkin.

'But you're right. Mason's the one I should be yelling at right now, not you.'

'But you aren't?'

Flora sniffed. 'No. I keep waiting to feel this wave of rage and humiliation and sadness. But it won't come. It's like it's blocked. I mean, I am sad. And shocked. But just not . . . '

'Enough?'

She shrugged. 'I guess not.'

'Maybe he wasn't the right guy for you,' said Henry softly.

He was standing behind Flora's chair, so she couldn't see his face. One hand was still absently stroking her hair. The other rested on her shoulder. All of a sudden the hand on her shoulder felt red-hot. Perhaps it was Flora's imagination, but it seemed a tension had descended out of nowhere, like a cloud over the two of them, so thick Flora could taste it.

Closing her eyes, she could feel her heart beat wildly like a trapped animal inside her chest. Then, just as she was about to bolt, to think up some excuse, any excuse, and get out of there, Henry stepped away.

'May I make a suggestion?' he asked, so coolly that Flora instantly felt foolish for thinking . . . whatever she'd been thinking.

'Sure,' she said, doing her best to match his even tone.

'Come out hunting with us tomorrow.'

It was so unexpected, Flora burst out laughing. 'Come out hunting? Me? What on earth for?'

'Because it's fun.' Henry grinned. 'It's also all-consuming and tiring and it gets you out of the house. I promise you, you will not have time to think about Mason when you're careering over the Downs after a fox. You weren't *really* going to marry someone called Mason, were you?' he added, as an afterthought. 'You have to admit it's a bloody awful name.'

Despite herself, Flora giggled. She'd missed this. Henry being charming and funny. Her allowing him to be charming and funny, without being permanently outraged.

'I can't,' she said. 'I appreciate the suggestion, but I haven't ridden in years.'

'All the more reason to get back on the horse,' said Henry. He'd never been good at taking no for an answer. 'I'll ask Seb to find you a nice, gentle mount. You'll love it, I promise. And, even if you don't, it's part of the whole English country experience. You'll miss all this when you're gone, you know.'

He was teasing her, trying to lift her spirits. But the truth was, he was right.

She would miss it.

That was part of the problem.

CHAPTER TWENTY-TWO

Saturday morning dawned bright and clear, the first glimpse of sunshine the Swell Valley had had in weeks. Flora opened her bedroom window to see fields stiffened by a pale grey frost, each blade of grass glittering in the sunlight like shards of glass.

Squeezing into the jodhpurs that Sebastian Saxton Brae had loaned her last night – 'They're actually designed for an older child but I 'spect they'll fit you all right' – and tucking in a white cotton shirt, she went downstairs to make a much-needed coffee.

Hunting! How on earth had she let Henry talk her into it? Mason had called her last night, to 'talk things through'. Stupidly, Flora had taken the call, and they'd ended up going round in circles till well past midnight. Mason was threatening to come to England and see her. He kept saying he didn't want to 'throw it all away', conveniently forgetting that by sleeping with Henrietta Branston he'd done exactly that, and had the gall to accuse Flora of being 'cold' towards him.

What did he expect? A thank-you note and a bottle of champagne?

After the call she'd been unable to sleep, and had ended up doing work emails into the small hours. The one bright spot was a note from Jason Cranley, thanking her for the 'miraculous' transformation of the townhouse, and informing her that a hundred and fifty thousand pounds had been transferred to her private account that morning.

'The adoption dragon came by yesterday and loved *everything*,' he gushed. 'We really can't thank you enough.'

A hundred and fifty thousand was a good start in Flora's book. Especially now that she wouldn't be marrying Mason and would have to rely on her own savings for security, at least for now. It bothered her that being poor again was probably the part of calling off her engagement that upset her the most. What did that say about her? That she'd never loved him? That she was venal, a gold-digger, no better than Henrietta and her cronies, sniffing around Mason for his money?

No. That's not true. I did love him.

But I loved the security too.

Flora had even briefly considered selling Mason's engagement ring rather than returning it to him before deciding it was beneath her dignity. Still, the lessons of her childhood, and what it meant to lose everything, ran deep. Mason had been Flora's rock, her provider. The cold, hard truth was that losing that was at least as terrifying as losing him.

Pulling on her boots, she opened the front door and took her coffee outside, letting the crisp morning air jolt her awake.

'Flora!'

Barney, looking fresh-faced and perky beneath his tartan woolly bobble hat, was walking Jeeves along the lane.

Flora hadn't seen Barney since breaking up with Mason,

but she assumed he knew by now. Swell Valley gossip was a ruthlessly efficient machine.

'How are you?' He walked over to the garden gate. 'I heard what happened.'

Flora came up the path to greet him. 'I figured.' She smiled. 'I'm fine.'

'Really?' Barney tried to look concerned, but it was hard to remove all traces of elation from his face. With the American boyfriend out of the way, he might finally stand a chance with Flora. 'I would have come over sooner, as soon as I heard. But I didn't want you to think I was . . . ' He paused, embarrassed. 'I thought you might want to be alone for a while.'

'Thanks.' Flora touched his arm gratefully.

He glanced curiously at her outfit.

'You're going riding?'

'Hunting, actually.' Flora pulled an *eek* face. 'Henry invited me and Seb's lent me a pony. They thought it might take my mind off things.'

Barney's face clouded over.

Shit, thought Flora, blushing. She'd forgotten how vehemently Barney disapproved of blood sports.

'I'd better be going,' he muttered, reaching down to clip Jeeves back onto his lead.

'Don't be angry,' said Flora. She didn't know why, but the thought of Barney being mad at her seemed terrible right now. 'I know how you feel about hunting. I'm not into it either. Henry just thought it would be a good distraction.'

Barney's frown deepened. Hunting wasn't just something that he 'wasn't into'. It was cruel and wrong, and he hated everything about it. And had done since he'd been a small boy. People being cruel to people was bad enough, but cruelty to helpless, innocent animals turned Barney's stomach. He wanted to think better of Flora. The fact that Henry Saxton Brae had encouraged her to do this, and that she'd let him, only made it worse.

'I really don't care what Henry thinks,' he snapped.

To Flora's dismay, he hurried away.

Thanks to the good weather, the meet was packed. By ten o'clock a large throng of riders, followers and general hangers-on had gathered up at Wraggsbottom Farm and were busy chatting, eating and fortifying themselves on Gabe and Laura Baxter's home-made cider before the off.

Henry rode casually over to where Lucy Smart was standing, struggling to tighten the girth on Hermione, a beautiful but flighty grey mare Richard had bought her as an anniversary present only last month.

'Let me help you,' said Henry, vaulting off his horse with the lithe grace of a gymnast.

'It's OK. I can manage,' said Lucy. But Henry was already beside her, his fingers brushing against hers on the leather strap. Leaning against her as he yanked the girth tighter, he whispered in her ear, 'I've missed you.'

Lucy closed her eyes, pushing hard against any residual feelings of longing. 'I've told you, for God's sake, Henry. Richard—'

'He can't see. No one can. I need to see you, Luce—'

'Ah, Henry, there you are!' Seb trotted over towards them, resplendent in his red master's jacket and antique 1920s hard hat.

Lucy and Henry shot apart like repelling magnets. Lucy swiftly mounted Hermione. Henry slipped off his jacket and held it in front of his groin to disguise his enormous erection.

'Come and help me with Flora, would you? She's getting panicky about Ned bolting.'

'You put her on Ned?' Henry laughed.

'You said she needed a gentle horse,' said Seb, defensively.

'Gentle, yes. I didn't say a *dead* horse. Does she know how old Ned is? She'll be lucky if he breaks a trot all day.'

'Well, quite. Anyway, do come and calm her down. We'll be off in a minute and I don't want her chickening out.'

'No,' said Henry, giving Lucy a meaningful look over his shoulder. 'No chickening out.'

Vaulting back up into the saddle, still carefully positioning his jacket to hide what was left of his hard-on, Henry rode off after his brother.

Today, he decided, was going to be a wonderful day.

Barney Griffith watched from his bedroom window as the hunt thundered across the Downs. He'd moved his desk up here from the study, in the hope that the view might inspire him to produce better material for his novel. Or, at any rate, to produce *some* material. In a fit of mid-book panic a few weeks ago, he'd ended up deleting more than a third of the material he'd produced so far, leaving him woefully behind his self-imposed deadline of 1st July for delivering the manuscript. If he didn't knuckle down soon, he'd be forced to admit that he had, in fact, wasted the last year entirely, fannying about taking photographs and failing miserably to make any headway with Flora Fitzwilliam.

Is that her? he wondered, leaning forward and narrowing his eyes in an attempt to zoom in on a petite figure on a lumbering black horse towards the back of one of the last groups of riders. Without binoculars he couldn't be sure.

Sighing heavily, he rubbed his eyes and forced himself to go back to his typing. He didn't know why he felt so depressed. Clearly he'd overreacted this morning, about Flora going out with the hunt. Was it the hunting part that bothered him, or the fact that Flora had gone out at Henry Saxton Brae's suggestion? It really was beyond Barney, this hold that Henry seemed to have over all these women who were in every way his superior. Sure, the guy was good-looking. But didn't being a total arsehole count for anything at all? At least Eva was principled enough to stick to her guns and not go out hunting, whatever Henry thought about it.

Ploughing on with the scene he was writing, Barney finally managed to push all thoughts of Flora, Henry and Eva out of his mind when he suddenly heard a horrendous, piercing scream. It wasn't a short, sharp cry of pain, but a long shrieking howl of terror. Leaping to his feet, Barney opened his bedroom window. The hunt had moved on, out of sight and earshot. But a lone rider exploded out of the woods and across the field above Barney's cottage at a terrifying speed. Slumped forward, her feet out of the stirrups, clinging on to the neck of her grey horse for dear life, the rider was screaming in panic as her horse bolted out of control towards the hedge at the top of the hill. It looked as if the horse was bleeding from its right flank and the rider's fear was clearly exacerbating the animal's panic.

Just then Seb Saxton Brae, instantly recognizable in his red coat and with his master's horn hanging at his side, tore across the field towards the grey. Standing in the saddle, whipping his own horse for all he was worth, like a Grand

National jockey in the home straight, he was gaining on them, but not fast enough. Barney watched frozen in horror as the grey lurched ever more urgently towards the top of the field, where the hedge loomed up, an impenetrable tangle of briars and bramble bushes.

'Pull up!' Seb was yelling. 'Pull up!'

But the woman on the grey either couldn't hear him or couldn't do what he asked.

Barney gasped as, with a split second's hesitation, her horse suddenly launched itself into the air. With a superhuman effort, Seb made up the last few yards between them and jumped after her, his perfect, event-rider form and control in direct contrast to the woman on the grey, who clung to her mount like a rag doll, still screaming.

After that everything seemed to happen in slow motion. The grey's forelegs flailed beneath it in the air like a cartoon character that has run off a cliff but doesn't realize the ground has disappeared. Miraculously, they cleared the top of the towering hedgerow. *They're going to make it*, thought Barney. But then there was another scream and a hideous thud as one of the grey's hind legs clipped Seb's head, knocking him off his horse like a bowling pin. Seb's horse sailed on into the next field as if nothing had happened. But the grey had been knocked off balance, twisting grotesquely, its rider still attached, before both disappeared from view on the other side of the rise.

Barney watched, stunned.

Seb's horse raced away across the next field. Seb lay motionless at the foot of the hedge. The grey and its rider seemed to have evaporated completely, swallowed up by the earth and the deathly silence that now descended.

Grabbing his phone, Barney ran downstairs and out of

the door, throwing himself over the gate, into the field and sprinting up the slope as fast as his legs could carry him.

Henry cantered into Brockhurst Woods after the pack, his heart pounding with exhilaration. The cold wind on his face, the wild, excited baying of the hounds as they neared the end of the chase, and the thought of meeting Lucy later all filled him with a primal thrill that made the hairs on his forearms stand on end.

All at once he was surrounded by huntsmen and riders. 'Fantastic!' A flushed Santiago de la Cruz was suddenly beside Henry, patting him on the shoulder.

'That was bloody good work by the whips at the end,' agreed Gabe Baxter, weaving his way through the throng of riders to join them. 'What happened to Seb, by the way?'

'No idea,' said Henry. 'Last I saw him was when we came past Coggins Mill.'

'Not like our illustrious master to miss the finish,' said Gabe, taking off his hard hat and wiping his brow with his sleeve. 'I don't know about you but I'm exhausted.'

'Is it over?' Flora asked, sweat pouring down her face after a long day spent trying to goad the elderly Ned into any sort of action.

'I'm afraid so,' said Henry, admiring the way Flora's bosom rose and fell beneath her white cotton shirt. 'Good day, wasn't it? Did you have fun?'

'There's been an accident!'

Everybody turned around. Penny de la Cruz, her white dress covered in mud and her tangled hair billowing in the wind, ran towards Santiago and Henry. Her Land Rover was parked by the gate, door open, engine still running.

Santiago went white. 'What's happened?'

'Lucy Smart . . . ' she panted. 'And Seb.'

'What about Seb?' Kate Saxton Brae rode over to see what all the commotion was about.

'Barney saw it,' said Penny. 'Lucy's horse bolted, apparently, tried to take some enormous hedge back at Fittlescombe. Seb was trying to stop her. They're both down.'

'Oh my God!' Kate gasped.

'Barney called an ambulance,' said Penny. 'And Richard Smart's there already.'

Her eyes were welling with tears. One look at her face told Henry it was serious.

Turning around, he jabbed his heels into his horse's side and thundered back in the direction of the village at breakneck speed.

Santiago put his arm around a shaking Kate. 'Come on. Seb'll be OK.'

'I'll drive you down there,' said Penny.

Nodding wordlessly, Kate followed her to the car.

Henry reached Fittlescombe just as Seb was being lifted into the ambulance. Lucy's horse, the grey whose girth he'd tightened just hours earlier, was sprawled on the ground dead, its neck broken at an almost ninety-degree angle. It was a ghastly sight, but Henry's gaze was fixed on Sebastian. He was in a spinal brace and he wasn't moving.

'I'm his brother!' Henry vaulted off his horse and ran towards the vehicle. 'Is he conscious?'

'No,' said one of the paramedics, putting a comforting hand on Henry's arm.

'Is he OK?' Henry looked at Sebastian's face in horror. The entire left side had been pulverized, and was a mess of blood and bone. His right eye was open but glazed. 'Is he . . . he's not dead?'

'No. He's heavily sedated,' said the paramedic. 'But we need to get him to hospital right away. You can come with him if you like, but we have to go now.'

Henry climbed into the back of the ambulance, resting his hand numbly on Seb's.

'What about the other rider? The woman?' he asked, belatedly. 'My brother was trying to stop her horse when it happened. Did they take her to A&E first?'

The paramedic signalled to the driver they were ready to go. As he jumped in and began closing the doors, Henry started as he caught sight of Richard Smart standing by the hedge like a statue, staring into space. Another ambulanceman was trying to talk to him, putting a blanket around his shoulders, but Richard didn't register at all.

'I'm afraid she died, sir,' the paramedic told Henry.

The doors closed and they drove away.

CHAPTER TWENTY-THREE

'Do you want me to drive?'

Eva stood next to the car while Henry loaded her suitcase into the boot. She was on her way to Sweden for her cousin's wedding. She and Henry had been supposed to attend together, but when Eva had asked him last weekend if he was still coming, Henry had looked at her as if she'd lost her mind.

'Don't be silly. I can't possibly leave Seb. Or Richard.'

Eva felt like saying that it had been three weeks since the accident that had rocked the valley to its core. That Seb's doctors had confirmed he would make a full recovery. That Seb had Kate to take care of him. And that Richard was still so poleaxed with grief over Lucy's death, he wouldn't notice whether Henry went away for one weekend, any more than he'd notice if the moon turned purple. But she didn't. Since the hunt tragedy, Eva had learned to avoid any sort of confrontation with Henry. Not because he overreacted, but because he didn't react at all. She might as well stand and scream at a statue for all the response she got.

'Henry?' She tapped him on the shoulder.

'Hmm?'

'I said I can drive if you like.'

In sweatpants, UGG boots and an oversized J.Crew hoodie, Eva looked comfortable and relaxed, if a little tired. Henry hadn't come to bed till almost three last night, breaking her sleep, something that was becoming a pattern. Henry, by contrast, looked like the walking dead, in the same jeans and Labatt's beer sweatshirt he'd been wearing for the last three days. His hair was dirty, his face unshaven and his gaze fixed, as usual, on some mysterious point in the middle distance.

'I'm fine to drive,' he said, closing the boot. 'Why wouldn't I be?'

'I don't know,' said Eva. Taking her life in her hands she added, 'Have you had a drink today?'

Henry's brow furrowed. 'I'm fine.'

'I'll take that as a yes,' said Eva, grabbing the keys out of his hand and sliding into the driver's seat. She didn't want to miss her plane. 'We'll get you a coffee at the airport before you drive back.'

The roads around Hanborough were clear – the scrum of reporters and TV crews who'd descended after the accident had finally moved on – and it wasn't long before they reached the M25. Henry spent most of the time staring out of the window.

'I wish you'd talk to me,' said Eva, keeping her eyes on the road. 'You can, you know.'

Henry sighed. 'There's nothing to say.'

Eva bit her lip. She tried not to take it personally, but it was hard. Of course Lucy Smart's death was awful, and it affected all of them. And Richard *was* Henry's best friend, so perhaps that added to the worry. But from the way Henry was acting, staggering around in a daze, neglecting his business, his relationship, the works at Hanborough – everything, you'd be forgiven for thinking that he was the one who'd just lost his wife. The only person who seemed able to reach him at all was Flora. Which also upset Eva, although at the same time she was grateful for Flora's help.

'Please talk to him while I'm gone,' Eva had begged her yesterday. The two women had been strolling in the castle grounds, talking. 'See if you can find out what's at the bottom of all this.'

'I'll try,' Flora said awkwardly. 'But I suspect he's just in shock. He really doesn't confide in me much, you know.'

'Well, he doesn't confide in me at all,' said Eva, unable completely to keep the bitterness out of her voice. 'Just do what you can.'

They drove the rest of the way to Heathrow in silence. At Terminal 5, Henry unloaded Eva's bag. To her surprise, he pulled her into his arms and hugged her fiercely.

'I'm sorry,' he whispered in her ear. 'I do love you.'

It was the first affectionate thing he'd said to her in weeks. Eva was shocked by how much relief she felt. 'I love you too,' she said, hugging him back tightly. 'Talk to Flora, Henry. Talk to somebody.'

Kissing him on the cheek, she turned and hurried towards the check-in.

Henry got back into the car, relieved to be alone. He stopped at the first service station to buy a cup of coffee. It tasted bitter and unpleasant, and reminded him how hungry he was, although at the same time he didn't feel able to eat. But he drank it anyway.

He would stop in at the hospital on his way back and

visit Seb. Henry hated hospitals. He hated the smell of disin-
fectant and floor polish and the institutional atmosphere, all
of which reminded him of prep school, and he never knew
what to say when sitting at someone's bedside. Especially
Seb's. But it was one of the few things that assuaged his
guilt, just a little bit. Going through the motions of being a
'good' brother. Doing something he actively disliked for
somebody else's sake, as a tiny penance for the huge wrongs
he'd done, that could never be undone.

Lucy was dead.

Dead.

Henry felt her loss like a punch to the stomach, a horrible
tangle of emotions lodged in his gut like a ball of thorns.
Had he loved her? He still didn't really know. All he knew
was that he had no right to feel anything; no right to grief
or pain or any emotion except the guilt that enveloped him
each night like a heavy, suffocating blanket, robbing him of
sleep to the point where he could barely function.

And meanwhile, of course, Richard was devastated, and
needed Henry's support. But how could Henry give it,
knowing what he'd done? Knowing the magnitude of his
betrayal?

He'd betrayed Sebastian too, of course. But that was
different. Kate wasn't dead, and nor was Seb, thank God.
Henry still had time to make it up to his brother. And Eva.

The list of people he owed a piece of his soul to was
getting longer and longer, dragging Henry down like chains
on a condemned prisoner. Since the accident, life had felt
like hell. The sun could shine, and Hanborough could dazzle,
and his business could soar and Eva could shower him with
love. But none of it mattered. None of it got through.

Henry didn't deserve to be happy. To be alive when Lucy was dead.

In the end, perhaps, it was as simple as that.

'Wot, no grapes?'

Seb grinned as Henry pulled up a chair at his bedside and sat down empty-handed.

'Sorry,' Henry said blankly.

Seb's room was nice, as far as hospital rooms went. There was a window overlooking the gardens and a Formica side table smothered with flowers, Get Well Soon cards and gifts, most of them related to hunting, including a large chocolate fox whose tail had already been half eaten.

In the days immediately after the accident, it had been unclear whether Sebastian would have permanent brain damage, or if his spine and leg injuries would end up confining him to a wheelchair for life. The strength and speed of his recovery had been remarkable, however, and his doctors had told Kate that, beyond using a walking stick to help with a slight limp, he should lead a completely normal life.

'You know, Lady Saxton Brae, I don't think I've ever met someone with quite such a relentlessly positive attitude,' Mr Crawford, Seb's surgeon, informed Kate. 'He's damned lucky to be alive.'

The worst part, for Seb, were the surgeries on his face, which were complicated and painful. He still needed at least two more procedures, which was one of the main reasons he was still in hospital now and not back home at Hatchings, much to his irritation.

'Are you hungry?' Henry asked. 'I should have stopped at Waitrose on the way here, I just totally forgot. Would you like me to run out and get you something now?'

'Don't be silly.' Sebastian frowned. 'I was only joking. Look, Henry old boy, are you all right?'

'Me?' Henry looked up, dazed. 'I'm fine. You're the one who broke both legs, fractured your spine and had your face pulverized like a crushed watermelon, remember?'

'Probably improved it,' muttered Seb good-naturedly. 'Let's face it, I was no oil painting before, was I? You definitely got the looks of the family.'

To Henry's own astonishment, not to mention embarrassment, he found himself starting to cry.

'Good heavens!' said Seb, attempting to sit up. 'What on earth's the matter?'

'Why are you so damn *nice* about everything? All the time?' Henry demanded.

Taking this to be a rhetorical question, Seb waited for Henry to go on.

'I've done some terrible things,' he said, running his hands through his hair frantically. Tears were still coursing down his cheeks. 'Unforgivable things.'

'Nonsense,' said Seb, almost angrily. 'You haven't killed anyone, have you?'

'Well, no,' admitted Henry. 'But—'

'If you're talking about what happened with Kate, I know,' said Seb, matter-of-factly.

Henry looked at him, mortified. 'You know? How?'

'Kate told me.'

'When?'

'When I came round after the brain surgery. So if that's what's brought all this on, for Christ's sake get over it. It's water under the bridge as far as I'm concerned.'

Henry shook his head, disbelieving. 'I'm your brother. I slept with your wife. How can you just forgive that?'

Sebastian sighed, then smiled. 'To be honest, Henry, I've never been as ballyhoo about sex as you are. I mean, I'm not saying I was happy about it. But Kate's sorry, and you're sorry, and well . . . that's an end to it, isn't it?'

'Is it?'

'I think so,' said Seb. 'There's nothing like getting your head kicked in by a horse and almost dying to put things in perspective. Especially when one thinks about the poor gal who *did* die. Richard and those children.' He shook his head sadly. '*That's* a bloody tragedy. If you want to blub about something, blub about that.'

Henry stared at his brother. He'd always loved Seb. But, at the same time, he'd also always viewed him as a bit of a buffoon. And he'd resented him, bitterly at times, for inheriting their father's title and the estate, when he, Henry, was so clearly the superior of the two brothers. More intelligent, more talented, more resourceful, more deserving.

Now he saw clearly just how wrong he'd been.

One of them was a fool all right, but it wasn't Sebastian. He was Henry's superior in every way.

'Nothing's unforgivable, Henry,' Seb told him now. 'Where there's life, there's hope and all that.'

Henry wiped his eyes, too moved to know what to say.

Hugging his brother wordlessly, he left the room.

Then he drove back to Hanborough, unearthed a bottle of twelve-year-old single malt, before sitting down at the kitchen table and drinking until he passed out.

'He's in there.'

Mrs French looked at Flora anxiously and pointed towards the kitchen.

'He hasn't been to bed. He won't let me go in, won't talk

to me, won't take any calls, not even from Eva. He's got a business meeting here this morning that I suppose I ought to cancel, but I don't even like to do that without his permission.'

'What makes you think he'll talk to me?' asked Flora. She'd woken up early again – ever since her break-up with Mason, a decent night's sleep seemed to be eluding her – and decided she might as well drive up to the castle and get started. Graydon had called her last night, their first conversation in weeks, and had presented her with a long list of demands, complaining again about the slow pace of progress on Hanborough's new, much more modern East Wing.

'I don't think you understand what a big deal this hunting accident was here,' Flora protested. 'Henry's brother almost died.'

'That's no reason for works to slow down,' insisted Graydon.

'Henry and Eva wanted some peace for a few weeks,' Flora explained patiently.

'Well, they can't have it!' Graydon snapped. 'You work for me, Flora, not them. Or had you forgotten?'

'Of course not,' said Flora. She couldn't understand why he was so angry.

'I'd have hoped that now you no longer have a wedding to distract you, or somebody else's money to fall back on, you'd have refocused your energies on your career,' Graydon observed cruelly. 'But perhaps there's something else on your mind? Something more important than GJD winning International Designer of the Year?'

It was almost as if he was alluding to something specific, although Flora had no idea what. She already spent every waking hour up at Hanborough. What more, exactly, did he want from her?

Mrs French put a hand on Flora's shoulder.

'You're the only one he ever talks to,' she said, answering Flora's earlier question. 'Well, you and Dr Smart. But he's in no position to help, poor man, and with Eva away . . . '

'All right,' said Flora. 'I'll give it a try.'

She waited till Henry's secretary had gone back into the office, then tapped on the kitchen door.

'For fuck's sake,' Henry barked. 'What part of "go away" do you not understand?'

'I understand it,' said Flora, turning the handle and entering the lion's den. 'I'm just choosing to ignore you.'

Henry was sitting on the floor, leaning back against the wall, his legs sprawled out in front of him. There was an almost empty bottle of whisky on the table, along with various discarded crisp packets, and a half-full crystal tumbler on the floor beside him. He wasn't slurring his words. And he hadn't actually been sick, thank goodness. But the glazed, belligerent look in his eyes made it clear he was very, very drunk.

Moving to the table, Flora started cleaning up, scrunching up the crisp packets and throwing them in the bin before reaching for the whisky bottle.

'Leave it,' growled Henry.

'I don't think so,' said Flora. 'That's not what friends do.'

Henry snorted what might have been a laugh. 'So we're friends, are we?'

'Aren't we?' said Flora, pouring the remnants of the bottle down the sink.

'What the hell are you doing?' protested Henry. 'That's a Glenfarclas 1962.'

Flora turned and looked at him.

'I don't care. It's still poison.'

In a fitted wine-red sweater dress and black boots, she looked more like a 1950s pin-up girl than ever. Even in his depleted state, Henry found it impossible not to let his eyes be drawn towards her full bosom and improbably tiny waist. She really was all curves, like a sexy but disapproving cello.

'You do realize you can't carry on like this?' she said, rinsing her hands under the tap and drying them on a Great Houses of West Sussex tea towel hanging over the rail of the Aga. 'Eva's worried to death about you. Everyone is.'

'Only because they don't know the truth,' muttered Henry, knocking back the four fingers of precious whisky in his glass before Flora could tip that down the drain as well. 'If they knew, they wouldn't worry about me. They'd hate me. Although probably not as much as I hate myself.'

Flora walked over slowly and sat down on the floor beside him.

'I know the truth,' she reminded him. 'I know about you and Lucy. And I don't hate you.'

'Well, you should,' said Henry, not meeting her eye. 'You threw me out of your house when you first found out, remember? You said it couldn't end well and that I was as bad as George Savile. That George and I were "two selfish peas in a pod".'

'I'm not saying it wasn't selfish,' Flora clarified. 'Affairs usually are. I'm saying I don't hate you for it. And hating yourself won't bring her back.'

'Oh God!' Henry wailed in pure anguish. Reaching out, he clung on to Flora, burying his head in her chest and sobbing like a child. Instinctively Flora started stroking his hair and making soothing, *shhhhh* noises. Henry was right that he didn't deserve sympathy. But Flora couldn't help giving it to him anyway. His remorse was so heartfelt and

327

so all encompassing, it was hard not to. And there was another reason too, one she'd tried to deny to herself for a long time, but which refused to be silenced now as she sat here with Henry in her arms.

I love him, she realized miserably.

'She was my friend's wife! My best friend's wife,' Henry rambled on. 'What does that make me?'

'Human?' said Flora. 'Look, it was wrong. It was. But we can't help who we fall in love with.'

Henry looked up at her. Still drunk, his pupils dilated, he reached up and touched her face. Flora felt as if she might pass out from the maelstrom of emotions she was feeling. The urge to lean down and press her lips to his was so powerful it hurt. With a superhuman effort, she resisted it.

You're Eva's friend, she told herself firmly. *He's grieving, and drunk, and out of his mind with guilt. None of this is real.*

'What's done is done,' she said, removing his hand and sitting up, extricating herself delicately from his vice-like grip. 'All you can do now is try to make it up to Eva. And Richard. Just . . . be a better person.'

'How?' asked Henry.

'By being one!' said Flora, exasperated. 'Stop all this for a start,' she said, removing his empty glass. 'Stop wallowing. Stop making Lucy's death about you. The more you drink, the more likely you are to blurt out something stupid.'

Henry looked horrified. Flora was right. Sometimes the urge to come clean, to confess his sins to Richard and Eva and the world felt hopelessly strong.

'The only person on earth who knows about you and Lucy is me,' said Flora.

'I know,' Henry murmured. 'That's why I can talk to you. You're the only person who sees me as I am.'

Flora half smiled. Was that a compliment? As usual with Henry, it was hard to tell.

'I'm never going to say anything. You have my word,' she told him. 'But I need you to promise the same thing. For your sake and everyone else's.'

Henry half smiled back. 'I promise. Thank you.'

He hugged her again, less desperately this time but just as tightly, his body expressing the depth of his gratitude more eloquently than any words. Flora closed her eyes and hugged him back, allowing herself that one, brief moment.

'Well, well.'

Georgina Savile's voice cut through the silence like a sharpened shard of glass.

'What *have* I interrupted? Perhaps you'd like me to come back another time?'

'Not really,' Henry drawled, reluctantly letting go of Flora. His head lolled forward as he tried to focus on George, who looked elegant and professional in a cream silk shirt and peach woollen pencil skirt from Armani's A/W collection, her long blonde hair swept up in a businesslike chignon.

'He had a tough night,' explained Flora, getting up awkwardly off the floor, feeling very inelegant all of a sudden, a dumpy spinster next to George's glamorous trophy wife.

'I can see that,' snapped George. 'Unfortunately he still has responsibilities. We have a business to run.' She dropped her briefcase on the table with a loud clatter that made Henry wince. 'Not that I'd expect you to understand,' she told Flora, adding rudely, 'Don't you have some tiles to grout or some cushions to arrange or something?'

'George!' Henry reprimanded her.

'What?' George shot back waspishly. 'You want your little girlfriend to stay and hold your hand?'

'She's not—'

'It's OK,' said Flora, mortified. 'I have to get on anyway. I'll leave you to it.'

She hurried out of the kitchen, closing the door behind her before Henry had the chance to say another word.

'Right then,' George said briskly, as soon as Flora had gone. 'Shall we get down to business?'

'She's not my girlfriend,' said Henry, rubbing his eyes wearily. 'There's nothing going on. At all.'

'I couldn't care less about your love life,' trilled George. 'I've driven all the way from London to finalize these contracts, and that's what we're bloody well going to do.'

Henry was too drunk to notice the small muscle twitching uncontrollably at the top of her jaw, or the look of raw venom in her eyes. He was also far too drunk to read a contract, or make any sort of sensible business decision. He should just tell George to go. To drive back to London, and to stick her stupid contracts where the sun don't shine. Or at least to wait until he was sober enough to know what he was signing.

But he didn't. All the fight had gone out of him suddenly. The path of least resistance had never looked so appealing.

'Fine,' he slurred, holding out a shaking hand. 'Just give me a damn pen.'

CHAPTER TWENTY-FOUR

Lucy Smart's funeral was held on the first Sunday in April, and drew the biggest crowds seen at St Hilda's Church in Fittlescombe since Logan Cranley's society wedding a couple of years earlier. While close family and friends packed the pews inside, well-wishers from the hunt and the local villages huddled outside in the graveyard under two specially erected awnings, spilling out onto the village green beyond.

Although officially spring, it was a grey and cold day. A light but persistent drizzle that began at dawn had yet to let up, and by mid-morning was made worse by bitter easterly winds, flattening the first few daffodils brave enough to unfurl their cheerful yellow petals, and battering the already damp mourners as they clustered together for warmth. Some enterprising young men from the cricket club had rigged up loudspeakers so that those outside the church could hear the service. But even artificially enhanced, the Reverend Clempson's voice was soon swallowed by the wind and rain, with only a few snatched phrases and occasional strains of the organ making it through the lugubrious howl of the weather.

Slightly to her embarrassment, Flora had been given a spot inside the church next to Henry and Eva, only a few rows back from Lucy's grieving family. On Flora's other side, Jen Clempson, the vicar's wife, had tears streaming down her face as she fed her baby daughter, Diana, from a bottle of formula.

'Sorry,' she whispered to Flora, accepting the offer of a fourth tissue. 'I think it's my hormones. We weren't even that close. I just can't bear the thought of those poor children.'

In the front row, flanking their father who looked as if he'd aged ten years, Lucy's sons Archie and Harry stood as solemnly as soldiers, their little backs ramrod straight. Neither of them was crying. Perhaps, by this point, they had no tears left? Flora thought back to her own father's funeral. Of course she had been much older than the Smart boys, and had already got used to life without her dad. Not that prison was remotely the same as death. Nothing was, nor could anything truly prepare you for the loss of a parent. She remembered standing beside her mother, staring at her father's coffin, waiting for the tears to come. But they never did. She felt guilty about it for years afterwards.

Thinking of guilt made her turn and look at Henry.

He too was staring straight ahead now, clasping Eva's hand tightly, singing 'Jerusalem', Lucy's 'favourite hymn', according to her mother, and doing a decent job of holding it together. There'd been a moment earlier when Flora had worried he might unravel. Richard Smart had walked over and hugged Henry as soon as he arrived at church.

'Thank God you're here, mate.'

'Of course I'm here,' said Henry.

'I bloody hate these things,' said Richard, while his

mother-in-law settled the boys into their places. 'Lucy hated them too, all the eulogizing and sanctimonious crap. The vicar asked me the other day what Lucy's favourite hymn was. I mean, really? She never came to church. That's like asking the Pope for his favourite Black Sabbath song.'

Henry tried to laugh, the way he would have in the old days, but his face just froze. Luckily Eva stepped in and hugged Richard before he had a chance to notice anything was wrong. Soon after that the service started. But Flora watched Henry standing there, fighting for breath, gripping the pew in front of him for support so tightly his knuckles went white.

After the final hymn, the Reverend Clempson led the mourners outside while the pallbearers followed with Lucy's coffin. Flora couldn't help but well up herself as the box was lowered into the earth and the grave covered over, Archie and Harry clinging tightly to their father, still not crying but unable to watch their mother being taken from them for the final time.

'Terrible thing,' muttered Sebastian Saxton Brae. Released from hospital a week earlier, he stood directly behind Flora in a heavy black overcoat, leaning slightly on a walking stick but otherwise in apparently good health. 'I'm not sure they should be here.' He nodded towards Lucy and Richard's boys. 'My father never let Henry come to our mother's funeral.'

'He didn't?' Flora's eyes widened.

Seb shook his head. 'He thought it would be too much for him. I think he was probably right.'

I don't know, thought Flora. Funerals were about acceptance, after all. About closure. Saying goodbye. If Henry had never really accepted his mother's death, was it any wonder his relationships with women were so hideously dysfunctional?

She smiled wryly. She'd always hated it when Mason played amateur psychologist with her, and now here she was doing the same thing to Henry.

On the other side of the grave, behind the vicar, Barney Griffith put a hand on Eva Gunnarson's shoulder.

'Hey.'

'Hey.' Eva spun around, smiling gratefully. She didn't know what she would have done without Barney's friendship these past few weeks. Flora had been a big help with Henry's depression, but it was only really Barney who had thought to ask Eva how *she* was doing. Their afternoon walks with the dogs had become the highlight of Eva's days when she was at Hanborough, a sad reflection on how gloomy life with Henry had become and how isolating country life could be for an 'outsider'.

'Are you going to The Fox afterwards?' Eva asked. Richard had laid on drinks and food at the Fittlescombe pub for everyone who'd come to pay their respects to Lucy.

'Probably not,' said Barney. It was common knowledge in the valley that Barney was the only person, other than Seb Saxton Brae, actually to have witnessed the accident. The thought of being accosted by one of Lucy's drunken, grief-stricken relatives and asked to relive that awful day had been filling Barney with panic for the last week. 'Would you mind awfully? I'm just not sure I can face it.'

'Of course not,' said Eva. 'I probably won't stay long myself. Flora and I thought we might walk back to Hanborough together, if the rain doesn't get worse. Clear our heads.'

'I'd hold that thought if I were you,' said Barney.

Eva followed his gaze. On the far side of the village green

a black limousine had pulled up. An immaculately dressed man in his early thirties stepped out of it, popping open a large black umbrella and setting out across the grass towards the church.

'You know who that is, don't you?' Barney asked, unable completely to keep the note of defeat out of his voice as the figure drew nearer.

'Who?' said Eva.

'It's Mason Parker.'

Eva gasped. He was right. She'd seen pictures of Mason before, although she'd never have recognized him from this distance. 'What's he doing here? And how do you even know what he looks like?' she added reproachfully to Barney, who blushed.

'I might have googled him once or twice,' he admitted.

They both watched as Mason reached the churchyard gate, hanging back discreetly until the crowds had dispersed. When Flora finally looked up and saw him there, she grabbed hold of Seb Saxton Brae's arm and went quite white, as if she'd seen a ghost.

'Are you all right?' Seb asked.

Lady Saxton Brae, aware of some sort of commotion, hurried over and hovered by her husband nervously, like an agitated queen bee protecting its hive. Kate felt relieved – now that Seb knew the truth about her fling with Henry – not to have the secret hanging over her like the sword of Damocles. But she knew that Flora also knew about it – that Eva had confided in her on that awful afternoon. She wouldn't feel completely comfortable until Flora Fitzwilliam had packed up and returned to the United States, where she so obviously belonged.

'I'm fine,' said Flora. She started to walk towards Mason

like someone in a trance, her feet acting quite independently of her brain.

A few moments later she was standing right in front of him, the rain stinging her cheeks as she looked up into his familiar, yet somehow incongruous features. Dark, wet figures streamed past them towards the pub or their homes or cars, but Flora felt them only as shadows, unreal creatures existing outside the bubble of herself and Mason and the church gate that had become, in that instant, the world.

'Hello, Flora.'

Even his voice sounded different. Or rather, it sounded the same, but wrong; as out of place here, outside St Hilda's Church, as a police siren would be in a Tibetan monastery or a bird call deep under the ocean.

'Hello.'

'I'm sorry, I didn't know . . . ' Mason looked at the gravesite awkwardly. 'Was it a friend of yours?'

Flora shook her head. 'Not really.'

'Can we talk?' asked Mason. 'Go somewhere? I've got my car.' He pointed across the green.

Flora nodded mutely. She wondered when, exactly, she was going to wake up.

Mason drove them into Chichester where he was staying at The Swan, a rather frou-frou hotel-cum-gastropub famous for its traditional afternoon teas.

'I don't understand how we're the most obese nation on earth when the British clog their arteries with afternoon tea,' Mason observed, as the waitress set down an impressive array of cakes, sandwiches, scones, clotted cream and jam in front of them on some sort of silver tower.

'Portion control.' Flora smiled, helping herself to a small

piece of Battenburg and a toasted teacake. 'They're not big on soda either. Why are you here, Mason?'

It wasn't asked angrily or aggressively, more in the tone of someone who genuinely wanted to know.

'I'm not entirely sure,' said Mason, equally genuine. 'I had to see you, I guess, face to face. To apologize.'

'Ah,' said Flora, not sure if she felt disappointed or relieved that this was the reason.

Reaching across the table, Mason took both her cold hands in his. 'I'm so sorry, Flora. I really am. It's over with me and Henrietta,' he added, almost as an afterthought, pouring himself a cup of tea from the Wedgwood pot between them.

'That was quick!' observed Flora, who still felt as if this were a conversation in a dream, or that it was happening to someone else.

'It was never going to last,' said Mason. 'I mean, it was never about Hen. It was always about us. I loved you,' he said, staring down at the steaming brown liquid in his cup, clearly struggling with his emotions. 'I still love you.'

'I still love you too,' said Flora, only realizing in that instant that she meant it. 'But it won't work, Mason.'

He forced himself to look up at her. 'Why won't it?'

Flora sighed. How to answer that question?

'I'm not saying I don't agree,' he clarified. 'I just want to know why. I want to hear it from your side, Flora. Because I don't think I've ever understood you, not really.'

That makes two of us, thought Flora. She tried to explain.

'It's lots of things. Your life, your family, the bank. Being a partner's wife. That's not me. I thought it was, for a while. I wanted it to be.'

Mason nodded. 'I know. The irony is, I fell in love with

337

you because you didn't fit the mould. But the problem with that is . . . '

'That I don't fit the mould?' Flora smiled ruefully.

'Right.'

'Coming back here, to England, that changed things too,' said Flora. 'It brought back a lot of stuff from my past, what happened to my dad, all of that.' She didn't mention Henry Saxton Brae, and her wildly conflicted feelings about him. 'And then there's my work.'

'Ah, yes. That.' Mason frowned. 'Your "artistic expression".'

'You see, exactly!' Flora sat back. 'You've never taken it seriously.'

Mason didn't deny it. Graydon James might think of himself as Michelangelo and Flora as his protégée. But Mason would never see interior design as 'real' art.

'I saw Graydon the other day at the Met,' he said, switching gears.

'Did he talk to you?' asked Flora.

'No. He was wearing, I don't know what you'd call it, some sort of headdress? He looked absolutely ridiculous. And he had three male models with him, trotting along behind him like chicks following their mother. I don't think he had time for the likes of me.'

'We're barely communicating at the moment.' Flora filled Mason in on Graydon's strange behaviour during his recent visit, and the radio silence followed by the angry outbursts. 'It doesn't help that he seems to have become thick as thieves with Georgina Savile, who wants my head on a spike.'

'Why?' asked Mason.

Flora's mind flew back to Henry, and George walking in on them in the kitchen at Hanborough. *Walking in on nothing.*

But it wasn't like George to let a little thing like facts get in the way of a good vendetta.

'Don't know,' Flora sighed. 'Don't care either.' She looked at her watch. 'I'd better go.'

Mason hesitated, as if thinking about trying to persuade her otherwise. But he didn't say anything.

'What will you do?' he said. 'Once Hanborough's finished, I mean.'

Flora bit her lip. 'I'm not sure.' She told him about the work she'd done for Jason Cranley and the free design advice she'd offered Penny de la Cruz for her Battersea gallery.

'A hundred and fifty grand for two weeks' work?' Mason was impressed. 'That's amazing, Flora. Good for you.'

'It doesn't mean I can repeat it, though,' she said cautiously.

'It doesn't mean you can't either,' said Mason. 'I've always thought you were better than Graydon. You should totally go it alone. Start your own business. Why not?'

'Oh, I don't know. It's not that easy.' Flora laughed nervously. 'Graydon's the one with the brand name. He's my security.'

Leaning across the table, Mason kissed her tenderly on the top of the head.

'*You*'re your security, Flora. That's why we aren't getting married. Remember?'

CHAPTER TWENTY-FIVE

'This is fantastic! There must be over two hundred people here.'

Laura Baxter scanned the room, crammed wall to wall with the great and the good from south London's buzzing art scene, all guzzling Penny de la Cruz's prosecco and stuffing themselves with Marks & Spencer's canapés.

'I know.' Penny beamed. 'And we didn't even use a PR firm. Can you believe it?'

Laura could. The only person surprised by Penny's success was Penny herself. Tonight was the official launch party for her new gallery, showing Penny's own work – large, abstract canvases in ethereal greens and blues – as well as pieces by a select few other artists, including some breathtaking photography by Barney Griffith.

'Is that Wraggsbottom?' Laura asked, catching sight of an enormous, stylized, staggered-shutter shot in black and white, showing shafts of sunlight breaking through clouds and hitting a tiled roof. 'I think that's our chimney!'

'Could well be,' said Penny. 'It's not sold yet. Do you want to make Barney an offer?'

'Definitely not,' said Gabe, kissing Penny and catching the fag end of their conversation. 'We're broke.'

'We are *not* broke,' said Laura crossly. 'You're just mean. There's a difference. How much is it?' she asked, ignoring Gabe's groans and moving closer to the photograph.

'Ladies and gentlemen, your attention, please!'

Santiago was dinging his wineglass loudly with a spoon, trying to make himself heard above the din.

'Saved by the bell,' Gabe whispered to Penny.

'Thank you all for coming.' In a dark suit and navy blue tie, with his black hair newly cut and his white teeth dazzling against his permanently bronzed skin, Santiago de la Cruz was still easily the most attractive man in the room, at least in Penny's opinion. Even after more than ten years together, she still had to pinch herself sometimes to think that he had chosen her. 'My beautiful wife would like to say a few words.'

'No, I wouldn't!' squealed Penny as a hush began to fall. 'Not yet!' But it was too late. With the entire room of artists, collectors and critics turned expectantly in her direction, there was no option but to step up to the dais.

'Welcome, everyone. This is an incredibly exciting day for all of us at the gallery. I promise to let you get back to your drinking, and hopefully cheque-writing, as soon as possible.' She smiled knowingly at Laura Baxter, and at Fast Eddie Wellesley, her former neighbour at Riverside Hall, where poor Richard Smart was still holed up, swathed in grief. Eddie had just flown in from the Bahamas with his wife Annabel, and had been eyeing a bronze sculpture of a sleeping whippet all evening, easily the most expensive piece in the gallery. 'But first I have a few important people to thank.'

At the back of the room, Flora smiled encouragingly at Barney Griffith as Penny singled him out for praise, not just for his photographs, but for the immense support and encouragement he'd offered as she got the gallery up and running. This was a big night for Barney, and he'd pulled out all the stops for the occasion. In a dark suit that actually fitted him for once, with his sandy hair cut short and his hazel eyes offset by a gorgeous, cornflower-blue silk tie, he looked positively dapper, if a little nervous. *How have I never noticed how good-looking he is?* Flora thought, as he flashed her a bashful smile. She was glad she was here to support him, especially as she'd almost cancelled just a few hours earlier.

It had been a terrible week. The nominations for the International Designer of the Year would be officially announced tomorrow, and the already frenzied pace of works up at the castle had now reached fever pitch. Every day Graydon demanded new images to submit to the committee, even though the rules clearly stated that no additional materials would be looked at by the judges until after the shortlist nominees had been announced.

'What the fuck is this?' Graydon had snarled down the line at an utterly exhausted Flora three days ago, after receiving the latest in a long line of shots of the party barn roof.

'It's what you asked for,' said Flora through gritted teeth. 'A night image of the interior, showing the retractable glass.'

'It's revolting. Offensively bad. It looks like something a six-year-old took on their mother's iPhone. Do it again.'

'OK.' Flora closed her eyes and thought of her happy place. 'I'll send you something tonight.'

'Not tonight. Now. I need it now!'

'Graydon, it's three in the afternoon here. It's broad daylight. I thought you wanted a night shot?'

'Don't *tell* me what I want. *Give* me what I want!' he bellowed.

Flora was used to Graydon's tantrums and unreasonableness under pressure, but this was ridiculous, even for him.

The work stress might be easier to bear if her personal life weren't also in utter tatters. She'd felt better about things after Mason's visit. It was good to clear the air and to part as friends and, although it was childish, Flora couldn't help but feel a little gratified that the poisonous Henrietta Branston had already been given the boot. On the other hand, closure with Mason meant exactly that. A huge, important chapter in Flora's life was closing. It didn't help that while Flora was busy dismantling the last pieces of what she'd believed would be her future with Mason, Henry was busy rebuilding his relationship with Eva.

Ten days ago, Henry had announced that he needed to get away, ostensibly from Hanborough and the works, but he confided to Flora that it was really about getting some distance from Lucy's death, not to mention George. So he had whisked Eva off to the Bahamas for a pre-wedding honeymoon, pictures of which were splashed all over the gossip magazines. Every morning Flora would drive back up to the castle, exhausted after the latest battle with Graydon and wracked with insomnia about her uncertain future, only to find Mono-Tony's workmen drooling over the latest picture of Eva in a barely there Heidi Klein bikini, draped over Henry like a groupie at a rock concert, radiating contentment and wealth and happy-ever-after.

Be happy for them, she told herself. *They're both your friends.* But it was hard.

'Don't beat yourself up,' Barney Griffith told her, turning up at Peony Cottage uninvited, and unannounced, as he was increasingly wont to do. 'No one likes seeing other people in love when their own love life's going down in flames.'

If only that were the only reason, thought Flora. But she wasn't ready to admit to herself that she might be in love with Henry Saxton Brae, never mind share that awful truth with anybody else.

'My love life isn't *going down in flames*,' she protested. 'It just changed direction.'

'Changed direction towards the completely burning building, you mean? The one that's a hundred per cent on fire?'

'That is not what I mean!' said Flora indignantly.

'You have to admit, it is smouldering a bit,' said Barney, unable to resist smiling just a little. Mason Parker being officially out of Flora's life was excellent news as far as Barney was concerned.

'Mason and I made a mature decision not to continue with something that wasn't working,' said Flora, po-faced.

'Right. So will you call the fire brigade or should I?' Barney grinned. 'Oh, come on. Lighten up! Your engagement tanked and you feel like shit. It's OK, I get it. I've been there, remember? Recently.'

Thank God for Barney, thought Flora. Looking at him now across the room, swatting away Penny's praise with an embarrassed frown that kept threatening to turn into a smile, Flora thought again how easy her life would be if she could fall for someone like him. Someone kind and talented, and not remotely alpha. But as much as she adored Barney as a friend, she simply couldn't find him attractive, even looking as dashing and Eddie Redmayne-ish as he did tonight. The fact remained, Barney wasn't really ready to take care of himself, never mind somebody else.

Perhaps Mason was right, and Flora should be her own security. But as much as she wanted her own career and life, the part of her that craved a man to look after her wouldn't be silenced so easily.

'Finally, I would like to say a heartfelt thanks to the lovely and talented Flora Fitzwilliam.'

Flora was miles away. Only when she heard her name did she realize Penny was still talking.

'When I asked Flora for advice on designing the gallery, this stunning place we're all standing in now, I was expecting a few sketches at most. Instead, and despite her own huge workload over at Hanborough Castle, she gave so generously of her ideas and her time and her vision, she ended up designing the entire space from scratch.'

Flora felt the panic rising up within her as the first ripple of applause rang out. There were a lot of famous and well-connected people at tonight's launch, not to mention a lot of journalists. If word reached Graydon that she'd been moonlighting for Penny de la Cruz behind his back, especially in his current mood, Flora dreaded to think what might happen.

'As I think you'll all agree, the final result is quite magical,' enthused Penny, to more applause. 'Flora, where are you?'

'She's over there!' Barney Griffith said loudly, pointing Flora out to anyone who might have missed her. To Barney, as always, Flora looked radiant, but a less biased observer might have remarked that she wasn't at her best tonight. That her cream pencil skirt and pale pink polka-dot blouse washed out an already wan, exhausted complexion, and that her decision to let her hair 'air-dry' on the train to London might well have made sense in terms of time, but less so in terms of pure aesthetics.

'I really didn't do anything,' Flora pleaded ineffectually. But Penny was on a roll.

'Nonsense! You did everything. And, as you didn't let me pay you for it, I'm afraid you must at least let me thank you tonight. Sasha?'

To Flora's horror, a pretty, Sloaney blonde approached the dais, teetering under the weight of the most enormous bouquet of flowers Flora had ever seen.

'On behalf of myself and everyone at the gallery.' Penny beamed, holding the flowers out towards Flora like a holy offering. 'Thank you, Flora, for giving us a space worthy of our fabulous artists.'

Cheers broke out again. Flora found herself moving inexorably forward towards the dais, swept on by countless well-meaning hands and nods and smiles. Before she knew it she was holding the ridiculously enormous bunch of flowers, as phone after phone snapped pictures of her.

She groaned inwardly, a rigor-mortis smile fixed on her face.

All it takes is one Instagram. One tweet.

Graydon's going to go ballistic.

Her only hope was that, with the International Designer of the Year nominations being announced tomorrow, he'd be too swept up in either excited joy or crushing disappointment to notice anything else.

If they were nominated for Hanborough, all the rancour and problems of the last few months would be behind them for good. For all his mood swings and capriciousness, Graydon had been an incredible mentor to Flora. When they worked together, they were a great team. Maybe even the best in the business.

Kissing Penny on the cheek through a veritable jungle of foliage, Flora said a silent prayer.

Please let us be nominated.

Please, please, please.

Flora stayed in London that night, at Jason Cranley's house. Jason and George had evolved from clients into friends, and it was lovely to wake up in a real home for once, rather than a soulless hotel room.

'Morning, sleepyhead.'

George smiled at Flora as she shuffled into the kitchen and handed her a just-brewed Nespresso.

'The built-in sofa works beautifully in here, doesn't it?' she observed happily, patting herself on the back for her own work. She was wearing the fluffy white dressing gown and matching slippers that Jason and George had provided, and feeling as pampered as an Egyptian queen. Like everything else in the guest bedroom suite, from the sheets and towels to the soap, scented candles, assortment of magazines and handmade chocolates from the sweet little shop on Hampstead Heath, the dressing gown was the last word in comfort. Flora felt as if she were wrapped in lightly warmed clouds.

'You know, if they don't give you another baby, you could always adopt me.' She looked at George hopefully, sipping the perfect coffee he'd just made her.

'You'll be too busy and important for the likes of us once you win that award,' said Jason, who was sitting at the table, deep in a *Guardian* piece on terrorism. Looking up at Flora he added, 'Today's the day, isn't it? What time are the nominees announced?'

'Not till ten,' said Flora, yawning and sitting down herself. Reaching forward, she helped herself to a slice of toast and some berries from the bowl in the middle of the table.

Jason looked at her, then at George.

'Er, Flora darling?' George said gently. 'It's a quarter past ten now.'

'*What?*' Flora spat out her coffee, promptly staining her perfect white robe. 'It can't be! I never sleep past eight.'

'That guest bed is *very* comfortable,' observed Jason mildly. 'I daresay you needed the rest.'

'Fuck!' Standing up, Flora spun around uselessly like a lost robot. 'Where's my phone? Where's my computer? Shit!'

'Calm down,' said George, putting a hand on her shoulder and guiding her back into her seat like a nurse helping a confused patient. 'You can use ours.'

Jason slid the already open MacBook Air across the table. With trembling fingers, Flora tapped out a search for this year's nominations.

The awards committee website opened. The very first image was a stunning shot of Hanborough Castle, shrouded in mist, the glass roof of the party barn just visible in the foreground against a backdrop of the original building's mellow stone.

Flora gasped. 'We got it!' Her hands flew to her mouth in delighted disbelief. 'We're nominated! We got it!'

'That's fantastic!' George beamed.

Jumping up, Flora allowed herself to be hugged, high-fived and twirled around in turn by each of them. It had been a terrible few months, really awful. She hadn't realized until this moment quite how down and exhausted she'd been. But this changed everything. She might not have Mason, or Henry, or any clear plan for the future. But her career was about to be catapulted onto a whole new level. Despite all the battles and problems they'd had on this job, Flora realized she owed a huge part of that triumph to Graydon.

'I need to call my boss,' she mumbled, sitting down again and scrolling further down the results page on the website. 'I wonder who else is nominated.'

George and Jason watched like proud parents as Flora read on. Quickly, though, they saw her expression turn from delighted to confused to horrified.

'What's the matter?' George asked. 'Is something wrong?'

'I don't believe it.' Flora stared at the screen, shaking her head. 'The bastard. The fucking *bastard*! How could he?'

Pushing the computer away from her in disgust, she got up again and headed for the stairs.

'Where are you going?' Jason called after her. 'Can we help?'

'To get dressed,' Flora called back, already halfway up the stairs. 'He's not getting away with this. Not this time.'

Jason looked up at George. 'What the hell was that about?'

George raised an eyebrow and turned the screen around for Jason to see.

Under 'Nominations, International Designer of the Year', six names and projects were listed, in alphabetical order. Hanborough Castle was third on the list. The entry read:

'Project: Hanborough Castle. Restoration, West Sussex, UK.
Designer: Graydon James.'

The receptionist at GJD's London offices looked as if she wished the ground beneath the front desk would open up and swallow her.

'I can't let you up there, Flora.' She bit her lower lip. 'I'm really sorry.'

'What do you mean you "can't let me up there",' Flora snapped. 'It isn't up to you.' She knew she was being unfair. None of this was Katie's fault. But right now she didn't care. The red mist that had descended the moment she read Graydon's name on that list and searched in vain for her own was the only thing holding her together. Without her anger, she felt her legs might literally give way beneath her.

Ignoring Katie, she walked around the desk to the bank of lifts and pressed the call button.

'There's security up there, waiting.' The poor girl was almost pleading. She sounded as if she might burst into tears. 'Graydon's told them to have you physically removed if necessary. He cancelled all your passwords and access codes.'

'Fuck this,' said Flora, banging her fist on the wall in frustration as the lift failed to arrive. 'I'll take the goddamned stairs.'

'Flora!' Katie shouted in desperation. 'Please. I'll be sacked.'

Flora hesitated, then stopped.

Damn him! Damn Graydon. The coward wouldn't even answer his phone. And now he wanted to use this clueless socialite *schoolgirl* like some sort of human shield, to get her to do his dirty work for him? To cast Flora out into the wilderness?

'I have a contract, you know,' Flora said calmly, turning around. 'He has no legal right to do this.'

Katie gave her a look that clearly expressed what Flora already knew. *I'm on your side. But I can't help you.*

'He can't fire me by proxy. He needs to serve a written notice of dismissal and it has to have a reason on it.'

The girl shrugged helplessly.

'Tell him to call me,' said Flora, tightening the belt of her coat in an effort to hold on to the last shreds of her dignity as she swept back out onto the street.

It was freezing outside. The bright blue spring sky of earlier had given way to grey clouds and a bitter east wind that chafed at Flora's skin like a slapping hand. Glancing at her phone she saw she had six messages and three missed calls. None was from Graydon. It was still only noon, just two hours since the nominations had been announced. It would take time for the news of Graydon's betrayal to filter through to the design world at large, but the first calls, from friends and colleagues back in New York, were already starting to trickle in.

Graydon's attempted betrayal, Flora reminded herself. He was trying to take sole credit for her work at Hanborough, and had made a bold grab for the International Designer of the Year award, but that didn't mean he would succeed. Flora would launch a formal appeal to the judging committee. She would certainly file for unfair dismissal, if Graydon was in fact sacking her and not just making some childish, melo-dramatic point by barring her from the London offices.

'Miss?' A cabbie had pulled up to the corner. Flora clearly looked as if she were waiting.

'Marylebone High Street, please,' she said spontaneously, jumping into the taxi. 'I need to pick up a bag. Then on to Victoria Station.'

Georgina Savile was having a wonderful day.

She'd spent the morning strolling through the grounds at Hanborough, giving interviews to journalists in Henry's absence. By lunchtime she felt like quite the chatelaine.

'I haven't spoken to Henry and Eva yet, no,' she told the breathless woman from *Elle Décor*. 'But I know they'll be delighted to see Hanborough nominated. Henry always felt that Graydon James was the most talented designer working today. After four decades in the business, it's wonderful to have that talent recognized.'

It had been a difficult few weeks for George, too. First came Henry's recalcitrance, his stubborn refusal to get behind a new business combining Gigtix's expertise and e-customer reach with Graydon's global brand. He knew it made sense to partner with GJD. Business-wise, it was a no-brainer. His refusal to move forward was clearly motivated by personal reasons, namely his growing dislike for George.

That hurt her. For years, George had accepted Henry's hostility towards her, the put-downs and the eye-rolls and the flat-out rudeness, as part and parcel of their sexual connection. It was the 'hate' part of the love/hate dynamic that had kept their affair so explosive and the sex so mind-blowingly good for so long. She told herself it was a game.

But she could no longer keep up that illusion. Like Flora, George had had to endure the loved-up pictures of Henry and Ikea frolicking in the crystal waters of the Bahamas, splashed all over the *Daily Mail*. But whereas in the past, Henry would always return to George's bed, now her perverse hold over him was fading fast. For this, George squarely blamed Flora Fitzwilliam.

Ever since Flora had turned up at Hanborough like a bad smell you couldn't get rid of, a dead rat in the pipes, Henry's relationship with George had curdled like sour milk. At first George had thought Henry and Flora were just friends. But walking in on them in the kitchen last month, seeing Henry curled up in Flora's arms like a little boy seeking comfort from his mother, a chill had shot through her.

That sly bitch; that preposterously proportioned, common,

American *scrubber*, Flora, was in love with Henry! With George's Henry. And some part of him at least was obviously starting to feel the same way. Worse, the embrace between them wasn't erotic, or at least not primarily. It was loving, affectionate. *Kind*. Kindness was something Henry had never given George, not even during the good times.

That hug in the kitchen was what had done it: tipped George over from sadness into anger, from passive dislike into determined action. The fact that screwing Flora over – and getting her own back on Henry – coincided so neatly with George's own business ambitions, was merely the icing on the cake. And Graydon, God bless him, had been so entirely amenable to all of George's suggestions. It really was incredible how quickly she'd been able to turn things around, to regain the upper hand in whatever game it was that she and Henry Saxton Brae were now playing.

George had just waved goodbye to a lovely man from the *Telegraph* and was heading inside to attend to some emails when her heart skipped a beat. Flora's red Mini Cooper was bumping up the drive, rain-streaked and dirty after two days parked at Hinton Station.

George and Graydon had expected Flora to show up at the castle, of course. Just not quite so soon.

Moments later, she pulled to a stop in front of the port-cullis and got out, slamming the driver's door shut behind her. In dark-wash jeans tucked into UGG boots and an oversized grey fisherman's sweater, with her blonde hair pushed back off her make-up-free face, Flora looked younger and more vulnerable than usual. Her stride, however, was determined, marching up the stone steps and across the drawbridge like Boudicca storming into battle.

Catching sight of Georgina Savile standing by the front

door in a chic black full-length coat and matching beret, Flora sighed. That was all she needed. What the hell was she doing here?

'Where's Tony?' she asked wearily.

'That's none of your concern.'

George had stepped forward, closing the front door of the castle behind her. She was smiling very oddly at Flora. With her waif-like figure and spiteful but delicate doll-like features, she made an incongruous gatekeeper. Besides, weren't trolls supposed to live *under* the bridge?

'I don't have time for this,' said Flora, pushing past her. 'What are you even doing here anyway?'

'Protecting my asset,' said George. She was still smiling as Flora tried the door but found it locked. 'I'm afraid I'm going to have to ask you to leave.'

Flora looked at her as if she were insane. 'Ask away,' she said, fumbling in her handbag for her keys. 'This is Henry's house, not yours. And I have a job to do.'

George laughed, an empty, tinkling sound utterly devoid of warmth, like an icicle shattering on hard ground.

'Wrong on both counts, I'm afraid. Henry bought Hanborough through his offshore trust, swapping out his equity stake for shares in Gigtix. It's far too complicated for you to grasp, but the gist is that the castle belongs to the company, not Henry personally. Which means it also belongs to *me*.'

'I don't believe you,' said Flora. 'Henry would have said something.'

But a dull fear began to creep over her. Henry *was* obsessed with making everything in his life tax efficient. It was one of the very few things he and Mason had in common. It wasn't beyond the bounds of imagination to think that he'd linked Hanborough in some way to his company. In fact, come to think of it, hadn't she heard rumours about English Heritage doing a 'behind closed doors' deal with some sort of trust when she first came to the village?

It was all so long ago now, she couldn't be sure. And it certainly wasn't beyond George to make something like that up.

'Clearly you're not as close to Henry as you imagined,' George observed spitefully. 'And I wouldn't bother looking for your keys either. Graydon and I took the precaution of changing the locks.'

Graydon and I?

Suddenly the penny dropped. Flora's eyes narrowed murderously.

'What did you do?' she hissed at George. 'What have you been saying to him?'

'Nothing that wasn't true.' George tossed back her long hair defiantly. In her new Charles Jourdan boots, she towered over Flora like the Wicked Witch of the West over an indignant Dorothy. 'I suggest you read these, before you make any more wild accusations.'

Reaching into her voluminous coat, George pulled out a slim white A4 envelope. The GJD New York office address was emblazoned on the front.

'What is it?' asked Flora, taking the envelope without thinking.

'Your notice of dismissal. You can read Graydon's complaints in detail at your leisure. Poaching clients. Illicit payments. Inefficient reporting—'

'What?' Flora exploded. 'That's crap and he knows it.'

'But you may not read them here,' George continued, ignoring her. 'You are to leave the property immediately. Any further attempts by you to access Hanborough or its grounds will be viewed as deliberate trespass and dealt with accordingly.'

'You can't do this,' said a shaking Flora. 'Henry won't allow it. Does he even know you're here?' she added, the thought suddenly occurring to her that perhaps all of this was bullshit, that George was acting solo on some sort of elaborate bluff.

'Goodbye, Flora,' said George, turning on her heel imperiously and pulling out her shiny new key to let herself back into the castle. 'Try not to make too much of a mess of the gravel on your way out.'

Watching her struggle with the stiff lock, her slender back turned to Flora as if she were nothing, nobody, Flora suddenly found herself overwhelmed with rage. It came upon her like a white, blinding light, filling her small body with waves of power and strength, and her spirit with an overwhelming desire to use them. Before she was even fully aware of what she was doing, Flora grabbed George from behind, clamping her arms around George's tiny, wasp-like waist and lifting her physically off the ground.

'Put me down!' George screeched. 'What in God's name do you think you're doing?'

Flora didn't answer. Instead she carried George to the edge of the low wall where the keep joined the drawbridge. Hoisting her up with astonishing ease – Flora wasn't a large person, but George felt as light as a Barbie doll – she held her over the side, enjoying a few delicious moments of George's utter panic, before dropping her into the moat with a satisfying *plop*.

It wasn't deep, five feet at most. But the water was thick with algae and slime. It was also, Flora assumed, breathtakingly cold.

George emerged from the fetid water, threw back her head and screamed, as much in shock as anything else. From all over the castle, workmen and staff came running to see what had happened.

'Are you all right, miss?' one of the men asked, struggling to suppress his giggles. Nobody at Hanborough liked Georgina Savile.

'All right? No! I . . . she . . . that woman . . . !' she spluttered.

Flora picked Graydon's letter up off the ground and walked quietly away.

Barney Griffith was elbow-deep in flour when he heard his door knocker hammering.

After a fun but drunken (and expensive) night up in London at Penny's gallery opening, ending in the triumphant sale of not one but two of his photographs, *hooray!*, Barney had returned to his cottage and a demented welcome from Jeeves, determined both to start saving more money (selling two pieces was a good start, but it was only a start) and to eat more healthily. No more cakes, no more booze. No more putting bank statements in sock drawers and pretending they hadn't arrived.

In a fit of enthusiasm for both these new resolutions, he'd slightly overdosed on *The River Cottage Cookbook* this afternoon, rushing out to the health food shop in Fittlescombe to buy organic flour, spelt, and various other previously unheard-of ingredients needed to make Hugh Fearnley-Whittingstall's 'healthy pastry'. Admittedly he had spent rather more than he meant to on this expedition. However, he argued to himself, you have to spend money to make money. By making copious amounts of home-made pastry and freezing it in advance, he would slash not only his budget for Mr Kipling cakes and expensive suppers at The Fox (from now on he would make his own steak and kidney pie), but his waist measurements, too. As a plan, it was foolproof, and not remotely compromised by the packet and a half of leftover Country Slices he'd eaten while 'prepping' his work space, or the two large glasses of wine he'd poured himself for courage, and to help channel his inner Keith Floyd as he cordon-bleu'd his way to svelteness and solvency.

It turned out, however, that pastry making wasn't quite as easy as Hugh F-W made it sound. Now on his second batch, and almost two hours into the attempt, Barney had two baking trays full of what looked and tasted like ready-mix concrete and a large mixing bowl full of grey, slightly lumpy glue. Or possibly the world's largest ball of spat-out chewing gum.

'Coming!' Wiping the worst of the flour from his hands onto a glue-encrusted tea towel, he raced to the door. His face lit up as soon as he opened it. 'Flora! What a lovely surprise. Come in.'

Following him inside, Flora was almost relieved that the smartly dressed photographer of the other night had been replaced by the scruffy Barney she knew and loved. He still looked remarkably handsome with the new haircut, notwithstanding the spelt liberally scattered through it. But Flora realized with a pang that she didn't want Barney to change, not ever. Standing in his tiny sitting room, looking around at the familiar paintings and photographs and tatty but welcoming furniture gave her a warm, safe feeling. A fire was dying in the grate, and in the kitchen sounds of the Test Match crackled through the air from Barney's old Roberts radio. It was all so comforting and cosy, apart from the oddly pervasive smell of burning . . . ?

Flora looked at Barney, covered in butter stains and flour, and suddenly burst into tears.

'Oh my goodness, what's wrong?' Barney asked, hugging her and depositing floury handprints all over her sweater and jeans. 'What's happened? I'm sure it can't be that bad.'

'It is,' Flora sobbed, completely letting herself go for once. 'It *is* that bad! I have nothing, Barney. No money, no home, no husband and now no career. In fact, it's worse than no career. It's like, I have a *minus* career. It wasn't enough for that *asshole* Graydon to steal my award and then sack me. He won't stop until he's ruined my reputation too! Can you believe he—'

'Graydon sacked you?' Barney interrupted, trying to latch on to the salient points in Flora's hysterical tirade before they were lost in the flood.

'Via Georgina bitch-of-the-goddamn-century Savile. She's behind all this, you realize? She stitched me up!'

'What did he sack you for?'

'Breach of contract!' shrieked Flora. 'Which is, I'm sorry, a *fucking joke* when you look at what *he's* done to *me*. He's given two interviews today, *today*, that I know of, accusing me outright of stealing his clients and undermining his business behind his back. He makes me out to be like this . . . this viper in the nest . . . like I'm some ungrateful . . . *Oooooof!*' She let out a weird strangled yelp of frustration. 'I hate him. I HATE him! But I also know him.' Her voice dropped to a doom-laden whisper. 'He's vengeful, Barney. He won't stop until he's ruined me. Until I can never work again as a designer. He's out to destroy me.'

'All right, calm down,' said Barney, not unsympathetically. 'You make him sound like some sort of Mafia super-boss or James Bond villain.'

'He is!' Flora yelled wildly.

'No, he isn't,' said Barney. 'He's a camp, geriatric has-been with a good eye for colour and a massive chip on his shoulder, egged on by a spoiled, jealous cow who's always hated you.'

Flora opened her mouth to protest, then realized that this was, in fact, a fairly accurate summary of Graydon and George's respective roles, and closed it again.

Leading her into the kitchen, Barney poured Flora a large glass of cooking wine. Taking a big gulp, Flora pulled a face. 'Good Lord, that is disgusting.'

'I know,' said Barney. 'I'm economizing. Spelt pastry?'

He offered Flora a small, squarish piece of concrete that he'd managed to chisel away from the rest earlier with the help of a sharp knife, a spatula, and considerable amounts of elbow grease.

She shook her head vigorously. 'I'm not eating that and nor should you.' Picking up the baking tray, she deposited its entire, rock-solid contents into the bin. 'I was about to say "don't give up the day job", but then I remembered you don't have one.'

'Ha ha,' said Barney, pleased she was able to crack a joke at least. 'Well, nor do you any more,' he teased her back. To his dismay, tears started streaming down Flora's face again.

'Oh God, I'm sorry,' she sniffed. 'I know you were joking. It's just the shock. When I saw Hanborough had been nominated, I was so happy. Just for a moment. I really thought everything was going to be OK, you know? But then it all came crashing down again, worse than before. What am I going to *do*?'

'Well, first you're going to sit down,' said Barney. 'Take a breath. I'll dig us out something edible and we'll come up with a plan. For one thing, you don't have "no money". Jason Cranley just paid you six figures, didn't he?'

'Which is one of the things Graydon's trying to use against me,' muttered Flora, curling up on Barney's sofa and kicking off her boots.

'That's six more figures than I currently have sitting in my bank account,' said Barney. 'It could be worse, Flora. Plus you haven't explored all your legal options.'

'What legal options?'

'I don't know yet,' said Barney. 'I haven't explored them either. But a good mate of mine from my old firm recently transferred to our New York office. Dan's a brilliant lawyer. He'll definitely give you some basic advice for free if I ask him to. Tell you honestly whether you have a case or not, under US law.'

'That's so kind,' said Flora sincerely. She doubted it would help. Graydon kept small flocks of lawyers as pets and considered litigation a pleasant, stress-relieving hobby. He would eat anybody Flora hired for lunch. But it was nice to feel that Barney was so unequivocally on her side.

Flora sipped her disgusting wine while Barney made them both some beans on toast with grated cheese. Watching him clatter around the tiny kitchen like a benevolent giant, she wished she could be a bit more like him. Broke but happy, cheerfully admitting to having nothing in the bank without the slightest twinge of fear. How did people do that? Flora wondered how different her life might look if she weren't always so panicked about money. If she could contemplate marrying a poor man like Barney, living on hope and baked beans.

I'd love to be like that, she thought. *I'd be a better person. But it's just not me.*

The more she drank, and ate, and chatted to Barney, the more relaxed she became. It was so warm and snug in the little sitting room, the heat from the fire filling every crevice of the room and lulling her into a sort of willing stupor. Occasionally thoughts of Henry would pop, unbidden, into her mind, and the sadness would creep back in. She really must get over her attraction to him. It had crept up on her, almost without her noticing, and it was making an already bad situation so much worse. She'd only just broken things off with Mason, after all. And Eva was her friend. And even if Henry were single, he was clearly utterly incapable of commitment—

'What are you thinking about?' asked Barney.

'Oh, nothing. Graydon, I suppose,' Flora lied. The room was starting to spin. She'd definitely had too much wine. 'Can I stay here tonight?' she heard herself asking Barney. 'I can't face going back to Peony Cottage on my own.'

'Of course. You know you're welcome any time. You can take my bed and I'll have the sofa.'

'Are you sure?' Flora sounded doubtful.

'Totally.' Barney smiled.

Despite himself, he felt a surge of happiness rise up inside him. He knew Flora saw him only as a friend, a big brother-cum-shoulder to cry on. After the fool he'd made of himself last Christmas, proclaiming his love for her, he wasn't about to ruin things by declaring himself again, or making a pass he knew would be rejected. But it still felt good that she'd come to him in her moment of crisis.

She trusts me.

Flora drifted in and out of sleep as Barney disappeared upstairs in search of spare blankets and a pillow to make her comfy on the sofa after all. The shrill ring of her cell phone jolted her awake.

Didn't I turn that off? Frowning, she reached down into her bag and grabbed the offending object.

'Hello?'

'Flora? It's me.' Mason's voice sounded distant. Strained.

'Hey.' It was nice to hear him, but strange at the same time. Through her half-drunk fog she struggled to reconcile being here, on Barney Griffith's sofa in the English countryside, with talking to Mason in New York City. It felt like one side of that equation had to be a dream. 'Are you calling about the award? You know Graydon screwed me, right?'

'Flora—'

'He fired me too. Locked me out of the London offices, and the Hanborough site. I need to talk to a lawyer. Barney Griffith has a friend who might—'

'Flora.' Mason raised his voice, cutting her off. 'It's not about that. It's your mother.'

'My mother?' The fog was coming back, swirling thicker and deeper now, clogging Flora's thoughts like wet cotton.

'They called the apartment.' Mason sounded choked. 'This was the number you gave, as next of kin. I'm so sorry, Flora, but Camila had a heart attack this afternoon at home. She died about an hour ago.'

PART THREE

CHAPTER TWENTY-SIX

Flora looked up at the cherry blossoms fluttering to the ground in the May breeze. It was a good day for a funeral, bright and clear and cool. St Agnes's Catholic Church in Brooklyn wasn't a particularly beautiful building, but its red-brick walls looked less severe in the spring sunshine, and the cherry trees lining the small rear churchyard gave it the feel of a private garden, the sort of space one might go to sit and read a novel on a quiet Sunday afternoon, or enjoy a peaceful sandwich on the simply carved stone bench.

Father Domingo's deep, resonant voice echoed through the still air.

'Our citizenship is in heaven, and from it we also await a saviour, the Lord Jesus Christ.'

Only Flora, the churchwarden, and Cecilia, Camila's cleaning lady, were at the graveside. Cecilia, poor thing, had found Flora's mother the day she died, collapsed in the hallway of her modest apartment. The two women had become friends of sorts over the years. As much as anyone could be a friend to a reclusive, alcoholic, borderline agora-phobic like Camila Fitzwilliam.

There was no one there from the old days. No one left who remembered Camila when she used to be a vibrant, engaging young woman, full of laughter and hopes and ideas, full of love. Sometimes Flora wasn't sure whether that version of her mother was something she actually remembered, or whether she'd invented that happy person after the fact, like an imaginary friend. All she knew for sure was that after her father went to prison, all the joy was gone. Later, with his death, there was another, more catastrophic descent. The drinking got worse. Sadness became depression, which in turn became paranoia and resentment. It was all so unnecessary, and so terribly, terribly sad.

Mason had offered to come with Flora to today's service, but she preferred to be alone. That was a good decision, she reflected now, as Father Domingo wrapped things up.

'Eternal rest grant to your daughter Camila, O Lord, and let perpetual light shine upon her. May she rest in peace.'

After thanking the priest and exchanging a few kind words with Cecilia, Flora decided to walk for a while. She had nowhere particular to be for the rest of the afternoon and it had been a long time since she'd walked through New York City alone; even longer since she'd looked around her and actually noticed things. Teenagers huddled together on brownstone stoops, laughing at something on their phones. Squirrels chasing each other madly along the sidewalks before leaping into trees, squawking like birds in some battle over mating or territory. The smell of fried onions wafting out from the restaurant kitchens on Franklin. The distant sound of sirens – someone else's tragedy today.

Her mother would never see or hear or smell any of these

things again. That was it. Camila had had her allotted days, her hours, her exact number of breaths, and now it was over. Some arbitrary higher power had clicked its fingers and turned out the lights, just like that. Flora hadn't been close to her mother for a long time. Perhaps, if she were honest, not ever. But Camila was still her mother. It still hurt, flying home to organize a funeral where the only mourners would be you and your mother's cleaning lady.

Flora couldn't help but compare today's mournful little gathering with the huge crowds that had turned out for Lucy Smart's funeral. Had that really been only six weeks ago? It felt like for ever. Of course Lucy was young, and a mother, and her death had been totally unexpected. But those weren't the only reasons that St Hilda's Church had been full to bursting that April day, while St Agnes's, Brooklyn, remained depressingly deserted.

Lucy Smart had been part of a family. Part of a village, a community, which came together in times of trouble or need or loss. Through her work at Hanborough Castle, and her friendships with Eva and Barney and Penny, and even Henry, Flora had felt briefly as if she, too, were part of that community. As if, for the first time in a long time, she wasn't completely alone.

Today's service had shown Flora in stark, brutal terms, just how alone her mother had been. *I can't let that happen to me*, she thought, sinking down slowly onto an empty seat at a bus stop. *I need a family. People to love me and mourn me. I need a life that means something.*

Terrifyingly, she had no idea what she was going to do now. Not today, not tomorrow, not in the weeks and months and years ahead. Her entire life was suddenly a blank sheet of paper. No wedding to plan, no job to rush back to, no family, no home. Nothing. Should she go back to England and fight for her share in the International Designer of the Year award? Fight for Hanborough, for her career, her reputation? She hadn't felt strong enough to speak to Henry since any of this happened, but she felt sure that both he and Eva would back her up if she did decide to take on Graydon.

Part of her wanted to. She had nothing left to lose at this point, after all, and the unfairness of what he was doing still rankled deeply.

But another part was tired of fighting. Deeply, deeply tired. Closing her eyes, Flora indulged that part, summoning up mental images of Barney Griffith's sofa, of the warmth of the fire, the soothing numbness of the cheap wine flooding through her bloodstream.

A passing drunk staggered in Flora's direction, collapsing on the seat next to her.

'Jesus, cheer up, would ya?' he slurred, in what might once have been an Irish accent. 'It might never happen.'

Flora looked at him, wide-eyed suddenly.

He's right, she thought miserably. *It might never happen.*

What if it never happens for me? Marriage. Family. A career. What if those things never happen?

Will I die alone and bitter and wasted, like my poor mom?

For the first time all day, she started to cry. Once she started, it was hard to stop.

Eva rested a tanned, diamond-encrusted hand on Henry's forearm as he got out of the car.

'Don't lose your temper,' she reminded him gently. 'Give George a chance to explain first, like we agreed.'

Had they agreed? Henry wondered, hauling their suitcases out of the car and staring up at his beloved castle, the first time he'd laid eyes on her in over three weeks. He didn't remember agreeing to anything. All he remembered was landing at Heathrow, after a blissful holiday in the Bahamas, to a barrage of messages, each making him more furious than the last.

Hanborough had been nominated for the big design award, but it was Graydon James's name on the nomination, not Flora's.

Worse, Graydon had sacked Flora, without so much as discussing the situation with Henry, and had actually had the nerve to ban her from the site at Hanborough, as a result of which the contractor had walked off the job and all works at the castle had ceased.

Most incendiary of all, however, was the news that Georgina Savile had taken it upon herself to enforce Graydon's instructions, installing herself at the castle – Henry's *home* – and declaring herself de facto decision-maker on everything in Henry's absence. After some sort of phys- ical fight with Flora, which ended with George taking an unexpected swim in the moat (even the saint-like Eva had raised a wry smile at that mental image), Flora had stormed off site and hadn't been seen at Hanborough since.

In the meantime, neither Flora nor George were answering their phones, which meant that for the long drive back to the Swell Valley, Henry had no one to rant to other than Eva, and the hapless Mrs French, who made the fatal mistake of answering the landline at the castle.

'Is George there now?' Henry demanded, so furious it was hard at times to make out what he was saying.

'She stayed again last night,' the flustered PA admitted. 'But she's not here right this second, no. I believe she's gone out riding.'

'Riding what?' Henry exploded. 'Who gave that bitch permission to touch my horses? How dare she!'

'I . . . I'm not *sure* she's riding,' poor Mrs French stammered helplessly. In the end Eva had convinced Henry to hang up and wait until they actually got to Hanborough to sort things out with Georgina.

'For all you know, she has a perfectly rational explanation,' Eva said, although she sounded less than convincing, even to herself. 'Of course we must reinstate Flora and sort all this out. But there's no point biting George's head off till we know exactly what happened and why.'

Striding across the drawbridge with a face like thunder, Henry stormed inside ahead of Eva.

'George?' he bellowed.

'There's no need to shout.'

George sauntered into the hall to meet him. In skin-tight jodhpurs and a crisp white shirt, with her long hair falling in tousled waves to her shoulders and her cheeks still flushed from the ride, she looked as desirable as she ever had.

'Welcome home.'

Henry glared at her with naked loathing.

'What the fuck do you think you're playing at?' he snarled. 'How dare you install yourself in my house? And how dare you fire Flora?'

George gave him a perplexed look. 'I don't know what you mean. I didn't fire anybody. Graydon fired Flora. As his business partner, and yours, I simply made sure his instructions were followed.'

Henry's eyes narrowed. 'What do you mean, "as his business partner"?'

'I haven't had a chance to tell you yet.' George smiled

sweetly. 'But while you were gone I finalized the deal with GJD. It really is a fantastic opportunity for us, Henry. When you read the terms, I know you'll agree that we—'

'Un-finalize it.' Henry's voice was quiet, but the anger quivered through every word.

'No can do, I'm afraid.' George was still smiling, but the steel in her tone matched Henry's. 'Gigtix.com and GJD are now officially partners. It's all legal, signed and watertight. So unless you want us to be sued for breach of contract—'

'You have no right to sign anything without me!' Henry thundered.

'On the contrary,' George replied confidently. 'Each of us has the right to act independently in the firm's best interests, which this deal certainly was. That's the joy of a 50/50 partnership. And while we're talking about rights, I didn't "install myself in *your* house". You listed Hanborough as a business asset, remember?'

'That was temporary, for tax purposes, and you know it,' snapped Henry. 'As soon as the renovations are completed and signed off, I'm buying it back for cash. We agreed all this a year ago.'

'Did we?' George scratched her head in mock confusion. 'I'm afraid I don't remember. I don't suppose you have anything in writing?'

'You know I don't,' Henry muttered murderously. 'We agreed on trust.'

'Ah, yes. Trust.' George's eyes flashed with anger and hurt. 'That goes both ways, doesn't it, darling?'

'Where's Flora?' Henry demanded.

'I have no idea.' George yawned pointedly. 'I believe she

was in New York last week for her mother's funeral. She should be back by now. I'm afraid I don't find fat Flora's whereabouts as fascinating as you do.'

Henry's eyes widened. 'Her mother died?'

'Didn't she tell you?' George asked. 'Perhaps the two of you aren't as close as you'd like to think?'

'You bitch.' Henry shook his head. What had he ever, *ever* seen in this awful, mean-spirited woman? 'For your information, I'm recontracting Flora as our designer, today, this afternoon. After that I'll call my lawyers and contest whatever bullshit you think you've sewn up with Graydon James. You won't get away with any of this, you know.'

George's jaw stiffened. 'If you so much as try to rehire Flora Fitzwilliam, I'll tell Eva about us. I'll leak it to the press too. Who knows, maybe my phone will be hacked and someone will come across some *very* intimate pictures?'

Henry stared at her. 'You wouldn't dare. You've got as much to lose as I have.'

'More. I'm married, remember?' George shot back. 'But I *would* dare, Henry. You think you can have your way with me whenever you want to and then treat me like a second-class citizen?' She was trembling with emotion, all the hurt and disappointment of the past two years pouring out of her like pus from an infected wound. 'Now that *Flora's* your new best friend, and you and Ikea are planning your big society wedding, you think I can be jettisoned like a used condom? Well, I can't!' she hissed. 'I'm here to stay, you bastard, whether you like it or not. Here in your business. Here in your precious castle. I'm the mouse that fucking roared! And that *bitch* Flora Fitzwilliam can go to hell.'

Henry looked at her in silence. He was still standing there, staring, when Eva walked in behind him.

'Hello, George,' she said, smiling politely. Then, noticing George had tears in her eyes, she asked anxiously, 'Is everything all right?'

'I don't know,' said George, not taking her eyes off Henry. 'Perhaps you'd better ask your fiancé. *Is* everything all right, Henry?'

'You're mentally ill,' Henry replied witheringly. 'You need help.'

'Screw you,' George whispered. Sweeping past both of them, she ran out of the castle with a stifled sob, got into her car and drove away.

Eva looked at Henry aghast. 'What on earth happened?'

'Don't worry about it,' he said. 'She's crazy.'

'You were only in here five minutes,' said Eva. 'I thought you were going to talk to her calmly?'

Mrs French hesitantly emerged from the office.

'Welcome back,' she said nervously to Eva. Turning to a stony-faced Henry she added, 'I'm so sorry about all of this. I just . . . I didn't know what to do. When Mrs Savile arrived . . . '

'It's not your fault,' said Henry. 'I'd like you to remove any of Mrs Savile's things she may have left here and put them outside the gates.'

'Now?' Mrs French asked.

'Now,' said Henry. 'And I want the locks and gate code changed. That woman is not to be allowed back on the property under any circumstances.'

'Come on, Henry,' Eva said reasonably. 'Let's not escalate this.'

Ignoring her, Henry headed back outside.

'Where are you *going?*' Eva called after him. 'We just got home. Don't you even want to unpack?'

'Out,' said Henry, blowing her a kiss. 'I won't be long.'

The drive to Peony Cottage took all of two minutes, but it took another fifteen for Henry to muster up the courage to get out of the car, walk up the path and knock on Flora's door.

Her mother had died. Everything else – George, Graydon, being fired, the award nominations – meant nothing in comparison to that one, awful fact. Henry knew that better than anyone. He'd told Flora all about his own mother's death and how devastating it had been for him. How present and raw her loss still felt, even all these years later.

Yet Flora hadn't confided in him. She hadn't called him on holiday, or emailed. She hadn't said a word. Was she trying to spare him her pain? To allow him and Eva their time away and their happiness, without tainting it with her own grief and misery? Or was George right? Were Henry and Flora simply not as close as Henry thought they were? The idea bothered him more than he cared to admit.

Then there was the whole situation with Flora's job. She would expect him to reinstate her at Hanborough, and of course he wanted to. But with George's threat hanging over him to expose their affair, never mind the legal quagmire surrounding ownership of the castle and his obligations vis-à-vis Graydon James Designs, his hands were tied, at least temporarily.

Would Flora understand?

Or would she feel Henry had let her down, right when she needed him the most?

He still had no idea what he was going to say when he knocked on the cottage door, gently at first, but then harder when there was no answer.

'Flora?'

He wandered round to the back garden, in case she was there, calling up towards the open bedroom window when he found it empty.

'Flora? Are you in there? It's me.'

Still no answer. Tentatively, he tried the kitchen door. It opened instantly.

Henry walked through the kitchen into the living room, but he didn't call out again. The basic furniture was still in the cottage, but all Flora's personal touches – the paintings on the wall, the bright Aztec throw cushions, the art deco clock – had gone. Walking upstairs in a daze, Henry stared at the stripped bed, its bare mattress lying forlorn on the white metal frame. Idly he pulled open the top drawer of the chest of drawers, but he already knew what he would find.

Nothing.

The house was empty.

Flora was gone.

CHAPTER TWENTY-SEVEN

It was a glorious June in the Swell Valley. As temperatures climbed into the eighties, schoolchildren sat at their desks, gazing out of the windows and longing for July. Locals stripped down to shorts and T-shirts, exposing limbs still white from the long, cold spring, and sat in their gardens delighting in the sunshine. Even larger crowds than usual descended on the valley for the annual Brockhurst-Fittlescombe cricket match. But all the usual events were overshadowed by the terrific excitement and anticipation surrounding this summer's celebrity wedding up at Hanborough Castle. The date was now set for 27 August, when legendary playboy Henry Saxton Brae would finally say 'I do' to the stunning Eva Gunnarson. Although the service and reception themselves would be private affairs, all the residents of the surrounding villages were invited up to the castle for celebratory champagne on the morning of the wedding, and to cheer on the bridal party as they made their way down the hill to St Hilda's Church. Not since Rory Flint-Hamilton's wedding to his society bride Victoria

Radcliffe-Gray back in the 1970s had there been so much excitement, or such a sense of the entire community coming together in celebration.

For Henry, it was a strange time. While Eva floated around in a halo of prenuptial bliss, strangers continually stopped him to offer congratulations, and the castle was filled with dress designers, florists, caterers, photographers and their various assistants from dawn till dusk, Henry's professional life was in a state of utter turmoil. His hopes of undoing George's deal with Graydon James, both to develop a design app and to bring out a line of Hanborough-inspired merchandise, had been roundly and swiftly dashed by his lawyer and old friend Peter Freeman.

'In a nutshell,' Pete said, in his refreshingly direct way, 'you're buggered. If you try to pull out now, GJD will certainly sue for breach of contract and material damages. You and George did give each other the right to act independently when you set up Gigtix, mate. The contract's pretty black and white.'

'Can't you make it greyer?'

'Not this time. On the plus side, this actually is a damn good deal for Gigtix. I know you hate her, but George is no pushover at the negotiating table. If you could get over the whole "control" thing, you might even see this as a good thing. Your business model was dying, Henry, whether you like to admit it or not. George and Gay-don just gave you the kiss of life.'

'And Hanborough?' Henry asked, through gritted teeth.

'Company property,' said Pete. 'My advice is to patch things up with George, make an over-generous cash offer and buy it back.'

'She won't sell it back to me. Not now we have this whole ridiculous merchandising boom going on.'

'Ridiculous, but very profitable already,' Pete reminded him, earning himself a glare of disapproval from Henry. 'Now that Graydon's won International Designer of the Year, it's gonna go through the roof. You do realize how huge that is?'

Henry sighed. He did know how huge it was. But all he could think about was poor Flora.

Last weekend Graydon had ascended the podium at the Grosvenor House Hotel in London and tearfully accepted the International Designer of the Year award, taking the opportunity to share with the audience how hurt he'd been by the betrayal of a 'close colleague' earlier in the year, and how receiving this award for Hanborough was all the sweeter as a result. He didn't mention Flora by name. He didn't have to. Everybody in the business knew who he was referring to, not least because he'd spent the last month employing his powerful global PR machine to brief against Flora, leaking negative stories to the press about her plagiarizing his work and abusing his generosity.

George had gone with Graydon as his 'date' for the evening, looking ravishing in a backless white gown, and together they had talked up GJD and Gigtix's new joint venture, milking the publicity for all it was worth.

Meanwhile Henry could do nothing but watch. He imagined Flora in a lonely hotel room somewhere doing the same. Was she depressed? Suicidal, even? It was possible. No one had seen hide nor hair of her since her trip to New York for her mother's funeral. Henry was desperately worried about her, and had even gone so far as to call Mason, her ex-fiancé, to ask for help tracking her down. But Mason hadn't heard from her either.

'I spoke to her when she was here, but not since. She

didn't want me at her mom's service. I think she just needed some space.'

A lot of space, apparently. Eva also seemed convinced that Flora would resurface 'when she's ready'. Only Barney Griffith shared Henry's deeper concerns, and though the two weren't friends, they'd promised to let each other know at once if either of them heard anything.

Pete Freeman gave Henry his sternest, most lawyerly face.

'Look, Henry. George won't sell the castle back to you while you keep telling her what a cunt she is. That's the bottom line. Can you really blame her?'

Henry's expression indicated that he could.

'Just play nice, for fuck's sake,' said Pete. 'This really is not rocket science. You scratch her back and she'll scratch yours. Can't you sleep with her again or something?'

Henry's eyebrows shot up.

'What?' Pete asked innocently. 'It seemed to work well before.'

'I'd rather stick my dick in a blender,' growled Henry. 'Besides, in case you hadn't heard, I'm about to get married.'

'Exactly,' said Pete, smiling broadly. 'Your business has been saved, you're making more money than you have in years, and you're about to marry the woman of your dreams. The woman of everybody else's dreams, too, come to that. You might want to consider cheering up.'

He was right, of course. Henry knew he had a lot to be thankful for, especially now. After Lucy's death and all the terrible things he'd done, the only way for him to make amends was to marry Eva and to make their marriage work. He was lucky still to have that chance. A second chance in his personal life *and* his business. Things could be a lot worse.

Even so, it was hard to feel happy with George lording

it over him, Flora being still missing in action, and the wedding in all its pomp and glamour and publicity hurtling towards him like a tulle-powered freight train.

Henry arrived home one evening after a particularly trying day in the office with Graydon James's UK press officer, a mincing little turd of an individual who would insist on talking endlessly about 'synergies', and who gloried in the name of Carlton Krepp, to find the vicar, his wife, and their noisily gurgling baby Diana installed in the drawing room with Eva.

'Ah, darling, there you are!' Eva beamed. 'Come and join us. We were just talking about Baby Einstein. Did you know that babies who first hear classical music in the womb are seven times more likely to graduate from a top university?'

'What utter drivel,' drawled Henry, unable to shake his bad mood. Eva, Bill and Jen all looked so smugly contented, cooing over the baby with their plates of fruit cake and half-drunk glasses of port.

'It's not drivel, actually,' said Jen. 'Plenty of studies bear it out.'

The vicar's wife had never thought much of Henry Saxton Brae. She considered him arrogant and self-centred, and nowhere near good enough for Eva, who remained irritatingly in thrall to him. Jen couldn't understand it.

'Name one,' said Henry rudely.

'The Newcastle University research in last month's *New Scientist*,' Jen shot back defiantly. 'There's quite a few long words in there, though, Henry. You may need Eva to explain the tricky bits.'

'*Jenny*!' The Reverend Clempson looked mortified. 'We'll get out of your way,' he added apologetically to Henry, hauling himself up out of the sofa and retrieving his drooling daughter from the tiger-skin rug. 'I daresay you and Eva were looking forward to a quiet evening.'

Once the Clempsons had left, Eva looked reproachfully at Henry. 'That wasn't very nice. Why do you always have to be so miserable?'

'I don't know,' snapped Henry. 'Why do you always have to fill the house with freeloaders?'

'He's the vicar, Henry! He's marrying us in a few weeks! And Jenny's a friend.'

'Was that my good port?' Henry asked gracelessly. 'How much did they have? I know Call-me-Bill's a lightweight, but that woman can drink for England.'

Eva stood up and pushed past him. 'I can't talk to you when you're like this.'

Grabbing her by the arm, Henry suddenly saw there were tears in her eyes.

'Oh God, I'm sorry. Really. It's not you, or them really. I had a godawful day at work. This phenomenally irritating little drag queen – who George seems to think is God's gift to PR – spent the entire day—'

'I'm pregnant,' Eva blurted.

Henry released her arm, lapsing into stunned silence.

'Aren't you going to say anything?'

'I . . . wow,' Henry stammered. 'Are you sure?'

Eva's hurt turned to anger. '*Are you sure?* That's what you have to say?'

'No, I mean, I'm just . . . I'm surprised.'

'And?' Eva's eyes widened. She was used to Henry disappointing her, but this took the biscuit.

'And . . . congratulations?' he offered hesitantly.

She shook her head at him in disgust. 'Congratulations?

Well, thank you very much. Congratulations to you too. Asshole.'

Pushing past him, more forcefully this time, she stormed out of the room.

'Eva!' Henry called after her. 'Eva, wait! I didn't mean—'

The slamming of the master bedroom door echoed all the way down the stone stairs, shaking the furniture below like the rattling of an old man's bones.

Fuck. Henry ran a hand through his hair.

He'd made a pig's ear of that one. He knew he should go up to Eva and make things right, and he would in a minute. But just for a moment, he let the import of what she'd told him sink in.

Eva was pregnant.

They were going to have a baby.

Was he happy? He should be happy. Perhaps he *was* happy, just too shocked and numb to realize it? He wished he could talk to Richard about it. Rich was a father, after all, an excellent father. But Henry still couldn't bring himself to confide in Richard Smart the way he used to. Every time he saw him, the guilt was unbearable. And the reminders of Lucy. Henry could have talked to her too, except that she was gone, gone for ever, and he would never see her or touch her or hear her voice again. All of a sudden, he felt tears prick his own eyes, as a torrent of different emotions swelled within him. Grief. Guilt. Fear.

Flora, he thought, for the hundredth time since she'd been gone.

I wish I could talk to Flora.

It frightened him how much he missed her. Henry realized now that during the months she'd worked at Hanborough, Flora had been a sort of buffer in his relationship with Eva. She'd become a friend in her own right too, to both of them. But she was also the glue that made them work, that held them together – comforting Eva when he hurt her, confronting Henry when he was in the wrong, listening to both of them. With Flora around all the time, Henry and Eva had rarely been completely alone.

But now they would be. A married couple.

More than that. They would be parents. A family.

Pulling himself together, Henry hurried upstairs, strings of apologies forming on his lips.

Two days later, Barney Griffith sat alone in the snug bar at The Fox, nursing his second Guinness of the day.

It was raining outside, the first shower the valley had seen in months, and a fitting backdrop to Barney's mood. Bad things, he decided, really did come in threes.

Having finally finished the first draft of his novel, he had sent it out two weeks ago to eight carefully selected London literary agents. This morning he had received his eighth and final rejection. ('Thank you for your manuscript, which we read with interest' . . . clearly translated to *'Thank you for your manuscript, which we didn't read at all/burned in a fire/ wiped our arses on . . .'*)

This latest rejection came hot on the heels of the announcement by his ex-girlfriend, Maud, that she was engaged to be married. And not just to anybody, but to Andrew Frasier-Bartlett, an old prep-school friend of Barney's whose father owned the better half of Hampshire.

'I hope you'll be happy for us,' Maud wrote, attaching pictures of a diamond engagement ring worth many multiples of Barney's house. 'And please don't take it personally that you're not invited to the wedding, but Andy feels it would be awkward and I think he's probably right.'

'Andy' was right. It wasn't even as if Barney still loved Maud, or even thought about her very much any more. It was more that in a dreadful, mean-spirited, unworthy way, he resented the fact that everybody else's life appeared to be following some sort of fairy-tale trajectory, while his own was a Woody Allen movie at best and a Lars von Trier sob-fest at worst.

True, his photographs were now selling steadily at Penny de la Cruz's gallery, a tiny chink of light in an otherwise gloom-laden sky, and useful in that it meant that he wouldn't starve – not this month, anyway. But the fact remained that he was a failed novelist with no real job, no prospects, no girlfriend. And now, worst of all, no Flora.

Barney's unrequited love for Flora had burned for so long it no longer hurt him. Rather, it provided a constant, gentle, warm glow, like a lit match in a carefully cupped hand. Just knowing Flora was there made him feel better.

But then, suddenly, she wasn't there. The last night Barney saw her, the night she learned her mother had died, he'd felt closer to her than ever. At the very least he had become her go-to friend in need, her top choice of shoulder to cry on.

But then she had gone to New York, come back, buggered off somewhere and stopped taking his calls. He knew he wasn't alone. No one had seen her on Facebook. No one had heard a word from her in weeks. Even Henry Saxton Brae, never Barney's favourite person, had come to see him, panicked that something terrible might have happened to Flora. Barney didn't really think it had, but the idea, once planted, worried him. So did the fact that Henry's worry was clearly sincere. As far as Barney knew, this was the first time Henry Saxton Brae had ever, in his life, been more focused on another person than on himself. He'd agreed to let Henry know if he heard from Flora.

But he hadn't heard. Not a peep.

'What what, old man? You look like you've lost a shilling and found sixpence.'

Barney glanced up. Sebastian Saxton Brae, ruddy-cheeked and moist-lipped, his eyebrows sprouting wildly out of his forehead like two especially hairy caterpillars, grinned down at him, revealing two rows of large, horsey, slightly yellowing teeth. Not for the first time, Barney marvelled that Seb and Henry were related – not only because Henry had got a hundred per cent of the good looks of the family, but because Seb had got a hundred per cent of the kind-heartedness. For a long time Barney had disliked Seb because of his support for hunting – he was master, after all – and what with Barney being an anti, the feeling had been mutual. But the accident had changed all that. Lucy Smart's death and Seb's own terrible injuries had brought the village together and put things into perspective.

Eva had always told Barney that Seb was a sweetheart. As with so many things, she was quite right.

'Can't be that bad, can it?' Pulling up a chair, Seb sat down at Barney's table without being asked. 'Is it money?'

'Not really.' Barney smiled ruefully. 'No more than usual anyway.'

'What then? A woman?'

Barney sighed heavily.

'She's not worth it y'know, whoever she is,' opined Seb. 'None of them are.'

'This one is.' Barney swirled the Guinness around and

around in his pint glass contemplatively. 'Flora's different.'

'Flora?' Seb looked surprised, then awkward. 'Yes, well. She is different, I agree. I had the wrong impression of her at first. But she's a lovely girl. Lovely. So are you and she, er . . . you know . . . ?'

Seb attempted a *nudge-nudge, wink-wink* expression that was so ridiculous Barney couldn't help but laugh out loud.

'No!' he said, recovering. 'I dearly wish we were "you know". But we aren't. And I don't think we ever will be. I just wish I knew where she *was*. We used to be such close friends. I'm awfully worried about her.'

Seb looked down, strumming his fingers on the table. Barney noticed he was biting his lower lip and looked terribly fidgety all of a sudden.

'Are you all right?' he asked.

'Hmm?' Seb was still miles away. 'All right, look,' he said, returning his attention suddenly to Barney. 'I said I wouldn't say anything. And I'd prefer if you didn't land me in it. But I know where Flora is.'

Barney gazed at him in frank astonishment.

'*You* do?'

'Yes,' said Seb, as if this were the most normal thing in the world. 'And I'll tell you if it will put your mind at rest. But I must also tell you, the young lady wants to be left alone. She's had a hell of a time of it with this tyrannical boss of hers, and breaking up with the boyfriend, and her mother kicking the bucket.'

'I know,' said Barney, unable to hide his amusement at Seb's choice of words. 'That's why I want to talk to her. Just talk. I won't pester her, I promise.'

Seb hesitated a moment, then scribbled an address on the back of an old betting slip and pressed it into Barney's palm.

'Mum's the word,' he whispered, tapping the side of his nose like Inspector Clouseau.

Barney watched him go, feeling inordinately happy all of a sudden. He looked at the paper in his hand. Perhaps he should go there first, talk to Flora, and *then* report back to Henry?

But no. A promise was a promise.

Downing the remnants of his pint, he set off for Hanborough.

'Barney!' Eva came to the door. With wet hair and no make-up on and wearing sweatpants, a loose-fitting green T-shirt that kept slipping off her shoulders, and a pair of oversized furry slippers, she looked oddly sexy. 'What a nice surprise. Come in.'

'Is Henry home?' Barney asked, taking off his jacket.

'I'm here.' Henry appeared at the top of the stairs. 'Have you heard something?'

'Actually, yes,' said Barney. 'You're not going to believe this, but Flora's in Yorkshire. Has been the whole time. Seb lent her his cottage up there weeks ago.'

'There you are,' said Eva. 'I told you she'd be fine.'

'We don't know she's fine,' Henry snapped, frowning as he came downstairs. 'Seb, *my* Seb?' he added to Barney, who nodded. 'I don't believe it. Why didn't he say anything? I've been going out of my mind.'

Barney shrugged. 'Flora asked him not to. She wanted to be alone. In any case, I just came to let you know. I'll drive up there in the morning and check on her, make sure she's really OK.'

'No,' Henry said, with a force and volume that made both Eva and Barney jump. 'I'll go. Tonight.'

Barney looked at him curiously. What had he missed? There could be no mistaking Henry's fervour, his desperation even, to be the one to race to Flora's side.

He's in love with her.

They're in love with each other.

As soon as the thought popped into his head, it all seemed blindingly obvious. Henry loved Flora. It explained his panic when she disappeared. His indifference to Eva. The increasing flashes of temper.

Poor Eva. She deserved so much better; it was heart-breaking.

Barney waited for the pangs of jealousy to hit him. He'd been infatuated with Flora for so long, surely he ought to feel dreadful at the idea of having Henry Love-God Saxton Brae, England's most lusted-after bachelor, as a rival? But instead all he could think about was Eva. He suddenly felt an overwhelming urge to protect her from the blow he knew must be coming.

Eva, however, seemed utterly unaware that anything was amiss.

'Don't be silly, darling,' she said lightly to Henry. 'Barney can go. I'm sure Flora's fine and we have our appointment tomorrow at ten, remember?'

Henry looked at her coldly. 'Stop saying that. You're not "sure" Flora's fine. You just don't care whether she is or not.'

'That's not fair!' said Eva, stung.

'No,' added Barney. 'It really isn't.'

'She just lost her mother, for fuck's sake,' muttered Henry.

'Then let Barney go to her,' said Eva, showing a rare flash of real anger.

'I'm happy to go, if it will help,' said Barney, putting a supportive hand on Eva's shoulder.

'It will help,' said Eva.

'No, it won't,' insisted Henry. '*I* will go. I'm not bloody debating it. I still can't believe Seb.'

'Why does it have to be *you*, Henry?' Eva raised her voice, but suddenly she sounded close to tears. 'When our baby's *first scan* is tomorrow?'

Barney's eyes widened. 'You're pregnant?'

Eva nodded.

Barney felt simultaneously delighted – he knew how much Eva had longed to become a mother – and as if the balled fist of fate had just sucker-punched him in the stomach. Spontaneously wrapping Eva in a bear hug, he lifted her up off the ground.

'That's amazing!'

His joy was infectious. Eva soon found herself grinning broadly, despite her anger at Henry.

'Congratulations!' said Barney.

'Thanks.'

Why couldn't Henry show even half as much excitement about his own baby as Barney could about somebody else's? thought Eva. The Bahamas trip had been magical, but ever since they got home a horrible distance had begun creeping back in between them. He was clearly more concerned about Flora than he was about her and their child. How could he even consider missing their first scan?

'Where are you going?' she asked, as Henry bounded back up the stairs, two at a time.

'To pack a bag,' Henry called over his shoulder.

Eva shook her head in disbelief. 'You're really going?'

'I'll call you when I get there.'

'Don't bother!' Eva muttered angrily after him, but he was already out of earshot.

Barney stood awkwardly watching this domestic fracas, feeling increasingly like a peeping Tom. He wished he could make everything OK for Eva. For all of them. But it was as if they were four puppets – himself, Eva, Henry and Flora – whose strings were being maliciously yanked and jerked by some careless and impish god.

'Are you OK?' he asked Eva.

'Not really,' she said. Barney half expected her to cry, but she didn't. Instead she let out a long, defeated sigh. In a way, it was worse.

'He's just worried about her,' said Barney, conscious of how unconvincing he sounded. 'I don't think he means to be short with you.'

'I don't care what he means,' said Eva bleakly.

'Yes, you do.' Barney wrapped a protective arm around her shoulder. 'Can I do anything?'

Eva looked up at him. 'Come to the scan with me tomorrow?'

Barney's face lit up. All of a sudden, it seemed, the gods had decided to let Barney go, setting him down gently upon the stage.

He beamed at Eva. 'I'd be honoured.'

Flora was in the garden, sipping coffee and working on some sketches, when Henry's Bugatti Veyron pulled up in the lane outside. It was still early, about nine in the morning, but the sun was already pleasantly warm and the birdsong and fresh morning smells were irresistible.

A former mineworkers' cottage in the idyllic village of Rosedale, set deep within the North York Moors national park, Seb Saxton Brae's fishing retreat had been the perfect bolthole. An hour's walk to the nearest pub and a twenty-minute drive from any sort of shop, school or other sign of civilization, it was about as remote as England got. And yet it wasn't lonely. The tiny community of farmers and writers and artists and fishermen kept quiet company with one another. A nod over the hedge as they worked in their gardens, a wave from the tractor as they headed up onto the moors. Despite the turmoil in her life, or perhaps because of it, Flora had felt happier in Rosedale than she would have imagined possible. Yes, she was living in a bubble. But it was a lovely bubble, peaceful and healing and productive and safe.

Henry's arrival popped it in an instant.

'I don't believe it. Seb told you,' said Flora as Henry unlatched the gate. In jeans and a dirty white T-shirt, Henry didn't look his best. He had heavy bags under his eyes from having driven through the night, and a grey-black shadow of stubble forming unevenly on the lower half of his face. Even so, and even after all the stern talking-tos Flora had given herself since her return from New York, the sight of him made her heart race unpleasantly and her palms start to sweat.

'Seb didn't tell me,' he said, stooping to kiss her cheek despite her less than welcoming expression. 'He accidentally let something slip to Barney.'

'So Barney told you?' Flora frowned. 'Since when are you two friends?'

'We aren't,' said Henry. 'But everyone's been worried about you.'

'I don't know why,' grumbled Flora. 'I'm fine.'

'Can I come in?' said Henry.

'Would it make a difference if I said "no"?'

He smiled. 'Of course not.'

'You'd better come in then,' said Flora.

Inside the cottage was a mess. Or, more specifically, a hive of activity. Flora's laptop was open on the dining-room table, surrounded by a sea of images, fabric samples, documents and box files, their contents spilling out everywhere. Two half-completed mood boards lay on the floor, amid piles of pins. In the kitchen a cheap white board now covered most of Kate's antique dresser, with headings such as 'Clients', 'Leads' and 'Cash Flow' scrawled in Magic Marker across the top, with columns of text, numbers and names below. Half-drunk cups of coffee littered every available surface.

'I wasn't expecting guests,' said Flora, catching Henry's bemused expression as she turned the kettle on.

'It looks like a war room,' he observed, throwing a three-day-old newspaper off the sofa in the kitchen so he could sit down. Now that he was here, Henry wasn't sure what, exactly, he had come to say, or what tone he should strike. He'd been so worried about Flora, so desperate to see her face and hear her voice, nothing else had mattered but reaching her as fast as he possibly could. But now that he'd arrived, and she was safe and here and sitting in front of him, he felt foolish. As if the Flora that needed his help and protection had been a figment of his imagination.

'I suppose it is, in a way,' said Flora. 'My battle plan.'

'And what battle are you planning?' Henry asked. 'A surprise attack on Graydon?'

Flora smiled. 'Not at all. Although if I were, I'm not sure I'd tell you. Not now you guys are partners.'

'Not my doing,' Henry said, raising his hands. 'Georgina went behind my back. Totally stitched me up. I would never do that to you,' he added, with a sincerity that took Flora aback. 'I hope you know that.'

'Of course,' said Flora, although she wasn't sure she knew any such thing. She'd seen so many versions of Henry. The spiteful and arrogant version, who messed around and betrayed those he loved with gay abandon. The loving and vulnerable Henry, who'd begged for her help to save his dog from the river and wept when Soda was safely back in his arms. The self-aware and guilty Henry, who continually promised to change but never quite seemed to make it. The lost, motherless son, desperate for love but too terrified to trust deeply enough in anyone, least of all himself. She wondered which version had driven all the way up here today, and what he wanted, really.

'What Graydon did to you over the Designer of the Year award, and afterwards at Hanborough, was outrageous,' Henry went on. 'I wanted to reinstate you but—'

Flora cut him off, pressing a mug of tea into his hand and sweeping more papers onto the floor to sit beside him.

'It's OK. I get it. I don't care about Graydon.'

Henry looked disbelieving. 'Honestly?'

'Honestly,' said Flora, with a cheerfulness Henry was starting to find disconcerting. All this time he'd been picturing her in a pit of despair, cut off from her friends and family, deranged with grief. It was difficult to adjust so quickly to such a different reality, one that left him with no role to play. The truth was, he realized now, he had wanted Flora to need him. To reach out to him, so he could reach out to *her*. To beg him for help.

Instead, she'd turned to Seb for help and had figured out everything for herself.

'None of this is about Graydon,' Flora explained, pointing to the chaos around them. ' It's about me. *My* future. What *I* want to do, where *I* want to be.'

Henry frowned. That was a lot too many I's for his liking.

'I'm planning to launch my own business. The details are still a little hazy. Totally hazy, actually.' Flora laughed.

'OK,' said Henry, cautiously. 'Well, that's good, I suppose.'

'It is. It's great.' Flora smiled broadly, but did he detect a certain edge to her voice? Henry still wasn't totally buying this new, upbeat, live-and-let-live Flora, any more than she was buying the completely honest, caring, upright version of him.

'I'm sorry about your mother,' he blurted.

Flora's expression instantly changed. 'Thank you,' she said stiffly.

Ah, thought Henry. *Now we're getting somewhere.*

'How was the funeral?'

'It was fine.'

Henry gave her a 'come on' look.

'It was sad,' said Flora. 'Small. Lonely. Her life was sad. But, you know, she made some bad choices. She lived in the past. She wouldn't let it go.'

'You could have talked to me about it,' said Henry, taking Flora's hand in his, feeling desperately close to her suddenly.

Meanwhile Flora felt something akin to panic. The physical contact, the warmth of his palm against hers, was unbearable. Wonderful and intoxicating and terrifying all at the same time. She quickly pulled her hand away.

'There was nothing to say,' she told him, the brisk smile of earlier now fixed back in place. 'I really am fine. I just needed to get away. Clear my head.'

'Hmm.' Henry looked disbelieving. And something else. Hurt? 'And have you?' he asked.

'I think so,' Flora said, truthfully. After all, clearing one's head was not the same as clearing one's heart. 'A lot has happened this year, and some of it's been hard. But I don't want to make the same mistake as my mother. I want to look forward, not back. Don't you?'

'Of course.'

Henry didn't know exactly why, but he felt horribly depressed all of a sudden. It was ridiculous really. He'd driven up the A1 in a blind panic, half expecting to find Flora strung up from a ceiling beam. But instead here she was – calm, sanguine, positive even; rising above Graydon James's spite and George Savile's scheming; moving on from her mother's death and her broken engagement, determined to focus on the silver lining among her clouds.

Am I sad because I'm jealous? Because I can't do the same? Can't count my blessings?

Or because I came here to rescue her, but she doesn't need rescuing after all?

Perhaps, Henry realized, he was the one who needed rescuing? But from what? Wasn't his life perfect, after all? The archetypal fairy tale, complete with princess and castle?

And yet something was wrong. Something was definitely wrong.

'Eva's pregnant,' he blurted out.

Flora felt her stomach lurch but her smile remained fixed. 'That's wonderful! Oh, congratulations, Henry. You must be thrilled.'

'Of course,' he nodded, smiling back.

Thrilled.

'A new life. A new start,' said Flora. 'That's exactly what you wanted. After Lucy and . . . everything. Right?'

'Right,' said Henry. 'Absolutely.'

Like two actors, trapped eternally in a play from which they could never escape, the two of them dully repeated their lines, each wishing that the other would break the spell.

'Please give Eva my love,' said Flora, bringing the scene to a close. 'When you go back.'

She's dismissing me, Henry thought bleakly. *I should never have come.* But he couldn't give up just yet. Turning to face her directly he asked:

'Why don't you give it to her yourself? Come home.'

'Hanborough isn't my home, Henry,' Flora reminded him as gently as she could, although she could see the hurt in his eyes again, the same, little-boy-lost expression he'd had before. 'It's yours. I was there for a job and the job is done. I already gave up my lease on Peony Cottage.'

'Well, you can't stay here for ever,' said Henry, his brow furrowing.

What Flora had said was true, of course, but he didn't want to hear it.

'And you're coming for the wedding anyway, so you may as well stay in the valley for the summer at least. Everybody's missed you.'

'Everybody?' Flora raised an eyebrow. She was fishing but she couldn't help it.

'Barney,' mumbled Henry, looking away. If Flora didn't know him better, she could have sworn she saw him blush. 'He's been moping about like Linus with a lost blanket for weeks.'

Flora stood up and walked over to the kitchen window. A bird feeder hung from the branch of a willow tree just a few feet from the house. She watched as a woodpecker flew down and attacked the nuts, his bright red head moving backwards and forwards like a particularly graceful jack-hammer.

Without turning around she announced: 'I'm not coming to the wedding, Henry.'

Henry felt the room starting to spin.

'What do you mean? Of course you're coming. You have to come.'

'I can't. I'm sorry.'

'This is ridiculous.' Henry stood up angrily. 'Why not?'

'I have a job,' said Flora. 'A job prospect anyway. Back in New York. It's too good to pass up.'

'What job?' Henry challenged her.

Reluctantly, Flora turned around. 'Does it matter?'

Henry could see there were tears in her eyes, but he couldn't feel compassion. Not when she was doing this to him. Not when she was leaving.

'Of course it bloody well matters!'

'Why?'

'Because I don't believe you!' he shouted.

A bleak, awful silence fell.

They looked at one another, sadness and love and longing and a whole host of other, repressed emotions hanging in the air between them, like a force field that neither of them could break through.

'Flora . . . ' Henry's voice cracked. 'Please. I . . . '

'You should go,' said Flora.

Henry shook his head, too choked to speak.

'You shouldn't have come.'

This was clearly true, but Henry couldn't admit it, not in words.

'You have a *baby* on the way, Henry.'

'I know.' He clutched his head as if in pain. 'I know, I know, I know.'

'Then go home,' said Flora. 'For my sake and for yours.

Go home to your family, Henry. You need to do the right thing this time. You can. I know you can.'

Afterwards, Henry couldn't remember leaving her. Did he say goodbye? Kiss her? Did he just turn and walk away? Did he run?

The only thing that stayed with him was sitting in his car on the motorway, somewhere past Ferrybridge, his mind filled with an image of Richard Smart's anguished face at Lucy's funeral, and his ears ringing with Flora's words.

'*You need to do the right thing this time. You can . . .* '

She was right. He did need to do the right thing.

And he would. For Eva, and their child.

Whatever feelings there were between him and Flora, they obviously weren't meant to be. Perhaps they were too similar? Too focused on protecting themselves? In different ways, their respective childhoods had taught them that. Don't open your heart. Don't get too close. Don't rely on others.

People let you down. People leave. People die.

And then you are on your own.

Again.

People like Eva didn't see the world that way. People who'd had happy childhoods, full of love, full of security.

It was time to let go and to grow up. Time to give his own child a childhood like that. Safe. Secure. Happy.

Flora had moved on. Now, so must he.

CHAPTER TWENTY-EIGHT

Georgina Savile carefully smoothed the seam of her midnight-blue Victoria Beckham dress, adjusting her vintage Philip Treacy hat to the perfect angle as she took her seat in the middle of the church.

On the downside, today was Henry and Ikea's wedding day. George still struggled to believe that Henry, her Henry, was seriously proposing to spend the rest of his life shackled to a woman with the IQ of a pickled walnut and the conversational skills of a rollmop herring. But the prospect of his marriage no longer upset her the way it used to. Marriage, after all, had never been any impediment to her own extra-curricular adventures. Glancing back at her husband, Robert, who'd been roped in at the last minute as an usher when one of Henry's school friends had come down with Norovirus and couldn't make it, George waved and smiled. Robert was a marvellous husband: loyal, hard-working, unsuspecting and malleable. Henry, on the other hand, would make a terrible husband. Being his mistress, George had decided, was a far more desirable proposition than being his wife.

The fact that she was *not* currently his mistress didn't concern her too much either. Step one in regaining that position had been to get rid of Flora Fitzwilliam, and in that George had succeeded brilliantly. Not only had she forced Flora out of Hanborough and destroyed her professional reputation, but she'd evidently managed to create enough of a wedge between her and Henry that Flora wasn't even attending today's ceremony. Her absence had raised one or two eyebrows, not least the bride's. But as far as George was concerned, it was the best possible news.

Step two had been reasserting her authority at work. She'd made a serious mistake, she now realized, in rolling over and letting Henry walk all over her for so long. In the early, passionate days of their affair, George and Henry had sparred and argued constantly. He was attracted to her because she was difficult, a challenge. Over time she had weakened, and his attraction had waned as a result. Now, however, with the GJD deal done and business booming, George was flexing her professional muscles once again. Coupled with her killer figure – if she did say so herself, she was easily the sexiest guest at today's wedding – George felt sure that her new-found confidence was bound to win Henry back. At least as far as her bed, which was where she wanted him.

George smiled regally at the other guests as they continued to file in. Being one of the first guests to arrive, not to mention the most ravishing, meant that George had had the entire press pack to herself. Paparazzi snapped away feverishly as she and Robert made their way slowly across the green and into St Hilda's churchyard, virtually ensuring that George's picture would earn a prominent place in the *Daily Mail's* gossip pages, as well as *Hello!*, *Tatler* and hopefully *Vogue*, all of whom were covering the Gunnarson/Saxton Brae nuptials.

It was a glorious day in the Swell Valley, and George's long bronzed legs and lithe figure, shown off to perfection in her fitted VB sheath, dazzled in the midday sunshine.

'Is it all right if we squeeze in next to you?'

Laura Baxter, the famous local TV producer, had been shown to George's pew by one of the other ushers, a lawyer friend of Henry's named Pete. Laura was attractive but middle-aged, and her chocolate brown knee-length dress wasn't doing her any great favours.

'Of course.' George flashed her the sweet smile she always gave less attractive women, especially the ones with good-looking husbands. Although, to be fair, Laura's husband Gabe was also not looking his best today, despite the morning suit.

'I told you we were early,' he grumbled to his wife as they eased past George to their seats. 'I could have had an extra half an hour in bed.'

'Oh, do stop moaning,' complained Laura, adding to George, 'He's on a diet. Honestly, you'd think it was a hunger strike, the fuss he's been making. It's like living with a teenage girl right before her period.'

George giggled. She enjoyed a good bitch with other women, just as long as she was prettier than they were.

With fifteen minutes to go before the service, the remaining guests began streaming in, with pews filling up thick and fast. Penny de la Cruz looked surprisingly beautiful in a flowing, grey silk dress with tiny white embroidered flowers, floating down the aisle with her long hair cascading down her back like the Lady of Shalott. Behind her, her daughter Emma Harwich, once a famous model and wild child, teetered along arm in arm with her latest husband, an Iranian oil magnate at least twice her age, and so greasy he looked as if you could fry chips in him. In a red minidress that looked

403

cheap but wasn't, and weighed down with a mountain of tacky but outrageously valuable diamond jewellery, the most striking thing about Emma was her face. She'd clearly done something deeply regrettable to her lips, which now bulged like two swollen balloons, smothered in glossy pink lip gloss.

'Bugger me,' Gabe Baxter 'whispered' far too loudly to his wife. 'Is that Emma Harwich? Her mouth literally looks like a vagina.'

'*Gabriel!*' Laura hissed, but not before everybody in the pews in front and behind them had collapsed with giggles.

One row behind Emma, Barney Griffith sat making polite conversation with Lady Saxton Brae, who bore an uncanny resemblance to Carole Middleton today in a naff champagne/peach-coloured dress and matching three-quarter-length coat, both purchased from Dominique's, a chichi boutique in Chichester.

'I simply can't bring myself to pay London prices,' she told Barney, who nodded with glazed eyes. 'I mean, obviously, we could afford it. But it's just so wasteful.'

'Right,' said Barney, looking around desperately for any means of escape but finding none.

'Especially when one thinks of all the other things one could do with the money.'

'Of course.'

'Starlight's crying out for a new dressage saddle, but you can't imagine what Equipe are charging these days for bespoke. Almost three thousand pounds!'

'Goodness,' said Barney, who felt as if he might cry, and not just from the boredom of Kate's conversation. He'd been ridiculously emotional all day. At first he put it down to disappointment, because Flora wasn't going to be here. She'd given Henry some spurious excuse about a work thing in

New York, apparently, a story she stuck to in her one, brief, deeply unsatisfying telephone conversation with Barney last week. She'd apologized, of course, for not being in touch, and the two of them had swapped stories about what they'd been up to. Flora asked Barney about his photography, and told him her ideas for a new business. But the old closeness, the connection they'd had before her mother's death – that seemed to have gone completely.

That accounted for part of Barney's sadness. But the more he examined his feelings, he realized it was the prospect of Eva and Henry marrying that was at the heart of his down mood. He'd grown closer to Eva than ever in the last few weeks, since she told him about the baby, and more convinced than ever that she and Henry were a terrible match. Going to her scan, particularly, had moved him more than he would have imagined possible. Seeing her baby on the screen, a new life, so innocent and full of hope, and watching Eva's face, anxious at first and then transfixed with wonder and love as the foetus started to move around.

Don't do it! he wanted to yell out. *Don't marry Henry. He'll let you down. He'll let you both down.*

But, of course, he hadn't. And the days and weeks had rushed by and now here they were, all playing their roles. Henry as groom. Eva as bride. Barney as honoured guest. It all felt horrible, sad and wrong but inevitable, like watching a tsunami roll in towards the shore.

Kate was still talking, her words floating around in Barney's brain like random ingredients bobbing up in soup he hadn't ordered and didn't want.

'Forelock . . . vet . . . Sebastian thinks . . . next season . . . hunt ball . . . Hanborough . . . '

Tuning her out, Barney looked towards the altar, where

405

Call-me-Bill was making small talk with Richard Smart, Henry's best man.

Richard looked a lot better than when Barney had last seen him. He was still too thin. His morning coat hung off him like a tramp's overcoat and his dress trousers swamped his legs, giving him a look of Charlie Chaplin. The lines and grey hairs that his wife's death had left him with were still there, making him look considerably older than his years. But when he nudged Henry in the ribs and grinned, his smile was genuine, reaching all the way to his eyes, and even his conversation with the vicar, a renowned windbag, seemed animated and engaged. Behind him, in the front pew, his sons were goofing around, stuffing kneeler cushions under their shirts and rubbing their backs, pretending to be pregnant. Richard told them off but you could see his heart wasn't it, that he was happy to see them happy again.

Life goes on, thought Barney. He wished to God he didn't feel so depressed. Maybe there was something actually wrong with him? Maybe he should see a doctor.

Next to Richard, Henry also looked well: happy and relaxed and as irritatingly handsome as ever in his perfectly tailored dark suit and tie. Whatever pre-wedding nerves he'd exhibited over the past few months seemed to have evaporated now. Even Eva had admitted that since he'd returned from his trip to Yorkshire to see Flora, Henry seemed different. Calmer. Happier. More at peace.

The organist struck up a few early chords as more of the bride's family started to arrive, Eva's mother Kaisa looking understatedly elegant in a jade green suit and ruffled cream silk blouse on the arm of Henry's brother, Seb.

It won't be long now, thought Barney, wondering idly what

Flora was doing right now. *In an hour and a half, Eva will officially be Mrs Henry Saxton Brae.*

'You look perfect. Just perfect.'

Erik Gunnarson's eyes welled up with tears as his only daughter appeared at the top of the stairs. In a bias-cut lace dress with long sleeves and a scooped back, which clung like gossamer to her sylph-like figure (at four months gone there was still no hint of a baby bump), her full-length veil held back from her face by an exquisite pearl and diamond tiara, Eva was breathtaking, every inch the fairy-tale princess. Over the years Erik had grown accustomed to the incredible life his daughter now led as a world-famous model. The six-figure earnings, the luxury cars and holidays, the private air travel and free couture clothes. Even so, seeing her now, descending the spiral stairs of an ancient English castle – *her* castle – on her wedding day, about to marry one of England's most eligible bachelors? It was quite something for a little girl from Vallentuna, the daughter of a Swedish postal worker.

'Thanks, Far.'

Eva smiled cautiously. She felt beautiful. The dress was a triumph, exactly what she'd wanted. Hanborough also looked ravishing, bedecked with white dahlias and sweet peas and every variation of greenery. Later, the party barn and great hall would both be illuminated by hundreds, if not thousands, of white church candles in miniature glass hurricane lamps. Graydon James may have stolen the credit, but Eva knew it was Flora's vision and hard work that had transformed the cold, bleak castle into the warm, romantic, utterly magical home that it was today.

Flora.

Flora was Eva's friend, probably her closest friend in the

Swell Valley, apart from Barney. But she wasn't coming to the wedding. Henry had passed on her excuses, something about work in New York. But Eva wasn't buying it.

There must be something else. Another reason. A real reason.

Barney had offered plenty of possibilities. Coming back to Hanborough was too painful after Graydon's betrayal. Flora was depressed after her mother's death and didn't want to have to field questions about her sacking and what happened and where she'd been.

'Maybe she can't face your wedding now that her own's been called off?'

All of these scenarios made sense. And yet, Eva couldn't shake the uneasy feeling that none of them was the truth, or at least not the whole truth.

Henry had been different since he'd returned from Yorkshire. Better, kinder, more interested in the baby and in their wedding plans. He'd apologized for his distance and snappiness before, blaming work and George and the stress of the new, unwanted merger with GJD.

These were all good things. And yet, Eva's unease grew.

Perhaps she was different, too?

Something had changed.

'Are you ready?' Her father offered her his arm as she reached the bottom of the stairs.

No.

'Yes, Far. Let's go.'

Outside, a vintage Daimler gleamed in the sunshine, a simple white ribbon draped across its polished black bonnet. The chauffeur opened the door, first for Eva and then for her father. Erik Gunnarson helped his daughter carefully smooth out her dress and veil before they set off for the church.

Holding her dad's hand, Eva gazed out of the window as

they made their slow, stately way along the castle drive. A not inconsiderable crowd of locals who had shown up for free champagne this morning now lined the sides of the road, waving and cheering and smiling at the bride as they passed. Once beyond the castle gates, the valley spread out below them, as lush and verdant as *Frozen*'s Arendelle. They drove through the tiny hamlet of Hanborough, bedecked in bunting for the occasion, then began the descent through the woods towards Fittlescombe and St Hilda's Church.

Tears filled Eva's eyes. She had come to love this place.

'Darling?' Erik asked anxiously, catching her sad expression. 'What's the matter?'

'Nothing.' Eva forced a smile. 'I'm fine. A bit emotional, that's all.'

Erik Gunnarson frowned. He knew his daughter.

'Eva?'

She wouldn't meet his eye.

'Eva!' he said, more sternly. 'Listen to me. You don't have to go through with this if you don't want to.'

'Yes, I do, Far,' she said, her smile genuine this time. 'There are over a hundred and fifty people in that church, and four hundred more heading to the reception later. Not to mention half the British press camped outside.'

'It doesn't matter,' Erik Gunnarson said, his voice quiet but deadly serious. 'I mean it, Eva. If you aren't sure, don't do it.'

'Is anybody ever "sure"?' Eva asked him. 'Really sure?'

'Yes,' he said firmly. 'They are. I was. Your mother was. Absolutely.'

Eva looked out of the window again. The moment was too intense and she couldn't hold her father's gaze.

Erik leaned forward to speak to the driver. 'Pull over.'

'I'm sorry?' The chauffeur sounded confused.

'I said stop the car,' said Erik. 'My daughter and I need to talk.'

'Where the hell is she?'

Henry leaned in and whispered to Richard, the same question being whispered in the pews and among the press pack and well-wishers camped outside.

'She's half an hour late. Eva's never late.'

'Bride's prerogative,' said Richard reassuringly, forcing a smile. 'She'll be here, mate.'

But he was worried too. Outside, the ushers scanned the horizon nervously for any sign of the bridal car. Someone had already been dispatched in the direction of Hanborough to look for them, but had not returned. Unsurprisingly, Erik Gunnarson's mobile was switched off.

Kaisa Gunnarson approached the vicar, an anxious look on her face. Keeping her voice low so as not to unduly panic Henry, she said, 'I think something's wrong. This is very unlike my daughter. And Erik's always on time, for everything.'

The Reverend Clempson looked more nervous than all of them. His forehead visibly glistened with sweat and he kept tugging anxiously at the gold-embroidered sleeves of his sacramental vestments, like a little boy on his first day at school worrying a loose thread on his blazer. Still, he did his best to sound positive.

'Brides do sometimes get last-minute nerves. Perhaps she and her father are talking things through. How did she seem this morning?'

Kaisa thought back to breakfast up at the castle. In keeping with tradition, Henry had spent the night before the wedding at Richard's house, so as not to see the bride until the church. The Gunnarsons had sat around the kitchen table at

Hanborough together, and Eva had seemed . . . calm? Or perhaps, with hindsight, subdued?

'I don't know,' she told the vicar. 'She was fine. Busy. People kept arriving and—'

Richard Smart interrupted them, holding his phone and looking deeply relieved.

'They're here. The car just pulled up outside.'

'Thank goodness!' Kaisa smiled broadly and returned to her seat. The vicar exhaled and a ripple of relief and excitement swept through the church by osmosis like a Mexican wave, as the organist finally struck up the opening chords of Bach's *Bist du bei mir*.

The double doors at the rear of St Hilda's swung open. A hundred and fifty necks craned and heads swivelled to catch a first glimpse of the bride. Henry stared down the aisle like a man staring down the barrel of a gun, the stress of the last hour still etched on his face.

This was it.

She's here.

We're getting married.

Erik Gunnarson appeared in the doorway. Alone. The organist hesitated, but continued playing as Eva's father walked purposefully up to the altar and spoke a few words to Henry and Richard. Henry's face turned green, then white. At a signal from Richard, the organ music stopped abruptly.

'I'm sorry everyone.' The father of the bride spoke clearly and in perfect English, his voice echoing off the walls in the sudden silence like a ricocheting bullet. Nobody spoke or even breathed. 'I'm afraid there won't be a wedding today. My daughter . . . '

There was a long pause. Erik looked at his wife, continuing directly to her.

'My daughter has changed her mind.'

Shock vibrated through the church like a clanged cymbal. Gabe Baxter looked at his wife in disbelief. Barney Griffith found himself gripping the pew in front of him so tightly his knuckles turned white.

Stepping down from the altar, Erik Gunnarson took his wife's hand, and the two elderly Swedes hurried out of the church together. The congregation watched in stunned silence until the doors closed behind them. Then came a collective exhale and a surge of noise as the implications of what had just happened sank in.

'Will there still be a party at the castle?' Penny de la Cruz's very old and very deaf mother observed loudly. 'Terribly disappointing if there isn't a party.'

Richard looked blankly at Henry.

'Shit,' he said, aghast. He wasn't sure what else to say. 'Are you OK?'

'I don't know,' said Henry truthfully.

Looking up, Henry caught Georgina Savile's eye. Everyone in the church was looking at him, their expressions ranging from shock to pity to concern. But George's face registered something else. Desire. Excitement. Hope.

She smiled. *Ikea must have gone mad. But her loss would be George's gain.*

Irrationally, instinctively, Henry smiled back, like a recovered meth addict remembering a past high. But only for a moment. He didn't know what he was feeling or even what was happening right now. But whatever it was, he knew George wasn't the answer.

He turned back to Richard.

'Get me the fuck out of here,' he whispered urgently. 'Now.'

CHAPTER TWENTY-NINE

Flora Fitzwilliam spread out her White Company picnic rug on the grass between two spreading oak trees and began unpacking her picnic lunch: a small game pie from Fortnum & Mason, a bag of perfectly ripe white cherries from Marks & Spencer's and an Innocent smoothie. Heaven.

It was early September, but summer still clung to London like the smell of woodsmoke after a long burning fire. Sitting here in Kensington Gardens, looking down the hill towards the Diana Memorial Fountain, Flora luxuriated in the warm sun on her bare legs, and the pleasant, leaf-dappled shade on her face. She felt profoundly happy. Her new design business, Fitz, had made a modestly successful start, with two solid commissions for private London houses already under her belt. More importantly, she was living completely independently for the first time in her life, without Mason or Graydon or any sort of a male safety net – professional or personal – underneath her. Working day and night from her tiny one-bedroom studio cottage in a mews off Ladbroke Grove, Flora almost had to pinch herself each morning at the idea that this new life in London, this *freedom*, was really hers. Of course, she still had to sort out something long term with her visa, and she was still having to endure Graydon's relentless attacks on her in the trade press, as well as his intermittent threats to sue. (For what, exactly, Flora wasn't sure, but she didn't doubt his deep pockets nor his vengeful nature. Graydon didn't just hold grudges. He acted on them, repeatedly and relentlessly, until his perceived enemy was extinguished.) But, all in all, from the dark days after her mother's death only a few months earlier, it was incredible how far she'd come. Getting away from the Swell Valley, and Henry and Eva's dramas, had been a huge piece of the puzzle. She still missed Henry. But she missed Eva and Barney and Penny too, and she told herself it was all part of the same thing, a lovely chapter in her life, but one that had had to come to a close.

Like the rest of the nation, Flora read about the saga of Henry and Eva's cancelled wedding with astonishment and fascination. She'd been in New York the day it happened, when Henry had actually been jilted at the altar, and had half expected to hear from him, or from someone. But her phone never rang. She returned to England two days later to find every newspaper and gossip magazine obsessed with the ongoing saga. There were pictures of Henry on his honeymoon in Tahiti with his best man, Richard Smart. Richard had apparently persuaded him they should go together, to get away from the media attention and/or to drown Henry's sorrows, although judging by the pictures of him surrounded by scantily clad Tahitian girls, he seemed to be bearing up admirably under the strain. Meanwhile, just as news of Eva's pregnancy leaked, she disappeared from public view entirely, sparking a week-long hunt to track her down, on a scale not seen since Liz Hurley 'went to ground' after Hugh Grant was caught with Divine Brown. The whole thing was like a soap opera, or an unusually gripping reality show. Despite knowing the protagonists intimately, Flora found herself swept along in the drama just like everybody else. It was as if she were reading about characters, not real people whom she knew and cared about.

Taking a bite of her ridiculously succulent and delicious pie, she opened today's early edition of the *Standard*, flipping it open at page two to catch up on the latest instalment. Things had taken a thrilling twist last night when Eva had been 'found' hiding out in a remote summer cabin in Skåne, in the south of Sweden, with a new man. Flora had almost choked on her gin and tonic when the man's name was announced on Capital FM as 'top British photographer Barnaby Griffith'.

Barney? And *Eva?*

Barney and Eva?

At first the thought of the two of them together seemed quite ridiculous. Barney, after all, had spent the last year professing his undying love for Flora. And in all the time Flora had spent with the two of them, she'd never seen the slightest spark of attraction. And yet, on many levels, they *were* a good match. Both kind, artistic and mellow, both dog lovers and country bumpkins at heart, notwithstanding Eva's glamorous, jet-set lifestyle. Flora had always had the sense that modelling had chosen Eva, rather than the other way around. That, had the cards fallen differently, Eva might have opted for a much, much quieter life. Looking at the grainy long-lens pictures of the two of them in the paper now, standing outside the cabin hugging and laughing, Eva's baby bump clearly visible in an old-fashioned, peasant-style dress, she looked as if she might have found it.

Now that Flora thought about it, Eva and Barney *had* spent an inordinate amount of time together in the time she'd known them. There were all those endless dog walks and long lunches at The Fox. Flora's mind went back to that awful day when she'd caught Henry and Lucy Smart at it in the woods and raced over to Barney's cottage in a panic, only to find Eva already there, looking far more at home than she ever had at Hanborough.

Now, rumours were swirling that the two of them had already secretly eloped and that the Skåne trip was a honeymoon. If it were true, Flora was happy for them both, although she couldn't help but worry about Henry. Eva was carrying his baby, after all. How was *that* going to work?

Part of her wanted to call him. She'd almost dialled his number scores of times. But she hadn't, and every time she'd been pleased afterwards that she'd resisted the temptation.

He has my number. He'll call if he needs me.

Clearly, he didn't. Flora wasn't the only one who was moving on.

The afternoon proved long and stressful. One of Flora's new clients, John Hamrick, a wealthy art dealer who'd been introduced to her and Fitz by George Wilkes, had decided to throw all his toys out of the pram about various finishes. The hand-painted Venetian tiles he'd ordered for the kitchen of his grand Nash apartment, overlooking Regent's Park, were suddenly 'too vulgar'. ('You should have advised me against them,' John snapped at Flora, his upper lip curling as the first tiles were unpacked. 'You must have known they were quite wrong.') As for the stone floor that Flora had painstakingly laid in the kitchen, it now looked 'too gnarly' and 'battered'.

'But, John, you specifically requested distressed limestone,' Flora tried to reason with him.

'Not that distressed.'

A fellow American, Hamrick had been charm personified up to this point: one of the easiest, most laid-back clients Flora had ever worked with. But evidently some big deal had gone wrong at work this week – a rare Dutch Impressionist had underperformed significantly at auction – and the art dealer had transformed overnight into a nit-picking, fault-finding, eternally dissatisfied monster.

At GJD, Flora would have fought her corner, agreeing to order different tiles or to rip up the floor, but only at the client's expense. But with Fitz barely off the starting blocks, and word-of-mouth recommendations vital to its survival, never mind growth, she had little choice but to accept John's histrionics and cave in. That would be expensive and time-consuming. Flora's resentment at his unreasonableness, coupled with her physical exhaustion and a cramped and sweltering Tube ride home all conspired to leave her in a frazzled mood by the time she finally sat down to a cold kitchen supper at almost nine.

No sooner had she cracked open her first bottle of Beck's than the telephone rang.

Flora sighed. Had she given John Hamrick her home number? She hoped not, but she couldn't remember. It was the sort of thing she might have done in a fit of misplaced efficiency weeks ago, back when he was still in his Dr Jekyll stage. Or was it Mr Hyde? The one who didn't eviscerate people and then eat their guts, anyway.

'Hello?' she answered wearily.

'Blimey. That's not much of a greeting. What's wrong, misery guts?'

Barney's voice rang in her ear like a half-remembered sound from another world. Flora's face lit up.

'Barney!'

'That's more like it.' On the other end of the line, his smile was audible.

'I can't believe it's you. It's been for ever! How did you get this number?'

'With difficulty, actually,' said Barney. 'You're not easy to track down.'

'You can talk!' laughed Flora. 'Half the world's press has been hunting for you and Eva. Or hadn't you noticed?'

'Hunting for Eva, not me,' he corrected her. 'But, yeah, it's been insane. I wish they'd sod off and leave us alone, to be honest. All the anxiety can't be good for Eva, or the baby.'

Grabbing her beer, Flora wandered into the living room with the phone, muted the TV and curled up on the couch. 'So how is Eva?'

'She's fine. She's at her grandmother's tonight but she sends you her love.'

'I send mine back,' said Flora. 'I still can't quite believe all this. Are the two of you really married?'

'We are.' Barney laughed, sounding happier than Flora had ever heard him. 'I'm not sure I can believe it myself.'

He told her how everything had unfolded. How he and Eva had grown closer, particularly since her pregnancy, but how he hadn't known until her wedding day that she was actually going to leave Henry.

'I'd told her I loved her. I think she knew anyway. But I wasn't sure if she felt the same way. Nothing had happened between us, not even a kiss. But then, after her no-show at the church she called me. About seven o'clock that night we met up at a hotel near Gatwick and talked. As soon as we saw each other again, we knew.'

'I can't bear it,' sighed Flora. 'That is so romantic.'

'Well, sort of,' said Barney. 'It's not exactly your classic love story. Eva's five months pregnant with another man's baby, don't forget. There's still a lot to be untangled.'

'How is Henry?' Flora couldn't hide the worry in her voice.

'I don't know,' said Barney. 'Eva's spoken to him a few times. He was angry at first, I think. And hurt. But a lot of that was wounded pride. Deep down he must have known things weren't right between them. Anyway, I'm sure you know more about his state of mind than I do.'

'Me?' said Flora. 'I don't know anything.'

'You mean you aren't talking?' Barney sounded surprised.

'No,' Flora said defensively. 'Why would we be?'

'Hmmm,' said Barney. 'Let me think. Maybe because you're obviously both madly in love with each other?'

'Don't be silly,' said Flora. Then, after a long pause, 'Do you really think he's in love with me?'

'Of course he is,' said Barney. 'Eva suspected it for a while, but I couldn't see it till much later. Not until after you slunk up to Seb's place in Yorkshire and disappeared. Henry was frantic.'

'Was he?' Flora hated the hope she heard in her own voice.

'Completely. That was when things really snapped for him and Eva. She was having his baby, but all he could think about was you. He wouldn't let me drive up to check on you; he insisted on going himself.'

Flora listened, lost in thought.

'I think that was also when it dawned on me that I'd fallen in love with Eva,' said Barney. 'Funny how these things creep up on you, isn't it? Or what it takes to make you realize what's right under your nose.'

'I suppose so,' said Flora, who hadn't really been listening to a word since 'you're obviously both madly in love with each other'.

'What happened up in Yorkshire, by the way?' Barney asked, nosily.

'Nothing happened!' Flora flushed. 'We just talked. He was only there for about twenty minutes. He was with Eva. Nothing has *ever* happened between Henry and me. And nothing ever will.'

'Why not?' asked Barney, 'now that you're both free?'

Flora sighed heavily. 'Have you seen the papers recently? The pictures of him in Tahiti and, last weekend, in LA? I've lost count of all the bimbos.'

'That doesn't mean anything,' said Barney, once again astonished to find himself defending Henry Saxton Brae. But, in this case, he meant it. 'He's just letting off steam.'

'I don't think so,' said Flora, sadly. 'Henry will never commit. He doesn't have it in him.'

'You don't know that.'

'I do. He hasn't even called me since it happened. Not once.'

'You haven't called him either,' Barney pointed out reasonably.

Finishing her beer, Flora shook her head. 'No,' she said firmly. 'Even if I *do* love him – and I'm not saying I do – that's one frying pan I am not about to jump into. I just got my life back, Barney. I'm free, from Mason, from Graydon, from my past, from everything. I'm starting a new business and that's all I care about right now. I'm happy.'

'If you say so, Flora.'

'I do say so.'

After she'd hung up, Flora sat there for a long time, clutching her empty beer bottle and staring into space, thinking. She was pleased Barney had called. Pleased that he and Eva were happy. They were a good match.

As for Henry, she meant what he said. Perhaps she did love him. Perhaps he loved her, too – as much as he was capable of loving anyone.

But the kind of love Henry Saxton Brae could give wasn't enough for Flora. It wouldn't make her happy. From now on she would be her own security, her own saviour, her own knight in shining armour.

Fitz would be her lover.

Work would be her children.

Too tired even to crawl into the bedroom, she closed her eyes where she was and fell into a deep and dreamless sleep.

CHAPTER THIRTY

Four months later . . .

'You're doing beautifully, Eva,' the midwife said encouragingly. 'Baby's head is out. One more push and you're there.'

'I can't!' Clinging on to the sides of the birthing pool for dear life, Eva looked at Barney, sweat pouring down her face, her jaw locked rigid with pain. It was unbearable, not being able to help her or do anything. Like watching a dying animal howling to be put out of its misery.

'You can,' said Barney, laying his hand over hers, trying his utmost not to cry himself.

Eva had asked Henry if he wanted to be present at the birth, booked months in advance at the Portland. In typical Swedish fashion, she'd already worked out a friendly, even warm relationship with her child's biological father, and even Barney and Henry were now on civil terms. For the time being, Eva and Barney had rented a farmhouse a few miles from Hanborough, so that Henry would be close to the child and able to visit regularly, as well as a London flat. Eventually they would probably buy in the Swell Valley and settle there permanently, but nothing was set in stone yet. So much had changed for all three of them in the last year – Eva, Barney and Henry, who was now totally single for the first time in many years. All that mattered was the safe arrival of the baby.

Despite these positive steps towards co-parenting, and Henry's new-found maturity, he had roundly rejected Eva's offer, explaining that he would rather stick hot pins in his eyes than hover around like a spare part amid the blood, pain and raw emotion of childbirth.

'Even if we were married, I'd give it a miss,' he said. 'I'll be there for the rest of his life. Just not for that.'

'Or her life,' Eva said archly.

'Whatever,' said Henry. The baby was a boy and that was that. He had a sixth sense about these things. 'I appreciate the offer, but I'm more the "cigars in the waiting room" type.'

At the time Barney had thought Henry a fool. What sort of a man would willingly miss out on the chance to see their child's arrival into the world? He, Barney, couldn't wait to see the baby. To hold it in his arms and look into its eyes and tell it how deeply and desperately it was already loved, by both of its putative fathers. But now that he'd spent ten gruelling hours watching Eva screaming in agony, unable to do anything other than hold her hand, he was starting to wish he'd had Henry's foresight. It was awful. Just *awful* – the most harrowing day of his life. And it still wasn't over.

'Aaaaaagh!' Eva let out a terrifying sound that was part scream, part roar and part heart-wrenching wail. Barney shot a panicked look at the midwife. He half expected the windows to shatter. But, to his amazement, the small, dumpy Liverpudlian overseeing the birth was smiling broadly.

'That's it, love! Go on! Shoulders are out!'

Seconds later, kicking its tiny legs back and forth like a tadpole flicking its tail, Eva's baby shot out of her body and into the water like a bullet from a gun. Barney stared, mute with shock, as the midwife reached into the birthing pool and scooped the infant out of the water, where it relieved everyone by crying loudly and immediately at the top of its lungs.

Slumping back against the side of the pool, her eyes closed, Eva asked weakly, 'What is it?'

Barney was still staring at the child as the midwife dried it with a towel. It had stopped crying now. All Barney could see were its huge eyes opening and closing as it was prodded and wrapped, and a shock of thick, dark hair protruding straight up from the top of its head, in the manner of a cartoon character after an electric shock.

'What is it?' Eva asked again, still too weak to move.

'It's got hair,' said Barney.

The midwife laughed. 'She's got hair.' Cutting and clamping the cord, she placed the wrapped child into his arms. 'You've got a lovely little gel.'

'Fuuuuuck.' Barney stepped backwards, gazing at the baby, sitting down gingerly and with infinite care in the armchair in the corner, as if he were holding a bomb. 'Oh my God. She's perfect. She is absolutely perfect. Hello, lovely.'

The baby blinked back at him, calm and curious, and all the worry of the last ten hours, all the worry of Barney's life up to that point, evaporated instantly and totally like a dewdrop in the sun. He knew in that moment that biology meant precisely nothing. He was looking at his daughter and he had never felt love like it.

'Have you got a name for her?' the midwife asked Eva, who was slowly coming back to life.

'Francesca,' said Barney firmly.

'Francesca?' Eva sounded surprised. They'd discussed a few names but Francesca had never come up. 'I like it,' she smiled.

'Francesca Eva.'

'Perfect.'

'Francesca Eva Griffith.'

Eva raised an eyebrow. 'One step at a time, my love.' Holding out her arms for her daughter, she added, 'Someone had better tell Henry.'

After a brief, half-hearted power struggle over the name (the truth was Henry liked the name Francesca, and he really didn't have any decent alternative suggestions, having focused all his energy on coming up with names for a boy), Henry quickly became as besotted by his daughter as Barney and Eva.

Though he didn't share Barney's enthusiasm for nappy changing, swaddling, burping and all the other daily ministrations Francesca apparently required, he was a regular visitor to the hospital during the ten days that Eva was there (she'd lost so much blood during the birth that she was kept at the Portland for observation), and was happy to spend hours 'chatting' to his daughter about everything from the racing results to politics and her predicted taste in music.

'You mustn't listen to too much of Mummy's Swedish crap,' he would tell the sleeping infant as they paced Eva's large private room.

'Why not?' protested Eva.

'Because it's crap,' Henry cooed in Francesca's ears.

'Your music *is* crap,' Barney agreed disloyally from behind an open copy of the *Telegraph*, where the crossword was defeating him utterly. 'I'll go and get a coffee,' he said, stretching his legs and yawning. 'Give you two some time on your own.'

'Actually,' said Henry, handing Francesca back to Eva and looking at his watch, 'I have to run. I've got a dinner at my club tonight – some fundraiser or other I got myself roped into. I can stop in tomorrow?'

'We're taking her home tomorrow,' said Barney.

For a split second Henry smarted at the word 'home'. Part of him felt instinctively that Hanborough was Francesca's home. But he restrained himself from snapping. Barney was Eva's husband, after all, and would be as much of a father to his daughter as he would. It was in everybody's interests that they continued to get along.

'All right, well, I'll come at the weekend then. Once you've had a chance to get settled.'

Barney opened his mouth to say something but Eva cut him off. 'That would be lovely,' she said. 'We'll see you then.'

After Henry left, Barney perched on the edge of the bed beside her and the baby.

'That's our first weekend home, as a family,' he grumbled.

'I know,' said Eva. 'But Henry's trying. I lived with him for three years and I'm telling you, this is him doing his best.'

'OK,' said Barney.

At the end of the day, Henry Saxton Brae had given him the greatest gift of his life. A few awkward weekends were a small price to pay.

Flora straightened her hair and brushed chocolate croissant crumbs off her Zara silk jacket as she rushed into the Portland.

As usual, she was late, this time after a meeting with Fitz's lawyers that had overrun by more than an hour and had been deeply depressing. Graydon James had launched yet another lawsuit against her, every bit as frivolous as the last. This time he was accusing her of ripping off his designs for a house they'd worked on together in the Hamptons years ago. Apparently the blue tiles Flora had chosen for a client's master bath, as featured in last month's UK *Elle Décor*, were 'almost identical' to the suite GJD had installed in East Hampton.

'You can't copyright blue tiles!' Flora complained in frustration to her lawyers.

'Of course you can't. Which is why he'll lose,' the lawyers assured her. The problem was that, even when Graydon lost, he won. His pockets were infinite, whereas Flora's most definitely had a bottom, a bottom that she'd hit at least two court cases ago. Even if she was awarded costs, they took time to come through, time that Fitz didn't have in terms of its urgent cash-flow needs. In less than a month Flora would be unable to pay her rent, or the interest on her business loans. Graydon was squeezing the life out of her fledgling company and there was nothing on earth she could do about it.

Forget about Graydon, she told herself, pressing the lift call button in the Portland lobby. *You're here to see Eva and the baby. Focus on that.*

Incredibly, Flora had only seen Eva and Barney once since they'd got back to England, and then only for a quick coffee on the King's Road between meetings. Eva was heavily pregnant, but still somehow managed to look utterly ravishing, her supermodel features as perfectly chiselled as ever and her long limbs still lithe, despite the enormous bump. Barney had sat beside her, beaming with pride, looking more svelte and healthier himself, and talking away nineteen to the dozen about the baby, their new farmhouse and his photographs, now evidently selling like hot cakes at Penny's gallery.

I wonder what the baby looks like? Flora thought, as the lift ground its slow way down to the lobby. *Francesca.*

Would she take after Eva or Henry? Either way, she was bound to be beautiful. It was a bit like having the Jolie Pitts for parents, or Blake Lively and Ryan What's-his-name.

Flora was still trying to think of Blake Lively's husband's surname – not Gosling, the other one – when the lift doors opened and she found herself face to face with Henry.

'Flora!'

She tried to read his expression. Was he happy to see her, or horrified? It was hard to focus on his face while her own heart threatened to leap out of her chest and start jumping up and down on the ground between them like a crazed basketball.

'Henry! I . . . Sorry, I didn't know,' she blurted.

'Didn't know what?'

'That you'd be here.'

They stood staring at one another in silence for so long, the lift doors started to close. Henry put a hand out to stop them, before stepping out into the lobby, so close to Flora she felt her knees turn to mush.

'I came to see the baby.' Flora held out the wilting bunch of peonies she was holding, along with a wrapped pink box from John Lewis with white storks printed on the ribbon.

'So I see.' Henry smiled, the same wolfish grin that Flora remembered, half teasing, half amused by her obvious discomfort. 'How are you?'

'I'm well.' Flora attempted a smile of her own, but she couldn't fully pull it off. Not after the day she'd had today.

'How's business?' Henry asked, too frightened to stray onto other, more meaningful topics, but desperate to prolong their encounter. In a pale pink silk jacket over a businesslike pencil skirt and blouse, and with her longer blonde hair still tousled from the stiff January wind, Flora looked even sexier than he remembered her. The urge to reach out and just touch her, smell her, breathe her in, was almost overpowering. But he resisted.

'Business is . . . ' She tried to think of something positive to say, but her mind went blank. Biting her lower lip she admitted, 'Actually, it's pretty awful.'

'Really?' Henry frowned. 'But I keep reading things about you. About the houses you've done. Just the other day I saw a piece about a restaurant you'd designed in Mayfair. Wasn't that in *Vogue*?'

'Yes,' Flora admitted. 'But none of that matters if you're bankrupt.'

She filled Henry in briefly on Graydon's ongoing vendetta and her expensive legal woes. Henry was no longer in business with Graydon, or George, so this was all news to him. After the humiliation of being jilted at the altar, and Eva's subsequent marriage to Barney Griffith, he'd been forced to take stock of all aspects of his life, and had decided he needed a completely fresh start. A venture capital firm had relieved him of his remaining stake in Gigtix and the GJD joint venture for a more than fair price. At thirty-one years old Henry found himself cash rich, footloose and fancy free. It wasn't a bad proposition. But listening to Flora he felt terrible and wracked with guilt. He might have escaped scot-free, but he'd left her behind, and the wolves were evidently tearing her to shreds.

'I'm thinking of moving back to the States,' she said, when she finished the whole sorry saga. 'Starting a new business back home that's not in interior design at all. Maybe event planning? I'm not sure yet. Something that Graydon can't touch, anyway.'

'Why?' Henry looked stricken. He hadn't seen or spoken to Flora in months. Yet somehow the idea of her leaving England felt terrible and wrong. The end of an era. The end of everything. 'I mean, why America? Couldn't you start a new venture here?'

'I could,' agreed Flora. 'But the bankruptcy laws are much easier in the US. And I have to go home eventually.'

Home. That was the second time today the word had offended Henry, and the second time he knew he was being ridiculous. America *was* Flora's home, just as Eva and Barney's rented farmhouse was Francesca's home.

It hit him then like a punch in the stomach.

None of the people I love live with me.

I've pushed them all away.

'I'd better go,' said Flora, looking down at her baby gifts. The woman standing next to her hit the call button for the lift and the doors opened immediately. Flora stepped inside. 'It was nice to see you.'

'And you,' replied Henry, automatically.

'Congratulations, by the way,' said Flora.

'Thanks.'

Their eyes met just as the lift doors closed.

Flora was gone.

Feeling utterly desolate, Henry walked out into the street and hailed a cab. He was about to head home to his flat to change for dinner, but as they pulled away from the hospital he changed his mind.

'The Boltons, please,' he told the cabbie.

He might have lost Flora. She might be returning to the States and he might never see her again. But there was one, last thing he could do for her. At the very least he could try.

George Savile's new house in The Boltons, a glamorous South Kensington enclave, stood behind grand electric gates set into a high stone wall. The joint venture with GJD, and in particular their new design app, Gridz, had catapulted George to the next level of wealth, and she'd wasted no time trading in her comfortable house in Fulham for this glitzy American-style new-build, complete with basement swimming-pool complex, media room and six-car garage. Security cameras swivelled from every corner. George was working out in her home gym when Henry's cab approached the gates. Seeing his familiar, handsome face on the monitor she stepped off her elliptical.

'Uh, uh, uh.' Her trainer, Matt, wagged an admonishing finger. 'Where do you think you're going? Six more minutes.'

'Sorry.' Wiping the sweat off her forehead, George kissed him on the cheek, allowing her warm, perfectly toned body to press against his for a moment. 'Something just came up.'

Sex with Matt, which she indulged in from time to time, was a workout in itself: intense, animal and blissfully uncomplicated. Today, however, she had more important fish to fry.

'I'll make up for it on Friday, I promise,' she cooed, allowing her fingers to brush lightly across the trainer's bulging crotch before disappearing into the changing room. She contemplated showering and changing, making Henry wait while she beautified herself. But a quick glance in the mirror convinced her she looked more than sexy enough in her skintight workout pants and bra top, with her hair a mess and beads of sweat glistening enticingly on the skin of her arms and the rounded tops of her breasts. Besides, Henry abhorred waiting.

Bounding up to the entrance hall, she got there just as the butler was showing Henry in.

'Hello, stranger.' She smiled sweetly, walking over and kissing him on the cheek. She smelled of sweat and sex and a perfume Henry dimly remembered. As always with George, he felt a strange mix of attraction and revulsion course through his body, like an alcoholic downing a shot of tequila while on Antabuse.

'What brings you to my humble abode?'

'Flora.' Henry looked at her coldly. 'I just ran into her at the hospital. She came to see Eva and Francesca.'

George's eyes narrowed. 'How sweet of her.'

'She told me about Graydon and these lawsuits. Did you know she was going bankrupt? He's forcing her business under.'

George shrugged. 'I didn't know that, no. But I don't see what it has to do with me. Or you, for that matter.'

'Call him off,' said Henry.

George frowned. 'What do you mean?'

'Just what I say. Call Graydon off. Tell him to stop hounding Flora.'

'You make him sound like my pet Rottweiler.' George

laughed, wandering into the drawing room, forcing Henry to follow her. Every step felt as if he was straying deeper into the Gorgon's lair. But he had to help Flora, if he could. He had to at least try. 'Graydon makes his own decisions.'

Coiling herself onto one of the suede sofas, she patted the seat beside her for Henry.

'You have influence,' Henry said, declining the invitation and folding his arms defensively. 'You could get him to leave her and Fitz alone.'

'And why would I do that?' asked George, bristling at his attitude.

'Because it's the right thing to do.'

'Says who?' George flicked back her hair defiantly. 'Flora blatantly plagiarized Graydon's work.'

'Bollocks.'

Getting up (if Muhammad wouldn't come to the mountain, after all), George slid slowly over to Henry. Snaking her arms around his neck, she pressed herself against him, tilting her beautiful, spiteful face up towards his so that their lips were inches apart.

'What is it, darling?' Her fingers expertly caressed the back of his neck, making the hairs on his skin stand on end. 'Why do you care so much about Flora? Are you still in love with her, Henry?' she taunted. 'Is that it? Is poor little easy-to-spread Flora Fitzwilliam the one who got away?'

Henry peeled off her arms like leeches.

'Yes,' he said matter-of-factly, knowing that the truth would hurt George more than anything else he could tell her. 'I am in love with Flora. And she *is* the one who got away. But you know what? That's OK. Because I know I'm not good enough for her. I know I couldn't make her happy. So I'm *glad* she got away. Just like I'm glad that I finally got away from you, and everything you stand for. Goodbye, George.'

He started walking away. Furious, George stormed after him.

'Everything *I* stand for? Who do you think you are, Henry? Fucking *Gandhi*? It takes two to have an affair you know. Or, in your case, multiple affairs. Henry! I'm talking to you!'

But Henry wasn't listening. He would never listen to Georgina Savile again. He couldn't force her to stop Graydon suing Flora. But he could cut her poison out of his life once and for all.

Flora would survive. She would recover. Rebuild.

And so would he.

George was still shouting as Henry climbed into his waiting cab and drove away. A free man, at last.

CHAPTER THIRTY-ONE

Sixteen months later . . .

'What do you mean, "it wasn't on the plane"?'

Flora Fitzwilliam ran her hand through her long hair and forced herself to take a long, calming breath.

The young man in front of her – was it Thomas? – looked perplexed. They were both standing in the gardens of one of Nantucket Island's grandest and oldest mansions, one of the 'Three Bricks' at the top of Main Street, staring at an empty trestle table and the spot where an intricate, six-tier wedding cake ought to be standing.

Mason Parker and his bride-to-be, Catherine Coffin, had ordered the twelve-thousand-dollar cake specially from Frederic James, Boston's world-famous patisserie. The wedding party was already at the church and would be returning for the reception at Catherine's parents' house within the hour. But when Flora summoned the cake to be brought out from the kitchens, the caterer had responded with a doom-laden, 'What cake?'

'Well, there was a plane from Boston,' Thomas explained to Flora patiently.

'Ri-i-i-ght.'

'I went to the airport to meet it.'

'OK.'

'But the cake wasn't on the plane.'

'So you . . . ?' Flora prompted him, hoping for *called the bakery* or *got it on the next flight out* or *sent someone to Boston to pick it up in person*.

'Came back here?' the boy offered, innocently.

Flora's head started to throb. She had a flashback to the last time she'd worked in Nantucket, doing up Lisa Kent's house in Siasconset (for which Graydon later took all the credit). She remembered the lazy workmen; entire crews failing to turn up from Boston; city planners who made it their life's mission to cause as much delay and throw up as many obstacles as possible. And then, of course, the weather: unpredictable and all-powerful. The fogs as thick as whipped cream, which descended out of nowhere and made escape from the island impossible. Storms that blew in from the Cape and literally knocked posts and beams out of the ground and sent them flying through the air like twigs. Summer rain that beat down so violently the drops could leave bruises on your skin. But nothing, *nothing*, could beat this level of incompetence.

Flora was organizing the Parker/Coffin wedding, *the* society nuptials of the summer – and there was no goddamned cake?

'This was last night, right?' she asked the hapless boy, trying to stay calm.

'Last night? No. This morning.'

A ray of hope flickered through the gloom.

'This morning? But the cake should have been flown in

last night. Call the airport. See if they're holding any packages. On second thoughts, I'll do it myself.'

Pacing through the perfectly dressed tables, Flora punched out the number for ACK baggage claim and spoke to the girl at Cape Air. Yes, they had a large box. Yes, she could open it, could Flora hold on? Yes, it was a cake. It looked gorgeous! Should they have someone drive it into town?

Flora contemplated going herself – at this point she didn't trust anybody on the island to perform even the simplest of tasks properly – but, deciding it was too late for her to leave and get back in time, opted to give Thomas a chance to redeem himself. Cake or no cake, it wouldn't do for the wedding planner not to be there when the bride and groom returned from the church.

The wedding planner. Flora was the wedding planner for Mason Parker's wedding. It should have felt weird, ridiculous, awful – only two years ago, she was supposed to be the bride, after all. But actually it felt oddly wonderful, the closing of a circle and a testament to what truly good friends they had become. She'd run into Mason about a year ago in New York, shortly after she'd moved back and launched her events company, Phoenix.

'It's a little cheesy,' she told him sheepishly. 'But I figured as it's sort of "rising from the ashes" of my last company . . .'

Fitz had folded a few months before, driven under by Graydon James's relentless lawsuits. But Flora hadn't let the grass grow under her feet. Event planning still allowed her to indulge her creative side, and it was a world in which Graydon couldn't touch her. Rather wonderfully, the same week that Fitz filed for bankruptcy, one of Graydon's ex-toy-boy lovers published a salacious take-down of the great designer in

Vanity Fair. As well as shamelessly exposing his vanity, mean-ness and sexual peccadilloes, the piece specifically mentioned Graydon's 'raging jealousy' about Flora and his paranoia that her work would eclipse his own.

'No one suffered more from Graydon's spite and caprice than Flora Fitzwilliam, whose reputation he systematically set out to destroy,' the author wrote. 'Ninety per cent of Graydon's best work in the last decade was down to Flora's designs.'

Of course, Graydon was suing the toy boy, too. And it wasn't an 'official' vindication. But the tide of public opinion – and industry opinion, which mattered far more to Flora – had definitely turned after the *Vanity Fair* piece. It had come too late to save Fitz, but it had been more than a small comfort to Flora. GJD would never again be the design powerhouse it once had been, and Graydon's own reputa-tion was the one in tatters now.

'That *is* cheesy!' Mason laughed, when she told him her new company name. 'But I like it anyway, and the logo's great. Say, I don't suppose you do weddings, do you?'

At first, Flora declined. So many of their old friends would be there. Other people would think it weird, even if they didn't. But a number of factors had swayed her. Mason's genuine enthusiasm was one. His fiancée being literally the sweetest, kindest, least jealous girl on planet earth was another. For the only daughter of one of Nantucket's oldest and wealthiest families to have turned out so down-to-earth and unaffected was little short of a miracle.

Then finally there was the publicity – Mason's wedding would be splashed all over every lifestyle magazine, celebrity gossip rag and fashion blog in New York and beyond – and, perhaps most beguilingly, the fee. Phoenix charged a flat 15 per cent of each event's total budget, and Mason and

Catherine's budget was eye-popping. For that sort of money, Flora could suffer a few raised eyebrows.

Not long after Thomas was dispatched to the airport, the bridal car arrived back at the house, swiftly followed by the first of the guests who had followed on foot up Nantucket's cobbled main street. The string quartet began playing, and Flora darted into the kitchen to make sure all was going smoothly with the canapés and champagne, which it was. Exhaling for the first time all day, she took a glass herself and wandered back outside to greet the bride and groom.

'Flora!'

Chuck Branston, Mason's best man, swooped down on her the moment she stepped outside. In a Ralph Lauren tuxedo jacket paired with Nantucket red pants and a bow tie with lobsters on it, Chuck couldn't have looked more preppy if he'd had a Brooks Brothers bar code printed on the back of his neck.

'How are you?' He beamed. 'I couldn't believe it when Mase told me you were doing the wedding. You look phenomenal, by the way.'

'Thanks.' Flora smiled. In a scoop-backed midnight-blue gown and sky-high Manolos and with her long hair worn tousled and loose, Flora *felt* good, but it was nice to have Chuck confirm it. She'd always liked him. It was only his bitch of a sister she had a problem with. Luckily Henrietta was not here today. Recently married herself, to some rich bore from Rhode Island, she was heavily pregnant and on bed rest. *Shame*.

'Look, I'm sorry about what happened with Mason and Henrietta,' he said, reading Flora's mind. 'It was so stupid. They both really regretted it afterwards.'

Flora waved a hand breezily. She doubted very much

whether Henrietta regretted anything, other than Mason dumping her. But it didn't matter now. 'There's nothing for you to apologize for. It's ancient history, anyway. And everything worked out for the best in the end.'

They both looked over to where Mason and Catherine were having their photograph taken beneath the arbour that Flora had had built especially. Leaning into one another and laughing, they looked adorably happy.

'They're good together, aren't they?' agreed Chuck.

But Flora was no longer listening. Her face draining of colour, she clutched Chuck's arm for support, so tightly that he could feel her fingernails through his jacket.

'Oh my God!' she gasped, downing the rest of her drink in one. 'It can't be.'

'What?' Chuck looked at her concerned. 'What's wrong?'

He followed Flora's horrified gaze. There, standing directly behind the happy couple, chatting and laughing with some other guests, was Henry Saxton Brae.

Sensing the two of them looking, Henry looked up. When his eyes met Flora's he smiled.

She felt her knees start to give way and clung on to Chuck Branston even tighter.

How? How is he here?

Still smiling, Henry was walking towards her.

'Oh God!' Flora moaned.

'Do you know that guy?' Chuck asked, holding her up.

Flora nodded mutely.

'Well, is there a problem? Do you want me to stay with you?'

'No,' she said, regaining control of herself and releasing Chuck's arm. 'It's fine. You go and mingle. Do your best man thing.'

Chuck looked sceptical. 'Are you sure?'

'Definitely,' said Flora. Henry was just yards away now. 'It's not a problem. Just someone I wasn't expecting, that's all. Go. Go go go.'

Chuck left, eyeing Henry suspiciously as they passed each other. Seconds later, Henry and Flora were face to face.

'Hello.'

His clipped, English accent sounded more pronounced than ever here.

'Hello,' said Flora.

They both stood in silence for a moment, drinking one another in. Henry spoke first. 'Can we talk? Alone?'

Flora frowned. 'I'm working.'

'I know. Just a few minutes,' Henry pleaded.

They walked down to the bottom of the garden. An old summerhouse was being used as a storeroom, full of dusty deckchairs and gardening tools, as well as various broken children's toys. A rattan couch with torn cushions had been shoved into a corner. Flora brushed the dead leaves off with her hands and sat down. Henry sat next to her, so close that their legs were almost touching.

'I don't have long,' said Flora, staring at the ground.

'That's OK,' said Henry, staring at her. The heavy blue silk of the dress clung to her body perfectly, accentuating her tanned skin and the soft curve of her breasts and thighs. Unable to stop himself he reached out and touched her hair. 'I like it longer,' he said, his breath heavy with desire. 'You look beautiful.'

Flora froze like a deer about to be shot.

'What are you doing here, Henry?' she said.

'Will Coffin's an old friend of mine,' he said, reluctantly withdrawing his hand from Flora's hair.

'Catherine's brother?' Flora sounded disbelieving.

'We met in London. He did a master's at LSE,' said Henry. 'Small world.'

'Very,' agreed Flora, suspiciously. 'So Will invited you? I only ask because I oversaw the seating plan and your name was definitely not on it.'

'It was a last-minute thing,' Henry said sheepishly. 'All right, look, I heard you were doing the wedding. OK? I asked Will to invite me.'

Flora took this in. 'You came to see me?'

'I came to see you.'

Now Henry looked at the floor. An awful silence fell.

'Did you hear about George?' Henry asked, breaking it at last with a jarring change of tone.

'No.' Flora looked up. 'What about her?'

'She and Graydon fell out, big time. Gridz shares are in free fall. Last I heard, they'd each filed separate lawsuits. *And*, Robert's divorcing her.'

'What?' Flora's eyes widened. 'Why?'

'Apparently he came home and caught her in flagrante with the trainer. Rumour has it they were doing something unspeakable with a rubberized dumbbell.'

Flora giggled. 'Good for Robert. Not that she cares, I imagine.'

'She cares about the money,' said Henry. 'Especially now the business is going down the tubes. I was lucky to get out when I did. Anyway, I thought you'd want to know.'

The tension had been broken, but the silence kept creeping back. This time, it was Flora who tried to break it.

'How's the baby?'

Henry's eyes lit up. Reaching into his wallet, he pulled out a picture of an exquisitely beautiful, dark-haired toddler with a cheeky grin and mesmerizing green eyes. Her colouring was Henry's but her features were all Eva.

'Oh my goodness! She's an angel,' said Flora.

'She's a horror.' Henry grinned. 'Her stepfather spoils her.'

'And you don't?' Flora laughed.

'Eva and Barney are expecting another in the autumn,' Henry told her. 'I think it'll be good for Cesca to have a sibling. She's becoming a little dictator.'

'And you?' Flora forced herself to ask. 'Are you . . . attached?'

'To what?' Henry asked, looking baffled.

Flora laughed loudly. 'I'll take that as a "no". So you're not seeing anyone then? Not settled?'

'No.' Henry looked at his shoes. 'I can't settle.'

I know you can't, Flora thought sadly.

'Not while I'm still in love with you.'

Before Flora had a chance to react he'd reached over, grabbing her hand and holding it tightly, his fingers stroking each of hers in turn. 'I love you, Flora. I tried not to, but I do.'

'Please. Don't.' She tried to remove her hand but he held it fast.

'Why not? I love you and I think you love me too.'

'It doesn't matter.'

'How doesn't it matter? I want to be with you.'

'No,' Flora said firmly, wrenching free from his grip and standing up, her heart pounding. 'You can't be faithful, Henry. Not for life. It's not in your nature. And I'm not like Eva. I couldn't just forgive.'

'Maybe it is in my nature?' said Henry. 'Maybe I just hadn't found the right woman yet?'

Flora looked at him sadly. 'I can't base my whole life on "maybe". I just can't. I need security, Henry. I need to be safe.'

Henry looked anguished. He opened his mouth to protest then closed it again, not sure what he could say in his defence.

'I have to go.' Flora pushed open the summer-house door. 'I have a wedding to run.'

'Please. Wait!' Henry called after her. 'Flora!'

'If you care about me at all,' she said, fighting back tears, 'go home. Don't stay for the dinner. It will only hurt us both. Let me do my job tonight, Henry.'

She began walking back up the garden.

'Flora!' Henry called after her.

But she didn't look back.

Two hours later, after the dinner and speeches, the dancing had begun. Mason led Flora onto the floor.

'Was that Henry Saxton Brae I saw here earlier?' he asked, after he'd thanked her again for the perfect night she'd given him and Catherine.

'Yeah.' Flora nodded. 'Did you know he was friends with Will?'

'I did not,' Mason admitted. 'I do know the guy's in love with you, though.'

Flora's eyes widened. 'Why do you say that?'

'Come on,' said Mason. 'He came all the way out here, didn't he?'

Flora was silent.

'Why don't you give him a chance?' said Mason, whirling her expertly around the floor.

Flora looked at him, incredulous. 'Are you insane?'

'Why is that insane?' Mason asked. 'You obviously love him too. I'd like to see you happy, Flora. You deserve to be happy.'

'I am happy.'

'You know what I mean.'

Flora sighed. 'I do. And I love you for saying it. But Henry's not like you. He'd be a terrible husband. He can't commit to anything. He's like a cat. You might think you own him, because you buy him a bowl and food and a bed to sleep in. But, as far as he's concerned, he's only ever passing through.'

'People change,' said Mason reasonably. 'Maybe he's changed?'

Maybe, thought Flora.

I really hate that word.

It was almost three a.m. by the time Flora finally got back to her rented cottage on North Water Street, overlooking the harbour. Even through her exhaustion, she was moved by the stillness and beauty of the view as she fumbled for her key. The lights from the boats reflected off the still water, echoing the brightly sparkling blanket of stars above, but beyond that all was darkness and peace.

Climbing the wooden steps to her front door, she jumped out of her skin when a figure emerged from the shadows.

'You took your time.'

'Jesus Christ, Henry!' She spun around, her heart hammering. 'You scared me half to death. What are you doing here?'

'I'm bringing you home.'

Flora rubbed her eyes, exhausted. She was too tired for this.

'What do you mean? I am home.'

'No.' Grabbing her suddenly by the waist he pulled her to him in the darkness, wrapping both his strong arms around her like bars on a cage. 'Your home is with me. It's with me.'

He kissed her then, his lips pressing hard against hers. He smelled of bourbon and some sort of English aftershave, and although her body squirmed in protest, Flora's lips seemed to have developed a mind of their own, returning his kiss with a passion she didn't know she was capable of. Were her feet even on the ground? The whole thing was terrifying, and blissful, and it seemed to go on for a long, long time.

When at last he released her, Flora started to speak, but Henry cut her off.

'I don't want to hear it!' he said angrily. 'This "security" you're looking for, Flora, this "safety". It doesn't exist! Not for you. Not for anyone. There's no such thing as a life without risk, never mind a love without it. And, if there were, it wouldn't be worth having. Can I promise to be faithful for ever, with a hundred per cent certainty? Of course I can't.'

'Exactly!' Flora was shaking.

'Exactly what?' Henry said, exasperated. 'Exactly nothing! You can't promise that either. No one can. Not truthfully. The best any of us can promise is to try our best. Isn't it?'

He pulled her close again, but she was resisting, shaking her head.

'Maybe,' she said, fighting back tears. 'Maybe that's true. But it's not enough for me. I can't live with that.'

'Yes, you can,' Henry said forcefully. 'And you bloody well will. Because I can't live without you and I'm tired of trying.'

He kissed her again, his hands roaming over her bare back and up into her hair. Flora staggered backwards till he was pressing her against the wall of the house. The pressure of his body against hers, the warmth and the power and the scent of him were too much. Kissing him back she let go, allowing three years of longing to flood out of her, losing herself in the incredible sensations.

'I won't . . . I won't give up my career,' she gasped as he slipped the dress off her shoulders and began kissing the tops of her breasts.

'Fine,' he murmured. 'Just open the fucking door.'

Flora handed him the key. Seconds later they were inside the cottage on the floor, clothes flying off them as if they'd been caught in a hurricane.

'You'll have to move to New York . . . ' Flora groaned as his hand slipped beneath the elastic of her underwear.

'New York. Fine,' said Henry, unzipping his fly to release his painfully huge erection.

'Really?' Flora wriggled backwards, desperate for him to be inside her but unable to stop testing him. 'You'd give up Hanborough for me?'

'We'll go there for holidays,' he said, burying his face between her incredible breasts. Glancing up, he added, 'With the kids.'

'The kids?' Flora's eyes widened.

Grinning, Henry seized his chance and eased himself inside her. Flora sighed with pleasure. Henry tried to slow himself down, to savour this moment he'd waited so very, very long for, but it was no use. Flora's hands were on his back, clawing at him, pulling him deeper and deeper into her as he thrust excitedly upwards. He responded joyously, harder and faster, until he came, far too quickly, but he didn't care.

'I love you,' he said, laughing and panting as he collapsed onto the floor beside her.

'I love you too,' said Flora, oddly relieved to be saying the words out loud at last. 'But we have to be practical.'

Henry rolled his eyes.

'I mean it,' said Flora, still gasping from the exertion of their incredible sex. 'There's Francesca to think about, and my company. It's all very well saying you'll move to New York. But your life is in England, Henry, and my life is here and—'

Propping himself up on one elbow, Henry gently but firmly put his hand over Flora's mouth.

'Shut. Up,' he whispered, beaming down at her. 'I love you. You love me. It will all be OK. Not perfect, maybe. But OK.'

And in that moment, Flora realized that he was right.

It would be.

Maybe even for the rest of their lives.

THIRTY-TWO

'Happy birthday to you, happy birthday to you, happy birthday, dear Frances-caaaa! Happy birthday to youoooo!'

It was hard to pinpoint who was singing more loudly, or more tunelessly – Barney or Henry.

'Do you think she'll be scarred for life?' Eva grimaced, wincing at Flora and covering her own ears as Cesca's two daddies belted out her birthday anthem to the packed barn at Hanborough. All of Francesca's little friends from nursery had come to see her turn two, as had a good number of her parents' friends and a smattering of villagers curious to see the latest changes up at the castle since Flora and Henry were last here at Christmas, and to enjoy some free tea, cake and champagne.

'I doubt it, judging by that grin,' said Flora, laughing as her stepdaughter blew out her candles before unceremoniously sinking her face into the elaborate Disney Princess icing and taking an enormous bite out of the top.

'Francesca!' Eva rushed forward with a horrified gasp. '*Sluta!* Stop that!'

'Oh, leave her alone,' said Henry, slipping a protective arm around Flora's waist and patting her growing baby bump proudly, while continuing to film Cesca on his iPhone with the other hand. 'It's her birthday.'

'That's not the point,' Barney said reprovingly, physically extracting Francesca from the cake, despite her loud protests, and handing her to Eva while he began cutting up slices for the other children. His new baby daughter, Violet, hung off his chest in a designer baby sling like a contented little monkey as he methodically handed out plates. 'She's the host.'

'She's two!' protested Henry.

'She might as well start as she means to go on,' muttered Barney, sounding very authoritative and grown-up all of a sudden.

Flora grinned. *Barney's such a good dad. Really a natural.*

Not that Henry wasn't. True, he would never be the world's most committed nappy changer. But he was utterly besotted with Francesca and saw her as often as he could, returning to Hanborough regularly. And he was also beside himself with joy over the prospect of his and Flora's new arrival, a little boy due in the summer.

Flora had particularly enjoyed Henry's desperate attempts to backtrack after she'd found out the baby's sex and told him, and he'd practically exploded with happiness, running around their New York apartment like an excited terrier after a rat, literally whooping with delight, punching the air and declaring it 'the happiest day of my life. Ever!'

The days of sincere 'of course, a girl would have been just as lovely' that followed were as endearing as they were obviously untrue.

'It's all right to want a son,' Flora reassured him.

'I'm just so happy,' Henry told her. 'Cesca. You. The baby. Everything is perfect.'

'Even New York?' Flora asked archly.

'I love New York,' Henry assured her.

Perhaps 'love' was an overstatement. But Henry had come to terms with their life in Manhattan, and enjoyed the energy of the city. Flora's business was going great guns, and Henry had started dabbling in some real-estate deals, which gave him something to do. He did miss Hanborough but, as Flora reminded him, he hadn't exactly excelled at full-time country life the last time he'd tried it. As compromises went, theirs felt like a pretty good one.

'Is that your second slice, darling?'

Jen Clempson, the vicar's wife, admonished her husband as poor old Bill edged towards the cake table. Call-me-Bill had definitely put on weight since they'd had Diana, and was looking distinctly fat and happy.

'Do leave some for the children.'

'Oh, shhhh.' The vicar patted his wife affectionately on the bottom, handing her a fresh glass of Bollinger. 'There's plenty for the children. In fact, I rather suspect they've had too much.' He wrinkled his nose in distaste, looking past Jen to the back of the room where Francesca's presents lay in a mountainous pile. 'Isn't that Gabe Baxter's boy being sick on the party bags?'

Luca Baxter was indeed throwing up mightily. His mother Laura rushed over to him, while a nearby father made the mistake of asking Henry for a mop.

'Do I look like a cleaner?' Henry replied drily. His arrogance was much improved in recent years, but he hadn't changed completely.

Tired suddenly, Flora pulled a chair into a quiet corner

and sat down, watching the party. Looking around the barn she'd been forced to build – she still considered it damn ugly, although she had to admit it was useful on days like today, and at least it had good views – it struck her just how very strange and wonderful it was that this place was now her home, and these people her family.

Not just Henry and Cesca – who had stopped wailing and was now singing along lustily to The Wiggles' rendition of 'Banana Phone' – but Barney and Eva and little Violet, too. Then there was Penny and Santiago, and the Clempsons, and the Baxters, and Max Bingley and Angela Cranley, and everyone who made the Swell Valley the special, magical place that it was. Today's party, like every party at Hanborough, was a village affair. A valley affair. There truly was nowhere else on earth quite like it.

My children will grow up here, Flora thought, rubbing her belly gratefully.

Henry and I will grow old here.

It felt hard now to remember the angst-ridden, commitment-shy girl she'd been when she'd first arrived here. Still less to think of Henry as the ultimate bad-boy bachelor.

Hanborough had worked its magic on both of them.

Long, long may it last.